Emma R. Carroll

Giant

BOOKS BY EDNA FERBER

Autobiography
A PECULIAR TREASURE

Short Stories
ONE BASKET · NOBODY'S IN TOWN
BUTTERED SIDE DOWN · CHEERFUL—BY REQUEST
HALF PORTIONS · GIGOLO · MOTHER KNOWS BEST
THEY BROUGHT THEIR WOMAN

The Emma McChesney Stories
ROAST BEEF MEDIUM · PERSONALITY PLUS
EMMA MCCHESNEY & COMPANY

Novels
GIANT · GREAT SON · SARATOGA TRUNK · DAWN O'HARA
FANNY HERSELF · THE GIRLS · SO BIG · SHOW BOAT
CIMARRON · AMERICAN BEAUTY · COME AND GET IT

Plays
THE ROYAL FAMILY (with George S. Kaufman)
MINICK (with George S. Kaufman)
DINNER AT EIGHT (with George S. Kaufman)
$1200 A YEAR (with Newman Levy)
STAGE DOOR (with George S. Kaufman)
THE LAND IS BRIGHT (with George S. Kaufman)

GIANT

by Edna Ferber

DOUBLEDAY & COMPANY, INC., 1952

Garden City, New York

Giant

1

THIS MARCH DAY the vast and brassy sky, always spangled with the silver glint of airplanes, roared and glittered with celestial traffic. Gigantic though they loomed against the white-hot heavens there was nothing martial about these winged mammoths. They were merely private vehicles bearing nice little alligator jewel cases and fabulous gowns and overbred furs. No sordid freight sullied these four-engined family jobs whose occupants were Dallas or Houston or Vientecito or Waco women in Paris gowns from Neiman-Marcus; and men from Amarillo or Corpus Christi or San Angelo or Benedict in boots and Stetsons and shirt sleeves.

All Texas was flying to Jett Rink's party. All Texas, that is, possessed of more than ten millions in cash or cattle or cotton or wheat or oil. Thus was created an aerial stampede. Monsters in a Jovian quadrille, the planes converged from the Timber Belt and the Rio Grande Valley, from the Llano Estacado and the Trans-Pecos; the Blacklands the Balcones Escarpment the Granite Mountains the Central Plains the Edwards Plateau the boundless Panhandle. High, high they soared above the skyscraper office buildings that rose idiotically out of the endless plain; above the sluggish rivers and the arroyos, above the lush new hotels and the anachronistic white-pillared mansions; the race horses in rich pasture, the swimming pools the drives of transplanted palms the huge motion picture palaces the cattle herds and the sheep and mountains and wild antelope and cotton fields and Martian chemical plants whose aluminum stacks gave back the airplanes glitter for glitter. And above the grey dust-bitten shanties of the Mexican barrios and the roadside barbecue shacks and the windmills and the water holes and the miles of mesquite and cactus.

There were, of course, a few party-goers so conservative or so sure of their position in society, or even so impecunious, as to make the journey by automobile, choosing to cover the distance at a leisurely ninety miles an hour along the flat concrete ribbon that spanned the thousand miles of Texas from north horizon to the Gulf.

Though the pitiless southwest sun glared down on the airborne and the groundling it met defeat in the vine-veiled veranda of Reata Ranch Main House. Even the ever present Gulf wind arriving dry and dust-laden after its journey from the coast here took on a pretense of cool moisture as it filtered through the green and spacious shade. Cushions of palest pastel sailcloth on couches and chairs refreshed the eye even before the heat-tortured body found comfort, and through the day there was always the tinkle of ice against glass to soothe the senses. Through the verdant screen one caught glimpses of a heaven-blue swimming pool and actually, too, a lake in this arid land. Radios yelped and brayed from automobiles and ranch houses, towns and cities throughout the length and breadth of this huge and lonely commonwealth from the Gulf of Mexico to the Oklahoma border, from the Rio Grande to Louisiana, but here at Reata Ranch no such raucous sounds intensified the heat waves. Jett Rink's name splintered the air everywhere else, but not here. It stalked in black three-inch headlines across the front page of every newspaper from El Paso to Bowie. It stared out from billboards and newsreels. It was emblazoned on the very heavens in skywriting. Omnipresent, like Jett Rink's oil derricks straddling the land. At every turn the ears and eyes were assaulted by the stale and contrived news of Jett Rink's munificence.

The JETT RINK AIRPORT . . . gift of JETT RINK to the city of Hermoso . . . biggest airport in the Southwest . . . private pre-opening celebration . . . two thousand invited guests . . . magnificent banquet in the Grand Concourse . . . most important citizens . . . champagne . . . motion picture stars . . . Name Bands . . . millions . . . first Texas billionaire . . . orchids . . . caviar flown from New York . . . zillions . . . lobster flown from Maine . . . millions . . . oil . . . strictly private . . . millions . . . biggestmillionsbiggestbillionsbiggesttrillionsbiggestzillions . . .

Mrs. Jordan Benedict, dressed for the air journey—blue shantung and no hat—sat in her bedroom at Reata Ranch, quiet, quiet. She sat very relaxed in the cool chintz slipper chair, her long slim hands loosely clasped in her lap. The quiet and the cool laved her. She sat storing coolness and quiet against the time when her senses would be hammered and racked by noise and heat; big men and bourbon, the high shrill voices of Texas women, blare of brass, crash of china, odors of profuse food, roar of plane motors.

Now, as she sat, little sounds came faintly to her ears, little accustomed soothing sounds. A light laugh from the far-off kitchen wing—one of the Mexican girls, Delfina probably, the gay careless one, the others were more serious about their work. The clip-snip of Dimodeo's garden shears—Dimodeo and his swarming crew who seemed to spend their days on their knees clip-snipping, coaxing fine grass to grow green, and hedges to flower and water to spurt in this desert country. The muffled thud of a horse's hoofs on sun-baked clay; one of the vaqueros who still despised the jeep or Ford as a means of locomotion. The clang of a bell, deep-throated, resonant, an ancient bell that announced the nooning at Reata Ranch schoolhouse. The soft plaint of the mourning doves. The town of Benedict, bustling and thriving, lay four miles distant but here at Reata Main House set back a mile from the highway there was no sound of traffic or commerce. So Leslie Benedict sat very still within this bubble of quiet suspended for the moment before it must burst at the onslaught of high-pitched voices and high-powered motors. For all the family was going, and all the guests up at the huge Guest House there at the other end of the drive. The big plane was in readiness at Reata Ranch airfield and the Cadillacs were waiting to take them all to the plane.

The giant kingdom that was the Reata Ranch lay dozing in the sun, its feet laved by the waters of the Gulf of Mexico many miles distant, its head in the cloud-wreathed mountains far far to the north, its gargantuan arms flung east and west in careless might.

2

THOUGH they had been only an hour on the road the thought of this verdant haven tormented Mrs. Mott Snyth as she and her husband tore with cycloramic speed past miles and miles of Reata fence and field and range. The highway poured into the maw of the big car, the torrid wind seared the purpling face of Vashti Snyth and—now that he had removed his big cream Stetson—tossed the little white curls that so incongruously crowned the unlined and seemingly guileless face of Pinky, her husband. Vashti Snyth's vast bosom heaved, her hands fluttered with the vague almost infantile gestures of the hypothyroid.

"My!" she whimpered in helpless repetition. "My! It's a hot of a day!"

"March, what do you expect?" The tiny high-heeled boot on the accelerator, the small strong hands on the wheel, the bland blue eyes seeming focused on nothing in particular, he appeared relaxed, almost lethargic; those eyes saw everything to the right to left and ahead, he was as relaxed as a steel spring. "Reata looks good. Salubrious. Bick must have had the stinger over this section again, not a mesquite far's you can see."

"Mott, let's stop by the house a minute, can't we?" This massive woman alone called him by his given name though to the rest of his world he was Pinky; she actually gave the effect of looking up at him though her elephantine bulk towered above his miniature frame; and in spite of the fact (or perhaps because of it) that she as Vashti Hake, inheritor of the third biggest ranch in all Texas, had years ago committed the unpardonable social crime of marrying one of her father's cow hands.

"Not if you're going to do a lot of shopping in Hermoso before we check in at the hotel we can't. Mathematically speaking."

"I'm only going to buy a little white mink cape throw."

"How long will that take?"

"Fifteen minutes."

"You said you didn't want to take the plane. You said you wanted to drive because the bluebonnets would be so pretty. It'll take us another five hours anyway to get to Hermoso. The dinner is seven. How do you figure——"

"I'm sick of bluebonnets. They're right pretty, but I'm sick of 'em miles back. We can leave the car at Reata, hitch a ride in the big plane with Les and Bick."

"How do you know?"

"They're taking their big plane. I know. That's why I didn't want to fly down. You wouldn't take the big plane. I won't come down in that little bitty old two-engine job, front of everybody in Texas."

"We'd look good, wouldn't we, just the two of us sitting in the

14

four-engine job holds fifty! Crew of four, gas and all, cost us about five thousand dollars to go four hundred miles."

"What of it!"

"How do you know how many they got going! Maybe they're full up."

"Company of course, up at the Guest House. But not more then ten or twenty, usually. Then there's Bick and Leslie and young Doctor Jordy and his wife probably and Luz——"

"Luz! Thought she was at school there in Switzerland somewheres."

"She quit it. Didn't like it."

"Like it! I should think if anybody didn't like it it'd be Bick. Heard her schooling there was costing him a heifer a day."

"Well, anyway, she's home and tearing up the place as usual, driving the jeeps like they were quarter horses they say, jumping mesquites with 'em, practically. You know Luz. But that's neither here nor there. Mott, I want to see what Leslie's wearing."

The cool blue eye turned from its task of pouring the road into the car to glance briefly at the beige mound palpitating beside him. "Whatever Leslie's wearing I want to tell you it's away yonder better than that sorry outfit you're carrying."

"Why Mott Snyth! This! What's wrong with it?"

"Plain. Plain as a fence post."

"Plain is the smart thing this year," Vashti boomed with the hauteur of one who knows her ground. "Shows what you men know. Neat and plain and expensive as all hell, like those pictures in *Harper's Bazaar* of the Duchess. That's the thing. Ask anybody. Ask Leslie. Nobody in Texas or anywhere knows better than Leslie what's being worn, she doesn't have to be told, she knows by instinct, the way you can pick a horse. Simple and girlish—" she flicked an imaginary speck off her big beige bosom—"is the keynote of this year's styles."

A flash of amusement wrinkled Pinky's guileless face. "Simple and girlish is all right for Leslie, maybe, ganted the way she is. But you're packing plenty tallow, Vash."

Mischievously he pronounced the abbreviation of her name so

that it became a French noun unflattering to her figure. She heard, she understood, she chose momentarily to ignore it. Blandly she resumed her description of the mode of the day.

"Everything but jewelry, that is. You're supposed to wear a hunk of a bracelet like this one I got on, no matter what, even with a sweater or a cotton wash dress. And a big clip with a lot of good stones or a flock of diamond or ruby or sapphire scatter pins is smart worn just stuck somewhere offhand like you'd jab safety pins into the front of your dress diapering a baby. But not even your engagement ring."

"How about wedding rings, Vash? Wedding rings still okay?"

"Oh sure. But no other jewelry daytimes. Only evenings."

He threw intense anxiety into his tone. "You got stuff with you, I hope?"

"Mott Snyth, I got enough rocks in that little bitty old handbag back there I'll bet if they take us on board Bick and the crew'll have to jettison some before they can lift the plane up in the air. Yes sir! Tonight I'm really going to rise and shine!"

Again Pinky Snyth turned a brief instant to survey the tentlike mound beside him. His glance was affectionate and possessive.

"Ruffles," he said. "I like ruffles on a female. But no matter what you wear you're sassy. You're as sassy as pink shoes."

Vashti, taking advantage of this rare approval, pressed her point. "Well then, we'll stop by like I said, see who's going and all and maybe catch a ride. And let me tell you, Mott Snyth, don't you go calling me Vash, like that, front of company. You and I ain't the only two in Texas know the French for cow. And one compliment don't cover an insult, either." But she was smiling upon him indulgently. "Look! There's the tower of the Big House. I bet it's crammed with company. We're not a mile away from the ranch."

"No place in all of Texas," Pinky announced without bitterness, "is more than a mile away from Reata Ranch somewheres."

Vashti bridled. "We are so! House to house we're more than ninety miles."

"House to house maybe. But fence lines, that's what counts.

Fence lines you adjoin as you know well and good. Like I said, nothing's a far piece from Reata, including Oklahoma one side and Mexico another and the Gulf and Louisiana throwed in. Here we are. My, those palms have took hold. Never know they'd been set in."

Any Texan overhearing this artless chitchat would have known that these two were talking Texas. Both had had a decent education, yet their conversation sounded like the dialogue in a third-rate parody of Texans. This was due partly to habit and partly to affectation born of a mixture of superiority and inferiority, as a certain type of Englishman becomes excessively Oxford or a Southern politician intensifies his drawl. Each was playing a role, deliberately. It was part of the Texas ritual. We're rich as son-of-a-bitch stew but look how homely we are, just as plain-folksy as Grandpappy back in 1836. We know about champagne and caviar but we talk hog and hominy.

They turned in at the open gateway with the Reata Ranch brand, the lariat—la reata as the Mexican vaquero wove it himself out of rawhide—copied in artful iron as an ornament for the gateposts. You saw its twists and coils over the gatehouse too, as it could be seen a thousand thousand times throughout this ranch empire with its millions of acres. Over the door of the Main House, the Big House, countless bunkhouses, line houses; burned into the hide of hundreds of thousands of bulls, steers, cows, calves; embroidered on the silks of the jockeys who rode the Reata race horses; monogramming the household linen, the table silver; wrought into andirons for the fireplaces; adorning the ranch business stationery and Leslie's own delicate blue-grey; stamped on the jeeps, the pickups, the station wagons, the Cadillacs, the saddles. A simple brand but difficult to distort. No cattle rustler of the old Texas days could successfully burn this braided loop into another pattern or symbol. It was for this reason that shrewd old Jordan Benedict had chosen it in 1855 with his first thousand acres of Texas land.

The nose of the Snyth car had not passed the gateway before Ezequiel was out of the gatehouse and into the road, barring the way with his outstretched left arm, his right hand close to his body. The black eyes pierced the windshield. Then the tense dark face relaxed, the arm dropped, the right hand came up in a gesture that was less a salute than an obeisance.

Pinky Snyth lifted his hand from the wheel, open-palmed. "Cómo estás, Ezequiel?"

The white teeth flashed. "Bienvenido! Señor Snyth! Señora!" He waved them on.

Vashti tossed her head. "About time Bick Benedict got over guarding his country like he was royalty."

"Now Vashti, you know he tried it and the place was stampeded like a fat stock show, the okies were fixing barbecue under every mesquite."

Up the long drive beneath the date palms so incredibly rich under the white-hot blaze. They stood row on orderly row, green-topped, mammoth, like pillars in a monumental cathedral. Only a brush-country Texan could even dimly realize what had gone into the planting and sustaining of these trees in this land. Between the rows were the clean straight lines of irrigation ditches. The fertilized soil lay in tidy ridges at the base of the tree trunks.

"Bick sets out to do something can't be done, why, he's possessed till he does it better than anybody," Pinky observed. "Be putting in a ski jump next, shouldn't wonder, middle of August middle of the range, bringing snow by air lift from Alaska."

Past the old whitewashed adobe schoolhouse, the Big House with its towers and intricate grillwork, past the old carriage house and the vast garage. But no cars stood waiting there, only the vine leaves stirred in the hot wind as the visitors drew up before the Main House and peered toward the shaded enclosure.

Vashti essayed a "Yoo-hoo!" It emerged a croak from her parched throat. "Either they're gone or they're all dead. Can't be gone, this hour." With amazing agility she climbed out of the car, smoothing her crumpled skirts, adjusting her belt, wiping her flushed face as she went toward the porch, her feet and ankles slim and small and neat beneath the ponderous superstructure.

"Leslie! Bick! Where've you all got to, anyway?"

18

Instantly it was as though the enchantment under which Reata Ranch had lain now was broken. The volley of shouts as the Mexican children were freed from the schoolroom; the crunch of gravel under heavy tires; a telephone ringing and a man's voice answering it; Dimodeo rising from where he had knelt near the pool and calling in Spanish to his men. "El mediodía! Noon!" A distant hum of noonday sounds from the houses of the Mexican section on the outskirts of the headquarters building.

Leslie Benedict emerged from the house, cool, slim; about her a sort of careless elegance. The Paris buyer at Neiman's in Dallas had said of Leslie Benedict that she wore indistinct clothes with utter distinction. The buyer was rather proud of this mot. Sometimes she elaborated on it. "What she wears never hits you in the eye. It sneaks up on you. No tough colors, ever. And no faddy stuff. You know. Never too long or too short or to full or too tight or bustles or busy doodads. My opinion, Mrs. Jordan Benedict's the best-dressed woman in Texas and doesn't even know it. Or care."

Now at sight of her guest Leslie's rather set smile of greeting became one of warmth and affection.

"Vashti! What a nice surprise!"

"Thought you'd all gone off and died."

"Where's Pinky?"

"In the car there. We're so hot we're spittin' cotton."

The contrast between the two voices was startling; the one low, vibrant; the other high, strident.

"I thought it was the others from the Big House. Come in, come in! Something cold to drink?"

"Hot coffee I'd druther if it's handy."

"Of course. After twenty years and more in Texas wouldn't you think I'd know it's always hot coffee?" She called in Spanish to someone unseen within the house. She went to the veranda entrance. "Pinky! Come in!"

"Where at's Bick?"

"He'll be here any minute. Come in out of the sun."

Vashti, sunk in the depths of a cool chartreuse chair, fanned

19

her flushed face with an unavailing handkerchief. Her inward eye on her own expanse of beige silk, her outward eye on Leslie's slim grey-blue shantung, she voiced the self-doubt that tormented her.

"Look, Les, does this look too fussy? Traveling, I mean. Light beige?"

"Well—beige is—is good in Texas. The dust." The soft dark eyes kind, friendly.

"I don't know," Vashti panted unhappily. She narrowed her baby-blue eyes to contemplate the entire effect of Leslie's costume. "Now, take you, piece by piece—shoes and stockings and dress and everything, why they're just right, every single thing. But to look at you quick you don't look like anything."

At the startled glance and then the quick flashing smile of the other woman Vashti's customary high color took on the scarlet of embarrassment. "Oh, Leslie, I didn't mean it mean! I just meant no matter what you've got on it doesn't hit you in the eye the first thing, but take you apart, why, everything is perfect. Just perfect."

On her way to greet Mott Snyth Leslie Benedict's hand rested a moment on the shoulder of her guest's moist and crumpled bulk. "Dear Vashti, that's the nicest thing any woman ever said to another woman."

"Coffee, Pinky?" she called to him. "Don't sit there under glass."

The little man, a Watteau figure in Western masquerade, emerged from the big car. Legs actually slightly bowed like those of a cowboy in a Grade B movie; the unvenerable white head was a dot beneath the great brimmed Stetson. "Me and Vashti got to mosey along, all that way to drive." This was a cunning opening wedge. "Where's Bick?"

"Out since five this morning. You know Jordan. He's probably down at the hangar now. He's always fussy about the big plane, I don't know why. You can fall just as far from a little one as a big one, but he's always casual about the little ones."

"Mott's the same way." Vashti had taken off one tiny beige slipper and was wriggling her toes ecstatically. "Climbs into the little Piper Cub, kind of flips his foot and shoves off like he was in a kiddiekar. Years back, when we first got a flock of planes and Mott used to fly the kids to school mornings—mmm, coffee!"

Delfina, soft-stepping, concealing her shyness with a childish insolence of bearing. As she placed the coffee tray on the glass-topped table she stared at the two women with the steady disconcerting gaze of a four-year-old, the bright dark eyes making leisurely appraisal from foot to throat encompassing their clothes. Their faces did not interest her. Masses of vital black hair hung about her shoulders, her blouse was low-cut, her stockingless feet shuffled in huaraches.

"Thank you, Delfina," Mrs. Benedict said—a shade too nicely —in English. Her eyes met Vashti's as the girl disappeared.

"New?" inquired Vashti over the scalding rim of her coffee cup.

"Alvaro's granddaughter. I can't do a thing about her hair! She copies the girls in the movies and the dime store in town. She's been working as elevator operator at the Hake. You must have seen her. Her cousin is a bellboy there. Raul Salazar. Alvaro asked Jordan to bring her back here to work in the house, she'd got into trouble——"

"Oh well, if you and Bick are going to look after all of old Alvaro's sons and daughters and grandchildren and great-grand-children, all that patriarchal Texas stuff."

Pinky choked over his coffee. "Listen at who's talking! Vashti's always up to her hocks in a Mexican wedding or a borning or a family ruckus. Takes enormous cantle off her life. How's old Alvaro, anyway? Must be pushing a hundred."

"Oh, who cares about who's pushing a hundred!" Vashti, now miraculously refreshed by the strong hot coffee, led up to the purpose of her visit. She peered through the vine leaves, her gaze squinting skyward. "Nice flying weather."

Quite as though she cared about the weather, about flying, about anything that had to do with this hideous day Leslie Benedict took her cue as hostess, she said smoothly, "Do you think so? What do you think, Pinky? Some of those fat black clouds look like rain."

21

"Rain!" Pinky scoffed. "Can easy tell you've only been twenty-five years in Texas. No rain in those clouds. They're just empties coming back from California. Come on now, Vashti. We got to get going. Vashti says she's got to pick up a new fur piece in Hermoso. White mink cape or some such doodad."

"How does it happen you're not flying?"

Hastily Pinky raised a protesting hand. "We better not go into that. Well, I didn't want to haul out the big plane, Vashti wouldn't hear to the little one." The rosy face crinkled in a grin. "They used to be a saying, in Texas a man is no better than his horse, and a man on foot is no man atall. Nowadays a fella without an airplane has got no rating, might as well be a Mexican."

At last. "Don't you want to leave the car here and fly down with us?"

"Oh, Leslie!" Vashti's tone of astonishment would not have deceived an amoeba.

"Well, say, if you're sure it wouldn't crowd you none——"

Quickly Vashti cinched it. "Love it! Just purely love it, and thank you kindly. Who all's going? Who's over at the Big House, h'm?"

As Leslie Benedict answered there was a half-smile on her lips, a rueful little smile. She thought, This is ludicrous I suppose. Twenty-five years ago I'd have said it was too fantastic to be true. When I introduce Pinky and Vashti, these good and kind people, there are no terms in which I can define them. They are of a world unknown outside Texas. Even as she answered Vashti she was seeing these two with the eye of one who would always be an outsider in this land. Pinky. As unlike the cowboy of the motion picture and the Western novel as one could be in the likeness of a man. Small, his bone structure as delicate as a woman's. His feet in their high-heeled ornately tooled cowboy boots were arched and slim as a girl's. Pink cheeks, pansy-blue eyes, white hair that waved in thick clusters of curls. In the dust-clouded past he had come to Texas from nowhere. They had deviled him and ridiculed him with their rough jokes and rougher horseplay. He must compensate for his miniature frame and his innocent blue eyes and pink cheeks. So he had been tougher, more daring than the biggest and most daredevil cow hand in the brush country. He used big words whose meaning they did not always understand, he spoke softly but at times his tongue was a whiplash. The small hands were steel-strong, there was no horse he could not gentle. He had come to the Hake ranch—the vast Double B—possessed of nothing but the saddle he carried under his arm—his ridin' riggin' in the ranch idiom. And Vashti Hake actually had married him on the rebound—this big booming woman who had been a big awkward girl—this daughter of old Cliff Hake, now long dead. Two million acres of ranch land, oil wells, cattle, millions.

"Who all's going, Les? Who's over at the Big House, h'm?"

Leslie walked to the veranda screen door, she listened a moment. "The cars went out to call for them."

"Yeh, but who, Les?"

"Well—uh—there's Cal Otter the cowboy movie star. You know—with the white hat and white buckskin chaps and white horse and all those white teeth. And the King and Queen of Sargovia and Joe Glotch the ex-heavyweight champion and Lona Lane that new movie girl and her husband and my sister Lady Karfrey——"

"She here! When'd she come?" Vashti interrupted.

"Leigh flew over from London on Tuesday and flew on here next day. And Jordan's brother Bowie and his sister from Buffalo——"

"Uh-uh! Trouble. And who else?"

"Well—the Moreys are here from Dallas, and Congressman Bale Clinch, and Gabe Target stopped on his way down and Judge Whiteside and a South American ex-Presidente who's Ambassador now—I've forgotten which country—and Tara Tarova and some others—and Cal Otter's taking his white horse." The absurd list gave her a mischievous pleasure.

"On the plane?" Vashti asked somewhat nervously.

"It's all right. In the forward compartment. He's used to flying. We'll be up only an hour or two, Jordan wants to show the

23

King and Queen something of the ranch from the air, they're thinking of buying a few thousand acres up north in the Panhandle. They spent a day or two at the King ranch. Jordan says they bought some of Bob Kleberg's prize Brahman bulls."

"Kind of nice selling foreign royalty a bill of goods for a change. They been taking us for a couple hundred years. They better watch out or Jett Rink'll be unloading one of his dusters on 'em."

"That's a funny thing for them to do, go to ranching," Vashti commented. "A real king and queen like that."

"Nothing so funny about it," Pinky said. "The Prince of Wales —Duke of Windsor he is now—he owns a big country up in Canada, don't he!" He ruminated a moment. "Don't know's I ever met a king and queen. Socially, I mean. Course, they're out of business now, those two, you might say. But what do you call them, talking to them I mean?"

But before Pinky could benefit by an elementary lesson in the etiquette of royalty a battered jeep crunched to a jolting stop in the driveway as though it had been lassoed and a gaunt girl in boots, jeans and a fifty-dollar shirt swung long legs around the side. "Hi!" she said. She was hatless, her sun-bleached hair was tied back into a sort of horse's tail. She entered the veranda, she went through a routine that was the perfection of pretty manners. So-and-so Mrs. Snyth . . . this-and-that Pinky . . . see you at the party it sounds horrible doesn't it . . . where's Dad . . . I'm off . . .

"Luz, they'll all be here in a minute. Why don't you go with us in the big plane?"

"Oh, Ma! That hearse!"

"Amador's packing the lunch. We're eating on the plane. Don't you want something before you go?"

"How you going?" Pinky asked, though he knew well enough.

"I'm flying the little Snazzy. I'll stop on my way to the field and grab a hamburger at Jerky's place."

Pinky wagged his head knowingly. "You taking any passengers in that footbath?"

"Don't be roguish, Pinky."

"He ain't going to the rumpus, for God's sake!"

"He wouldn't be seen dead at it."

"He sure would if he went," Pinky asserted, quite solemnly. She was off with a neat little clatter of scuffed boots. Pinky called after her. "I am informed that Jerky's hamburgers are made of horse meat. Old beat-up quarter horses shot for their hides."

She stuck her head out of the jeep. "Plenty of onions and barbecue sauce, it'll be better than tough Texas beef." To the shouts of remonstrance at this heresy the jeep scuttled off like a frightened bug.

The eyes of the three followed her out of sight. They looked at each other. Silence hung momentarily between them. Vashti was not given to silences.

"Honey, she ain't serious about that dirt farmer, is she?"

But before Leslie could answer Pinky cut in, deftly.

"Now, Vashti, look who's talking. You married a low-down cow hand, didn't you?"

"Cow hand is different. This fella works afoot. Telling everybody, going around lecturing at Grange halls about this grass and that, blue grama—yella bluestem—side-oats grama—telling Texans been ranching all their life and their fathers and grandfathers how to run things. He don't even act like a Texan. Cornell University! Texas U. ain't good enough."

"What you think of Bob Dietz, Leslie?" Pinky asked baldly. "Might as well ask out, now Vashti's been and choused things up. Me, I got the opinion that boy is an unexception."

Very quietly Leslie Benedict said, "I think Bob Dietz may change the whole face of Texas—its system and its politics and its future."

Vashti Snyth gave a little yelp of shock. "Why Leslie Benedict, he ain't got five hundred dollars cash to his name!"

"I'd have said a hundred," Leslie replied quietly.

Now there came an acceleration of sound and movement from within the house and without. It was like the quickening of the tempo in a discordant modern symphony. From the dim interior of one of the rooms along the veranda emerged young Jordy Benedict with the Mexican girl who was his wife. They were hand in hand, like children afraid. There was between them a resemblance so marked that they might have been brother and sister. His hair was black but hers was blacker. He had inherited his from Leslie, his mother; she from centuries of Spanish forebears. Her skin was camellia-white, the Texas sun had hurled its red rays in vain. In their bearing, too, this young pair had a strange diffidence in common. Withdrawn, these two, as though alien to this familiar group. So young, so beautiful, they bore themselves with a shy uncertainty. Nothing about them of the confidence with which Luz had come and gone. The girl was dressed in black, very simple in cut, a strand of small pearls at her throat; and that throat and the face above it seemed almost translucent, as though a light were glowing behind them.

They knew their manners. Hers were quaintly old-world in their formality. She had been born in Texas, as he had been. Her father and mother, her grandfather and grandmother, her great-grandfather and great-grandmother and their forebears had been native to this land centuries before the word Texas had ever been heard. In a vortex of airplanes and bourbon and Brahman cattle and millions and little white mink capes and Cadillac cars and oil rigs and skyscrapers this girl moved and spoke in the manner of an ancient people in an ancient land.

"Hiyah, honey!" yelled Vashti as though addressing a deaf foreigner. "My, you sure look pretty."

To this the girl said nothing. With grave dignity she gave her hand to Vashti Snyth, to Pinky. "Sure do," echoed Pinky, and took her hand in his bone-crushing grip. She gave a little yelp, then she laughed like a child at sight of Jordan's startled look. For the moment the tension that had followed their entrance was broken.

"What do you think you're doing!" Jordy Benedict said, laughing, and pretending to shy away from Pinky's extended hand. "Bulldogging a steer?" He spoke with a slight stammer—not always marked when he was at ease, but now noticeable as he negotiated the word bulldogging.

"Hiyah, Jordan!" Pinky pronounced it Jurden, Texas fashion. "You and Juana flying down to the big blow, Doc?"

"No," Jordy said and turned away. He sat then on the arm of his wife's chair and flung one arm across the back. There was something defiant, something protective about the gesture. "We're driving—if we go."

Leslie put her hand lightly on the girl's knee. "Juana doesn't like flying. But then," she added quickly, "neither do I, really. I never have learned to take it for granted. I guess I belong to the generation that still thinks the automobile is a wonderful invention."

"What you wearing black for all the time, anyway?" Vashti shrilled at the girl. "Like a Mex——" She stopped, appalled. "I mean a little bitty thing like you, whyn't you wearing bright stuff, look at me, I got age on me but I go busting out like a rainbow."

Pinky shook his head in a mood of ruminant wonder. "Funny thing about women folks like Vashti here. Her young'uns growed up and married away, she's got to be riding herd on everybody else's."

"Mott Snyth!" The vast bosom heaved, the plump pink face crinkled like a baby's who is about to cry. "You go to saying things like that, mean, I've a good mind to——"

But at the sound of the quick drum of horse's hoofs the infantile face cleared magically. As Bick Benedict leaped off his horse a Mexican boy sprang from nowhere to mount the brisk little animal and, wheeling, clatter off to the stables.

There was nothing regal, certainly, in the outer aspect of this broad-shouldered figure in the everyday clothes of a Texas cowman. Yet here was the ruler of an empire. His high-heeled boots of black leather were stitched in colored thread, scuffed by hard wear, handmade, had cost perhaps sixty dollars; tight brown canvas pants tucked into the boot tops; brown shirt open at the throat; a canvas brush jacket; a Stetson, dust-stained, and rolled at the brim to make an exaggerated tricorne. Every garment he

27

wore was suited to the work and the climate of his world; and everything from his lariat to his saddle, from his boots to his hat, had been copied from the Mexican horsemen whose land this Texas had been little more than a century ago.

Just below the leather belt with its hand-tooled design of the reata the hard lean body was beginning to show a suspicion of a bulge. Sun wind dust had etched Bick Benedict's face, tanned the skin to warm russet. A strangely contradictory face, benign and arrogant. Benevolent and ruthless. The smile was nervous rather than mirthful. His was a deceptive gentleness; soft-spoken, almost mild. The eyes were completely baffling; guileless, visionary; calculating, shrewd.

Up since five, he was late, he was weary, he was beset, he had nicked his right forefinger in a magic new weighing machine they were installing down at the main corral. He threw a lot of Texas into his greeting now.

"Vashti! And Pinky! Well! This is mighty nice!" He clasped Pinky's little hand of steel, he took Vashti's plump fingers in his hand that was tough as rawhide. Vashti's color, normally pink, now became enriched by a maroon overlay. She had blushed in this way, painfully, at sight or touch of him ever since the day, over twenty years ago, when he had surprised Nueces County and the whole of Texas by bringing this Leslie, this Virginia girl unknown to them all, to Reata Ranch as his wife. Jilted they said. At least the same as jilted Vashti Hake. Even his sister Luz had as much as admitted they'd be married someday and you know how she glared if any woman so much as looked at him.

"Nearly winded Pronto getting here. Anything wrong, Leslie?" He poured a cup of coffee, drank it black and hot with the eagerness of need. People frequently were annoyed by the fact that as they talked to him he appeared not to be listening. He listened to nothing that did not vitally interest him; and nothing held his interest that was not vitally connected with this vast this fantastic kingdom over which he and his father and his grandfather had reigned for a hundred years. His was the detachment, the aloofness, the politely absent-minded isolation of royalty.

28

"They're late too," Leslie now said. "The cars went to the Big House half an hour ago."

He tensed to a distant sound. "There they are now. I'll change and be back before they're out of the cars."

"Pinky and Vashti are going with us. I thought we could drive down now, and all these people needn't get out of the cars———"

Over his shoulder as he strode indoors. "Better not do that. But I'll only be five minutes. Shave on the plane." He vanished into the shaded recesses of the house whose dim rooms seen from the veranda seemed to have a pale green quality like a scene glimpsed under water.

The gaze of the two older women followed him. In Vashti's eyes were bafflement and adoration and poignant hurt; in Leslie's wisdom and tenderness and the steady glowing warmth of a wife who, after many years of marriage and disillusionment, is still deeply in love with her husband.

A covey of long sleek grey cars; talk, over-hearty laughter. Two people only occupied the passenger space of the roomy first car though each following car held six or seven.

Leslie stood up. It was not merely the act of rising to her feet; there was about the simple act something that communicated itself to Vashti, relaxed and bountifully disposed in the depths of her chair, and to Pinky, squatting on his haunches as he tousled and played with the frisking dog, and to the two young people so silent and politely aloof.

A tall thin man in a black Homburg scrambled hastily down from the front seat which he had occupied with the Mexican driver and opened the door of the lead car. The urban incongruity of the black Homburg in that scene and climate gave the wearer the comic aspect of a masquerader. The King and Queen of Sargovia stepped out of the car. A thin somewhat horse-faced sad girl in a not very new French dress and a long double string of large genuine pearls which dangled drearily and looked dated because all the women were wearing two-strand chokers of cultured pearls that looked smarter and more genuine. The man was shorter than she with a long neck as though he had stretched it in an attempt to appear taller; and his Habsburg blood showed in his prognathous jaw which should have looked strong but didn't. He wore one of those suits carefully made by a Central European tailor who long ago had served an apprenticeship in London's Savile Row. But he had apparently lost the knack of line for the suit was tight where it should have been easy.

Leslie went forward to meet them as Vashti scrambled for the slipper at the side of her chair.

"I hope you slept, Sir. And you, Ma'am. Everyone was warned to be very quiet on pain of death, but you know . . . ranch noises are so . . . Sir, may I present Mrs. Mott Snyth. Mr. Mott Snyth . . . Ma'am, may I present . . ."

3

"IT ISN'T FAR," Bick Benedict assured them. "Four hundred miles. We're early. We can cruise around. I'd like to show you something of the Pecos section of Reata—from the air, of course. And you could have a look at historic old Beaumont later. That's the site of old Spindletop, you know."

"Spindletop?" said Miss Lona Lane, the movie girl. "Is that a mountain or something? I don't like flying over mountains very much."

The Texans present looked very serious which meant that they were bursting inside with laughter. The Dallas Moreys and

Congressman Bale Clinch and Gabe Target of Houston and Judge
Whiteside did not glance at each other. It was as though a tourist
in Paris had asked if Notre Dame was a football team.

"Uh—no," Bick Benedict said, turning on all his charm which
was considerable. Miss Lona Lane was extremely photogenic.
"Spindletop was the first big oil gusher in Texas. It dates back to
1901."

The Texans relaxed.

"What's this San Antone?" inquired Joe Glotch, the former
heavyweight champion turned sportsman and New Jersey res-
taurateur. "I heard that's quite a spot."

"Nothing there but Randolph Field," the Congressman assured him.

Bick Benedict addressed himself to the King.

"Perhaps tomorrow we can fly up to Deaf Smith County in
the Panhandle. There are some Herefords up there I'd like to
show you——"

"That would be interesting. What is the distance?"

"About eight hundred miles."

The young man smiled nervously, he fingered his neat dark
necktie. "To tell you the truth, I am not as accustomed to this
flying as you Texans. You see, my little country could be hidden
in one corner of your Texas. At home I rarely flew. It was considered too great a risk. Of course, that was when kings were . . .
Our pilots were always falling into the Aegean Sea. Or somewhere. Perhaps it is because we are not the natural mechanics
that you here in the great industrial United States——"

His English was precise and correct as was his wife's, clearly
the triumph of the Oxford tutor and English governess system
over the mid-European consonant.

"That's right," said Congressman Bale Clinch. "Here every
kid's got a car or anyway a motorbike. And a tractor or a jeep
is child's play. Flying comes natural, like walking, to these kids."

The group had been whisked to the ranch airfield where the
vast winged ship stood awaiting them. A miniature airport, complete, set down like an extravagant toy in the midst of the endless

plain. The airport station itself in the Spanish style, brilliantly white in the sunlight with its control tower and its sky deck and its neat pocket-handkerchief square of coarse grass and specimen cactus and the wind-sock bellying in the tireless Texas wind. A flock of small planes, two medium large Company planes, and the mammoth private plane of Jordan Benedict. Down the runway Luz was warming up for her flight, you could see the trembling of the little bright yellow bug, its wings glinting in the sun, gay as a clip in a Fifth Avenue jeweler's window.

They all climbed the metal steps, jauntily, into the hot shade of the plane's interior.

"It'll be cooler as soon as we get up," Bick Benedict called out. "We're pressurized." Seats upholstered in brilliant blue and yellow and rose and green, very modern and capacious. It was startling to see that they did not stand in orderly rows like the seats in a commercial plane, but were firmly fixed near the windows as casually as you would place chairs in a living room. The safety belts were in bright colors to match and the metal clasps bore the Reata brand. In the tail was a cozy section with banquettes upholstered in crimson leather and a circular table in the center for cards or for dining.

And there at the door as they entered was a slim dark-haired young steward in a smart French-blue uniform and beside him stood the blonde young stewardess in her slick skirted version of the same, and in the inner distance an assistant steward busy with wraps and little jewel cases and magazines.

A vibration, a humming, a buzzing a roaring; they lifted they soared, the strained expression left the faces of the King, the Queen, the Motion Picture Star, the Congressman, the South American—all the passengers who did not feel secure in life, whether up in the air or down on the ground.

"Bourbon!" boomed a big male voice. It was Judge Whiteside in reply to a question from the steward standing before him with tray and glasses.

The royal pair jumped perceptibly. The steward turned to them. "Bourbon? Scotch? Old-fashioned? Martini?"

"Oh, it's a—it's something to drink!" It was the first time the Queen had spoken since leaving the house.

"Well, sure," said Bale Clinch, "bourbon whiskey, what else would it be?"

"I have some relatives whose family name this is, in a way of speaking. May I know how the name of Bourbon came to be used for a whiskey?" the girl asked shyly.

"Well, ma'am," the Congressman began to explain, quite unconsciously addressing her correctly as he used the Texas colloquialism, "it's the best old whiskey there is, and it's made of mash that's better than fifty percent corn. It's named because they say it was first made in Bourbon County, Kentucky. My opinion, it was originally made in Texas."

Vashti Snyth's shrill voice came through with the piercing quality of a calliope whistle. "He'll tell you everything was originally made in Texas. Texas brag. Worse than the Russians."

Leslie made herself heard above the roar of the motors. "Here in the United States the word has still another meaning. Anyone who is extremely conservative—well, reactionary you know. We say he is a Bourbon. I hope you don't mind."

"Not at all," said the girl with an effort at gaiety. "But to have a good whiskey named after one is more flattering."

Fascinated, the two watched the male Texans tossing down straight bourbon. Bent on pleasing though they were, they refused it themselves knowing that this was no refreshment for a royal stomach, sedentary by habit and weak by inheritance. On the wagon, said the heavyweight ex-champion. Not before six P.M., said the cowboy movie star.

For Leslie Benedict there was about this vast and improbable vehicle and its motley company a dreamlike quality. Her sister Lady Karfrey was being studiedly rude to royalty, she had no time for the deposed or unsuccessful. They're behaving like refugees, Leslie thought. Worried and uncertain and insecure and over-anxious to please. Kings and queens deposed once were called exiles—splendid romantic exiles. Now they're only refugees, I suppose.

34

They alone stared out of the plane windows, in their eyes fright and unbelief mingled. Seen from the sky the arid landscape lay, a lovely thing. The plains were gold and purple, the clouds cast great blue-black shadows, there were toy boxes in a dark green patch that marked the oasis of an occasional ranch house, and near by the jade-green circlets that meant water holes. So, in the almost unbearably brilliant blue sky, they soared and roared aloft in a giant iridescent bubble. The ship was steady as a bathtub, the stewards were preparing lunch, there was a tantalizing scent of coffee. Everybody said everything was wonderful.

The casual arrangement of the seats and the roar of the engines made conversation difficult. So the company sat for the most part in a splendor of aerial isolation, earthly mortals helplessly caught up in a godlike environment.

The canny and taciturn Gabe Target, who was said to hold the mortgage on every skyscraper in Texas and to own at least half of all the oil leases, now turned conversationally to the royal pair. His face was benign and mild, his abundant white hair parted very precisely in the middle, he resembled a good old baby until he lifted the hooded eyelids and you saw the twin cold grey phlegms through which his ophidian soul regarded the world. His voice was low and somewhat drawling. Understand you're fixing to buy a ranch, you and the—uh—your good lady here. Takes a powerful sight of work, ranching. What you aiming to stock? Herefords?

Frantically the King snatched at the one familiar word which had emerged audibly from the rest.

"Ah yes, work! Everyone in your country works that is one of the wonderful things." In a panic lest Gabe Target should make further inaudible offerings he turned to encounter the fascinated stare of Lona Lane's husband seated just across the way. His royal training, drilled into him from the age of six, had taught him to file diplomatically in his memory names faces careers. At a loss now he regarded the tall moonfaced man smelling faintly of antiseptic. The eyes were myopically enlarged behind thick octagonal lenses, his maroon necktie matched his socks, his socks matched the faint stripe of his shirt. His beautifully manicured fingernails bore little white flecks under their glistening surface.

The King's voice was high and plangent, it had the effect of a hoot in a cave. "I know of your charming wife's career of course who does not but tell me what is your work your profession. Everyone works in this marvelous country of yours. And your name—I did not quite——"

The man, caught off guard, took a too hasty sip from the glass in his hand, coughed, managed to bow apologetically though seated. Recovering, "Lamax!" he roared. "G. Irwin Lamax. Oral specialist."

An expression of absolute incomprehension glazed his listener's face. Noting this, G. Irwin Lamax smiled and nodded understandingly. "Say, pardon *me*. I clean forgot you were a foreigner. I didn't go for to get you buffaloed with American talk." Smiling still more broadly he tapped his large even front teeth with a polished fingernail. "Oral specialist. Extractions. Teeth. Dentist."

The King stared, stiffened, remembered, smiled a frosty smile, he was trying hard to say democracy democracy in his mind. He glanced at the lovely Lona Lane, he looked out of the window at the seemingly endless reaches of Bick Benedict's empire, he closed his world-weary eyes a moment and wished himself quietly dead.

Bick Benedict, in response to a summoning glance from Leslie, came swiftly up the broad aisle between the seats. "Feeling all right, Sir? Well, I just thought . . . We're flying over the south section now, we always buzz them a little when we go over." He turned to face the assembled company, he stood an easy handsome figure in his very good tropical suit and his high-heeled polished tan boots; that boyish rather shy smile. He raised his voice. "Hold your hats, boys and girls! Hang on to your drinks. We're going to give the south section a little buzz. Here we go!"

For perhaps thirty seconds then the huge ship did a series of banks, swoops and dives. It was an utterly idiotic and wantonly frightening performance, Leslie thought. Unadult and cruel. Some of the women visitors from outside Texas screamed. The Texas men grinned, they said, "Now nothing to be scared of, honey. This ship's just feeling frisky as a cutting horse." The Texas-bred women looked unruffled and resigned like mothers who are accustomed to the antics of high-spirited children.

From her aloof place near the tail of the big room the aquiline Lady Karfrey barked, "Why don't you Texans grow up!"

Bick Benedict's brother Bowie and Bick's sister Maudie Placer from Buffalo turned upon her the gaze which native Texans usually reserve for rattlesnakes.

The ship righted itself, Leslie's lovely voice projected itself miraculously above the roar and the chatter. She pointed toward the windows and the plains below. "They're using the stinger on the mesquite. You might like to see it—those of you who aren't Texans."

"Stinger? What is a stinger?" the South American asked. Obedient faces were pressed against the windows, they surveyed a toy world.

"It's that yellow speck. Now we're a bit lower, you can see. The black patch is brush. The little thing moving along is the stinger, it's a kind of tank with great knives and arms and head like a steel monster. It's called a tree dozer too. It's rather fascinating to watch."

Up there, high in the sky, they could see the green patch of brushland that was a wilderness of mesquite. The trees were large and the thickness was dense and the yellow monster snorted and clanked and backed and attacked but they could not hear the snorts or sense the power. There was the green patch and then a path no longer green as the trees fell right and left like ninepins.

The King turned a shocked face away from the window. "But why do you cut down a forest like that!"

"That's no forest," Bick Benedict said. "That's mesquite."

"But these are trees. Trees."

Leslie turned from the window, she began to explain, brightly. "You see, the whole country's overrun with mesquite."

"Really! The whole of the United States!"

Oh dear! Leslie thought. Now I'm talking that way too. "No,

37

I meant only Texas. All this once was open prairie. Grazing country. Then the mesquite came in a little, it wasn't bad because
there are no trees to speak of, you know. Then they brought
cattle in from Mexico where the mesquite was growing. Some
say that the cattle droppings carried the seed. Others say that
when they built all these thousands of miles of automobile roads
they stopped the prairie fires that used to sweep the earth clean
of everything but grass——"

The voice of Maudie Placer, Bick's perpetually angry sister,
broke in with a sneering quality of almost comic dimensions.
"Really, Leslie, you're getting to be quite a rancher, aren't you!
You must have been reading books again." But no one heeded
this or even heard it except the three women who knew—Leslie
herself, and her good friend Adarene Morey and the outspoken
amiable Vashti Snyth.

"But your serfs," said the King. "The peons I see everywhere
here. Could they not have removed this mesquite with hand labor
before it grew to such——"

"Serfs!" roared Bale Clinch. "Why, we got no serfs here in this
country! Everybody here is a free American."

"Yes, of course," agreed the King hastily. "Certainly. I see. I
see."

He does see, Leslie thought. He's only a frightened little king
without a kingdom but he sees.

"Lunch!" cried Vashti happily as the steward and the stewardess and the assistant steward appeared, quite a little procession,
with trays. "Mm! Leslie, you do have the loveliest food! Nobody
in Texas has food like Leslie's. Avocados stuffed with crab meat
to begin with! My!"

It was midafternoon as they came down at the Hermoso airport, the shabby old municipal airport. As they buckled their
seat belts for the landing their faces were pressed against the
windows, they beheld glittering beside the scrofulous old airport
the splendid white and silver palace which Jett Rink had flung
down on the prairie. Spanning the roof of the building was a gigantic silver sign that, treated with some magic chemical, shone

38

day and night so that the words JETT RINK AIRPORT could be seen from the air and from the ground for miles across the flat plains from noon to midnight to noon.

"Oh, look!" cried Adarene Morey. A trail of heaven-blue as if a streamer of sky had been tossed like a scarf to the earth spelled out the omnipresent name of Jett Rink.

"It's bluebonnets!" Leslie said, and her voice vibrated with resentment. "He has had bluebonnets planted and clipped and they spell his name. In bluebonnets!"

"How cute!" said Lona Lane. "It's simply fabulous! I'm dying to meet him."

It was the pallid Queen who put forward the query this time. "We ask a great many questions, I am afraid. But bluebonnets—what is it that this is?" In a literal translation from the French.

"Why girlie!" bawled Bale Clinch—he had had three bourbons—"girlie, you been neglected in your Texas education down there at the Benedicts'. Bick, you old sonofagun, what's a matter with that old schoolhouse you got on your country you're always bragging on!" He beamed now on the Queen. "Bluebonnets! Everybody knows they're the national state flower of Texas. The most beautiful flower in the most wonderful state in the world. That's all bluebonnets is." He pondered a moment. "Are."

The huge craft touched the runway as delicately, as sensitively as a moth on a windowpane. The clank of metal as straps were unbuckled. The Texans strolled to the door as casually as one would proceed from the house to the street. The visitors breathed a sigh of relief. They stood ready to disembark, huddled at the door, king and cowboy and rancher and politician and actress and statesman and shrewd operator and housewife. Royalty in the lead.

At the door, smiling but military in bearing, stood the slim young steward and the pretty stewardess. "Come back quick now!" the girl chirped.

"I beg your pardon!" said the King, startled.

"It's a—a phrase," Leslie explained. "It's the Texas way of saying good-bye."

39

Just before they descended the aluminum stairway that had been trundled quickly across the field for their landing Bick Benedict made a little speech, as host.

"Look, I'm going to brief you, kind of. Those of you who aren't Texians. This is the old airport, you know. The new one isn't open for traffic until after tonight. That's where the party's to be. I'm afraid there'll be photographers and so forth waiting out there; and reporters."

"You don't think Jett Rink's going to lose a chance like this for publicity, do you, Bick?" Lucius Morey called out, and a little laugh went up among the Texans.

"This is going to be a stampede," Gabe Target predicted.

"No, now, Gabe. Everything'll be fine if you'll just trail me, you know I'm a good top hand, Gabe. There's a flock of cars waiting, we'll pile right in and head for the hotel. And remember, everything's pilone. No one touches a pocket—except to pull a gun of course."

Even the outsiders knew this was a standard laugh. But, "Pilone?" inquired Joe Glotch.

"Means everything free," yelled Congressman Bale Clinch, "from Jett Rink's hotel and back again."

"Yes," drawled Pinky Snyth. "And I'll give anybody odds that Gabe Target here will own the hotel and the airport and the whole outfit away from Jett Rink inside of three years."

There were the photographers kneeling for close shots, standing on trucks for far shots. There were planes and planes and planes overhead and underfoot. A Texas big town commercial airfield. Squalling kids, cattlemen in big hats and high-heeled boots—the old-timers. The modern young business and professional men, hatless, their faces set and serious behind bone-rimmed spectacles, their brief cases under their arms as they descended the planes from Dallas and Lubbock and Austin and El Paso. Local air lines with cosmic names tacked to and fro between cotton towns and oil towns, wheat towns and vegetable valleys. Hatless housewives in jeans or ginghams with an infant on one arm and a child by the hand flew a few hundred miles to do a bit of shopping and see the home folks. Everywhere you saw the pilots in uniform—slightly balding young men who had been godlike young aviators with war records of incredible courage. Years ago they had come down out of the wild blue yonder; and now they found themselves staring out at the Southwest sky in two-engined jobs that ferried from Nacogdoches to Midland, from Brownsville on the Mexican border to Corpus Christi on the Gulf. In the duller intervals of the trip they would emerge from the cockpit to chat with a sympathetic passenger and to display the photograph of the thin and anxious-looking young wife and the three kids, the oldest of these invariably a boy and always of an age to make the beholder certain that he had been born of their frantic love and their agonized parting in '42 and '43.

The Wonder Bird, the dazzling invention of the twentieth century, had become a common carrier, as unremarkable here in Texas as the bus line of another day.

"This way!" Bick Benedict called. "Just follow me through this gate, it's supposed to be closed but I know the . . . right through here . . . those are our cars lined up out there. . . ."

There were signs printed in large black letters on the walls. One sign read DAMAS. Another, CABALLEROS. "What's that?" inquired Lona Lane scurrying by. "What's that sign mean?"

"Sh-sh!" Vashti Snyth hissed as she puffed along. "That's Spanish. Means toilets for the Mexicans. Men and women, it means."

Through the motor entrance another sign read RECLAME SU EQUIPAJE AFUERA A SU DERECHA. Miss Lane glanced at this, decided against inquiring.

"H'm," said the ex-Presidente. "I find this interesting, these signs in Spanish. It is like another country, a foreign country in the midst of the United States."

"Texas!" protested old Judge Whiteside puffing along, red-faced and potbellied. "Why, sir, Texas is the most American country in the whole United States."

"I should have thought New England, or perhaps the Middle West. Kansas or even Illinois."

"East!" scoffed Judge Whiteside. "The East stinks."

Through the withering blast of the white-hot sun again and then into the inferno of the waiting motorcars that had been standing so long in the glare. The newspaper men and women crowded around the windows, they said lean forward a little will you king, as they tried for another picture.

Bick Benedict's eyes blazed blue-black. "Look here, you fellas!" But Leslie put a hand on his arm, she was the diplomatic buffer between Bick and his rages against the intruding world forever trying to peer into the windows of his life.

"We'll see you all later," she called in that soft clear voice of hers. "Tonight." She pressed her husband's arm.

"See you later, boys," Bick muttered grumpily, not looking at them. He climbed into the huge car in which the King and Queen were seated in solitary grandeur except for the driver and their aide in the front.

"You all going to be at the Conky?" one of the reporters yelled after them as they moved off. Leslie, with the others about to step into one of the line of waiting cars, smiled over her shoulder at the cluster of reporters and cameramen. "Conky," she repeated after them with distaste. She caught a glimpse of the royal pair, an artificial smile still pasted, slightly askew, on their faces. Then their car picked up speed and was away like the lead car in a funeral cortege. The grimace of forced amiability faded from their weary features. With a gesture Leslie seemed to wipe the smile from her own countenance, she thought, I'm one of a family of rulers, too, by marriage. The Benedicts of Texas. I wonder how soon we're going to be deposed.

Somehow the first formality of the earlier hours was gone. Helter-skelter they had piled into the capacious cars and now there mingled affably in one big interior the prize fighter and Vashti and Pinky, Leslie, the South American and the Congressman. The car doors were slammed with the rich unctuous sound of heavy costly mechanism.

"Do you object," inquired the ex-Presidente as the cortege

drove off, "that I ask so many questions? After all, I am here to learn. We are Good Neighbors, are we not?"

"Oh, please!" Leslie said quickly. "Please do."

"Uh—Conqui? However it is spelled. Is that the name of a man like this Jettrink?"

"That's two names, you know. His first name is Jett. His last name is Rink. Conky. Well, they just call it that, it's a sort of nickname for the big new hotel. The Conquistador. Jett Rink built that too."

"Mm! The Spanish is very popular here, I can see. And this Jett Rink whose name I hear so often. He is a great figure in the United States of America?"

"Say, that's a good one," said Mott Snyth. Then, at a nudge from his wife, "Pardon me." A little cloud of ominous quiet settled down upon the occupants of the car.

Through this Leslie Benedict spoke coolly. "This Jett Rink about whom you hear so much—he's a spectacular figure here in Texas."

"They say he was weaned on loco weed when he was a baby," Vashti babbled. "He's always trying to do something bigger or costs more money than anybody else. They say this Hermoso airport's bigger than any in the whole United States. La Guardia, even. And this hotel we're going to, why, ever since he saw the Shamrock in Houston he said he was going to put up a hotel bigger and fancier and costing more than even it did. And that's the way he always does. Ants," she concluded, smiling her cherubic smile at the gravely attentive South American diplomat, "in his pants."

Congressman Bale Clinch spoke cautiously. "You'd be put to it, trying to explain Jett Rink outside of Texas."

Whirling along the broad roads, past the huddled clusters of barbecue shacks and sun-baked little dwellings like boxes strewn on the prairie. Oleanders grew weed-wild by the roadside, the green leaves and pink blossoms uniformly grey with dust.

Little Pinky Snyth, grinning impishly, addressed himself to the visitors. He spoke in the Texas patois, perhaps perversely perhaps because instinct told him that this was the proper sauce with which to serve up a story about Jett Rink.

"Well, say, maybe this'll give you some notion of Jett."

Congressman Bale Clinch cleared his throat, obviously in warning.

"Pinky, you ain't aiming to tell about that little trouble with the veteran, are you, I wouldn't if I was you, it's liable to give a wrong notion of Texas."

"No. No this is nothing serious, this is about that fellow up to Dalhart," he addressed himself to the Ambassador, and to Joe Glotch, impartially. "That's way up in Dallam County in the Panhandle. This fella, name of Mody—yes, Mody, that was it— he had a little barbecue shack by the road up on Route 87. He got a knack of fixing barbecued ribs they say it had a different taste from anybody else's and nobody can get the hang of the flavor even tasting it and nobody's wangled the receipt off of him, he won't give. So Jett Rink he hears about these ribs and one night when he's good and stinking he gets in his plane with a couple of other umbrys, he always travels with a bunch of body- guards, they fly up to Dalhart it's as good as a thousand miles or nearly and the place is closed the fella's gone to bed. Jett and the others they rout him out they make him fix them a mess of barbecued ribs and they eat it and Jett says it's larrupin' and what has he got in the barbecue sauce makes it taste different. This Mody says it's his receipt it's his own original mix and he don't give it out to nobody. Well, Jett gets hot the way he does, he started out just rawhiding but now he gets wild the way he does when he's by-passed, he gets serious he starts fighting like he does when he's been drinking they had beer and whiskey too with the barbecue. He hits the fella over the head with a beer bottle, the fella dies, Jett has to pay his widow ten fifteen thousand dollars besides all the other expenses and lawyers and fixers and the plane trip and all, why it must of cost Jett Rink better than twenty-five thousand dollars to eat that plate of barbecue. It'd been cheaper for Jett to buy that fella and his barbecue shack and all that part of town including the grain elevator. Funny thing about Jett. If he can get a thing he don't want it. But if he wants it and can't get it, watch out."

"That's right," ruminated Congressman Bale Clinch. "Yes sir. You got to say this for Jett Rink. He goes after what he wants."

A heavy silence fell upon the occupants of the great rich car as it swept along the sun-drenched streets of Hermoso's outskirts.

Leslie Benedict had been sitting with her eyes shut. Vashti Snyth reached over and patted her hand almost protectively as a mother might touch a child. She ignored the presence of the others.

"Mott got one fault, it's talking. Talktalktalk. What he missed out in growing he makes up in gab."

Congressman Bale Clinch smiled chidingly upon her. "Now now, Vashti. You hadn't ought to talk about your lord and master thataway." He then roared as at an exquisitely original witticism.

"We will soon be there," Leslie said to the Ambassador. "Just another minute or two. The Conquistador isn't in the heart of the city, you know. Like the other hotels. It's almost like a big resort hotel. Very lavish."

"Air-conditioned," shrilled Vashti, "from cellar to roof, every inch of it—except the help's quarters, a course. They say there's guests there never had their faces outdoors since Jett flang it open —or sealed it shut, you might put it."

"And the recipe for the barbecue," the South American persisted gently. "Did he get it then?"

Pinky looked doubtful. "Well sir, I never rightly heard. The place was closed down or sold out. Jett he felt terrible about the whole thing when he sobered up. There was a daughter, girl about eighteen, she got a job in Jett's outfit somewheres. In the office in Hermoso or Houston or Dallas or somewheres. Did real well."

"She sure did!" said Vashti with more bite than her speech usually carried.

Silence again. The streets were broad boulevards now, the houses were larger, they became pretentious. Hermoso oil and

45

cattle society had gone in for azaleas, the motorcars flashed past masses of brilliant salmon-pink and white and orchid and now you could see the towers of the Conqueror, the Conquistador, rising so incongruously there in suburban Hermoso thirty stories up from the flat Texas plain. Towers, balconies, penthouses, palm trees, swimming pool. Flags and pennants swirled and flirted in the hot Gulf breeze—the single-starred flag of the Lone Star State, the Stars and Stripes above this, but grudgingly; and fluttering from every corner and entrance and tower the personal flag of Jett Rink, the emblem of his success and his arrogance and his power, with his ranch brand centered gold on royal blue as he had sketched it years ago in his own hand—years and years before he had owned so much as a maverick cow or a gallon of oil: the J and the R combined to make the brand JR. Houses had been razed, families dispossessed, businesses uprooted, streets demolished to make way for this giant edifice. All about it, clustered near—but not too near—like poor relations and servitors around a reigning despot, were the little structures that served the giant one.

4

ROYAL BLUE and gold smote the eye, the air swam with it. The doorman's uniform, the porter, the swarm of bellboys that sprang up like locusts. Royal-blue carpet in the vast lobby. Gold pillars. Masses of hothouse blue hydrangeas and yellow lilies. The distinguished guests were engulfed in a maelstrom of boots, spurs, ten-gallon hats, six-foot men; high shrill voices of women, soft drawling voices of sunburned men; deep-cushioned couches and chairs hidden under their burden of lolling figures staring slack-jawed at the milling throng, their aching feet wide-flung on the thick-piled carpet. An unavailing vacuum cleaner whined

47

in a corner, an orchestra (in blue and gold) sawed discordantly against a cacophony of canned music which someone had senselessly turned on and which now streamed from outlets throughout the gigantic room and the corridors and shops that bounded it. The Conquistador was a city in itself, self-contained, self-complacent, almost majestically vulgar. Downstairs and upstairs, inside and out, on awnings carpets couches chairs desks rugs; towels linen; metal cloth wood china glass, the brand JR was stamped etched embroidered embossed woven painted inlaid.

Later, over a soothing bourbon consumed in the privacy of the Snyth suite together with ten or twelve neighboring guests who had drifted in from this floor or that, Pinky incautiously observed, "Jett's sure got his brand on everything. Prolly got his initials cut in the palm trees out there. Puts me in mind of a little feist dog gets excited and leaves his mark on everything he can lift his leg against."

What with Bick Benedict's familiarity with fiestas such as this, and Leslie Benedict's clear orderly sense of situation, the members of their group had, for the most part, been safely disposed in their Conquistador quarters, each according to his importance as seen through the eyes of the Manager, the Assistant Manager and the Room Clerk, guided perhaps for this very special occasion by the bloodshot orb of Jett Rink himself. Protean couches could magically transform single sitting rooms into bedrooms. Good enough for an ex-Presidente, the hard-pressed Management instantly decided. Sitting room and bedroom in a nice spot for the heavyweight ex-champion. Nice little suite for Cal Otter the Cowboy Movie Star, where the crowd could get at him for autographs and so on. Snappy little balcony job for Lona Lane where the photographers could catch her for outside shots if the swimming pool section got too rough. Never could tell with a gang like this, liquored up and out with the bridle off. The Coronado penthouse suite for the Bick Benedicts and the Hernando de Soto apartment for the King and Queen, ex or not, the Management said in solemn discussion, they were a bona fide king and queen even if they had been cut out, you couldn't laugh that off and it would look good in publicity. This festive opening of Hermoso's airport, gift of the fabulous Jett Rink, had turned Jett Rink's hotel (mortgaged or not, as gossip said, for something like thirty millions) into a vast and horrendous house party. There wasn't a room or a closet or a cupboard to be had by an outsider. From lobby to roof the structure was crammed with guests each of whom had a precious pasteboard, named and numbered, which would identify and place him at Jett Rink's gigantic airport banquet tonight.

The contrast between the blazing white-hot atmosphere of Hermoso's streets and the air-conditioned chill of every Conquistador room, restaurant, hall, was breath-taking, like encountering a glacier in the tropics. From every corridor, hurtling out through every room whether open-doored or closed, you heard the shrieks of high shrill laughter, booming guffaws, the tinkle of glass, a babble of voices; and through and above it all the unceasing chatter of radios, the twang and throb of cheap music, the rumble of rolling tables laden with food or drink trundled along the halls by stiffly starched blue-and-gold waiters or tightly tailored blue-and-gold bellboys bearing themselves like the militia, discreet as secret service men; wise, tough, avaricious, baby-faced.

Tee-hee ho-ho yak-yak. Wham. Whoop-ee!

"I wish we had friends as amusing as that," Leslie Benedict said to her husband across the vast spaces of the Coronado suite.

"No you don't," said Bick Benedict. "And don't be like that."

"Like what?" Leslie said. She was standing at the window which was tightly closed because of the air conditioning, and looking out at the view which consisted of nothing—unless one found refreshing an endless expanse of flat prairie pushing the horizon into obscurity.

"Like the kind of person you aren't. Like dear Lady Karfrey your bitter bitchy sister. Bitterness doesn't become you."

"What's the opposite of lebensraum, Bick? That's what's the matter with them. They've got too much space. It gives them delusions of grandeur. In the plane they kept on yelling about it being the most wonderful place in the world—the most wonderful people in the world, the biggest cattle, fruit, flowers, vegetables, climate, horses. It isn't. They aren't. And what's so important about bigness, anyway? Bigness doesn't make a thing better."

"All right. I'll bite. What is?" He was at the telephone. "Room Clerk. . . . Well, I'll hold on. . . . Don't say that damned Riviera. Or California."

"No. No, I think the temperate climate of the United States. New York, or Pennsylvania, or Virginia or even Ohio. Cold in the winter with lemon-yellow sunshine and enough snow to make you long for spring. Hot in summer, cool in the spring, tangy in the autumn. You know where you are and you don't have to explain about it all the time and try to sell it as they do here in Texas."

". . . Hello! Room Clerk? . . . This is Bick Benedict. . . . Oh, fine fine! . . . No, I don't want to speak to the Manager, I just want to know if . . . Oh, God, he's connecting me with the . . . Hello there, Liggett! . . . Yes, everything's wonderful . . . yes, she's here looking at the view . . . yes, she thinks the furnishings are wonderful . . . no, don't bother to send anything up thanks just the same we brought a lot of stuff with us . . . sure sure if we need anything we'll . . . Look, I called the Room Clerk to find out if my daughter Luz—uh—Miss Luz Benedict you know—had come in yet, I . . . Oh, for . . . he's putting me back on the Room Clerk. . . . Hello! Look, can you tell me if Miss Luz Benedict . . ."

They were in the enormous bedroom. Blond wood, bleached like a Broadway chorus girl. Their feet seemed to flounder ankle-deep in chenille. "They ought to give you snowshoes for these carpets," Bick said. "Or skis. Liable to get in up to your neck and never get out."

A half acre of dressing table laden with perfumes, china, glass. A dining room of bleached mahogany but vaguely oriental in defiance of Coronado. The dining table could seat thirty. There was a metal kitchen complete and as virgin as the culinary unit in a utilities company window. Vast consoles in the entrance hall and living room. Overpowering lamps with tent-size shades.

Three bedrooms. Terraces. A bathroom in pink tile, a bathroom in yellow tile, a bathroom in aquamarine, and here deference was done to Coronado in terms of brilliant varnished wallpaper depicting conquistadores in armor dallying with maidens of obscure origin amongst flora not now indigenous to Texas.

Leslie had taken off the blue shantung and was making a tour of the vast and absurd living room, so cold in its metal and satin and brocade and glass and pale wood and air conditioning. She surveyed this splendor with an accustomed eye. It had been theirs on the occasion of the hotel's opening a year earlier. With one hand Leslie hugged her peignoir more tightly about her for warmth while with the other hand she patted cold cream on her face, walking slowly the length of the room and pausing now and then before some monstrous structure of porcelain or carved wood or painting.

"There's no JR on the Meissen or the pictures," she called back to Bick. "What must Coronado think! Except for a few liquor spots on the carpet and cigarette burns on the wood everything has stood up wonderfully this past year. I hope Hernando de Soto has done as well for the King and Queen."

"You were all right on the plane. You promised me you would be and you were." He stood in the great doorway in shirt and shorts and bedroom slippers, a costume becoming only to males of twenty and those in the men's underwear advertisements. "I know you didn't want to come but we had to and you damn well know why. Even if millions are dross to you. I don't bother you with business affairs but you had to know that and now I'm telling you again. . . . And where's Luz I'd like to know! And Jordy and Juana. Why couldn't they come with us the way other people's kids would! No, Luz had to fly her own, and Jordan and Juana had to drive. And now where are they! And you stand there and talk about the climate of Pennsylvania and Meissen and Coronado and what's the opposite of lebensraum. And spots on the carpet."

She went to him, she had to stand on tiptoe, tall though she was.

GIANT

"If you don't mind the cold cream I can stand the shaving soap." She kissed him not at all gingerly. "No soap there, at least."

"You hate the whole thing, don't you? As much as ever. That's why you talk like a—like a——"

"Like one of those women in the Marquand novels you don't read. Very quippy. Don't worry about the children. They'll make the dinner. Their behavior is odd but their manners are beautiful."

"Like their mother, wouldn't you say?"

"That's right, amigo. We'd better dress. Entacucharse, eh?"

"Now listen, Leslie. It's bad enough having Luz talking pachuco. Where do you hear it? The boys on our place don't talk like that."

"Oh, yes they do. The young ones. The kids in the garage. And on the street corners in Benedict. Just today in the kitchen that young Domingo Quiroz, Ezequiel's grandson, was looking at a leaky pipe that needed welding. He said, 'La paipa está likeando hay que hueldearla.' That's the sort of Spanish the kids are speaking."

"Entacucharse, eh? Dress to kill. Well, I haven't a zoot suit, have I?"

"I had Eusebio pack your white dinner clothes and black cummerbund and I've even ordered a deep red carnation for your buttonhole—probably the only red carnation in Texas. You'll be smart as paint."

He glanced down at himself, he contracted his stomach muscles sharply. "Riding does it. Everybody else lolling around in cars all the time. Even the vaqueros ride herd in jeeps half the time."

"Just remember to tuck in like that when you wrap your lithe frame into your cummerbund or you'll never make the first button. Look. We'll have to dress."

Here in southern Texas as in the tropics, there was little lingering twilight. It was glaring daylight, it was dark.

"Where're those damned kids!"

"Luz is probably out at the airfield chumming with the me-

52

chanics. Perhaps Jordy and Juana decided not to come. And even if they did, you know they're driving. That takes——"

"Thanks. I know how long it takes. I'm kind of from Texas too, remember?"

He was like that now. On the defensive, moody.

"Yes, dear. Get into our clothes and then we'd better give our Noah's Ark a roll call. Shall we go as we came out—you with the King and Queen and I with—doesn't it sound silly!"

Hermoso's old airport, so soon to be discarded, seemed a dim and dated thing huddling shabbily, wistfully, outside the glow and sparkle of the Jett Rink palace. Planes were coming and going on the old strip. Against the solid fences that separated the two fields were massed thousands of townspeople staring, staring, their white faces almost luminous in the reflected light. They talked and milled and shoved and drank Coca-Cola and the small children chased each other round and about their elders' legs, and the men shifted the sleeping babies hanging limp on their shoulders. "Lookit," they said. "Lookit the big lights up yonder. . . . I bet that's the Governor coming in there. . . . Stop that stompin' around, Alvin. Come here, I say, afore I whup you."

"Biggest airport in the whole state of Texas. Texas hell! In the whole United States Hermoso's the biggest. They say it makes anything they got in the East—New York or anywheres—look like a prairie-dog hole."

And in the deeper shadows stood the Hermosans of Mexican heritage, their darker faces almost indistinguishable in the gloom. These were quiet, the children did not run about with squawking catcalls; the boys and girls of sixteen, seventeen, sometimes stood with their arms about each other's waists, but demurely, almost primly, with their parents' eyes approvingly upon them. The roads beyond were choked with every kind of motorcar and in these, too, the people stood up and stared and wondered and applauded in their curious psychological consciousness, which was a mixture of childlike hope and provincial self-satisfaction.

"They lease that piece I got up in Tom Green County and it

53

don't come in a duster I can be in there next year along with any of 'em, Jett Rink or any of 'em. All you need is one good break. What was he but a ranch hand, and not even a riding hand. Afoot. And now lookit!"

Lookit indeed. The guests came in cars the size of hearses and these were not stuck in the common traffic. Each carried a magic card and whole streets and outlying roads were open only to them. The women had got their dresses in New York or at Neiman's in Dallas or Opper-Schlink's in Houston. Given three plumes, they could have been presented just as they stood at the Court of St. James's. Their jewels were the blazing plaques and chains you see in a Fifth Avenue window outside of which a special policeman with a bulge on his hip is stationed on eight-hour duty. Slim, even chic, there still was lacking in these women an almost indefinable quality that was inherent in the women of the Eastern and Midwestern United States. Leslie Benedict thought she could define it. In the early days of her marriage she had tried to discuss it with her husband as she had been accustomed to talk with her father during her girlhood and young womanhood—freely and gaily and intelligently, lunge and riposte, very exhilarating, adult to adult.

"They lack confidence," she had said in the tones of one who has made a discovery after long search. "That's it. Unsure and sort of deferential. Like oriental women."

"What do you think they should be? Masculine?"

"I was just speaking impersonally, darling. You know. Even their voices go up at the end of a declarative sentence, instead of down. It's sort of touching, as though they weren't sure you'd like what they've said and were willing to withdraw it. Like this. I asked that Mrs. Skaggs where she lived and she said, 'Uvalde?' with the rising inflection. It's appealing but sort of maddening, too."

"Well, you know the old Texas saying. In Texas the cattle come first, then the men, then the horses and last the women."

Now, as they drove into the vast airfield and stopped at the floodlighted entrance, Leslie was thinking of these things without

54

emotion, but almost clinically as she had learned she must if she would survive. Mindful of their two most distinguished guests in the crush and glare and clamor of the entrance they had somehow lost the South American. "It's all right," Bick said. "We'll pick him up inside. And we're all at the same table."

"Oh, Bick!" Leslie called through the roar and din. "Did you give him his card, I think it would have been better to give everyone a card just in case they were lost—oh, there he is in the doorway. Why—what——!"

The olive-skinned aquiline face, the slim and elegant figure in full evening dress, was easily distinguishable in the midst of the gigantic Texans in cream-colored suits, in dun-colored tropicals, in Texas boots and great cream Stetsons, worn in arrogance and in defiance of the negligible universe outside their private world. Even in the welter of waving arms, the shrill greetings, the booming laughter, the shoving and milling, the handshaking the back-slapping, "Well, if it ain't Lutch, you old sonofagun! You telling me you left that wind-blown sand-stung Muleshoe town of yours and all those cow critters to come to this——" even in the midst of this hullabaloo it was plain that something was wrong.

"Hurry, Bick. What is it?"

The men behind the door ropes were none of your oily head-waiters full of false deference and distaste for the human race in evening clothes. Giants in khaki guarded the entrance, and on their slim hips their guns, black and evil, gleamed above the holster flaps. And now, as Bick Benedict elbowed his way through the throng near the doorway, he heard one of the most gigantic of these guardians say, as he snapped with a contemptuous thumb and middle finger the stiff card in his other hand: "Well, you sure look like a cholo to me, and no Mexicans allowed at this party, that's orders and besides none's invited that's sure."

"Oh God, no!" cried Bick Benedict, and battered his way past resistant flesh and muscle to reach the giant cerberus. He called to him as he came. "Hi, Tod! Tod! Hold that, will you! Hold on there!" And the other man's head turning toward him, a curious greyish tone like a film over the olive skin, his dark eyes stony with outrage. Bick reached them, he put a hand on the faultlessly tailored sleeve, the other on Tod's steely wrist. "Look, Tod, this gentleman is one of the honored guests this evening, he's going to be the new Ambassador from Nuevo Bandera, down in South America. He's come all the way from Washington to——" His voice was low, insistent.

Tod's sunburned face broke into a grin that rippled from the lips to the eyes, he spoke in the soft winning drawl of his native region. "Well, I'm a hollow horn! I sure didn't go for to hurt your feelings. I made a lot of mistakes in my day but this does take the rag off the bush." He held out his great hand. "Glad to make your acquaintance. Sure sorry, Bick. Pass right along, gentlemen. Hi there, Miz Benedict, you're looking mighty purty."

There isn't anything to do, Leslie said to herself as she slipped her hand through her guest's arm, there isn't anything to do but ignore the whole thing unless he speaks of it.

She chatted gaily. "It's going to be a shambles, so crowded. We don't have to stay late after the dinner if you want to leave—you and the others. It's just one of those things—everybody's supposed to show up—you know—like a Washington reception when you can't get near the buffet. You've probably never before in your life seen Stetsons worn with black dinner coats or women in Mainbocher evening gowns escorted by men in shirt sleeves and boots." She looked about her. "Perhaps escorted isn't exactly the word."

Dinner, presaged by a jungle of tables and tables and tables, was to be served in the great domed main concourse. A bedlam, designated on the engraved invitations as a reception, was in progress in great sections and halls and rooms that next week would be restaurants, lunch rooms, baggage rooms, shops, offices. Every ticket and travel counter tonight was a bar. Travel signs were up, neat placards bearing the names of a half dozen air lines. And off the main hall were arrowed signs that said LADIES and others that said COLORED WOMEN. Orchids and great palms and tubs of blossoming trees. Banners, pennants, blinding lights. The reception now was spilling over into the concourse, into the patio and out to the runways. Kin Kollomore's Band over there. Oddie Boogen's Band over here. The loudspeakers were on, the blare was frightening, it beat on the brain like a pile driver.

Perhaps escorted isn't the word, Leslie had said somewhat maliciously. The men—the great mahogany-faced men bred on beef—who somehow had taken on physical dimensions in proportion to the vast empire they had conquered—stood close together, shoulder to shoulder, as male as bulls; massive of shoulder, slim of flank, powerful, quiet and purposeful as diesel engines. On the opposite side of the room, huddled too, but restless, electric, yearning, stood the women in their satins and chiffons and jewels. The men talked together quietly, their voices low and almost musical in tone. The women were shrill as peacocks, they spread their handmade flounces and ruffles; white arms waved and beckoned.

"Ay-yud!" a wife called to a recalcitrant husband. "Mary Lou Ellen says at Jett's big bowil last year at the Conky opening they was ten thousand——"

"Sure nuff," Ed calls back, nodding and smiling agreeably, though no sound is heard above the din. He remains with the men.

"Ay-yud's had the one over the eight he's feelin' no pain," his wife says philosophically, turning back to her women friends.

The Ambassador regarded this with an impassive face. "It is interesting," he said, "that the people of this country of Texas——"

"Country!"

"It is like a country apart. It is different from any other North American state I have seen and I have traveled very widely here in the United States. It is curious that the citizens of Texas have adopted so many of the ways and customs of the people they despise."

"How do you mean?" Leslie asked as though politely conversational. She knew.

"In Latin countries—in Mexico and in Spain and Brazil and other South American countries including my own Nuevo Ban-

57

dera—you often will find the men gathered separately from the women, they are talking politics and business and war and national affairs in which the women are assumed not to be interested."

"Or informed?"

Leslie, the outspoken, looked at him, she felt admiration and almost affection for this man who had met insult with such dignity. "Here in Texas we are very modern in matters of machinery and agriculture and certain ways of living. Very high buildings on very broad prairies. But very little high thinking or broad viewpoint. But they're the most hospitable people, they love entertaining visitors——"

He inclined toward her in a little formal diplomatic bow. "I am happily aware of that, madame."

"Oh, I didn't mean—I just—sometimes I forget I'm a Texan by marriage. But thank you. I—you see they're really wonderful in a crisis. In the last war—and the First World War too—the Texans were the most patriotic and courageous——"

"Yes. I know. But war is, as you say, a crisis—an excrescence, a cancer on the body of civilization. It is what a people do and think in the time of health and peace that is most important." He was very quiet and collected and somehow aloof in the midst of the turmoil all about them. Like Jordy's wife Juana, she thought suddenly. Remote, like Juana. He was speaking again, through the uproar. "But you are not a Texan?"

"No. But my husband is, of course, and all his people since the beginning of—— Oh, it must be dinner. They're moving toward the other room. Our party is all at the same table, it's Number One on the dais with our host, Jett Rink."

"Ah yes, the host who spends twenty-five thousand dollars for a dish of barbecue." He glanced about at the incredible scene. "I can well believe it now."

"There's Jordan—there's my husband—with the others. Now if only we can stay together." She raised her voice to reach her husband struggling toward them. "Luz? Jordy?"

His shoulders were making a path for the royal pair behind

him. "Haven't seen them," he shouted. "Catch on like a conga line and we'll make it."

Breathless, disheveled, they found themselves half an hour later seated on a platform at an orchid-covered table like a huge catafalque. From the hundreds of tables below a foam of faces stared up at them. Flashlights seared the air. Bands blared. The loudspeakers created pandemonium.

"And when," said the King seated beside Leslie, "does our host appear?"

With awful suddenness the loudspeaker system went off. It had exaggerated every sound. Conversation had necessarily been carried on at a shout. Now the abrupt quiet was as shocking as the noise had been. The comparative silence stunned one. From the dais where he sat with the guests of honor boomed the unctuous voice of Congressman Bale Clinch in tones which, under stress of the megaphones, had been meant for the confidential ear of his dinner neighbor alone. In the sudden silence they now rang out with all the strength and authority with which, in Washington Congress assembled, he frequently addressed his compatriots on the subject of Texas oil rights in general and Jett Rink's claims in particular.

"That wildcattin' son-of-a-bitch Jett Rink is drunk again or I'll eat a live rattlesnake. They're soberin' him up in there——" He stopped, aghast, as a thousand faces turned toward him like balloons in a breeze.

Big though his voice was it had carried only through a fraction of the great concourse. But the repetition from mouth to mouth had taken only a few seconds. A roar, a Niagara of laughter, shook the room.

In the midst of this Luz Benedict appeared suddenly at the main table, she had not made her way through the main room, she seemed to have materialized out of the air. She was wearing a white chiffon gown, not quite fresh; no jewelry, her fair hair still tied back in the absurd horse's tail coiffure, though now a little spray of tiny fresh white orchids replaced the black ribbon that had held it.

59

She leaned over her father's chair as casually as though she were in the dining room at the ranch. "Who told the joke?" she inquired casually. "I could use a laugh."

Bick Benedict turned his head slightly, he bit the words out of the corner of his mouth. "Where've you been? And Jordan?"

"Parn me, lady," said a waiter, and placed a huge slab of rare roast beef before Bick Benedict. It almost covered the large plate, it was an inch thick, astonishingly like the map of Texas in shape, and it had been cut from the prime carcasses flown by refrigerated plane from Kansas City. Luz viewed it with distaste as she leaned over her father's shoulder.

"Listen. Jordy's looking for Jett, he says he's going to beat him up he——"

A girl in a strapless scarlet evening dress appeared on the platform at the far end of the great hall, she began to sing to the accompaniment of the orchestra, her lips formed words but no note was heard in the absence of the sound mechanism, there was an absurd quality in her mute coquetry as she mouthed the words of the familiar Texas song that now opened the evening's program.

Bick Benedict jerked around in his chair to face his daughter. "You're crazy! Where is he?"

"Louder!" yelled a man in the audience. "Louder!" someone echoed from a far corner. "What's the matter with the loudspeaker! Jett! Jett, get busy in there!" With knives and forks they began to tap the sides of their water glasses or wineglasses or bourbon tumblers, the clinking rose to an anvil chorus. The girl in the red dress faltered, stopped, smiled uncertainly, went on with her soundless song.

From the far far end of the room young Jordan Benedict strode down through the jungle of tables close-packed as mesquite on the plains. He was alone. A neat grey suit, a neat blue bow tie, his blue-black hair that was so like his mother's seemed a heavy black cap above his white face. Straight toward the table marked Number One—the table on the dais.

Bick Benedict muttered an apology to the right to the left, quickly he pushed back his chair and stood facing Luz. He grasped her wrist. "What's the matter with him! What happened!" He shook her arm a little as though to hurry her into speech.

"He smashed up the Beauty Parlor at the hotel, he threw chairs into the mirrors and shot out the lights like an old Western movie——"

"Beauty Parlor! What the hell do you m——"

"Oh, you know—where we have our hair done and everything. Don't be—anyway, he wrecked it and now he's looking for Jett he says he's going to smash his face he says it's Jett's hotel and his orders——"

"Why! Why! Why! Quick!"

"Juana went down to keep an appointment to have her nails done. She'd telephoned, and given her name of course. When she got down there the girl at the desk looked at her and said they didn't take Mexicans, she came upstairs and Jordy went——" She stopped abruptly. "There comes Jett. Look. He's been drinking."

With a sudden blare that jolted the eardrums the loudspeaker went on. From the two bands there was a ruffle of the drums. Jett Rink came through the door marked Office. Private. White dinner clothes, a tight little boutonniere of bluebonnets on his lapel. The curiously square face, thin-lipped, ruthless, the head set too low on the neck that in turn was too massive for the small-boned body. He walked, not as a man who has authority and power but as a man does who boasts of these. On his right walked a man, on his left walked a man, the two looked oddly alike in an indefinable way, as though the resemblance came from some quality within them rather than from any facial kinship. Their clothes seemed too tight as though they covered muscles permanently flexed, and their shaves were fresh, close and unavailing. Their faces impassive, the cold hard eyes regnant as searchlights.

"Hi, Jett!" bawled the cowboy movie star.

"Which is he?" the King inquired, not very astutely.

61

Congressman Bale Clinch answered somewhat impatiently. "The middle one of course. The other two are strong-arms."

Now that the sound system had been restored the girl in red and the accompanying band were in full swing with a childish song which the state had adopted as its own. The tune was that of the old ballad, "I've Been Working on the Railroad" to words which someone had written.

> *The eyes of Texas are upon you,*
> *All the live-long day.*
> *The eyes of Texas are upon you,*
> *You cannot get away. . . .*

Jordy Benedict reached the dais, he leaped upon it nimbly, crept beneath the table opposite his father's empty chair like a boy playing hide-and-seek, he bobbed up to face Jett Rink. At the tables below the dais the diners had got to their feet leaving the slabs of red roast to congeal on their plates.

Jordy Benedict called no names. He looked absurdly young and slim as he faced the three burly figures.

"Stand away," he said quietly, "and fight." His arm came back and up like a piston. A spurt of crimson from Jett Rink's nose made a bizarre red white and blue of his costume. A dozen hands pinned Jordy's arms, the flint-faced men held Jett Rink, the two glaring antagonists, pinioned thus, strained toward each other like caged and maddened animals.

Jett Rink jumped then, swinging hammock-like between the two guards whose arms held his. His feet, with all his powerful bulk behind them, struck Jordy low with practiced vicious aim so that the grunt as the boy fell could be heard by the guests of honor on the dais even above the blare of the band.

Quick though Bick was, Leslie was there before him, kneeling on the floor beside her son. For the moment he was mercifully unconscious. The first exquisite agony of this blow had distorted the boy's face, his body was twisted with it. His eyes were closed.

Bick, kneeling, made as though to rise now. His eyes were terrible as he looked at the panting Jett Rink. But Leslie reached across the boy's crumpled form, she gripped Bick's arm so that her fingers bit into his muscles. Quietly, as though continuing a conversation, she said, "You see. It's caught up with you, it's caught up with us. It always does."

But now the boy stirred and groaned and his eyes opened and his face was a mask of hideous pain as he looked up into the two stricken faces bent over him. The physician in him rose valiantly to meet the moment, the distorted lips spoke the truth to reassure them.

"Morphine . . . pain . . . horrible . . . not serious . . . morphine . . ."

5

THOUGH the three Lynnton girls always were spoken of as the Beautiful Lynnton Sisters of Virginia they weren't really beautiful. For that matter, they weren't Virginians, having been born in Ohio. But undeniably there was about these three young women an aura, a glow, a dash of what used to be called diablerie that served as handily as beauty and sometimes handier. These exhilarating qualities wore well, too, for they lasted the girls their lifetime, which beauty frequently fails to do.

The three Lynntons were always doing things first or better or more outrageously than other girls of their age and station in

Virginia and Washington society. Leigh, the eldest—the one who married Sir Alfred Karfrey and went to England to live—scandalized Washington when, as a young woman in that capital's society circles, she had smoked a cigarette in public long before her friend Alice Roosevelt Longworth shocked the whole United States with a puff or two. Leigh certainly was the least lovely of the three Lynnton Lovelies as they sometimes were fatuously called. She had the long aquiline face of her mother—horse-faced, her feminine detractors said—and she was further handicapped for dalliance by a mordant tongue that should have scared the wits out of the young male Virginians who came courting with Southern sweet talk. People said that with her scarifying wit she actually had whiplashed the timorous Karfrey into marrying her.

Leslie the second sister was, as the term went, a bluestocking. She was forever reading books, but not the sort of books which other Southern young women consumed like bonbons as they lay, indolent and slightly liverish from too many hot breads, in the well-worn hammock under the trees. Leslie Lynnton had opinions of her own, she conversed and even argued with her distinguished father and his friends on matters political, sociological, medical and literary just as if she were a man. Though her eyes were large, dark, and warmly lustrous there undeniably was a slight cast in the left one which gave her, at times, a sort of stricken look. Oddly enough, men found this attractive, perhaps because it imparted a momentarily helpless and appealing aspect.

The third girl, Lacey, was seven years younger than her second sister and represented Mrs. Lynnton's last try for a son. Lacey turned out a tomboy and small wonder. As each of the three had been intended by their parents to be males only masculine names had been provided for them before birth. With the advent of the third girl Mrs. Lynnton, admitting final defeat, had hastily attempted to change the name from Lacey to Laura. But Lacey it remained.

You were always seeing photographs of the three in airy organdies and sashes posed with arms about one another's waists in front of white-columned porticoes with a well-bred hunting dog or two crouched in the foreground. But Race Lynnton—Doctor Horace Lynnton in all the encyclopedias and Who's Whos and medical journals—had really brought them up with a free hand and an open mind. Though the girls moved with grace and distinction they were generally considered too thin. Theirs were long clever-looking hands rather than little dimpled ones; theirs a spirited manner; little money and small prospect of more, being daughters of a very dedicated surgeon-physician-scientist.

In spite of these handicaps the Lynnton ladies somehow emerged feminine and alluring. The life juices were strong in them, they possessed the gifts of warmth and sympathetic understanding which tempered their wit. Sometimes, talking before the fire with a gay and friendly group, Leslie had a way of sitting on the hearth rug, her shoulder and arm pillowed against her father's knee, her face turned up to him as he talked, her fine intelligent eyes seeming to absorb the light in his face. At such times the younger men present were likely to take their handkerchiefs furtively from their pockets and wipe their brows. Electra, even in that fairly recent day, was merely a Greek legend, together with the equally bemused Oedipus.

"I declare," Mrs. Lynnton would say—she frequently prefaced her statements with a warning salvo such as I declare or I must say or if you want my opinion—"I declare, Leslie, I sometimes think your father and I will have you on our hands as an old maid. Leigh was late enough, twenty-three when she married, but look at her now, Lady Karfrey! So it turned out well enough in spite of her sarcastic ways when she was a girl."

"But Mama, you didn't marry Papa until you were past twenty. And you did pretty well for yourself, you will admit. Married to the most wonderful man in the world, that's all."

"I married your father because he asked me, and that's the truth. I was no beauty and neither are you. You treat men as if they were girl friends, though you've had a hundred chances I must say."

"Not quite a hundred, Mama. Perhaps ten."

"Most girls have one, and snatch at it, and don't let them tell you anything different. If you're not married next year I'm going to dress up Lacey and put her in the parlor. She'll be seventeen soon and there she is out at the stables day and night. It's time she learned that all males aren't quadrupeds." She had a somewhat tangy tongue of her own, Nancy Lynnton.

Equipped thus rather meagerly for matrimony, one would justifiably have thought the three Lynnton sisters fated for spinsterhood. On the contrary the big shabby Virginia house was clogged with yearning swains. Young Washington career men; slightly balding European sub-diplomats and embassy secretaries in striped trousers and cutaways; Virginia and Maryland squires of the huntin' ridin' and slightly run-down set; with a sprinkling of New York lawyers and Wall Street men and even an occasional Midwestern businessman. Doctors who came ostensibly to confer with Horace Lynnton ended up in the vast hospitable kitchen (for the Lynntons were famous cooks in defiance of a day and place in which cooking was considered menial). Beaux haunted the verandas the parlors the stables. They swarmed all over the place—to the dismay of neighboring beauties—much as bees will sometimes desert the stately cool rose for a field of heady wild red clover.

As for the boasted Virginia background, this lay so far in the past as to be misted by the centuries and discernible only to Mrs. Lynnton's somewhat bemused eye. A great-great-great-grandfather had sailed overseas to Virginia in the 1600s, one of those indentured servants or jail bait whose descendants later became First Families of Virginia perhaps as legitimately as their more aristocratic contemporaries. But this traveler's son too had possessed the spirit of roving adventure. He had moved with the tide of travel from Virginia to Kentucky to Indiana to Ohio. Mrs. Lynnton always skipped lightly over these geographical intervals when she spoke of herself as having descended from one of the F.F.V.s. Leslie and Lacey made nothing of this, or at best regarded it as a family joke. Leigh—now Lady Karfrey—having inherited something of her mother's snobbishness, took the doubtful distinction more seriously. As for Doctor Horace Lynnton, late of Ohio, here was a great human being and a dedicated spirit disguised as a tall somewhat shambling man in a crumpled suit and a bow tie slightly askew so that his wife or one of three daughters seemed always to be busy under his chin. When finally he had moved with his family to the once stately but now rather ramshackle house in Virginia it was because he could give his brilliant brain his surgical genius and his magic hands to the rehabilitation of the thousands of broken boys who, veterans of the gruesome 1917–18 war years, filled the nearby hospitals of Washington Virginia and Maryland. Offered the cushiony post of White House Physician, he had refused it as casually as though he had been handed an over-sweet dessert.

Though there was only a physician's income behind it, profusion was characteristic of the Lynnton ménage. Horses in the weathered stables; the most delicate and savory of American cooking in the kitchen with no Southern grease-fried indigestibles to mar it. There were succulent soft-shell crabs from Maryland, smoked Virginia hams, Ohio maple sugar and pancakes, little plump white chickens, button-size hot biscuits with golden pools of butter between their brown cheeks. Terrapin. Oysters. Succotash. Devil's food cake. Profusion not only of food but of gaiety and laughter; of good talk at dinner and after; of guests, of servants, of books, of courtesy, of horses and dogs and crystal and silver. Sweet-scented flowers in the rambling garden, deep-cushioned shabby handsome chairs, vast beds and capacious fireplaces, sherry on the sideboard, leisure in the air, and wit to spice the whole of this.

Bick Benedict was no fool, and he hadn't been twenty minutes on the place before he realized that this was a run-down old Southern shebang in need of about fifty thousand dollars in repairs. Not that he was there in the role of anything but guest, and that of the most transitory nature. In Washington on business he had come down to the Lynnton place in Virginia to look at a horse and to buy it if possible.

By the purest of accidents Doctor Horace Lynnton had found

himself owner of a long-legged rangy filly who had turned out to
be a gold mine. As horses, to him, were four-legged animals
meant for riding or for driving he was more bewildered than
pleased. He was forever evading gifts from moneyed patients who
sent them in gratitude, or from insolvent patients who proffered
them in lieu of cash. The filly had come from a long-standing
friend who fell just between these two classifications. Doctor
Lynnton had good-naturedly accepted the unwanted animal offered in part payment of a bill already absurdly small.

"She's an accident," the owner had confessed. "And I won't
say she's any good except for one of your girls to ride. She's one
of Wind Wings'."

"But I can't accept her," Doctor Lynnton had in the beginning
protested. "You say her sire was Wind Wings!"

"Yes, but the dam was a stray plug that we kept for my little
Betsy to jog around on. She got into the paddock by mistake, and
the damage was done. Not that it matters, except that I want you
to know that on her mother's side she hasn't a drop of good blood
in her that I know of. She'll never run."

"Prince and peasant girl," said Horace Lynnton. "A combination that has been known to produce amazing results. Sire for
speed, they say. Dam for stamina."

They named her My Mistake but in spite of this by the time
she was three years old it began to appear that she would soon
romp away with everything from New York to Mexico.

Bick Benedict of Texas had sought out Horace Lynnton in
Washington not as the famous man of science but as the owner
of My Mistake.

"Is she for sale?" he had asked.

"I suppose so. I don't go in for racing. She was meant for my
youngest daughter—to ride around the country roads. Turned
out to be a lightning bolt."

"Could I see her?"

"Drive out with me this afternoon, if you care to, stay for
dinner and overnight."

70

"Thanks, I'll be glad to drive out but I can't stay. I've got business engagements here in Washington——"

But he never left—or practically never—until he and Leslie were off for their honeymoon and Texas.

In the first twenty-four hours of his stay at the Lynntons' Jordan Benedict experienced a series of shocks which left him dazed but strangely exhilarated too. The first shock to his Southwest sensibilities came when Doctor Lynnton introduced the young Negro who drove them down to Virginia. The little ceremony was as casual (but also as formal) as though he were introducing any two friends or acquaintances.

"Benedict, this is Jefferson Swazey who'll drive us down. Jeff, this is Mr. Jordan Benedict from Texas."

Well I'll be damned, thought Jordan Benedict. On the way down the two men talked of this and that—of the freakish little filly; of the dead Harding, that pitiful and scandal-ridden figure with his imposing façade concealing the termite-riddled interior; of Coolidge, the new President of the United States; the rigid and vinegary Vermonter.

Arrived, "Jeff will show us the filly," Horace Lynnton said, "or perhaps one of the girls will, though they don't ride her nowadays. She's in training, very hoity-toity and has ideas about who's in the saddle."

Jordan Benedict's eye, trained to estimate millions of acres and dozens of dwellings as a single unit, made brief work of the wistaria and honeysuckle. They did not hide from his expert gaze the sagging columns or disguise the fact that the outbuildings were in urgent need of repair. But then the family, as he met them one by one, made no effort at disguise, either.

It was almost dusk as they arrived. The two men entered the house. A wide and beautifully proportioned hall ran from front to back with great arched doorways opening off it. Shabby rugs on a caramel floor. Riding crops, tennis racquets; books and papers and magazines on the overflowing hall table; a friendly lean and lazy dog; a delicious scent of something baking or broil-

71

ing or both. They peered into the big living room. Here was a feminine world, all crystal and flowers and faded yellow satin curtains. Bits of jade. The ruby glow of Bohemian glass. The flicker of flame in the fireplace.

Doctor Lynnton shook his head. "The girls are somewhere around, but they're probably busy. Perhaps you'd like to wash up."

"I'd like to have a look at the filly while it's still light."

"Yes—the horse," Doctor Lynnton agreed somewhat vaguely. From a nearby room there came the sound of voices. He raised his voice to a shout. "Leslie!" Then, still more loudly, "Leslie!"

Bick Benedict turned expecting to see a son, perhaps, or a man-servant answering to this name. There emerged from the room that later he was to know as the library two figures, a man and a woman. The woman was wearing riding clothes, he was startled to see that it was a sidesaddle habit complete with glistening black boots, crop, white-starched stock. He had seen nothing like this in years—certainly not in Texas. A tall slim girl, not pretty.

"Leslie, this is Jordan Benedict, here from Texas. My daughter Leslie."

The young man with her was in riding clothes and not only riding clothes but actually a pink coat of the hunting variety. Well I'm damned, Jordan Benedict said to himself for the second time in an hour. Then his ear was caught by the girl's voice, which was lovely, warm and vibrant.

"Texas! How interesting! Father, you know Nicky Rorik. Mr. Benedict, this is Count Nicholas Rorik, Mr. Jordan Benedict."

Doctor Lynnton moved toward the rear doorway. "We're on our way to the paddock. Mr. Benedict's come to look at My Mistake."

"I'm coming along," said Leslie, "to tell you all her bad points. I don't want anyone to buy her."

"Dear daughter, kindly remember that Mr. Benedict is a Texan and your father is a country doctor. You two go on down to the stable. I'll join you directly, Jordan."

Rorik, Benedict was saying in his mind. Rorik. Now let's see.

He comes from one of those kicked-around kingdoms, or a midget principality or something, it's one of those musical-comedy places.

Then the slim dark young man said something about seeing everyone at dinner. And vanished with a bow that gave the impression of heel-clicking, though nothing of the sort took place. Weeks later Jordan Benedict dredged the young man up from the depths of his memory and put to his wife Leslie the questions which even now were stirring in his thoughts.

"That first day I met you, Leslie, when I came into the house with your father. You were tucked away in the library with that Rorik guy. What kind of hanky-panky was going on, anyway? Quiet as mice until your father called you."

"Oh, that. Well, I never quite knew myself. It was a serious proposal of a sort, but it had a morganatic tinge. When his uncle dies he'll become ruler or Grand Duke or whatever it's called—if any. I've lost track."

Now, on their way to the paddock he waited for her to speak. In Texas the women talked a lot, they chattered on and on about little inconsequential things calculated to please but not strain the masculine mind. Leslie Lynnton did not start the conversation. She strolled composedly and quietly beside him in her absurdly chic riding clothes. All about them were the ancient trees, the scent of flowers whose perfume yielded itself to the cool evening air. The orchard was cloudy with blossoms.

"How green it is!" he said inadequately.

"Isn't it green in Texas?"

The girl must be a fool. "Don't you know about Texas?"

"No. Except that it's big. And the men wear hats like yours."

"Yes, I suppose this does look funny to you. But then that rigging you're wearing looks funny to me." For some reason he wanted to jar her composure. "And your friend's red coat."

She laughed and paused a moment in her walk and looked directly at him for the first time. And he thought, She might be kind of pretty if she filled out a little. Lovely eyes but there's a little kind of thing about one of them. A cast in it. She was saying, "They're called pink, not red. Don't ask me why. And you're

73

right about these riding clothes of mine. They're ridiculous. I never wear them, really."

"But you're wearing——"

"I mean I never wear them for riding. Just today. It's a special day down here. Once a year they do a lot of rather silly stuff that was Virginia a century or two ago. You know—scarlet coats and floating veils and yoicks. The men dig their pink coats out of moth balls and the women wear this of thing out of the attic if they still can stick on a sidesaddle. Tonight's the Hunt Ball— not at our house, thank heaven!—and you're invited."

"How veddy veddy British!"

"I was born in Ohio so don't be sneery."

"I'd look good at a Hunt Ball in these clothes."

"Oh well. We're having dinner here—just the family and two or three others. Do stay for that."

He muttered something about an engagement in Washington, to which she said politely, well, another time perhaps. And there they were at the stables and My Mistake was being paced in the paddock by a young Negro boy. Bick saw instantly that the satin-coated sorrel had the proper conformation; long of leg, neat of hoof, long muscular neck, deep chest. Her hoofs seemed scarcely to touch the ground, they flicked the earth as delicately as a ballet dancer's toes.

"Well, there she is," said Doctor Lynnton, coming up behind them.

Horses had been a vital part of Jordan Benedict's life since birth. "And way before," he sometimes said. "They tell me that when I was born my mother slid off her horse and into bed at practically the same moment. She had been taking part in an equestrian quadrille at the rodeo in Benedict. All the young women for miles around tried for the quadrille, but only the top riders made it. The women rode in divided skirts those days."

It could not be said that he prided himself on his horsemanship any more than he could be said to be proud of his breathing or walking. Certainly walking was more foreign to this Texan than riding.

"I'd like to try her out if you've no objection," he said to Doctor Lynnton.

"Of course. How would you like to try her on the track? We've rigged up a little half-mile track there just beyond."

"How about your clothes?" Leslie called to him as he mounted in his Texas tans, his great wide-brimmed Texas Stetson, his brown oxfords.

He flung up his arm. "My grandmother could rope a steer in hoop skirts."

Perhaps it was the upflung arm that startled My Mistake. Jordan had ridden a thousand quarter horses, bucking ponies, racing horses. This filly was a live electric wire carrying a thousand volts. She was out of the gate and on the track like a lightning flash. Accustomed all his life to the high-pommeled Western saddle, he sat the Eastern saddle well enough but his style was a revelation to Eastern eyes. The stable boys stared, their eyes their mouths making three wide circles in each amazed face. Jordan's arms were akimbo, he held the reins high, his loose-jointed seat in the saddle irked the little filly, she jerked her head around to glare at him with rolling resentful eyeballs, she skittered sidewise. She gave him a nasty five minutes. Damned girl, watching. He knew he must master her, he did master her, he took her twice around, drew up before his startled audience and dismounted before the animal had come to a stop.

Leslie Lynnton was laughing like a child, peal on peal of helpless spontaneous laughter.

"Now Leslie," her father said chidingly, "don't you tease Mr. Benedict. That's the way they ride in Texas. Informal, their riding."

Leslie drew a deep breath and choked a little. "That wasn't riding. That was scuffling with a horse."

He was deeply offended, it was almost as if a man had impugned his honor—a phrase still used in Texas editorials. Instantly she sensed this, she went to him she spoke so that the grinning boys could hear. "I'm sorry. Forgive me. I'm ignorant about your part of the country. Our way of riding seems queer to you too. You'd laugh at me if you saw me in this habit all bunched up on the side of a horse."

He was furious. He said nothing. There was a little frown between his eyes and his eyes were steel.

"All right, boys!" Doctor Lynnton called to the stablemen, and waved away the horse, the attendants, the stable, the whole incident. "Thanks. Come on, Jordan—let's go up to the house and have a little drink before dinner."

"Oh, I'm afraid I'll have to——" Jordan began stiffly.

"You must have a wife or a mother or a—or someone who has spoiled you terribly," Leslie said. "You take teasing so hard."

"My sister," he found himself saying to his own intense astonishment. "I'm not married. My sister—I live with my sister."

"Oh well, that accounts for it. Why aren't you married, Jordan?"

"Now Leslie!" Doctor Lynnton remonstrated again.

He ignored this. "It seems strange to hear you call me Jordan." He pronounced it with a *u*, Jurden, Texas fashion. "Almost no one does. There's always been a Jordan in the family, but everyone calls me Bick." I'm talking too much, he told himself. What the hell does she care whether there's always been a Jordan and they call me Bick.

"Bick Benedict," Leslie tried the sound of it. "No, I like your own name. Jordan Benedict. Why do they call you Bick?"

He began to feel really foolish. "Oh, when I was a little kid I suppose I couldn't say Benedict, the nearest I could manage was Bick, and it stuck as a nickname."

"Jordan," she said stubbornly. "You're staying to dinner. And the night. You can drive back to Washington tomorrow morning with Papa, he gets up at a ghastly hour and starts poking at people's insides before the world is awake."

"I came here to buy a horse," Bick announced rudely. "I won't go to any Hunt Ball."

Walking between the two men Leslie linked an arm into her father's arm, into Bick's. "I'll get up early and have breakfast with you two. There's Mama. We're late I suppose."

On the veranda steps stood Mrs. Lynnton and beside her a girl of sixteen or seventeen in men's pants—at least that was what Bick Benedict called them. Benedict was shocked. Even the professional rodeo girls wore full divided skirts in Texas. Even Joella Kilso who was champion woman bronco buster of the Southwest wore a buckskin skirt with fringed trimming and bright brass nailheads.

"Well, really," began Mrs. Lynnton with considerably less than storied Southern hospitality, "it's half past seven, dinner's at eight and you're not even———"

"Mama, Mr. Jordan Benedict from Texas. . . . Lacey—my sister Lacey."

Leslie performed the introductions at a clip which left her mother's complaint far behind. Mrs. Lynnton had made instant appraisal of this tall broad-shouldered visitor in the ten-gallon hat and dismissed him as negligible.

"Are you the man who wants to buy My Mistake?" Lacey asked bluntly.

Mrs. Lynnton acknowledged his presence for the first time. "I hope so, before Lacey here kills herself riding her."

"No, Mr. Benedict's not buying her," Leslie said, without reason.

"Oh, yes ma'am, I am," Bick said with a great deal of drawl as always when angry. Too many damned bossy women around here, he thought. And he decided that Mrs. Lynnton looked like a longhorn with that lantern face, her hair in two sort of winged horns at the side, and her long lean wiry frame.

Doctor Lynnton waved a placating hand. "Let's not decide anything now. We'll have a drink and then we'll all clean up and see you downstairs at about eight, Jordan. Uh, Bick. Is that better?"

Stuck, he thought as he entered his room, but then instantly there came over him a sensation very strange—a mingling of peace and exhilaration. A large square high-ceilinged room, cool, quiet. Chintz curtains, flowers in a vase, a fire in the fireplace, a bathroom to himself, shaving things and sweet-smelling stuff in bottles in the bathroom, and big thick soft towels. Nothing like this at Reata in spite of the millions of acres and dozens of rooms and scores of servants and "hands."

Later in the evening when he mentioned the comfort of his room to Leslie she said flippantly, "Yes, who cares about the necessities, it's the luxuries that count. What if the dishpan does leak!"

Now he still could telephone Washington and have someone drive out to fetch him. What was the sense in staying? He'd made up his mind to buy the filly, if only (he told himself parenthetically) to show those women that they couldn't run him the way they ran Doctor Lynnton.

He stared at himself in the mirror, decided to bathe and shave, decided against it, the hell with it, dinner was at eight it was quarter to eight now, he couldn't make it if he wanted to. Whereupon he peeled off his clothes, jerked on the shower, shaved, cut himself, got into his clothes distastefully because they were the crumpled garments he had just kicked off, rushed downstairs to find no one there but Mrs. Lynnton in rustling silk doing something to chair cushions and looking surprisingly handsome. She greeted him politely, she looked at him fleetingly, the rumpled Texas tans the tan shoes that he had hurriedly wiped with a corner of the bath towel. Not only did she mentally dismiss him as an eligible or even a possible suitor for her daughter—she regarded him as a male nobody with whom she could relax cozily without pretense as one would in the company of a sympathetic servant or an old friend with whom one had nothing to gain and nothing to lose.

"You're from Nebraska, Mr. Beckwith?"

"Texas, ma'am. Uh—Benedict."

"Texas, really!" As though he had said Timbuctoo.

Old harpy. "You're from Ohio your daughter tells me."

"Well, we did live there at one time. But I'm a Virginian, my ancestors really settled Virginia, they were among the First Families."

78

"I've read about them," he said, too dryly. "A very interesting, uh, type, some of them."

She looked at him sharply but his blue eyes seemed guileless, his smile winning. Here was someone a nobody, to whom she could unburden herself momentarily, a fresh receptacle. "My daughter Leslie makes fun of me, and so does the Doctor and even Lacey, for that matter, because I am proud of my ancestry. The Doctor calls me Mrs. Nickleby. Leslie's the worst. Daughters are a real problem, Mr. Uh. Of course Leigh wasn't. She's Lady Karfrey, you know."

"No, I didn't know."

"My, yes! She married Sir Alfred Karfrey, they live in England of course, he's a member of Parliament."

"Like our Congress," Bick said smoothly. I'm really being bitchy as a woman, he thought. But she had not heard, she heard nothing that she did not want to hear.

"Leslie could have married—well, anybody you might say. Goodness knows she's no beauty, skinny as a bird dog, and a slight cast in her left eye at times perhaps you've noticed, well, you'd think it would put men off her but they're bees around a honeypot. I don't know what it is, Doctor says Leslie has something that transcends beauty but I can't see it myself——"

Why, the old girl's jealous of her daughter, Bick said to himself.

"—and she has her nose in a book all day long and talks to the servants as if they were her equal—so does the Doctor for that matter—and she argues about what she calls democracy and human rights and stuff like that, I declare I should think the men would run the other way at mention of her name——"

"I think she's fascinating," Bick Benedict heard himself saying, to his own astonishment. It was a word he had never used—certainly never in connection with a woman.

Mrs. Lynnton blinked a little as though coming out of a trance, it was plain that she had been talking to relieve her feelings, this man might as well have been, so far as she considered him of importance, an old uncle or a piece of furniture. She seemed even to resent his interruption as though he had committed an impertinence. She put this horse trader in his place. "So others say. Count Rorik. He'll be practically a king when his uncle dies. A principality they call it."

He was cursing himself for having stayed when suddenly, like a badly directed stage scene, there were voices on the stairs, in the hall, on the veranda, there were a dozen people in the room and introductions were being performed and trays were being passed. Sherry! I'll bet that's the old girl's doings. And there was Leslie, late but leisurely.

He looked at Leslie, he was startled by the rush of protective loyalty he felt toward her. She was wearing the disfiguring evening dress that was in vogue—the absurdly short skirt and loose hip-length waistline that so foreshortened the figure. Long slim legs, lovely shoulders, and now that she was rid of the white piqué stock and the rest of those stuffy riding clothes he saw how exquisitely her head was set on her throat and how, in some mysterious way, she was really a beauty in disguise. He couldn't make up his mind whether there really was a slight cast in her eye or whether her eyes were so large that there wasn't quite room enough for them in the socket. Another part of his mind was recalling that he had once seen an actress in New York—what was her name?—Ferguson, that was it—Elsie Ferguson. Her eyes had been like that, very large and liquid, not those stiff eyes that most women had, and there had been a little sort of quirk in one of them and he had been strongly attracted by this blemish.

Dinner. The colored man in white cotton gloves announced dinner. In later years Jordan Benedict sometimes referred to this evening as That Hell of an Evening When I First Met You.

6

ACROSS THE TABLE from him—across all those lighted candles and the flowers—were Leslie and that Rorik fellow still in the red coat. Only it looked dressier now and his hair very black above the red. Career man he'd been called. Bick disliked him for no reason. He was irritated by the way the man ate his dinner, using his knife and fork in the European fashion, a busy gathering of food with both utensils, a finicky little clatter of metal against china. He ate quickly, almost daintily, he talked and looked into Leslie's eyes very directly, and smiled. Since the war Washington was full of them, Bick thought, and scuffled his feet a little under the table; always hanging around the foreign embassies and legations. The food was very good. Wonderful, really. Run-down place, though. How could they afford it? Three daughters. Lady Karfrey, eh? Nuts to that!

The women did a great deal of talking, they were leading the conversation, especially that Leslie girl, it wasn't the formal sort of dinner-table talk that he had sometimes encountered in Washington on his infrequent business trips there. He rarely took active part in the Washington end of Texas affairs, that was his cousin Roady Benedict's business, that was why he had been sent to Washington. They were talking about everything from that crazy Scopes trial in Tennessee, with its monkey glands and its Bryan and its Darrow, to a book called *An American Tragedy* (which Bick hadn't read) to a play called *Desire Under the Elms* (which Bick hadn't seen). Bick Benedict ate his flavorsome duck and talked politely when necessary to the young woman on his right (whose name he hadn't caught) and the middle-aged woman on his left (whose name he hadn't caught).

Someone at the other end of the table must have asked Nicholas Rorik a question for now he paused in the sprightly business of the knife and fork, he raised his voice to carry down the line of dinner guests, and smiled deprecatingly and shrugged his shoulders as he replied in his very good Oxford English. "It isn't a large country as you know, it is a principality, my country. Our little kingdom, as you call it, is only—" he cast up his eyes ceilingward to juggle the figures into American terms—"it would be in your miles less than eight hundred square miles. Very small, as you consider size in this country."

"My goodness," said his questioner at the other end of the table, laughing a little and then turning to look at Jordan Benedict, "Texas is bigger than that, isn't it, Mr. Benedict!"

"Texas!" said Doctor Lynnton. "Why, Mr. Benedict's ranch is bigger than that. Sorry, Nicky. No offense."

"I've always heard these tall tales from Texas," said one of the men across the table—he, too, was wearing one of those red coats with a red face above it, "and now I'd like to have it right from the hor—right from headquarters, Mr. Benedict. Just how many acres have you got, or miles or whatever it is you folks reckon in? It's the biggest ranch in Texas, isn't it?"

Jordan Benedict never could accustom himself to the habit these Yankees had of asking a man how much land he had. Why, damit, it was the same as coming right out and asking a man how much money he had! How would that redcoat like it if he, Bick Benedict, were to shout across the table to ask him how much money he had in the bank?

"No," he said quietly, "it isn't the largest. It is one of the large ranches but there are others as large. One or two larger, up in the Panhandle and down in the brush country."

He felt that Leslie Lynnton was looking at him and he sensed that she understood his resentment though he didn't know how or why. That girl isn't only smart, he thought. She understands everything, that's why her eyes are so warm and lovely that's what her father meant when he said she's got something that transcends beauty.

"Yes," the fellow was saying persistently. "Yes, but how many acres, actually? I'd like to hear those figures really rolling out and know that it's authentic. I never could bring myself to believe them. A million? Is that right? A million acres?"

Jordan Benedict felt his face reddening. Still, a straight question like that, aimed at a man's head. You had to answer it or insult a man at your host's table. He had seen men killed for much less. There was a lull in the table talk. He looked squarely into Leslie's eyes, she smiled at him ever so faintly as a mother smiles at a shy child, in encouragement. He heard himself saying, "Something over two million acres. Two million and a half, to be exact."

Doctor Lynnton nodded interestedly. "Yes, I remember my father saying something about it when I was a young fellow. It used to be four or five million acres, wasn't it? Years ago."

"Yes." God damn the man and his family and his friends.

"There you are, Nicky!" yelped the man who originally had asked the questions. "I guess that makes you look like a sharecropper." Nicky shrugged his shoulders again and spread his hands in deprecation and smiled at Leslie Lynnton beseechingly.

Mrs. Lynnton's head had been slightly turned away from the table to speak over her shoulder to a servant. She turned now to look at Jordan Benedict. It was a stunned look, the look of one who has heard but who rejects the words as incredible. She turned her head again automatically to speak to the servant, then again she faced forward with a jerk to stare at Jordan as though the sense of the words had just now penetrated. Her mouth was open before she began to speak.

"How many acres did you say, Mr. Benedict?"

"He said two and a half million acres, Mama," Leslie said with exquisite distinctness. "And you should see the greedy look on your face."

But Mrs. Lynnton was not one to be diverted from her quarry, once she had the scent.

"Are there," she persisted, "any cities on the premises?"

Choking a little, "Why, yes ma'am, there are a few."

"Do you own those too?"

The company could no longer be contained. A roar went up. Bick Benedict's reply, "Not rightly own, no ma'am," was lost in the waves of laughter. Mrs. Lynnton turned her gaze upon her husband then. Her expression was one of the most bitter reproach and rage.

"Nobody owns a city," Bick persisted virtuously. Controller of every vote in the town of Benedict, and most of the county.

From across the table Leslie said, "How about Tammany?"

"Oh, now, Leslie!" pleaded a man seated beside Mrs. Lynnton. A New Yorker, Bick decided not very astutely. And anyway, what does a woman want to go and get mixed up in political talk for?

There followed, then, in that household between the hours of ten-thirty P.M. and seven A.M. three scenes which made up in variety what they may have lacked in dramatic quality.

At ten o'clock the dinner guests departed, bound for the Hunt

84

Ball. Jordan Benedict declined politely to go, pleading no proper clothes and a very early Washington appointment. At ten-thirty Doctor Lynnton was in his own bedroom after a half hour's chat and a nightcap with Jordan Benedict. At ten-thirty Mrs. Lynnton opened fire.

"Well, Doctor Lynnton, I must say you seem to care very little about what becomes of your daughters!"

"What have the girls done now, Nancy?"

"It's you!" Then, at his look of amazement, "Bringing that Benedict here and never telling me a word about him. Not a syllable."

"Why, Nancy, he's a nice enough young fella. Texans are different. You can't judge a man by his hat. They're used to big open ways, lots of everything. He's a nice enough young fella."

"Nice! He said he owns two million acres of land! And more!"

"You're not going to hold that against him, are you?"

"Horace Lynnton, you know very well that there isn't a young man in Virginia, Washington, Maryland and the whole of Ohio she hasn't laughed at from the time she was thirteen. She's past twenty. I can't keep Lacey in pigtails forever waiting for Leslie to marry." She was becoming incoherent. "Look at her! She says I'm feudal. And I said to him right out that she was skinny as a bird dog and her eyes—how did I know he had millions of acres and everybody knew about him—you bring a man into the house and you never even . . ."

"But Lacey's only a kid and she isn't skinny she's over-plump if anything. What's she got to do with it?"

"Lacey! Who's talking about Lacey! Leslie! Leslie! For years she's been going on about how silly Washington society is and how she hates dinners and teas and calling cards and why can't things be big and real and American and here is this man with millions of land why it's an empire and you never even mentioned to me . . ."

At quarter of eleven Leslie Lynnton pleaded a crashing headache together with various other racking complications and left the Hunt Ball flat, returning to her home under the somewhat dazed escort of a bewildered young man who had long been a willing but unrewarded victim. She went straight to the library but seemed disappointed in what she found—or failed to find—there. But she made three silent trips between the library and her bedroom, her arms loaded each time with books of assorted sizes. These she plumped down on her bed and it was surrounded by these tomes that her sister Lacey in the room next door came upon her in a spirit of investigation, having seen her light and heard her moving about.

Lacey poked her head in at the door. "I thought it was burglars or a lover," she said.

Leslie glanced up from the book she was reading. "Well, it would have been nice to see you in either case. And where do you learn such talk!"

"What are you home for!"

"To read. About Texas."

"You mean you came home from the Hunt Ball just to have a read! About Texas!"

"Go along to bed," Leslie said. "There's a good child."

Lacey gave her a hard look. "Aha!" she said. "Likewise oho! Texas, huh?"

The Lynnton family knew what Leslie meant when she said she was going to have a read. Her bed in the old Virginia house was by no means the meager maiden couch upon which the un-wed usually compose themselves to sleep. Leslie had seized upon a vast four-poster that had reposed for years in the jungleland of the attic. Originally it must have been meant for at least one pair of ancestors and a suckling infant. A vast plateau, as broad as it was long and as long as any six-foot Virginian could have wished, it stood, not with its headboard against the wall as is the custom of all well-behaved beds, but in the middle of the room for reasons that no one of the family could fathom and that Leslie never explained. The headboard soared almost to the ceiling. Above blazed a crystal chandelier, full blast, and on either side were lamps. All over the bed and in piles on the floor were books large and small, making a sort of stockade in the confines of which Leslie Lynnton had composed herself to read for hours. Books of history, encyclopedias, pamphlets, almanacs, even fiction. Leslie Lynnton read and as she read she twined and untwined a lock of hair between her fingers until tendrils curls and wisps stood up, medusa-like, all over her head.

Upon this spectacle Lacey gazed without astonishment.

"Oh, Leslie, are you in love with him!"

"Perhaps. Yes, I think so. He says Texas is different from any other state in the whole United States."

"Pooh! Everybody says that about their own state. That's what Papa says about Ohio and Mama about Virginia."

"Not like that. He talks as if it were a different country altogether. A country all by itself that just happens to be in the middle of the United States."

"It isn't in the middle. It's way down near Mexico or something."

Leslie ignored this. "He calls it 'my country' when he means Texas. I asked him about that and he said all Texans—he says Texians—call their state their country and they even call their own ranches their country as if they were kings. I never was so interested in my life. Never. I've got all the books I could find in the library that might have something about Texas and Pa's files and the Congressional Records since way back and the encyclopedia and a lot of histories and *Your Southwest* and *How to Run a Ranch* and *Life of a Texas Ranch Wife* and *The Texas Rangers* and *Texas, a Description of Its Geographical, Social and Other Conditions with Special Reference to——*"

"Good night!" said Lacey, and closed the door firmly. Lacey awoke once during the night and heard the great clock in the downstairs hall strike three. Turning over drowsily she saw the thin line of light still grinning beneath Leslie's closed door.

Breakfast at the Lynntons' was a pleasant thing. The dining room itself was perhaps the friendliest room in that openhanded house. A noble old room, high-ceilinged, many-windowed. On a sunny day such as this it was no room for a woman who preferred to shun the early morning light. A brilliant bay at the south end led to a terrace and the haphazard garden. Inside shone mahogany and silver and crystal.

Bick Benedict, entering the room rather diffidently, noted that the napkins were neatly darned, the flower-patterned carpet threadbare. It's the luxuries that matter, Leslie had said. Who cares about the necessities.

Breakfast here was done in the English fashion, a movable feast. Doctor Lynnton was likely to breakfast at six and Lacey Lynnton at five or at ten, while other members of the family and assorted guests might appear between seven and eleven. On the long sideboard were the hot dishes cozily covered and freshly replenished from time to time but certainly the early risers had the best of it. Eggs, kippers, sausages. Hot biscuits toast muffins. Tea coffee jam honey. You helped yourself, you sat and you talked or you sat and ate if you had awakened grumpy or you sat and read your paper, the sun streamed in, the coffee was strong and hot, there was an air of leisure mingled with a pleasant bustle of coming and going.

Leslie Lynnton came in with a rush which she checked at once. Early as she was, Doctor Lynnton and Bick Benedict were there before her. She looked very young and pale in the little blue dress with the white collars and cuffs, her black hair tied with a ribbon. She had had three hours of sleep.

"Hello!" she said. "Good morning!"

"Why Leslie!" said Doctor Lynnton.

She hurriedly blotted this out by saying, as she helped herself to coffee, "I almost always breakfast with Papa." She looked very straight at Bick Benedict and he at her. She saw in the morning light that his eyes were crinkled at the corners from sun and wind; he looked even taller and broader of shoulder there at breakfast in the sunny room.

"You're looking mighty pert, Miss Leslie," he said inadequately. "You don't look as if you'd been dancing all night."

She drank her entire cup of coffee, black, she set the cup down carefully in the saucer and sat a moment very still as though ignoring the little compliment, so that the two men as they regarded her so admiringly and thought of her, the one with the love and affection of many years, the other with an emotion that bewildered and exhilarated him, felt momentarily puzzled.

She made her decision. "I came home at quarter to eleven," she said quietly, "and I read about Texas until four this morning."

"Oh, Leslie!" groaned Doctor Lynnton. "Leave the poor boy to eat his breakfast in peace."

Bick Benedict was astonished and he did not believe her. He smiled rather patronizingly. "Well, what did you learn? It takes a lot of reading, Texas does."

"We really stole Texas, didn't we? I mean. Away from Mexico."

He jumped as if he had touched a live wire. His eyes were agate. He waited a moment before he trusted himself to speak. "I don't understand the joke," he finally said through stiff lips. He thought how many men had been killed in Texas for saying so much less than this thing that had been said to him.

"I'm not joking, Mr. Benedict. It's right there in the history books, isn't it? This Mr. Austin moved down there with two or three hundred families from the East, it says, and the Mexicans were polite and said they could settle and homestead if they wanted to, under the rule of Mexico. And the next thing you know they're claiming they want to free themselves from Mexico and they fight and take it. Really! How impolite. I don't mean to be rude, but really! Of course the Spanish explorers, and the French, that was different. There was nobody around and there they were tramping and riding across the hot desert in all those iron clothes, with steel helmets and plumes. They must have been terribly uncomfortable. Those Conquistadores—isn't it a lovely word!—Coronado and De Soto and Whatshisname De Vaca, poor dears, looking for the Seven Cities of Cibola like children on a treasure hunt. Still, they didn't actually grab the land away from anyone, the way we did. Of course there were the Indians, but perhaps they didn't count."

89

Doctor Lynnton glanced at Benedict. He was startled to see that the man was rigid with suppressed anger. The muscles of his jaw stood out hard and stiff. For a moment it was as though he would rise and leave the room. Or throw the cup in his hand. These Texans.

"Now now, Leslie," Doctor Lynnton murmured soothingly. "You mustn't talk like that to a Texan. They're touchy. They feel very strongly about their state." He smiled. "Their country, you might almost say. To some of them the United States is their second country. Isn't that so, Benedict?"

"Oh, but I didn't mean to be impolite!" Leslie said before Bick could voice his pent anger. "I was just talking impersonally —about history." She picked up her cup and saucer and came over and sat beside him, cozily, her elbow on the table, she leaned toward him, she peered into his face like an eager child. It was disconcerting, it was maddening, if she had been a man he would have hit her, he told himself. "It's all in the books, it's news to me, I just meant it's so fascinating. It's another world, it sounds so big and new and different. I love it. The cactus and the cowboys and the Alamo and the sky and the horses and the Mexicans and the freedom. It's really America, isn't it. I'm—I'm in love with it."

Bick Benedict's heart gave a lurch. Watch out, he said to himself. Rattlesnakes.

Women did not talk like that. Certainly Texas women didn't talk like that. Of course, in those two years he had spent at Harvard because the Benedict men always had a couple of years at Harvard so that no one could say they were provincial, he had met a few girls who had a lot of opinions of their own but they weren't popular girls, they weren't girls you saw at the football games or the prom. Well, if she wanted to talk about Texas he'd talk to her as if she were a man.

"I never saw anything as ignorant as you Easterners. All you know about American history is what's happened east of Philadelphia. Valley Forge and Bunker Hill and Washington crossing the Delaware. The Delaware! Did you ever hear of the Rio

Grande! I'll bet they don't even teach about the Alamo and San Jacinto in your schools."

"No, they don't. Do they, Papa?" Doctor Lynnton passed his hand over his face with a gesture like that of brushing off cobwebs. But she went on without waiting for his confirmation. "And anyway, we're not Easterners, Mr. Benedict." With earnestness she had grown formal. "Not at all. Are we, Papa?" A rhetorical question, purely. "Tell him."

"Hell no!" said Horace Lynnton. "Ohioans are no Easterners. But now don't you get into any fracas with a Texan, Leslie. They're touchier than a hornet, didn't you know that? Besides, you came near being a Texan yourself."

"She did!" Bick exclaimed in a surprisingly pleased tone of voice.

"Maybe you've forgotten, Leslie. I guess I haven't mentioned it since you were a very little girl and you didn't pay much attention."

He reached for a hot biscuit and split it and placed a great gob of butter in the center of the upper half and on top of this he perched a large gobbet of strawberry jam. He gazed admiringly at the brilliant gold and ruby picture before he bit into it.

Leslie said, very low, with a concern more wifely than filial, "You know not so much starch and sugar and fat."

"I know," he agreed ruefully, as though speaking of something beyond his powers of accomplishment. "My patients mind when I tell them but I don't." And went on eating and talking with enjoyment. He looked at Bick, genially. "My father was a doctor too, you know. Scotch-Irish stock. He heard the talk about Texas when he was living in Ohio about 1870, before I was born. When I was a kid I used to hear him say he went to Texas to settle down there and grow with the country. He fell in love with it, like Leslie here, before he ever laid eyes on it. Well sir, he stayed about six months and worked up quite a practice, there weren't many doctors then in Texas. He didn't mind the climate. The heat. And the northers. And the dust. But he packed up and went back to Ohio. He said his digestion was ruined for life in those six months. Fried steak. Fried potatoes. Fried bread. Fried beans. Said that people who fried everything they ate, and fried it in grease and cared as little about good food and knew as little about cooking as the Texans, would take all of another hundred years to catch up with the rest of the civilized world. No offense I hope, Jordan." He had a thin pink curl of Virginia ham on his fork and now he used it to chase a few buttery biscuit crumbs around his plate before dispatching it. He eyed the covered dishes on the sideboard, caught Leslie's disapproving gaze and sat back with a sigh of renunciation. "The Lynntons all set too much store by their palates, I suppose. Leslie here would rather try a new recipe than a new dress."

"You're worse than any of us," Leslie retorted. She turned to Bick. "Everyone knows there's been a feud for years between Papa and Caroline the cook about which can make the most delicate crème brûlé."

"What," inquired Bick Benedict, "is crème brûlé?" At sight of their stricken faces he laughed, but not very heartily. "One thing you'll say for us—we never bragged on our food. But I like it." Then, to his own surprise, "Texas would be a good place for Virginia women. They're pampered and spoiled out of all reason."

"I'm not. Am I, Papa? But then, I'm not a Virginian."

Horace Lynnton turned to look at his daughter with the appraising gaze of one who is freshly curious. "Oh, you, Leslie. You were born out of your time. You'd have been good in the Civil War, hiding slaves in the Underground or, before that, pioneering, maybe, in a covered wagon crossing the prairie with an ox team."

Leslie, stirring her second cup of coffee, considered this and rejected it. "I wouldn't have liked it, except the freedom and no Washington society and all that nonsense. Nothing to fear except scalping by the Indians, no household worries except whether you'd find water on the way. It does sound rather lovely, doesn't it? But awfully uncomfortable. You've brought me up wrong, Papa. I love old silver and Maryland crabs and plenty of hot water day and night with bath salts, and one glass of very cold very dry champagne."

Bick Benedict waved an arm that dismissed silver, hot water, house, garden, champagne, and the entire Eastern seaboard.

"All this is decadent," he said. "Dying. Or good and dead."

"It isn't!" Leslie contested. "It's been sick, but now it's just coming back to life. If Lincoln had lived another two years. He had plans. The South would have been better after the Civil War instead of broken because a lot of ignorant greedy——"

"Well," Doctor Lynnton interrupted, very leisurely, and brushing the crumbs off his vest. "I won't have time for this, if the Civil War's going to be fought again."

Leslie looked directly into Bick's eyes. He thought, What's coming now? "Do you read Carlyle?"

"My God no!" Bick said.

Horace Lynnton stood up. "Look here, Leslie. It's all right to attack a Texan about Texas in the early morning but you can't batter a guest at breakfast with Carlyle."

"I don't know much about Carlyle," Bick said, and he, too, stood up as Leslie rose, so that the three made a curiously electric group without actually being conscious that they were standing. The two young people faced each other. Their talk became disjointed like the dialogue in a bad English translation of a Chekhov play. "My Mistake. The filly, I mean. I've bought her. If you ever come to Texas, Miss Leslie."

Sadly, "I never will." Her eyes turned to the open door and the apple orchard beyond where the blossoming trees in their bouffant white skirts stood like ballet dancers a-tiptoe, row on row.

His eyes followed hers. "Those apple blossoms. You can smell them way in here."

"I read about those yellow blossoms on your trees—or are they shrubs? Are they sweet-smelling?"

"Retama?"

93

"Huisache. If that's the way it's pronounced."

"After the spring rains there are desert flowers. Miles of them, like a carpet."

"Then it is a desert, Texas?"

"No. You can grow anything. From grapefruit to wheat. Pretty soon there won't be anything you can't grow better in Texas." Then, to his own horror, he heard himself saying, "If it's freedom you want, come to Texas. No one there tells you what to do and how you have to do it. No calling cards there and young squirts in red coats. Cattle and prairie and horses and sun and sky and plenty of good plain——"

"Plenty of good plain cactus and ticks and drought," Doctor Lynnton interrupted good-naturedly. "And northers and snakes. You Texans!" He shook his head in wonderment. "Don't you think you ought to look at My Mistake again before we go? I don't think you ought to buy her unless you're dead sure. You'll have to watch out for that trick she has of doing fancy dance steps just when she's supposed to be getting near the post. Ten thousand dollars is a lot of money."

"I've paid double that for a good bull," Bick said, but not boastfully. Absently, as though this were something unimportant, to be dismissed for more pressing things. "Do you like it living here in Virginia?" he asked Leslie.

"Yes, I suppose so."

"Everything looks so little."

"Big doesn't necessarily mean better. Sunflowers aren't better than violets."

"How far west have you been?"

"Kansas City once, with Papa."

"Kansas City! That's east! And little. In Texas there's everything. There's no end to it."

"Perhaps too much of everything is as bad as too little. I suppose I'm used to everything being sort of cozy. I don't mean little and cramped. But sort of near me. Family and books and friends and the kitchen if I want to go out and try something new and Caroline doesn't mind."

Doctor Lynnton cleared his throat to remind them of his presence. They were weaving a pattern, warily, of which he was no part. "We'll have to be getting along, Bick," he said. "Unless you would like to stay on, we'd be happy to have you but I'm due at the hospital——"

"Good morning!" cried Mrs. Lynnton from the dining-room doorway in clear ringing tones. "Good morning, everybody." She looked straight at Bick. "Good morning, Lochinvar!"

Bick Benedict, rather red, stammered, "Uh—good—uh——"

"Don't mind Mama," Leslie said, not at all embarrassed. "She's been trying to marry me off for years. And anyway, Mama, if you're going to be geographical, Lochinvar came out of the West, not the Southwest. It wouldn't have scanned."

"Leslie reads too much," Mrs. Lynnton explained blandly. "Horace dear, fetch me a sliver of that ham, will you? For a young girl, I mean. But it's her only fault and you wouldn't really call it a fault. Leslie dear, if Mr. Benedict has finished breakfast don't you want to show him the stables?"

"He saw them yesterday, Mama. Besides, we've just quarreled in a polite way about Texas so it's no use your trying to palm me off on him. And anyway Mr. Benedict has three million acres and five hundred thousand cows or whatever they're called in Texas——"

"Head of cattle," Bick suggested, "and not quite five——"

"—head of cattle then. And hundreds of vaqueros and consequently he's engaged to marry the daughter of the owner of the adjoining ranch who, though comparatively poor, is beautiful and has only one million acres and fifteen thousand horses and two hundred thousand head of cattle and six hundred vaqueros."

"What is a vaquero?" Mrs. Lynnton demanded, dignified in defeat.

Jordan Benedict walked round the table to stand beside Leslie as though he were talking to her rather than to her mother. "A vaquero is a Mexican cowboy," he said crisply, with no trace of a drawl. "Did you ever hear the word buckaroo? That's what the old Texas pioneers made of vaquero, they couldn't get the

95

hang of the Spanish word vaquero. You see—vaca, cow. Vaquero —fellow who tends cows."

"Is she pretty?" demanded Mrs. Lynnton, turning the knife in her wound.

Doctor Lynnton bent over his wife's chair and kissed her lightly on the cheek. "Good-bye, dear. Mr. Benedict and I are going now. I'm late."

Baffled, Mrs. Lynnton must still know the worst. "What, may I ask, is the name of the lucky young lady you are marrying, with all those cows?"

Then even Leslie was moved to protest. "Oh dear Mrs. Nickleby, that was just my little joke."

Bick Benedict just touched her hand with his forefinger. "It's more or less true—or was. My next-door neighbor does have a daughter—only a next-door neighbor in Texas is fifty miles away, usually. And he does have just about all that land and those horses and the cattle. And perhaps there was some idea of my marrying his daughter like the fellow in a book. But I'm not."

A radiance lighted Mrs. Lynnton's austere features. "Dear me, it all sounds so romantic. I never knew anyone from Texas before, it's very refreshing, of course it's quite a distance, Texas."

"It is a far piece, ma'am," Bick agreed, still looking at Leslie. "But when you get there you never want to live anywhere else."

"Yes," Mrs. Lynnton agreed happily, "with those new fast trains and all you can visit back East in no time at all. And you're going back tomorrow. Dear me, what a pity. I don't know when I've met any young man that seemed so much like one of the family."

7

AFTER thirty-six hours of travel the bride and bridegroom seemed to have set up miniature housekeeping in their drawing room on the Missouri Pacific's crack Sunshine Special. Books and papers and bundles and bags were heaped on couches and racks. A towering edifice of fruit in a basket, untouched, was turning brown under the hot blasts that poured through the screened window. A vast box of Maillard's candy, open on the couch, was coated with the fine sift of dust that filmed the little room. A bottle of bourbon clinked against a bottle of water in the wall bracket. Railroad folders and maps of Texas splashed their brilliant pinks and blues and orange and scarlet against the drab green of the car upholstery and the grim maroon of the woodwork. The door of the compartment adjoining the drawing room was open, and this was piled with a formidable array of luggage.

They had been traveling hours, days, yet Texas was not in sight. Bick Benedict did not appear eager for a glimpse of that fabulous commonwealth from which he had been three weeks absent. He lolled on the hot plush seat, the withering southwest blasts poured over him, the dust clogged his throat, the electric fan set the cinders to spinning more merrily in the stifling little room.

He had been bred on heat and dust. This was nothing.

He looked at Leslie and he was like a man fanned by ocean breezes, laved in the perfumes of fresh-cut meadows. But now and then when he leaned against the gritty cushion and shut his eyes his face muscles tensed, his fingers clenched, and it was obvious that his inner vision presented a picture less than idyllic.

The bride was reading a railroad timetable. Bick Benedict eyed her through narrowed lids. "I've married a bookworm." They both laughed as though the timeworn joke were new-minted.

It was incredible that any woman could appear as cool and fresh as she after thirty-six hours in the gritty luxury of a train drawing room. She seemed to have an unlimited supply of fresh blouses and just to watch her open a filmy handkerchief and to catch the scent that emanated from it as she shook out its white folds was a refreshment to the onlooker. She brushed her hair a great deal. She poured eau de cologne into the lavatory wash basin and bathed her wrists and her temples and the scent of this, too, pricked the grateful nostrils.

"I don't know how other brides feel on their honeymoon," she now said, "Mr. Benedict sir. But I'm having a lovely time."

"Well, thanks."

"It isn't only you. It's traveling. I love train-riding even if it's hot and dusty."

"If we'd had the private car as I wanted———"

"Private cars for two people are immoral. And anyway, they're dull."

"Well, thanks again."

"I'll bet you," said the bride, "that this minute, sight unseen, I know more about Texas than you do."

"Mrs. Benedict, if I may call you that, I am taking the filly known as My Mistake and the young woman formerly known as Leslie Lynnton, off the hands of Doctor and Mrs. Lynnton, respectively. The understanding was that the one can run and the other is intelligent as well as lovely. Perhaps one of you has got the wrong name."

"Leslie Benedict," she mused. "It isn't as pretty as Leslie Lynnton."

"But you're prettier. I don't say that I'm taking full credit. But you are."

"It's the fresh air," she said. "And the regular hours. Darling, will you let me know the minute we reach Texas?"

"Texas isn't exactly a secret."

"It's different from other states, isn't it? It looks different?"

He was seated opposite her on one of the grim settees. Now he leaned forward and clasped his hands between his knees and smiled up at her, so earnest so eager so alive. "You're a funny girl. You didn't marry me just for the trip to Texas, did you?"

"I won't say I didn't."

He laughed aloud then and held out his hand for hers and swung around so that he sat beside her on the seat that had been facing him. They looked at one another a moment, smiling, and then they became serious and silent.

The sound of the drawing-room door buzzer was like an electric shock. Bick Benedict passed a hand over his forehead and shouted, "Come in!" It was the dining-car steward, sallow and sleek and obsequious.

He purred. He bowed. "Parn me," he said. "But I figured you'd want to get your order in early, before the rush. You can just run your eye over the menu, but I have a couple of suggestions. Our last stop we took on some——"

"Oh, let's have dinner in the dining car," Leslie said. "With the rest of the world. Let's have olives—the big black ones—in a bowl of cracked ice with celery. And melons. And brook trout."

"Brook trout!" Bick protested doubtfully. "They don't have
——"

"But we do," interrupted the steward with injured dignity. "I
was just trying to tell Mrs. Benedict. We took them on at Baxter
just for our special passengers."

It had been like that from the moment they had turned their
faces toward the West. Passenger agents had come aboard at
various stops for the sole purpose of inquiring about their comfort.

"They behave as if you were royalty," Leslie had said. "Do
they always do that? Or just for brides and bridegrooms?"

"The Benedicts have been around these parts a long time,"
Bick explained. "And we travel a lot. And Reata beef travels a lot
too. They're the really important passengers when it comes to
railroad arithmetic."

It seemed to Leslie that the conductors, the stewards, the
porters the station agents knew more about the members of the
Benedict family of Texas—their names, habits, characteristics
and whereabouts—than they knew about President Coolidge and
his family in the White House.

The Pullman conductor, benign and spectacled, with all those
stripes on his sleeve and the Elks charm and the little gold nugget
dangling from his watch chain, was introduced with friendly
formality.

"Leslie, I want you to know Mr. McCullough. The newest
member of the family, Ed. Mrs. Benedict."

"Well, say, Bick! I heard, last trip up. Certainly pleased to
make your acquaintance, Mrs. Benedict. This is great news. The
girls are all fit to be tied, I bet. They had just about given him
up, I guess. But say!" His tone was jocose, his manner almost paternal. He turned, beaming, to Bick. "Yessir, great news
this is. How's Miz Maudie Lou? She come for the wedding? She
hasn't ridden with us here lately. How's Miz Luz? Did she get
over that nasty fall she took? How's Uncle Bawley? Bowie was
riding with us last week, never let out a yip about the wedding,

and prolly on his way to be best man. Awful closemouthed, Bowie is."

Leslie thought that her mother would have loved all this kow-towing on the part of railroad crew and officials. In those brief days before the hurried wedding Mrs. Lynnton had chanted her refrain endlessly.

"Jordan Benedict of the famous Benedict ranch in Texas, you know. Jordan Benedict Third. Everybody knows about the Benedict ranch. It's practically a kingdom. It's a kind of legend Doctor Lynnton says."

The Benedict family had not come to the wedding in great numbers. Bick's younger brother Bowie had come as best man and of course his cousin Roady in Washington and his sister Maudie Lou Placer and her husband Clint. But his older sister Luz, the one who kept house for him at the ranch, the one who never had married, caught the grippe or something at the last minute and couldn't come. Nor did Uncle Bawley, who practically never left his big untidy bachelor house from which he ran the five hundred thousand acres of the Holgado Division. Assorted aunts and uncles and cousins had not been urged to come. There had been no time, really.

The Virginia newspapers and the Washington society columns referred to it as a whirlwind courtship—a phrase that delighted Mrs. Lynnton. Rushed though she was with the wedding preparations, Mrs Lynnton snipped out all the newspaper clichés and pasted them in a Bride's Book—white leather with gold tooling—which she presented to Leslie and which, years later, Leslie's daughter Luz came upon with whoops of mirth at the knee-length skirts and the ear-hugging coiffures.

The lovely Leslie Lynnton. The dashing Texan. Virginia belle. Cattle King. Bick Benedict had battered down everyone's opposition to such haste.

"Wait for what!" he demanded of Leslie, of Doctor Lynnton of Mrs. Lynnton. "Now!" he insisted. "Now, while I'm here. Suppose I do go home and come back here again in a month—two months. What for!"

"Trousseau," Mrs. Lynnton insisted. "There are a million things a bride has to have, besides clothes. Linens and——"

"There are a million things at the ranch. There's everything anybody needs and no one there to use them—except my sister Luz. Boxes of stuff, barrels of them, closets stuffed with them. Fifty beds, and sheets for a hundred, and all the rest of it."

"My daughter Leslie will be married as befits a Lynnton of Virginia. And her clothes will be as carefully chosen as those of her sister Lady Karfrey."

But here Leslie took over. "Mama dear, you are talking like someone out of Jane Austen. Anyway, I'm not a Lynnton of Virginia. I just live here. I was born in Ohio, remember? And Texas isn't England."

"What has that to do with it?" Mrs. Lynnton demanded unreasonably.

"Nothing. Not a thing. For some reason Jordan wants us to be married next week. And he's here. And why not!"

"It's odd. People will talk."

Leslie linked her arm through Jordan's and together the two faced Nancy Lynnton. Horace Lynnton, never doubting the outcome, smoked a calming pipe and surveyed the battle with interest at once paternal and professional. Long ago he had learned, a male surrounded by females, to take on the protective coloration of the absent-minded professor.

Somehow it filtered through to Mrs. Lynnton that it was now or never. She looked at her husband, so maddeningly noncommittal; at Leslie who somehow, suddenly, had taken on a baffling mixture of soft bloom and hard resolution; at Jordan Benedict a man of thirty bewildered and in love for the first time.

It had not been much of a wedding, as society weddings go. The striped trousers and cutaway coats knew about Bick Benedict, and seemed somewhat pale beside him, not only from chagrin but because they hadn't a century of Texas sun and dust and wind behind them for coloration. The girls said, "Oh, Leslie, he reminds me of Tom Mix a little, only blond of course."

Bick's sister Maudie Lou Placer turned out to be something of a bombshell. Very chic. She and Clint Placer arrived the morning of the wedding and departed immediately afterward, leaving a somewhat stricken Mrs. Lynnton to digest the utterances of the strangely resentful Maudie Lou.

She had given Mrs. Lynnton a grisly five minutes. That doughty lady, recognizing an adversary when she saw one, had said, "It's a pity they will have such a short honeymoon. Just ten days. It would have been nice if they could have gone to visit my daughter Lady Karfrey in England. But Jordan says he must get back to his ranch."

"His ranch!" Maudie Lou had echoed, and with a peculiarly nasty laugh. "It isn't his ranch."

Nancy Lynnton had turned white and faint. "What do you mean by that!"

"Well, it's no more his than mine or Luz's or Bowie's or Roady's for that matter. Bick runs it. Manages, with Luz of course. But we all own it. Though if he keeps on with——"

"Of course," said Mrs. Lynnton feebly. "So many millions of acres."

"Though if he keeps on the way he is," Maudie Lou concluded angrily, "putting all the profits back into the ranch and going on with his crazy breeding and fads and experiments there'll be nothing left for any of us pretty soon."

Bick's oldest sister Luz did not come to the wedding. "She brought me up, really," Bick had told Leslie. "She has been like a mother to me. She had to be. She's nineteen years older than I am. She looks like Great-grandma Benedict. She even tries to look like her. Once she got the old hoop skirts out of the attic and went out into the pasture and tried roping in that crazy outfit because the story goes that that's what Great-grandma Benedict did back in the late fifties. She does her hair like her, too. Two braids in a kind of crown on top of her head."

"Like pictures of Mrs. Lincoln," Leslie observed thoughtfully. "Luz. What an unusual name."

"It's Spanish. It means light."

When the actual week of the wedding arrived there was a

telegram. Luz was ill with the grippe, she had a fever of one hundred and two. The doctor said she absolutely must not travel. . . .

Bick Benedict seemed perturbed by this out of all proportion to its importance, the Lynntons thought. An elderly sister is ill and can't come to the wedding. How sad. But in another way how convenient, Mrs. Lynnton thought privately. A middle-aged woman, a bedroom alone of course, the house was crowded. It would have added to the difficulties without contributing anything to the festivities.

Bick had talked a great deal about this older sister. "She's wonderful, really," he had said, as though someone had said she was not. "Right out of a Western movie, you'll think. She can do anything a cowboy can. The boys are all crazy about her, but they're scared of her too."

Doctor Horace Lynnton, in these past few years, had related to this favorite daughter of his some of the phenomena which had emerged in the trial practice of a rather new branch of therapeutics called psychiatry. He was using it to help some of the broken boys who sat staring into space in the corridors and rooms of the crowded veterans' hospitals in Washington, Maryland, Virginia. He had given Leslie books to read, he introduced her to the writings of the giants in this new and inexact science. "Our thoughts, our dreams, our entire lives are influenced by the unconscious," he explained.

Leslie had found this new instruction fascinating, she had accepted it with calm. "I suppose," she said thoughtfully, "that I've been in love with you all these years, Papa, and that's why I haven't married."

"Quite likely," Doctor Lynnton agreed. Then, with a wry smile, "I wouldn't try, if I were you, to explain this to your mother."

Now, with the wedding only three days distant, it was with a certain amused thoughtfulness that Leslie received the news of her future sister-in-law's sudden illness.

Bick said with excusable stiffness, "I don't see why you find this amusing."

"I didn't know I was looking amused. Forgive me. I was thinking. You know it's just possible that your sister Luz is sick to order. Sometimes those things happen when people are upset. Papa says he often encounters cases like that."

"I suppose Luz got a hundred and two just to order. Is that what you mean?"

"Lots of mothers do."

"Luz isn't my mother. What's the matter with you, Leslie!"

"Wives, I mean."

"Look, Leslie, have you gone loco!"

"Big sisters sometimes think they're wives. Or mothers. And mothers do too, Papa says."

This somewhat confused utterance was a maddening climax for Bick.

"I think you must be sick yourself," he had said with a harshness unusual in a prospective bridegroom.

But certainly Bick Benedict had no cause for complaint once the furor of the wedding was past. His bride was ardent and lovely and incredibly understanding. Three days of their honeymoon were spent in New York where the tall Texan in the big white Stetson and the starry-eyed girl in bridal grey caused a turning of heads even on Manhattan's blasé Fifth Avenue. They had stayed at the Plaza.

He seemed, curiously enough, in no great hurry to start the journey home. Strangely, too, he seemed not to have a great deal of ready money. They went to the theatre, they ate well, they drove in the Park, they shopped a little but there was none of the lavish moneyed carelessness that one would expect from the possessor of millions of acres of land and hundreds of thousands of cattle.

Not that Leslie expected or coveted the brilliant baubles with which the Fifth Avenue windows were bedecked. But perhaps he felt that some sort of explanation was called for.

"Cattle men don't have a lot of ready cash," he said not at all apologetically. "We put it back into the ranch. More beef cattle,

GIANT

better stock, experimenting with new breeds. A good bull can cost twenty thousand dollars."

The bride had her practical side. "He can bring in twenty thousand too, can't he? If you sell him. Or his—uh—sons?"

"You don't sell a bull like that. You buy him."

At the unreasonableness of this she laughed. But then she said seriously enough, "I hope you're not stingy by nature, Jordan darling. Because that's very bad for you. We've never had any money but we've always been lavish."

"Perhaps that's why."

"Why what? Oh. Just for that perhaps you'd better buy me something very expensive. Not that I want it. But as a lesson to you. Not the price of a bull but a calf, say."

Now, as they neared the end of their journey, the little luxury room on the train grew hotter, hotter, became stifling, the electric fan paddled the heat and slapped their face with it, the whole body was fevered with heat and dust. Too, another kind of fever possessed Leslie, it was the fire of deep interest and anticipation so that she quite ignored the physical discomfort of the stuffy train.

"You can see miles!" she said. "Miles and miles and miles!" She had her flushed face at the ineffectually screened window, like a child.

"It's sort of frightening, isn't it—like something that defies you to conquer it? So huge. Why, we've been riding in it for days. And ugly, too, isn't it! I thought it would be beautiful. Oh, now, don't be sulky. I'm not talking about your ancestors or something, dearest. I'm being interested. And clinical."

"Like your father."

"Yes, I suppose so. Oh, I'm so excited. Look! There at that little station we're passing—that's a cowboy, isn't it, it must be, I was just feeling cheated because I hadn't seen a single cowboy. Are they like that at the ranch, at Reata?"

He eyed her with fond amusement. "Sometimes I think you're ten years old and not real bright."

"I can't help it. Geography always excites me when it's new places, and I love trains and being married to you, and seeing

106

Texas. When your grandfather came here it was wilderness really, wasn't it? Imagine! What courage!"

"They were great old boys. Tough."

"No trees, except that little fluffy stuff, it's rather sweet. What's it called? Is there some at the ranch?"

His smile was grim. "That little sweet fluffy stuff is the damnedest nuisance in Texas. It's called mesquite and if you can find a way to get rid of it you'll be the toast of Texas, sure enough."

As far as her eyes could see she beheld the American desert land which once had waved knee-high with lush grasses. She had never seen the great open plains and the prairies. It was endless, it was another world, bare vast menacing to her Eastern eyes. Later she was to know the brilliant blurred pattern of the spring flowers, she was to look for the first yellow blossoms of the retama against the sky, the wild cherry and the heavy cream white of the Spanish dagger flower like vast camellias.

"How big is it, really? Not in figures, I can't understand figures, but tell me in a kind of picture."

This was home again, this was what he knew and loved. "Well, let's see now. How can I—— Look, you know the way the map of the United States looks? Well, if you take all of New England —the whole of the New England states—and then add New York State and New Jersey and Pennsylvania and Ohio and Illinois, and put the whole thing together in one block, why, you'd have a state the size of Texas. That's how big it is." He was triumphant as though he himself had created this vast area in a godlike gesture.

It was late afternoon when their train arrived at Vientecito. "Here we are!" he said and peered out through the window to scan the platform and the vehicles beyond in the swirling dust.

"What's it mean? How do you pronounce it?"

"Vientecito? Means gentle breeze. We call it Viento for short. The wind blows all the time, nearly. The Spanish explorers arrived here way back in 1519 before you were born I think, honey. Alonso Alvarez de Pinedo, if you want to know in round numbers.

You see I did go to school. He and his crowd swung around hereabouts and liked the layout and claimed it for king and Spain. But they didn't know enough to hang onto it." He pointed at some object. "There we are. But who's that!" A huge Packard. In the driver's seat was a stocky young Mexican with powerful shoulders. About twenty, Leslie thought; a square face a square brow, his hair like a brush growing thick thick and up from his forehead. He was very dark very quiet he did not smile.

There was no one else in the car. There was no one to meet them. The man got out of the car, he stood at the open door looking uncertainly at Bick. He did not glance at Leslie. Bick's face was cold with anger, there was a curious underlay of white beneath his deep-coated tan, his jaw muscle swelled as he set his teeth. The two men spoke in Spanish.

"What are you doing here? Where is Jett?"

"Señorita Luz said she needed him. She sent me in his place."

"You don't know about a car. Here. Pile these bags in the back. Where's the pickup? There are trunks."

"Nothing was said about sending the pickup."

Bick Benedict's lips were a straight thin line, his fists were clenched.

This phenomenon Leslie surveyed with lively interest and no alarm.

"Bick, you look bursting. I must learn Spanish."

The boy, very serious and dignified, was inexpertly piling suitcases into the rear baggage section. This accomplished, he was about to take the driver's seat. "Out!" barked Bick. The boy paused, turned. Bick gave him the baggage checks. In Spanish he said, "You will wait here. The pickup will be sent. It may be two hours it may be midnight. You will wait here."

The boy inclined his head. Leslie came toward him, she put out her hand. "I am Mrs. Benedict," she said. "What is your name?"

The dark eyes met hers. Then they swung like a startled child's to encounter Bick Benedict's ice-blue stare. The boy bent over her hand, he did not touch it, he bowed in a curiously formal gesture, his hand over his heart, like a courtier. His eyes were cast down.

"What eyelashes!" Leslie said over her shoulder to Bick. "I wish I had them!"

"Dimodeo," the boy said in English. "I am called Dimodeo Rivas!"

"That's a beautiful name," Leslie said.

"Leslie! Get into the car, please. We're leaving." His voice was a command. She smiled at the boy, she turned leisurely, she was somewhat surprised to see her husband's face scowling from the driver's seat.

"Coming!" she called gaily. She looked about her as she came —at the railway station so Spanish with its Romanesque towers, its slim pillars and useless grillwork. The sun burned like a stab-wound, the hot unceasing wind gave no relief. The dark faces of the station loungers were unlike the submissive masks of the Negroes she knew so well in Virginia. No green anywhere other than the grey-green of the cactus, spiked and stark. Dust dust dust, stinging in the wind. Nothing followed the look or pattern of the life she had left behind her.

"It's like Spain," she called to Bick. "I've never been in Spain but it's like it." She stood a moment by the car door, hesitant, waiting for Bick to leap out. He sat looking straight ahead. The boy Dimodeo ran to her, he opened the Packard's half-door, she placed her hand delicately on his arm. "Thank you, Dimodeo. Uh—gracias—uh—muchas gracias! There! I can speak Spanish too. How did I happen to remember that? Ouch!" As she settled herself on the hot leather seat. "Read it somewhere I suppose."

With a neck-cracking jerk the car leaped away. Never a timorous woman their speed now seemed to her to be maniacal. She glanced at her husband's hands on the wheel. Nothing could go wrong when hands like that were guiding your life. He was silent, his face set and stern. Well, she knew that when men looked like that you pretended not to notice and pretty soon they forgot all about it.

"How flat it is! And big. And the horizon is—well, there just isn't any it's so far away. I thought there would be lots of cows. I don't see any."

"Cows!" he said in a tone of utter rage.

She was, after all, still one of the tart-tongued Lynnton girls. "I don't see why you're so put out because that boy came instead of someone else. Or the family. After all, it's so far from the railroad."

"Far!" In that same furious tone. "It's only ninety miles."

She glanced at the speedometer. It pointed to eighty-five. Well, no wonder! At this rate they'd be home in an hour or so. Home. For an engulfing moment she had a monstrous feeling of being alone with a strange man in an unknown world—a world of dust and desert and heat and glare and some indefinable thing she never before had experienced. Maybe all brides feel like this, she thought. Suddenly wanting to go home to their mother and father and their own bed.

He was speaking again in a lower tone now, but a controlled anger vibrated beneath it. "We don't behave like that down here."

"Behave?"

"Making a fuss over that Mexican boy. We don't do that here in Texas."

"But this still is the United States, isn't it? You were being mean to him. What did he do?"

The speedometer leaped to ninety. "We have our own way of doing things. You're a Texan now. Please remember that."

"But I'm not anyone I wasn't. I'm myself. What's geography to do with it!"

"Texas isn't geography. It's history. It's a world in itself."

She said something far in advance of her day. "There is no world in itself."

"You've read too damn many books."

She began to laugh suddenly—a laugh of surprise and discovery. "We're quarreling! Jordan, we're having our first quarrel. Well, it's nice to get it over with before we reach—home."

To her horror then he brought his head down to his hands on the wheel, a gesture of utter contrition and one that might have killed them both. At her cry of alarm he straightened. His right hand reached over to cover her hands clasped so tightly in her fright. "My darling," he said. "My darling girl." Then, strangely, "We mustn't quarrel. We've got to stand together."

Against the brassy sky there rose like a mirage a vast edifice all towers and domes and balconies and porticoes and iron fretwork. In size and general architecture it somewhat resembled the palace known as the Alhambra, with a dash of the Missouri Pacific Railroad station which they had just left behind them.

"What's that! Is it—are we near the ranch, Jordan?"

"We've been on it the last eighty miles, practically ever since we got outside Viento. That's Reata. That's home."

"But you said it was a ranch! You said Reata was a ranch!"

8

AND THERE ahead of them was the town. The town of Benedict. A huge square-lettered sign said:

WELCOME TO BENEDICT!
pop. 4739

"Is that for us, Jordan? How sweet of them!"

"No, honey. It's just the Chamber of Commerce saying howdy to any visitors who come by."

"Oh. Well, it's all been so regal, and everyone has done so much forehead-bumping I thought—— Oh, look! Look, Jordan."

They had flashed into town, they were streaking down the wide main street. "Please drive slower, darling. I want to see. What a wide street for such a little—I mean——"

"It's wide because it was a cattle trail. We used to drive thousands of head of cattle to market along this trail, way up to Kansas. That was long before this was a town. Just a huddle of shacks on the prairie."

Now the vast white mansion had vanished, obscured for the moment by the town with its Ranchers and Drovers Bank, its Red Front Grocery, its hardware store, garage, drugstore, lunch room. But even as they roared through the town Leslie felt herself in a strange exciting new land. Dark faces everywhere, but not like the ebony faces of the Virginia streets. These were Latin faces; fine-boned Spanish faces; darker heavier Mexican Indian faces. Even the store-front signs were exhilaratingly different. Leslie hugged herself and bounced a little in her seat, like a child. Boots and Saddles Hand Made. . . . Come to Hermoso for the Fat Stock Show. . . . Quarter Horses For Sale. What was a quarter horse? . . . A little sun-baked dry-goods store whose sign said BARATO. Bargain Sale. She knew enough Spanish for that, at least. Sallow women in black with little black shawls over their heads under the blasting sun. Dusty oleanders by the roadside. Big beef-fed men in wide-brimmed Stetsons and shirt sleeves and high-heeled boots that gave their feet a deceptive arched elegance. Dark little men squatting on their haunches at the street corners. Lean sunburned tall men propped up against store buildings, their stance a peculiar one; one foot on the ground, the opposite knee bent so that the other foot rested flat against the wall. Small houses baking, grassless, by the road. Dust-bitten houses grey as desert bones.

"What's that! What in the world is that!"

In the courthouse square facing the street was a monstrous plate-glass case as large as a sizable room made of thick transparent glass on all sides. Within this, staring moodily out at a modern world, stood a stuffed and mounted Longhorn steer. A huge animal, his horn-spread was easily nine feet from tip to tip.

Wrinkled ancient horns like those of some mythical monster.

"You've just got to stop. I must see him."

"You'll have the rest of your life to see him."

"I can't believe it. A—a cow stuffed and put into a glass case on the street."

He touched her flushed cheek tenderly and laughed a little.

"You're in Texas, honey. Anyway, they have lions outside the New York Public Library, don't they?"

"But this is real."

"Everything's real in Texas."

"What's it for? Do they worship it, or something?"

"He's a Longhorn—the last of the Reata Longhorn herd. They roamed the range wild a hundred years ago. Now they're as extinct as the buffalo, or more. Way back in the days of the Spanish Missions in the 1600s the Spanish brought the first livestock with them. When the Missions were abandoned the stock was left behind and pretty soon there were thousands and thousands of head covering the whole country. Tough mean animals. Hoofs and horns and hide like iron and the meat like leather. That's what we used to call beef, not so many years ago. And now there's the last Longhorn a museum piece in a glass case."

"Who'd have thought a cow could be so romantic! What are they like now—the Reata cows? And where are they? I haven't seen any. I don't believe you really have any. You've dragged me down here under false pretenses."

He laughed wholeheartedly and the sound delighted her. She was not used to morose faces, the Virginia house had been a gay lighthearted place. "Oh, we've still got one or two," he said airily, "hiding out in the mesquite and around. Wait till you see the new breed. We've been ten years experimenting and I think now we've just about got it. We brought Herefords from England and bred them to the best of the native stock. And now I'm breeding the cream of that to the big Kashmirs. Oriental stock. They can take the heat and they've got a body oil that discourages ticks and fleas. The King ranch crowd and some of the other boys are experimenting with Brahmans but I'm the Kashmir Kid.

Wait till you see some of those Kashmir-Hereford bulls. They look like a house on legs. There's never been anything like them in the world. In the world!"

His face was brilliant with life, the silent man of an hour ago was a young eager boy. Some deep inner instinct pinched her heart sharply. That is his real love, it said. Reata and its past and its future are his life. You are just an incident, you are a figure in a pattern you don't even understand.

Now the town was behind them, they were again in the open country. Again and again, in the past hour, she had seen pools of water in the road ahead. But once the spot was reached the pool had vanished and another glinted a hundred yards beyond the speeding car.

"The water. The little pools of water in the middle of the road. And then they're not there."

"A mirage. Texas is full of mirages."

She looked at him quickly, smiling, but his face was serious. He was merely stating a fact. Now again she saw the house, its great bulk against the brassy sky, its walls shimmering in the heat. She stared at it in a sort of panic but she asked quietly enough, "Did you build it?"

"The Big House. God, no! My father built it. He said he built it for Ma but I reckon he really built it to show the cotton crowd that he wasn't just a big high-powered cattle man. He wanted to show them that he was in high cotton too."

"High cotton?"

"Here in Texas the cotton rich always snooted the cattle rich. And now if this oil keeps coming into Texas the old cattle crowd will look down their noses at the oil upstarts. You know, like the old New York De Peysters snooting the Vanderbilts and the Vanderbilts cutting the Astors." He pointed with his left hand. "See that low greyish building about half a mile from the Big House? That's the old ranch house. That's where I was born. It's always been called the Main House."

She stared for a long minute at the low rambling outlines of the old house, so small and colorless in comparison with the magnificence and ornamentation of the great mansion. She leaned toward him gently, her arm pressed his arm. "I like it. It looks like a house to be born in." He was silent again. She glanced sidewise at him. "Who lives in it now? Your sister Luz, does she—will she live there?"

"Luz lives with me," he said. "With us. In the Big House. She's run it ever since Ma died twenty-five years ago." He laughed a short mirthless little laugh. "Some say she runs the ranch."

"It will all be strange to me at first. Of course at first I'll have to learn how things are done here. I hope she won't—mind."

"Hard to say what Luz will or won't mind. Let's just relax and be happy we're home."

She longed to say, But a wife runs her house, doesn't she? A wife wants to manage her own household and plan things and decide things and be alone with her husband. Some new wisdom told her to say nothing.

He was speaking again, rather hurriedly for him, as though he felt she must have certain knowledge squarely placed. "Texians are openhanded kind of folks you know, Leslie. Hospitable. Tell you something that maybe you don't know. Texas—the word, I mean—comes from the word Tejas, that's an Indian word that the old confederacy of Indian tribes used to use, and it means Friend."

"Nice," she murmured drowsily, for she was very weary. "Nice."

"So the Big House is usually full of folks. Every ranch is the same all through Texas, Panhandle to the Gulf. Folks drop in, sometimes two, sometimes ten, sometimes twenty. Feed 'em, bed 'em, mount 'em."

"People you don't even know!"

"Sometimes. Interested in ranching, or breeding, or feed crops. Open house. Old Waggoner was the same, and all of us. Tejas."

"My goodness! And I thought Virginians were hospitable!"

A turn of his wrist, the car ground to a halt before high iron gates. A man ran out of a little gatehouse and he seemed to bow as he ran. He opened the gates, he raised his hand in salute and his teeth flashed, his face was joyous with welcome.

"Bienvenido! Bienvenido, señor, señora!" A dusky skin, the face square, the features finely cut; an ageless face, perhaps forty perhaps sixty. He had limped a little as he ran, so that between the running and the bowing and the limping he had a hobgoblin aspect, but there was dignity, too, in his bearing, you saw pride in his face.

Bick Benedict raised a hand from the wheel in greeting. "Cómo estás, Arcadio!"

"Muy bien, gracias. Gracias!" He looked at Leslie, his hand went to his forehead, he saluted gravely, ceremoniously.

"Hello, Arcadio," Leslie called to him. She smiled and waved. As they moved on and the gates closed behind them she pinched her husband just a little nip. "Is that all right? Tell me if I do something wrong, darling. I feel as if I were in a foreign country. I'm not used to acting queenly."

"Don't be silly. This is Texas. Everything free and open. You're home."

"I shall simply burst if I don't ask questions. Darling, is his name really Arcadio, how enchanting, and why does he limp so terribly and is the gate always closed you said everything's free and open in Texas I don't mean to be critical I'm just so interested I can't wait till I write Papa——"

"It's really Arcadio, though I don't know why that's enchanting. He was just twelve when they put him in the corrida, and so was I. They gave us old horses to ride, we were only kids. One day when he was helping hold the herd his horse stumbled and fell on him, his right leg was pinned beneath it and then the horse's hoofs began to dig into him and tear him apart. His father was a ranchero but they were out on the range, there wasn't a doctor within fifty miles——"

"Poor little boy," she said. "Poor little man, limping and bobbing."

"You can't be sentimental on a ranch."

She thought, I don't even know what a corrida is.

Up the long drive. An old adobe building on this side. Another on that. Big square buildings, small squatted buildings. She longed to say what's that what's that what's that? Something restrained her.

Far off across the flat land she saw what seemed to be another town made up of toy houses huddled on the prairie.

"Do you remember that first night at dinner? When Mama asked if there were any cities on the premises? Is that another town—all those little houses way off there?"

"That? That's no town. That's just where some of the ranch help live—some of the married ones with families. Some of the vaqueros live there and a few of the rancheros. Most of the rancheros live out on the ranchitos, they're spread about ten or fifteen miles apart, of course."

"Of course," Leslie echoed solemnly. Then she giggled, what with nerves, travel-weariness, and some amusement. "Mr. Benedict, sir, your bride wouldn't know a vaquero from a ranchero when she saw one—if she ever saw one."

"You will." Then, as they made a sharp turn in the drive, "You're going to see a heap of vaqueros right now. Old Polo has put on a show for you."

They were approaching another gate—a wooden one, cross-barred—and a line of fence that stretched away endlessly. On the other side of the fence, facing them, were perhaps fifty men on horseback. They sat like bronze equestrian statues. Erect, vital, they made a dazzling frieze against prairie and sky. Their great hats shaded the dark ardent eyes. Their high-heeled boots were polished to a glitter; narrow, pointed, they fitted like a glove. Their saddles, their hatbands, their belts were hand-tooled. Their costumes lacked, perhaps, the silver, the silks, the embroidery, the braid, but in every basic item this was the uniform that the Mexican charro had worn three hundred years before and that every American cowboy all the way from Montana down to Arizona and Texas had copied from the Mexican.

On either side of the gate they made a single line, reined up side by side like cavalry on parade. Immobile they sat in their

GIANT

saddles, they did not smile, they did not raise a hand in greeting. Only their dark eyes spoke. At the gate, mounted on a splendid palomino, was a man of middle age, dark like the others but with an almost indefinable difference. Authority was in his bearing. Slim and small, he was a figure of striking elegance. Now his horse moved daintily forward with little mincing steps like those of a ballet dancer on her toes. The man swung low in his saddle and opened the gate, he drew up squarely then in the path of the car.

He spoke the greeting. "Viva el señor! Vivan los novios!"

From the men then, like a chant, "Viva el señor! Vivan los novios!"

She tweaked his coat sleeve. "Jordan, what's it mean—los novios? What do I do?"

But Bick Benedict nodded carelessly to the men, he raised a hand in greeting and gravely he spoke his thanks in the Spanish tongue. Then, out of the corner of his mouth, to Leslie, "They've put on a real show for you, honey. Welcome to the bridal couple. Say gracias, will you?"

She was enchanted, she opened the car door, she stepped to the fender and leaned far out. "Thank you!" she called, and her voice was warm and lovely with emotion. "Gracias! Gracias! Thank you for the beautiful welcome!"

"Don't overdo it please, Leslie."

"Can't I blow them a kiss! I'm in love with all of them."

"Come in and sit down. We're moving."

"Especially that beautiful café-au-lait Buffalo Bill."

"Polo's got ten grandchildren. He'd be shocked to his Mexican core."

"Why were they so stern and silent? They hardly looked at us."

"They saw you all right," he said as he shifted gears. "They'll tell their families everything you wore, what you said, how you look. The grapevine will carry it to every barrio, through the ranchitos out to the West Division where our Holgado ranch is, and south to Hermoso and up to La Piedra that's the North Division and over east to the——"

120

"But you told me to say thank you. I thought it was picturesque and wonderful. Did I do something wrong?"

"No. No. Perhaps you overdid it just a little."

"But you didn't marry me because I was like the girls you know in Texas. You'd have married one of those if you'd wanted your wife to behave like a Texan."

Behind them the thunder of hoofs on hard-baked clay. The sun flashed on stirrup and spur, was reflected dartingly in iron and silver. The horsemen spoke together softly as they rode, the one to the other very softly. Now the hoofbeats were like an echo.

"No está mal. Not bad."

"Sí, pero le faltan carnes. A little thin for my taste."

"Tuerta?"

"No, you fool. Her eyes are soft and dark like the eyes of a gentle heifer, but with spirit, too, in them. That little flaw in the eye it is a mark of beauty in a woman, very stirring to men."

Now the car made the last curve in the long drive and there they were at the foot of the great broad stone steps that led to the doorway of the house. She looked up at it. She had hoped that when they actually came upon it the whole thing would vanish miraculously like the mirages she had seen on the road. But now it was real enough, yet about it there hung a ghostly quality in spite of the blinding sun, in spite of the bulk of walls and columns and towers. No one came to the car, no one stood in the doorway, all was quiet, breathless, waiting, like the castle of the Sleeping Beauty. Nothing could be really sinister in sunlight, she said to herself. And aloud, "It's siesta time, isn't it? Just like in Ol' Virginny, though we never paid much attention to it."

He held out his hand to her, his hand was hard, was crushing. "Neither do we." He looked up at the house, together they began to mount the steps.

"Would it sound too sickening and coy if I asked you to carry me through the doorway, just for luck?" And she smiled. "Of course I'm a big girl———"

He stared at her incredulously, he saw that her lips were trembling. His hands were on her shoulders, he swung her around and picked her up in his arms as if she had been a child, and so up the steps, across the broad veranda and through the doorway, her arm about his neck, her cheek against his. He pretended to be panting as they came into the shade of the huge entrance hall, dim after the glare outside. They were laughing, and the sound echoed against the high grey walls. Her arm went more tightly about his neck, he still held her in his arms. He bent his head impetuously and they kissed long and silently.

Like a vast flue the great doors east and west drew the prevailing wind from the Mexican Gulf. "Oh, it's cool!" she said inadequately. He tipped her to her feet and she staggered a little and leaned against him and looked about her, blinking with the sudden change from glare to shade. Then she saw against the grey-white background the six flags of Texas, draped and brilliant in a burst of color upon the wall that faced them. The Spanish flag, the French flag, the Mexican flag, the flag of the Republic of Texas, the flag of the Confederacy, the flag of the United States of America.

No sound disturbed the utter silence of the enormous room. Yet Leslie had a feeling that on the other side of every door and wall there were ears listening, listening. They stood in the middle of the great hall like tourists, Leslie thought. Or like guests who have mistaken the time at which they were expected. "The flags," she said. "Against the wall like that. They're history, alive. They're so lovely. Gay like the flags in the cathedral at St. Denis."

"What's going on here!" yelled Bick. He clapped his hands. "Tomás! Vincente! Lupe! Petra!" Then, in a great bawl that topped all the rest, "Luz! Luz, what the hell is this! Come out here before I come and get you."

From nowhere there appeared a little plump woman. Until this moment Leslie had not been aware that she had pictured this older sister of Jordan's as a tall dark woman—swarthy, almost—with straight black hair and straight black brows. But this Luz who came toward them was a pink-cheeked bustling little body in a pink ruffled dress and a bright red hat. Thick plaits of grey-white hair and, in unexpected contrast, very black

eyes that gave the effect of having been mistakenly placed in a
face meant for blue eyes. Their hard brightness startled the beholder like sudden forked lightning in a sunny summer sky.

Her voice was shrill and high, she walked with a little clatter
and rush of short steps, hers were the smallest feet Leslie had
ever seen.

"Jurden! Stop that bawling like a calf's just been branded."
Her manner was brisk, not to say hearty. She kissed her brother
on the cheek, a mere peck. She came to Leslie. "Howdy, Miss
Lynnton," said Luz Benedict. "Excuse my being late." An added
flush suffused the pink rouged cheek.

Bick Benedict put one hand on his wife's shoulder. "Now Luz,
don't you go roweling Leslie first thing. This is Mrs. Jordan
Benedict, and don't you forget it."

9

"WE LOOKED for you a week ago," said Luz. She took Leslie's hand in a grip of steel and smiled up at her.

"But we didn't plan to come sooner," Leslie said. "What made you think we did?"

"I didn't figure Bick would stay away. All the spring work to be done. It's the worst time of the year to be away. The big spring roundup."

"But this is—was—our honeymoon!"

"No honeymoon's as important as roundup at Reata."

Leslie felt suddenly inadequate in an argument involving the relative importance of a honeymoon and a roundup. She was mildly amused to hear herself saying, "Yes, it must seem so to all but the two involved." She stood with her arm through Bick's, she turned to smile at him tenderly, she was startled to see that he apparently had heard none of this exchange, he was staring at the big doorway through which they had just entered. There was the sound of a motor in the drive.

"Jett!" yelled Bick, and released his arm with a jerk as he started toward the door. "Jett! Come on in here."

"Don't you want to see the house?" Luz said hurriedly. "Let me show you the house." She grasped Leslie's arm firmly.

"Yes. Yes, of course," said Leslie. "But I'll wait. I'd rather wait for my—for Jordan."

"Oh, Jordan and Jett are everlastingly jangling about something. Come on." It was plain that she was anxious to be off. The sound of the men's voices rose in argument. Leslie glimpsed this Jett Rink in the doorway now—a muscular young fellow with a curiously powerful bull-like neck and shoulders. He wore the dust-colored canvas and the high-heeled boots of the region, his big sweat-stained hat was pushed back from his forehead and you saw his damp dark curls. His attitude, his tone were belligerent. About twenty, Leslie decided. She decided, too, that he was an unpleasant young man.

"She wanted for him to go, not me. It was her doing. I don't like for Dimodeo to drive the big car any more'n you do. Ever time he does I got to spend two days patching her up."

"You'll do as I say."

"Tell that to Madama. How am I going to know what to do? Her hauling one way and you another. Tell me who's boss around here and I'll do like they say."

Leslie turned away, annoyed at the boy's hard insolence. Her eyes had become accustomed now to the dimness of the great hall. Through open double doors she glimpsed other rooms, they seemed as vast as this. She looked about her, interestedly. Luz Benedict had disappeared. Madama. The boy Jett had called her Madama. Funny, her going off like that.

Glancing about, she smiled as she thought of the first line of the letter she would write to her father tonight or tomorrow. Dear Papa, do you remember when I was about ten the time you took me to the Natural History Museum in New York? Well, that's where I'm living now, only it's been moved to Texas.

Everywhere on the walls were the mounted heads of deer, of buffalo, of catamounts, coyotes, mountain lions; the vicious tusked faces of javelina or wild hog, red fox, grey fox, and two sad-eyed Longhorns whose antlered spread and long morose muzzle dwarfed all the other masks. In the space not occupied by these mortuary mementos were large gold-framed paintings of cows (Herefords) of Longhorns (extinct) of sky and prairies and prairie and sky—of all that which the sun-tortured eye could see if it so much as peered through a crack in a window blind in this land of cattle and sun and sky and burning hot prairie.

Through the wide door at the rear she saw the patio and a glimpse of green, she walked toward it inhaling a deep breath as she walked, feeling suddenly shut in and stifling. As she went she said, aloud, socially, "Oh, how lovely, there's a terrace do let me see that," though there was no one to hear her. Oleanders in tubs stood disconsolately about, the white walls under the glare of the sun glared back gold at their tormentor. Leslie sank for a moment into one of the big wicker chairs and sprang up with a little screech. It was like sitting on a bed of red-hot coals. She began to know why Texans never sat out of doors, why they sought the dim shade of inner rooms.

She came back into the hall and stood there and now Bick joined her, he took her hand. "Leslie! I thought you'd gone upstairs with Luz."

"I was waiting for you."

"You must be hot and tired. Where's Luz?"

"She was very nice, she wanted to show me the house." Suddenly she had a horrible feeling that she was going to cry—she who so rarely wept even when a child. She raised her swimming eyes and looked at him. "I waited for you. I want my husband to show me his house."

"Of course, my darling, of course. Things have kind of gone loco around here while I've been gone. Luz can get the whole place in a——"

The tap-tap-tap of Luz Benedict's little feet sounded on the stone floor. "Oh, there you are, Bick! Going off and leaving this poor little bride of yours alone. She wouldn't come with me. Come on, Bick. You show her the house. I'll tag along."

Leslie was to become accustomed to the clatter of men's high-heeled boots on these tiled floors, and the clank and jingle of spurs and the creak of leather. Texas sounds. Everywhere the creak of leather. The staccato tap-tap of Luz Benedict's little heels were to stay in her mind long after they had ceased forever. She and Bick went hand in hand but Luz chattered and clattered close behind them. "And this is the big room and that there is the little sitting room and this is the library and this is the music room and over there is the dining room and that is the men's den."

And "How wonderful!" Leslie exclaimed. "How interesting!" as they walked through the dim vast rooms. Everything was on a gargantuan scale, as though the house had been built and furnished for a race of giants. Chairs were the size of couches, couches the size of beds. There were chairs of cowhide with fanciful backs fashioned from horns. Luz was displaying the monolithic rooms as a hostess guides a guest whose stay is so temporary that all must be crowded into a brief time.

Leslie was weary, warm, her face was burning, her eyes smarted. The three ascended the great stone stairway now. Leslie put a hand on the balustrade and it seemed damp to the touch. She was to learn many things about this pseudo-Spanish palace of stone and concrete and iron that was foreign to the Texas land and that had been rejected by it. The elements had turned upon it to destroy it. The battle was constant, day after day, summer and winter. In a norther the concrete would break out in a cold sweat. Patches of mold followed the spring rains. Fungi sprang up in dark places, shoes in closets were covered with a slippery white mildew. Plumbing rusted. There seemed forever to be a tap-tapping and clink-clinking as workmen busied themselves with leaky roof, sprung floor, cracked wall, burst pipe.

Fifty bedrooms Bick had said in his argument with Mrs. Lynnton. Leslie had assumed that this was a figure of speech. Now it seemed to her that there were acres of dull bare bedrooms with their neat utility beds and their drab utility chests of drawers and one armchair and one straight chair and a drab utility table and an electric light bulb in the middle of the ceiling. A hotel. A big, bare unattractive hotel with no guests. A terrible thought occurred to Leslie.

"Have they ever been filled—all these rooms?"

"My yes!" Luz shrilled happily. "And then some. Times we had 'em sleeping in cots out here in the hall. Sitting-room couches too. Bick, remember that time of the big rodeo in Viento, Kale Beebe blew in late and stepping a little high, laid down on the big tapestry sofa with his spurs on and must have been riding nightmares all night because in the morning the sofa was ribbons and the stuffing all over him like a store Santa Claus."

Luz clattered on down the hall, she pointed briskly to a big room whose door stood open. Two Mexican women and a man were bending over open suitcases which Leslie recognized as Jordan's.

"That's Bick's room," Luz said breezily. She marched on down the hall, turned right, turned left. "And this," she said, "is your room."

There was the fraction of a moment of utter silence. Then Leslie began to laugh. She laughed as helplessly as one does who has been under fearful strain and then Bick too was laughing, they laughed leaning against each other, the tears streaming with their laughter; they laughed as two people laugh who love each other and who have been apart in spirit and now suddenly are brought together again by the stupendous absurdity of the situation at which they are laughing. And oh! they whooped, and ugh! they groaned in a pain of combined laughter and relief.

The black eyes stared at them, the pink face was rigid with the resentment of one who does not share the joke.

Bick wiped his eyes, he patted Luz's shoulder. "Look, sis, Leslie and I are married. We're having these two big front connecting rooms where the breeze'll get us, one for a bedroom and one a kind of sitting room where we can sit and talk if we want to."

"Away from me, I suppose."

"Why no, honey, we don't mean——"

"Yes," said Leslie then, with terrible distinctness. "Away from anyone when we want to be. When we want to talk together." Then, at the look on the woman's face, "Not secrets, Luz. Just husband and wife talk." Poor dear, she doesn't know.

"Get Lupe and one of the other girls," Bick said hastily. "They'll fix us up. I hope those trunks get here. They could un-pack while we're eating supper."

"Supper!" Leslie repeated rather faintly.

"Supper's at six," Luz announced firmly. "How'd you like a cup of coffee right now? I clean forgot, with Bick yapping at Jett."

"Oh, I'd love it. But could it be tea?"

"Tea!" Doubtfully.

"Or coffee, if it's—coffee will be wonderful." She realized now that she had vaguely envisaged a tea table on their arrival, with hot tea for the wise and a pitcher of cold lemonade for the foolish, and little thin sandwiches and a deceptively plain-looking pound cake. And decanters for the men. That was tea at the Lynntons' when you were hot and tired and thirsty at five or at six.

Bick now pressed a wall button. "That'll fetch somebody. Leslie, I'm going to take a look at the ruin that's gone on while I've been away. . . . Now Luz, don't you get sore again. . . . The girls will help with your things, Leslie . . . I'll see you at supper. Anything you need, just tell Luz."

He was gone. "Well now," said Luz, and settled herself in a chair, "the girls will fix you up in a jiffy. I hope you didn't bring too much fussy stuff. We're plain folks out here. I ain't got enough clothes to dust a fiddle."

It came to Leslie with a shock that this woman was acting a part. Was purposely talking a kind of native lingo. The black eyes were darting here and there as the suitcases and bags were opened. Lupe had come in with a tray on which was coffee.

"I hope it won't spoil my dinner," Leslie said.

"Coffee never spoiled anything. Here in Texas everybody drinks coffee morning to night and night to morning."

"It's the climate," Leslie thought suddenly, but thinking aloud. "That's it. Hot and flat and humid. They have to have it as a stimulant."

"Nothing wrong with Texas climate I know of," Luz countered belligerently.

"No, no, I just meant—you know, the English drink a lot of tea. Uh—Bick told me you went to Wellesley when you were a girl."

"Yes, the Benedict girls go to Wellesley for anyway two years and the boys to Harvard, but it never takes. I don't talk like college, do I?"

"Perhaps not. I don't know."

"Where did you go? Vassar, I suppose. Or one of those places up on the Hudson."

"No. In fact my sisters and I had the sketchiest kind of education. Papa didn't believe in separate schools for boys and girls. He said they were tribal vestigial."

She felt better now that she had had the coffee. She had gulped it down, hot and strong. "That was lovely," she said. Lupe was taking things out of the bags. She was a dark silent woman in a shapeless clean dress of no definable color pattern or material. A covering. On her feet were soft shapeless black sandals. Her garments, her face, her hair were decent yet she gave a general effect of untidiness as though she had thrown on her clothes in a hurry and had not since had time to adjust them. Leslie was to grow accustomed to this look in the house servants, as to so much besides. The young girl Petra had joined the older woman. Now the clean bare room with its big white bed, its neat wooden chairs, its stark table burst suddenly into bloom like a spring garden released from winter. Lacy filmy silken things. Soft beribboned flowered things. Scent. Color.

"My!" Luz exclaimed inadequately. "Where you fixing to wear those?"

With a sinking heart Leslie thought of the trunks that were even now on the road from Vientecito—trunks crammed with more dresses, more chiffons, silks, laces. The woman Lupe and the girl Petra were not being very helpful. They caught up the scented silken things and gazed at them as a child would look at a toy, in wonderment. They held them and stroked them, making little crooning sounds of admiration and amazement. As they hung the garments in the inadequate closets they chattered to each other in Spanish, hard and fast, the sound of the consonants falling on the ear like hailstones on a tin roof. Leslie began to hate the filmy bits of lace and ribbon that Nancy Lynnton had insisted were the proper garments for a bride's trousseau, Texas or no Texas. Suddenly, too, she felt an unbearable weariness and lassitude. She wanted to be alone. More than anything in the world she wanted to be alone. It was not an urge merely, it was a necessity. For over two weeks now she had not had an hour, a moment alone. She longed to be alone in the big bright room and rid of the two chattering women, the little pink-frocked woman still wearing the red hat beneath which her tight round little pink face was like a baked apple bursting its skin.

"Do you know," she began haltingly, "it's the queerest thing but I feel so—so terribly tired. And sleepy, too. I can hardly——"

"Texas," Luz said triumphantly. "Lots of strangers from up North feel like that. Thin-blooded is what's wrong with them. Texas air is so rich you can nourish off it like it was food."

"That must be it. And everything so new and strange."

"Texas is different, all right. But you'll have to get the hang of it."

"Oh, I will. I'm going to love it. It's so big and new and different—as you say. I just thought if I could have a tiny nap before dinner—supper."

"Well, sure. You go right ahead."

"And a bath. That will be lovely."

Luz took charge. "Lupe! Un baño caliente."

"No. No, thanks so much. I'll just take my time and perhaps sleep a little first and then have the bath, or perhaps the other way around. I don't know." She was growing incoherent with weariness.

"Go at once," Luz commanded the two women. Leslie caught the Spanish inmediato. "Cierra la puerta."

As they went Leslie remembered her two-word Spanish vocabulary. "Gracias! Muy gracias!"

They were gone. The door was closed. She stood with her back against it for a moment like a woman in a melodrama. Don't be silly. Where did you think you were going to live? Paris? This is all strange and wonderful and tomorrow you'll love it, but you're tired and tense. That's all that's wrong with you, Leslie Lynnton. Benedict.

A bath, that was what she wanted after all that grit and grime of the train journey and the dust of the drive. The immense tub was a man's tub, when she tried to relax in it her toes were six inches from the tub end. The immense towels were men's towels. It was as though no arrangements were made for the comfort of women in this man's world of Texas. Everything in the bathroom and the bedroom was good, utilitarian, and plain as a piece of canvas and as durable. Well, she argued to herself, this is a ranch, isn't it? You and your silly trousseau—what do you expect!

She went through the pleasant relaxing ritual of the bath, the powder, the lotions, the creams. Nancy Lynnton had made a warning din about cold cream. "That Texas climate is frightful for the complexion. Remember to use cold cream all the time, every minute, or your face will look like leather." Leslie had laughed at the mental picture of her face grinning socially through a mask of oily white cream. Still, it wasn't advice to be sneered at, she thought now as she patted the smooth stuff on cheeks and chin and was startled to see it vanish like water into thirsty earth. She put on a plain silk dressing gown, stood blinking a moment in the disordered bedroom and was reassured by the scent of the perfume that Leigh Karfrey had sent her from Paris, by the look of the pink bottles and jars ranged neatly on the grim bureau, by her own small frilled and lacy pillow, the satin mules, the peignoir flung across a chair, by all this fluff of feminine belongings that had turned the dour chamber into a woman's room.

She threw herself in a fine Gulf draft across the great double bed and was immediately asleep in spite of the strong coffee and the bewildering day.

She awoke to a bedlam of sound, she sat up terrified, her terror mounting as she stared about her at the unfamiliar room and did not know where she was or how she had got there. Now she remembered and now she translated the sounds that had shocked her into wakefulness as the clamor of metal on metal. A brazen gong was beating within the house. An iron-tongued bell was shattering the air outside. She sprang up, she ran a comb through her short clipped hair and arranged its waves tenderly over each cheek in the mode of the day. I don't care, she argued to herself, I'm going to put on a pretty tea gown for dinner, that's what they're for, I'm not going to dress in linsey-woolsey just because I live on a ranch, what's linsey-woolsey I wonder, anyway I'm going to dress as if I were having dinner with the family at home. At home. You are at home, you little fool. Hurry.

She put on the filmy tea gown with the lace fishtail in the back though it came just below her knees in the front. The clamor had ceased, the sound of the brazen gong had died away. Suddenly it was cooler—not actually chill but the fierce heat of the day was gone. She shivered a little standing there in her transparent chiffon gown, she wondered if perhaps she should have worn something heavier. They'll have a fire in the fireplace, she told herself, and a glass of sherry. Perhaps Jordan hadn't come in yet, that's why they rang that big bell outside. She went carefully to the hall and peered over the banisters. The vast hall below was empty but she heard the murmur of voices and now they were raised in something very near a shout. Here I am, Leslie Lynnton —Leslie Lynnton Benedict—tiptoeing around and peeking over stair rails like a schoolgirl afraid to go down to her first party. She stepped slowly down the great stone stairway in her slim pointed satin slippers with the brilliant buckles and the high heels.

The javelinas and the jaguars and the buffalo glowered down upon her from the stairway and the hall, their lips curled back from their teeth in sneering distaste.

She stood a moment in the center of the hall. Then she followed the direction of the voices. Jordan and Luz Benedict were talking with considerable animation in the room that Luz had designated as the music room. Curiously, it was Luz who was standing in front of the fireplace facing the door and Jordan who was seated. Their voices were loud and, Leslie sensed, angry.

"Maudie's a hog for money," Luz was saying, "she wouldn't care if the ranch was put in sheep if she could get more out of it. And Placer—well—Placer! A pair of fools, but Maudie's the worst, because she knows better." At this somewhat ambiguous statement she saw Leslie in the doorway. "Well, come on in. Where's the party at? My!"

For one terrible instant Leslie sensed that her husband had momentarily forgotten that he was married, had forgotten that she was in the house, had forgotten that she existed.

Now he jumped up, he came to her and took her two hands in his and held her off to look at her. "You're prettier than a sunrise. Just look at her, Luz!"

She came closer to him. "I fell asleep."

"Don't I know it! I came up and there you were stretched across the bed, dead to the world, and the room looking as if a norther had struck it."

"Really! Really were you there while I was asleep?"

"I didn't have the heart to wake you, I sneaked out and washed up in the next room."

"You look kind of wonderful yourself," she said, and meant it though he wore boots, brown canvas pants and brush jacket, a brown shirt open at the throat. Luz was as she had been through the day. Leslie was relieved to see that she had taken off the red hat. Her hair was wound quaintly in neat slick braids like a crown round her head, just as Jordan Benedict once had described it.

No fire in the fireplace. No sherry. A concert grand piano

dominated the room, it bore the Steinway stamp. "What a beautiful piano!" Leslie exclaimed. "I haven't seen one like that since I heard Paderewski play in Washington years and years ago. Who plays? You, Luz?" She opened the lid, the keys were yellow, she ran a tentative handful of notes, it was badly out of tune.

"The strings go to rusting," Luz said. "Bick plays a little and so do I, Ma made us all take lessons, like it or not, but there's no time for piano playing on a ranch."

"Why not?" Leslie inquired innocently.

"There's too much work to do." Luz, in spite of the baby-pink cheeks and the plump comfortable body, seemed always to speak with belligerence. Now the gong sounded again furiously from the dining room. "Come on," said Luz, "let's go eat." She led the way, scudding across the tiled floor. The two followed slowly, his arm about her, her shoulder nestled in his shoulder. The lace fishtail slithered after them, absurdly. From the upper hall dark eyes watched it, wondering.

She pressed her cheek against his arm. "I'll have to learn to be a rancher's wife. Look at me!" She kicked up a satin-shod foot. "Ridiculous."

"No it isn't. I love it. Don't change. There are too many ranchers around here already."

The great table would have seated twenty, it was covered with a white tablecloth, a mammoth spread that could have been rigged as a sizable tent. Down its middle, at five-foot intervals, were clustered little colonies of ketchup, bottles, chili sauce, vinegar, oil, salt, pepper, sugar bowl, cream pitcher.

Luz took charge. "Bick sits there of course. You sit there. I sit here." The three huddled at one end of the table, Bick at the head. Places were laid for ten.

Leslie sat down, she tucked her absurd chiffons about her, she shivered a little in the damp air of the vast vaulted room through which the Gulf wind blew a ceaseless stream. She eyed the empty places with their expectant china and glass and silver. "Is there company?"

"No, thank goodness for once," Luz said. "But you never know on a ranch whether there's going to be two or twenty. Folks stop by."

Leslie smiled at Luz, at Bick. "We're like that at home. There's always enough for sudden guests. But not quite twenty."

Bick reached forward to cover her cool fingers with his big hand. "You're cold! You must be starved. I remember now you hardly ate a bite at lunch."

"I was so excited. I couldn't. We had just half an hour before time to leave the train. But now I do feel kind of hollow and limp."

Two Mexican girls came in, very quiet and neat in dark dresses and white aprons, their feet slip-slapping in sandals. They carried platters and vegetable dishes. There was steak—not the broiled steaks of the Eastern seaboard, crisp on the outside, pink on the inside, juicy and tender and thick. These were enormous fried slabs, flat, grey, served with a thick flour gravy. Mashed potatoes. Canned peas. Pickles. Huge soft rolls. Jelly. Canned peaches. Chocolate cake. It was fundamental American food cooked and served at its worst, without taste or imagination.

Wrestling, Leslie found that the steak once cut could not be chewed. She felt her face flushing scarlet, she tried to swallow the leathery mass, it would not go down, she choked a little, took a sip of cold water, chewed again resolutely, swallowed with a final fearsome gulp and thought what a surprise it would be for her stomach when the door opened and that rude mass of rubber beef tumbled in. She ate her mashed potatoes, she ate her peas, she worried the steak around her plate and tried not to think of little broilers and strawberry meringue and lobster bisque and spoon bread. She looked with wide bright eyes that still did not seem, somehow, to envision things very well, at the clump of ketchup chili sauce vinegar and other condiments that served this particular corner of the long white expanse which spread like a roadway down the room.

"Doesn't she look lovely, Luz!" Bick was saying.

"Certainly does," Luz agreed, without enthusiasm. "I was just wondering where at she was fixing to wear all those party dresses."

"She's going to wear them for me, aren't you, Leslie? I'll feel like a maharajah. Run cattle all day and when I come in evenings there you'll be all satin and sweet."

"I was thinking of sending them all back home to Lacey," Leslie said, "and swapping them for her blue denims."

"Don't let Luz fool you, just because she goes around looking like an old daguerreotype. It's a pose of hers. Texas girls are mighty dressy. Wait till you see them, they go to Chicago and New York for their doodads."

Here Luz made a bewildering about-face. "They don't have to," she said spiritedly. "We've got plenty of stores right in Hermoso and Houston and Dallas and around."

"That's so," Bick agreed. "I heard that Neiman-Marcus dresses the cotton crowd up in Dallas now and the new oil rich. They say they've got stuff there makes Bergdorf and Saks in New York look like Indian trading posts."

Luz smiled a little secret smile. "You'll have a chance to see for yourself tomorrow."

Bick leaned forward. "Leslie's going out with me tomorrow. . . . There's a roomful of riding clothes here in the house, Leslie. All sizes, all shapes."

"But won't my own things be here by then?"

"Well, yes. They're probably here now, unless Dimodeo and Jett Rink want the hides skinned off 'em. But your kind of riding clothes out on the range——"

Luz cut in. "The girls are coming. We've fixed up a real old-fashioned barbecue tomorrow noon. Out at Number Two."

"Call it off."

"Likely. With some of them on the way this minute from every which place. It's a welcome for the bride."

"How lovely!" Leslie said weakly. She was afraid to look at the fuming Bick.

"Damn it, Luz! Why don't you mind your own business! Leslie wants to see the ranch."

"She'll be seeing it on the way."

"I don't think she'd like a barbecue."

Leslie began to laugh a little hysterically. "If it's me you're talking about I'm right here. Remember? And of course I'd love a barbecue. It's like a picnic, isn't it? And cooking out of doors?"

Dinner was finished. Bick rose abruptly. "This is different."

"How?"

"Well—different. I know what you Virginians mean by a picnic. Chicken and ham and champagne cup and peach ice cream and a darky in a white coat to hand it around."

She went to him, she linked her arm through his, she looked up into his eyes. "But if that was the kind of picnic I wanted for the rest of my life I wouldn't be here, would I?"

The little clatter of Luz Benedict's heels, the high shrill voice. "Gill Dace is waiting on you, he phoned twice."

"Yes, I know. I'm going down now."

To her horror she heard herself cry out. "No. No, don't go away. Stay with me, Jordan. Don't leave me alone."

"Why honey, Luz is here."

"Where are you going? I'll go with you."

"You can't go down there in those clothes."

"Where is it?"

"Gill Dace is the vet. He's the man who doctors all the four-footed characters and there isn't a more important man on the ranch. I'll take you down someday soon." He kissed her lightly on the cheek, the friendly placating kiss of a husband of ten years' standing, whose thoughts are elsewhere. He was off down the hall and out into the twilight, she heard the sound of the car roaring down the road. She stood in the center of the great hall with the stuffed animal heads goggling down at her in her trailing tea gown. Luz was standing on the stairway waiting for her to ascend and as Leslie looked up at her it seemed to her weary and confused gaze that this face had in it much of the quality of those others eying her from the walls.

"I guess you'll find things different out here from what you're used to."

Leslie managed a light gaiety. "I want it to be different."

"I suppose you're all tired out, traveling and all. You'll want to turn in quick, be all raring to go for tomorrow. The girls are wild to see you."

Solemnly they were ascending the stairs. Leslie heard herself making polite conversation and she began to feel very odd; light in the head and heavy in the legs. "Are they all nearby neighbors —the girls?"

Luz laughed a sharp little cackle. "Texas, anything less than a hundred miles is considered next door. Only real nearby one is Vashti Hake and she's better than sixty miles. The Hake ranch."

Leslie was tempted to ask if this Vashti Hake was the girl whom Jordan in spite of family pressure had not married. Better not. I'll know when I see her. Luz was still rattling on, Leslie forced herself to listen, standing there in the upper hall, a politely interested smile on her lips, the light glaring down on her tired eyes.

"Texas ranch folks, a lot of them, have gone to living in town and only come out to the ranch when they feel like it. The Hakes and us and two three more around are about the only ones left hereabouts who live on the place, summer and winter, day and night, the year around. Of the big countries, that is. Of course the Klebergs over to the King ranch they do too. There used to be a saying the Benedict men and the Hake and Beezer men, they were married to their ranches, any wife coming in would be only morganatic."

Leslie held out her hand. "Good night, Luz. You're right, I do seem to be awfully tired. I'll write to Mama and Papa and then I think I'll——" Her voice trailed off, emptily.

"Sure I can't help you with anything?"

"No. No really."

"Good night." The heels pounded down the hallways. Over her shoulder she tossed a final word. "I'll wait up have coffee with Bick like always."

Her trunks had come, the two women were slip-slapping about in her bedroom, the lights were blazing, it was horribly hot. They had hung away most of the gowns; the bureau drawers, open, showed neat rows of pink and blue and white, but a froth of lace and silk on chairs and bed testified to the inadequacy of the room's cupboards and chests and the fantastic unreality of Mrs. Lynnton's geographical knowledge.

Leslie, standing in the doorway, began to laugh for no reason at all and the two women, with quick Latin sympathy, laughed to keep her company so that an outsider coming upon the scene might have mistaken the moment for one of girlish merriment.

Leslie clapped a hand to her head. "I am very tired. Will you go away now. And take these things somewhere. Anywhere."

They were full of little murmurs and nods of understanding. "Sí sí sí! Dolor de cabeza. Rendida." They looked about the room rather wildly, they snatched up armfuls of delicate clothing, they bowed gravely. "Buenas noches, señora." They were gone, the slip-slip of their feet on the tiled floors. Silence in the great house.

From somewhere outside the hum of a stringed instrument—a guitar? A scent drifted in—a sweet dusty scent. The wind had not stopped blowing, she had hoped it would by nightfall. Hot winds made her nervous and irritable. I must ask Jordan if the wind always blows like this in Texas. Perhaps this was just a windy day. Tomorrow I'll take a walk. A nice long walk, I've been cooped up in that train for days and days.

There was a little glass-fronted bookcase and in it perhaps a dozen books leaning disconsolately against each other or fallen flat in zigzag disorder. She opened the glass door. A little pile of magazines, the *Cattleman's Gazette*. Webster's Unabridged Dictionary. *A Girl of the Limberlost. The Sheik. Wild Animals I Have Known*. The Texas Almanac for 1919. She closed the little glass door.

She went to the door and listened. Nothing. She went through the bedtime ritual of her adult life in Virginia; brushed her hair, washed and creamed her face, wiped it carefully and canceled the process by dusting it over with powder. Men, she had learned, found cold-creamed wives distasteful. She sat down at the little table-desk, she took from the drawer the stationery engraved with the reata, she thought, Lacey would love this.

Dear Papa and Mama and Lacey. She stared at this for a long time. I am camping out in a Spanish castle. But how did you go about writing a letter in which you thought one thing and wrote another?

When Bick came in an hour later she was still seated there with her pen in her hand drawing curlicues on the paper before her—the sheet of paper that said only Dear Papa and Mama and Lacey.

"You still up, honey!"

"It's only a little past ten—on my beautiful watch that my husband bought for me in New York."

The dusty clothes he had worn at dinner were a trifle dustier now and as he bent to kiss her there was a horsy smell that was not too unfamiliar to her Virginia background, nor too repugnant. But she made a little face. "Phew! You certainly have been down to see the vet."

"Gone about a month and you'd think I'd been away a year. Luz always gets the whole place to milling when I'm off." He paused at the door. "Coming?"

"Where?"

"I'm going down to have some coffee."

"Can't you have them bring it up here, all cozy? I don't think I'll have any. I'm dead for sleep, suddenly. Do you think it's the change in climate?"

"Sure. Texas air's too heady for you after that thin Virginia stuff. Texas air's so rich you can practically live off it."

"Darling, you Texans have a kind of folklore, haven't you?"

"Why, I don't know exactly. What——"

"Nothing. Uh—look, dear, I must order a lot of books from Brentano's in Washington."

"Oh, you won't do much reading out here."

"But I always read. I read a lot. It's like saying you won't do much breathing out here." Her tone was a trifle sharp for a bride.

"Here in Texas there's so much more to do. You won't have time to read."

142

"The house, you mean? Yes, I suppose there must be a lot to do, just running a big house like this."

"Oh, I didn't mean that. Luz runs the house."

"But Jordan! I mean—I'm quite good, you know. Really. I know about food and servants and furniture and I'm even a pretty good cook. I'd like to——"

"We'll let Luz tend to all that. She wouldn't like anyone else to run the house. She and old Uncle Bawley out at the Holgado Division they can't bear to have anybody mess in with their way of doing things."

"But I'm your wife!" Her sense of the ridiculous told her that she was talking like a woman in a melodrama. She began to laugh, rather helplessly. "Let's not be silly. This is my—this is our house, isn't it!"

"As long as we live and want it, honey. And you're going to be happy in it, and relax and have fun. You're going to love it down here, all the space in the world——"

"Space! Some of the happiest moments of my life have been spent in a telephone booth."

Bick pulled off his brush jacket and tossed it on a chair, he yawned a shade too carelessly and stretched his arms high above his great hard lean body. There was nothing amorous in the glance his bride bestowed upon this fine male frame. "I'm going down for a cup of coffee. Come on."

"Jordan Benedict, do you mean you're going downstairs to have your coffee!"

"I've got to talk to her anyway about something. We'll have to give her time. Luz is used to being the point, she'll have to have time to get used to being the drag."

"I don't know what you're talking about. I don't know what those words mean."

"That's so, you don't," he agreed genially. "In a roundup—you know what a roundup is—everybody knows what a roundup is—a man—on a horse of course—a man is posted one east one south one west. In a kind of triangle. The front man, the man at the front tip of the triangle, is the point. The other two men at the base of the triangle, at the rear end, they're the drag. Of course the swing men, they're stationed behind the point man they've got to swing in the herd when they scatter. You know we've got a saying here in Texas if you owe money or somebody is after you hot on your trail we say, 'He's right on your drag.' "

She flew to him, she twined her arms about him, the lace and silk and ribbons were crushed against his dusty boots his crumpled shirt. "You don't wish you had married a Texas girl, do you, Jordan? That Texas girl. Do you? Jordan!"

"You're the one I wanted to marry, the only one. Sweet. Wonderful."

"I'm frightened. For the first time in my life I'm frightened."

"Frightened of what, honey!"

"I don't know about all those things. Those Texas things."

"You will. You're just tired out. Look, I'll just run down and see———"

"Stay with me!"

"I'll be back in a minute. Come on down with me. Come on, Leslie, unless you're too tired."

"Yes, I am. I am too tired. I'll finish my letter and then I'll pop into bed. I think I never was so tired in my life."

She stood a moment after he was gone, listening to the sharp click-clack of the high-heeled boots on the hard floors. She went to the desk, she stared a moment at the words on the paper. Dear Papa and Mama and Lacey. She took up the pen and went on.

I love it. Texas is so different and wonderful. Jordan's house is huge but then everything's big here. Luz, Jordan's sister, the one who was ill, is here with us and I know we're going to be great friends she's so refreshing. And all those picturesque vaqueros and the stuffed heads I must write you all about them when I'm feeling more rested after the long journey down.

She began to cry and the tears plopped on the sheet of paper and she quickly dried them with a blotter but they left a little raised spot anyway.

10

SHE AWOKE to the most exquisite of morning smells—hot fresh coffee and baking bread. Piercing shafts of light stabbed the drawn window blinds. The wind again. The wind the wind hot and dry. Faraway shouts. The thud of horses' hoofs. And from somewhere below in the house the mumble of voices talking talking talking an endless flow of talk.

She glanced at the wedding-gift bedside clock, a charming bijou. It was six o'clock. Curiously enough she felt rested, refreshed. Bick was not beside her, he was not in the bathroom, he was nowhere to be seen or heard. In her slippers and robe she tiptoed into the hall. Then she remembered that this was her home, that she was mistress here. She ceased to tiptoe, her slipper heels clip-clapped on the stone floors like every Texan's. She leaned over the banister as she had done the night before and again she heard the little rustling and stirring near by, but when she turned she saw no one. So she called, very clearly, "Lupe! Petra! Tomás!"

And there was Lupe the silent one and behind her Petra, the younger one, less somber and secret. Buenos días, señora. Buenos días, señora. Buenos días Petra buenos días Lupe if this keeps on I'll be speaking Spanish in no time. On the little tray in Petra's hand was the ubiquitous coffee. The delicious aroma pricked the senses. Leslie drank the brew sweet and black and hot, two of the little cups that were the size of after-dinner cups in Virginia.

"Mmm! Delicious!" she said.

The two nodded violently, their faces broke into smiles, they seemed delighted out of all proportion. "Delicioso, sí! Delicioso!" And Leslie repeated delicioso after them and added a word to her Spanish vocabulary.

It was the nearest approach to friendliness that they had shown. She wondered about them a little. It was curious, their manner, not unfriendly but withdrawn even for a servant—strange, as though they wished to be as unnoticeable as possible. They moved silently, fluidly and with remarkable inefficiency. It was much as though children were trying to help and only succeeding in getting in the way.

But Leslie had decided that nothing would upset her today. A new day, a new home, a new life. Adventure and strangeness and novelty, that was what she always had wanted—freedom from convention and custom grown meaningless. And here it was.

She bathed, listening for Bick's returning footsteps. She dressed, one ear cocked. She decided on one of the plainer daytime frocks, a little silk, her mother had called this sort of dress. Anything inexpensive was "little"—a little dress, a little dressmaker, a little tailor, a little piece of jewelry. This little dress was of soft blue silk, quite simple. The white suede shoes with the smart blue kid tips and the not too high heels. There was a blue head-hugging hat to match—a cloche, it was called. She was hurrying now, she was listening for departing hoofbeats. But he wouldn't leave without seeing her.

When she had clattered downstairs there was no one about. The dining room, of course. There was the long table and the same islands of ketchup and chili sauce and vinegar and sugar and oil and cream. The tablecloth, she noticed, had lost the pristine freshness of the night before. She decided that she'd soon attend to that. Spotted tablecloths indeed!

Seated at the table were two men and a woman; the men in boots, canvas trousers and shirts, the woman in what, in Virginia, they called a wash dress. They were eating T-bone steaks with fried eggs on top; and grits and enormous rolls and there were big cups of coffee and large bowls of jams, yellow and purple and scarlet. The three glanced up from the business of eating and looked at her amiably as she entered.

"Howdy!" they said. "Howdy!" And went on eating.

So Texans actually did say howdy like that. She decided to try it herself but shied away from it at the moment of test and said "good morning" instead. "Isn't it a lovely morning!"

At this they again looked up from their plates but now they regarded her thoughtfully, their gaze more searching and direct.

One of the men—the older one—said, "You visiting from the East, ma'am? Kansas City or around?"

She hesitated a moment. She did not want to embarrass them. "I'm from Virginia. I'm Mrs. Benedict."

They seemed to find this in no way remarkable. "How-do!" said the young woman, a little more in the way of formality. "Howdy, ma'am," the men said. And the older one again took the lead. "Hodgins is my name. Clay Hodgins." He pointed with the tip of his knife. "My boy Gib and his wife Essie Lou. We're from up in Deaf Smith County, we been taking in the Fat Stock Show down to Hermoso."

Leslie had seated herself at an empty place at table, she leaned forward, her face alight with interest. "Why that sounds fascinating. I'd love to go to a fat stock show." And she meant it.

"Well, it's over, honey," the girl said.

A Mexican girl placed a platter before Leslie. On it was a slab of flat greyish steak that bore a nightmarish resemblance to its twin of the night before. Two fried eggs atop it glared at her with angry yellow eyes. Hot thick biscuits in a little baking crock, they bubbled a little with heat and butter. Coffee. Hurriedly Leslie poured the coffee, she regarded the three bright-eyed over the cup's steaming fragrance. "Tell me about it," she said. "Do they have to be fat—and how fat?"

They all laughed politely at that and she realized that they thought she was being humorous. The young man now spoke rather shyly in a charmingly soft musical voice, he blushed a little as he spoke. Leslie thought him most engaging. "We figured we'd best get an early start, we lit out of Hermoso three this morning it looked to be such a hot of a day down here, we figured to make three four hundred miles before daylight and we sure enough did."

"How nice," Leslie murmured inadequately.

Now the girl spoke up again, her voice was a shrill rasp after the man's low soft drawl. "We come away without what we went down after, mostly, though."

"What a pity," Leslie said. "What was that, do you mind telling me?"

"Appaloosas," the girl said.

Defeated in this, Leslie was girding herself for further enlightenment when the younger man unwittingly came to her rescue.

"You wouldn't believe, would you," he demanded, rather heatedly for one whose voiced indignation was so gentle and slow-spoken, "that they wasn't a bunch of appaloosas I'd cut up into horse meat! All we was looking for was five six real using horses that rein good and work a rope."

"Well, now," the older man ventured gently. "I wouldn't go so far's to say they wasn't some might have fitted in, but not what you'd call real outstanding individuals."

"So," the younger man concluded, ignoring this defense of the four-footed humans, "we said well, look, we're riding right by Bick Benedict's country we could easy drop in see what he can show and sure enough we got just what we come for, we could of saved ourselves a heap of time and trouble down to Hermoso."

"Yes, but," the girl protested, "I had a real time for myself with the stores and the shows and all."

"Well," the man named Clay said, and rose from the table. "We got to be going along." Gib and Essie Lou pushed back their chairs. "Next time you come up to Deaf Smith you come and pay us a visit we'd sure be glad to see you, we're up there outside Umbarger. Course it's kind of wildish up there, not like here, and we only got a small place—couple hundred thousand acres—it ain't what you'd call a braggin' ranch—but it's all deeded, no lease land, and like I say to Gib and Essie Lou, it's home." He drew a long breath after this speech and glanced at the others in a kind of oratorical triumph.

"I'd love to," Leslie said. "Perhaps someday when my husband is out that way he'll take me along. I want to see every bit of Texas. Is it far?"

Gib considered this question a moment as though loath to be less than strictly accurate. "It's a far piece, yes ma'am. But then again, not too far. About eight hundred miles if you come right along——"

Taptaptap. Swift high-heeled boots. Luz Benedict. "Well, howdy!" she cried. "Sure nice to see you! When'd you blow in? You been treated right?"

"Sure have, ma'am."

"Hope you're aiming to stay awhile."

"That's mighty kind of you," Clay Hodgins said with great earnestness. "But we got to mosey along. You know how it is this time of year."

As they stood the men were enormously tall and quietly powerful and graceful, too, in a monolithic way, Leslie thought. The girl was rangy, she seemed to have too many bones around the elbows, the hips and the shoulders. Leslie, in her mind's eye, tried various dresses on the lank frame, did her hair over, corseted her, shod her, and gave it up. "Good-bye," she said. "Do drop in again soon."

The older man's face crinkled good-naturedly. "I wouldn't rightly promise soon, ma'am. Maybe a year from now we might be down this way, I wouldn't say for sure."

They clattered out, the men with their great hats in their great hands, their walk leisurely almost cautious, as though this were an unaccustomed form of locomotion.

The two women, left alone, regarded each other warily. "They're sweet," Leslie said. "Are they great friends of Jordan's —and yours?"

"Hodgins? Don't scarcely know 'em. They just dropped by. They got a little place up in the Panhandle."

"Little!"

"But they sure had a run of luck," Luz went on, resentment in her tone. "They had a little bitty on account piece up near Luling and a gusher came in on their land last year, must bring in a million."

"A million gallons!" Leslie exclaimed, fascinated.

"Dollars."

"A million dollars in one year!"

Luz Benedict looked at her pityingly. "A million a month."

"How terrible!"

Luz ignored this. "My, you sure look dolled up in all that silk dress and citified shoes and all. You must of got up before breakfast to get all that on, as we say here."

Leslie laughed, but not very merrily. "I was just going to say that you look as fresh as if you'd slept twelve hours. But I heard you and Jordan—it was you, wasn't it?—talking at six this morning."

"Sure was. Bick and me, we have our coffee and talkee every morning of our lives at five, sit and talk and get things rounded up for the day. Any other way we'd never get a head start."

Leslie stood at the long table's edge, her smile sweet, her eyes steady. "I know. There must be such a lot to do on an enormous ranch like this. And this house. Now I'll be able to take a lot of the household duties off your hands. I thought we might have a little talk perhaps this morning——"

"Now don't you go getting yourself beat out." Luz sat smiling up at her from the chair into which she had dropped at the table. She poured herself a cup of coffee from the massive pot, she slopped a great dollop of cream into it and two heaping teaspoons of sugar. "You look real ganted I was saying to Bick. Not real strong. We want for you to get a little meat on your bones, and have a nice time."

Leslie felt the color rush into her face. Careful now, she heard her father's voice say. Slow now. This is new country for you, this is that Texas I told you about, remember? "That's so good of you, Luz. But I'm just naturally slim, we all are, but I'm really very strong and well. I'm never ill."

"Me too," Luz agreed, her manner all amiability. "Never sick a day in my life. Course you don't count being throwed by a horse and tromped by a mean——"

"But you were ill. You had the grippe and couldn't come to the wedding." And could have bitten her tongue for having yielded to an impulse so childish.

Luz laughed a great hearty guffaw. "That's so, I guess I didn't want to let on I remembered ever being sick. The Benedicts are that way, always bragging on their health. When Pa died he made us promise he wouldn't have any slow funeral, solemn and slow wasn't his way. I want for you to promise you'll gallop the horses all the way, Pa said, as if I was riding, and I will be. You never saw such a funeral, streaking down the highway and across the prairie to our family cemetery, the family and the boys and the chuck wagon and all, like he wanted it, all going like possessed, and we promised him we'd eat out there off the chuck wagon, his last roundup, and so we did. No automobiles, Pa said. Horses. The family and the vaqueros and the neighbors and half the county. It was better than a movie. Poor Pa."

Leslie was entranced. "All this is so new and exciting to me." She hesitated a moment. "I hope you won't mind if I seem a little strange at first. I've never been West before—really West, I mean. I'll soon learn Texas ways. And in a little while I'll be able to run the house too." She must know. It was unthinkable that she could go on like a guest in her husband's house. Better to settle things definitely and at once.

Luz had set her coffee cup down with a sharp clack. "The house runs itself, honey, with me giving it a little shove and a push now and again. I know how to handle the Mexicans, I been living with 'em all my life, and my pa and ma and grampa and gramma before me. They'd be squatting on their honkers all day if I didn't keep after them. Now you just run along and enjoy yourself." She shoved back her chair with a grating sound.

She had boundless vitality. No, it wasn't vitality, Leslie decided. It was energy. Luz bustled. She ran bounced hurried scurried. Energy was merely motion, wearying to witness. True vitality was a deep inner strength that sustained anyone who came in contact with it. Later, trying to describe her to her father, Leslie said, "She makes you long to sit quietly in a low chair in a dim peaceful room with your eyes shut listening to nothing, not even to a faraway string quartette."

Leslie stood very still in the middle of the big dining room with the hot Gulf draft blowing through four doors. "I think I'll go up and attend to my room—I mean put away——"

She was a little girl again, uncertain, talking to her domineering mother, without the understanding and sustaining protection of her father.

Luz patted her shoulder as she trotted briskly by. "The girls'll have you all fixed up by now and prob'ly know every hook and eye on every dress, and every button and shoelace. But they never sweep the dust that's under the bed."

"I'm going to take a walk," Leslie announced.

Luz turned at the door. "A what!"

"A nice long walk, perhaps into town and look around at things. Or perhaps around the—the garden—the—to see the place and poke into some of those quaint buildings——"

Luz came back into the room. Her round pink face looked sharp. "You can't do that."

"Why not?"

"People don't walk in Texas. Only Mexicans. If you want to ride one of the boys'll saddle you a nice gentled riding pony."

"I'll let you know," loftily. "I'll speak to my husband about it later in the morning."

Luz laughed, a short little bark of a laugh. "Honey, if you think Bick's got nothing to do only take people around the ranch. He's been away weeks now, he's got to catch up if he's ever going to. Now honey, you just do some sewing or something or reading, Bick says you're a great hand to read. H'm?"

She bustled out of the room, click-clack click-clack. Leslie felt a surge of murderous rage. She turned sharply and walked out of the room out of the great front door through which she had been carried so gaily the day before. She walked out into the blazing Texas morning.

She almost ran down the dusty roadway. The young fellow who had met them at the Vientecito station was on his knees at the edge of a small lawn of tough coarse grass. Through many years she was to see him thus coaxing green growing things and brilliant colorful flowers to thrive in spite of the withering sun and the Gulf winds that shriveled them with the heat and the sudden icy northers that blasted them with the cold.

To see him was like encountering a friend, she was dizzy with the sudden rush of gratitude as the boy's face lighted with recognition, his eyes his smile became radiant.

"Hello!" she said. "Hello, Dimodeo!"

The boy rose from his knees in one graceful fluid motion, he bowed low. "Señora. Buenos días señora."

"How far is it to the village?" At the blank look on his face, "You speak English, Dimodeo. You understood me yesterday."

"Yes, señora, I speak English, certainly. I am only more in the way of Spanish. . . . Village?"

"Yes. The town. Benedict. How far is it to the town? I want to walk there."

153

"But you cannot walk to the town." He was genuinely shocked. He looked toward the house. "I will tell them the automobile. Or a horse. No, you are not dressed for riding. The automobile."

"No. I want to go alone and—and just look around and see things. I don't want to sit in an automobile. I'm sick of sitting and sitting and sitting, here's a million miles of land and doesn't anyone ever walk on it!"

"We walk," he said. "The Mexicans walk."

"Where is the schoolhouse? Yesterday we passed a schoolhouse. Down there. Is that the building? Down the road."

"It is the school. It is the school where the children go who live on Reata Ranch. The little ones. Until they are ten or twelve and can work well."

"How many?"

"Oh, many, señora. And many in other schools on other divisions."

She waved good-bye with a gaiety she did not feel, she trudged down the road in the blue silk dress and the white suede shoes. It was fearfully hot and dusty, she saw no one, nothing moved. She reached the schoolhouse, she sauntered past it and heard the drowsy bee-hum of children's voices. Abruptly she turned up the little path that led to the whitewashed adobe house. It looked very old and picturesque like pictures she had seen of missions built by the exploring Spanish priests centuries ago. Perhaps it had once been a mission, she thought.

There was a tiny whitewashed vestibule, surprisingly cool. She was to learn to appreciate the coolness of these thick-walled adobe buildings, she was to learn to stay through the day in the dim cool shelter of a house interior.

She knocked at the closed door. The humming and buzzing ceased abruptly. Silence like the listening silence of the upper hall at the Big House. She knocked again with some authority now. She had a feeling of exhilaration and discovery.

The door was opened by a woman of about thirty, a thin sallow woman in a drab dark dress. A fretful-looking woman with fine black eyes whose heavy brows met over her nose in a dark forbidding brush. She stood, the door open a few inches only, her hand on the doorknob.

"What do you want?" she said.

"I'm Mrs. Jordan Benedict," Leslie said, smiling. And extended her hand. "Perhaps I shouldn't disturb you. I was passing by and I couldn't resist dropping in——" The woman was staring at her so fixedly that Leslie was puzzled, then startled. "You are the schoolteacher, aren't you?"

"Yes."

Leslie decided not to be annoyed. This was, she told herself, a gauche girl who possibly was not accustomed to visitors during school hours. The woman was looking at her with the slow appraising stare of the Mexican girls, but she was not Mexican. She looked at Leslie's white shoes, dusty now; at the blue silk dress that now was a little damp with dark spots here and there. Leslie could feel tiny rivulets slithering wetly down her spine.

All very interesting and different and she was enjoying herself immensely. It was wonderful to say, "I am Mrs. Jordan Benedict." She said it again because she thought the woman had not understood. It was a shock to see a look of pure hate flick into the woman's eyes like the red darting flash of a snake's tongue. It came to Leslie that the teacher was actually barring her way.

"I just thought I'd drop in and see the children," she said then. "I'm out for a little walk."

"Walk!" the woman repeated after her as the others had done, as Luz and Dimodeo had done. It was becoming slightly annoying. Leslie took a firm step forward feeling suddenly tall and dignified and very important and for one dreadful moment she thought the woman was actually going to stop her.

"What is your name!"

"Cora. Cora Dart."

What was everyone so cross about? Leslie stepped rather too briskly into the room. A vast whitewashed room crammed with children. Children of from four to fifteen. Their eyes were fixed on her with a steady stare that combined to give the effect of a searchlight. Immediately Leslie was struck with the fanciful thought that the seated children made a pattern like that of a gigantic piano keyboard. The faces shaded from ivory to almost black, and the lighter ones seemed to occupy the front rows, the darker the back.

Cora Dart seemed to have recovered from the shock of a visitor, she placed a chair for Leslie and suddenly Leslie was frantic to be gone. The room was stifling, she felt unbearably drowsy, as though drugged.

"Go back to your work," Cora Dart said in English. "Go back to your work," she then said in Spanish. The battery of eyes turned briefly down to the desks, the next instant was lifted again.

"I won't stay, really," Leslie said hurriedly. She felt she should ask some intelligent questions, she remembered the way grownups used to behave when they had visited her childhood public school in Ohio. "Uh, are the pupils the children of people who work— who live on the ranch?" You know they are, how silly. She moved toward the door, she smiled at the children, feeling foolish, she smiled at the dour Miss Dart.

"Thank you so much, it is all so interesting, you must come up some afternoon after school or perhaps on a Saturday and have tea with me."

"Tea!" echoed Cora Dart as one would say opium.

Leslie's nightmarish feeling of being an interloper now drove her to the point of being unable to terminate a distasteful encounter.

"Or coffee," she corrected herself hastily. "Coffee I've learned seems to be the national drink of Texas—I mean they seem to prefer it here—uh—have you been teaching here a long time?"

"Too long for my own good," Cora Dart said with extraordinary venom. "They've had about a million teachers here, first and last."

"But that's too bad. I should think it would be upsetting for the children—the pupils."

The woman stared at her with the eyes of pure hate. "You'd better speak to your husband about that. Your husband is the person to speak to about that, Mrs. Jordan Benedict."

The woman's mad, Leslie thought as she turned abruptly to go. Stark staring mad, literally.

Outside again in the glaring heat Leslie glanced at her watch and incredulously saw that it now was ten minutes past nine. Her day was just beginning but she felt she had been up for many hours. She wondered where Jordan was, she longed to see him, she looked out and out toward the endless haze of prairie and sky. He was miles and miles off somewhere with those thousands and thousands of cows.

There was so much to learn, so much to see. She supposed she was what they called a tenderfoot, she realized now what a good and descriptive word this was. She wished that she felt more like moving briskly about and not so listless and inclined to lie down and sleep somewhere in the shade. The shade. May. May in Virginia. Cool and sunny in Virginia with a breeze from the Blue Ridge and the grass always richly green in the meadows and pastures, the apple blossoms all gone now but the late spring flowers bravely abloom. The Rivers of Virginia. Walking in the dust and glare of the Texas road, stubbornly, she thought of the Rivers of Virginia, the very sound of them was cool and fresh and clear as she said them over in a little murmur, it was like dipping her fingers in their limpid softness and laving her throbbing brow. The sound of them rippled and flowed. Shenandoah. Roanoke. Rappahannock. Potomac . . . And the flowers . . . Mountain laurel . . . Wisteria . . . Rhododendron . . . White alder . . . Wax myrtle . . . Trumpet flower . . . What were the rivers of Texas? Rio Grande. Nueces. Diablo. Brazos. Hot Spanish names. Don't be like that, silly.

She must have taken a wrong turning, what with the heat, the glare and her weariness, for she found herself off on a smaller rougher road lined with rows of shanties, small and tumble-down. Flimsier, even, than the Negro cabins she had seen so familiarly in Virginia. These were on stilts, there were no green or growing things about them. It was strange that there seemed to be no pleasant human hum of life from within these shacks.

A thin wailing sound. From within one of the hovels an infant crying. Leslie turned and looked about her. In her resentment and bewilderment she had come farther than she knew. There was the Big House shimmering in the heat, but it seemed terribly far away. She wondered if she should telephone and ask them to come for her. The thought of walking back under the blazing sun made her feel a little sick.

The Girls. Luz had said the Girls would be there early. A barbecue, a great hot red barbecue. Of course there wouldn't be a telephone in any of these crazy dwellings. But perhaps someone could be sent to fetch a car. . . . She followed the sound of the wailing infant, she ascended the rickety steps and knocked at the doorway hung with strips of flyspecked paper. The baby cried without ceasing—a high-pitched kitten-like mewing. She knocked again.

"Entre!" A woman's voice.

She brushed aside the paper strips, she entered the dark close-smelling room. For a moment, blinded by the transition from glaring sun to gloom, she could see nothing. She put her hand over her smarting eyes.

"I am Mrs. Benedict," she said to no one in particular.

"Sí, sí," said a woman's voice, low and soft, with a note of weakness in it. "Perdóneme. Pardon me that I do not rise. I am ill." This in Spanish. Miraculously, Leslie thought, she caught a word—two words—and translated their meaning. Perdóneme. Enferma. Now she looked about her. A woman on the bed in the little front room. A girl, really, black-haired, big-bosomed, her eyes bright with fever. The girl half sat up, she even essayed a little bow as she sat there in the disordered bed. "I have a fever," she said in Spanish. "Fiebre." Leslie nodded. The infant's shrill cry came from a tiny second room at the rear; the lean-to kitchen of the shack. This front room evidently was bedroom and sitting room. In one corner an altar, all pink crepe paper and bits of ribbon and gilt and paper flowers, with a gilt cross in the center and a bright pink and blue and scarlet picture of the Christ and the Madonna, gilt-framed.

Dimodeo had understood English, and spoken it. This girl must, surely. "I am so sorry. Is the baby ill?"

The girl nodded sadly. "He is ill because I am ill. My milk is not good."

"Well for heaven's sake!" Leslie said. "You just get a formula and feed him that." The girl said nothing. The child's wailing pulsed through the hot low room. Leslie went to him. He lay in a basket, very wet; dark mahogany beneath the brown skin, very angry. There was no water tap, no pump, no sink. He smelled badly. She took off his clothes, she found some water in a pitcher, she wiped him with a damp rag, the woman, bare-footed, came shakily across the sagging floor to hand her a diaper. "Go back to bed," Leslie said, and smiled at her a little ruefully. "I'm not very good at this, but it's better than having him so wet and—so wet." She diapered him inexpertly and he never stopped crying, looking up at her with great black swimming eyes. She felt like someone in a Victorian novel. Lady of the manse. How old-fashioned. She ought to have—what was it?—calf's-foot jelly, revolting stuff it must have been that they were always bringing in napkin-covered baskets for the defenseless poor. The floor of the little wood and adobe hut was broken so that you actually could see the earth over which it stood. Rats must come through those gaps, Leslie thought, looking at the squirming infant. Rats and mice and every sort of awful creeping thing.

She returned the child to the basket and his screams were shattering. The woman on the bed looked up at her submissively. Leslie felt helpless and somehow foolish.

"What is your name?"

"Deluvina."

"What does your husband do here—what is his work?" She wished she didn't sound like a social worker invading someone's decent privacy.

"He is Angel Obregon. He is vaquero." So this splintered shanty was the home of one of those splendid bronze gods on horseback. "He is vaquero. My father too and my father's father are vaquero here on Reata Ranch." She said this with enormous pride.

Leslie longed to ask what his wage was. She told herself this would be disloyal to Jordan. She must ask him.

There was the sound of a motorcar stopping outside, a horn brayed, quick steps on the broken wooden stairs.

"Miz Benedict!" called a man's voice. "Ma'am! Miz Luz says you come along home with me, they're waiting on you Madama says."

At the door stood Jett Rink. "You ain't supposed to be in there," he said. "Bick'll be mad as all hell. And Madama's fit to be tied."

11

SHE SAID NOTHING, she stood there, she looked at him, he stared at her, she thought, almost insolently. The eyes that were too small, very blue; the curiously damp-looking curls with one lock falling across the forehead. Those pagan goatlike young gods in the Greek pictures—that was it.

"I am Mrs. Benedict," she said needlessly and very formally.

"Well, sure." He waved a hand toward the car, a new Ford, dust-coated. "We'd better get moseying."

She was relieved to have been sent for, she welcomed the

sight of the car. He had spoken of her husband as Bick. Coolly she said, "Did Mr. Benedict send you here for me?"

"No. She did."

Leslie stifled the impulse to say, haughtily, And who is she? She looked back at the woman on the bed. The child yelled. In silence she entered the car. Now she looked down at herself. The little blue silk was a mess. A great stain on her lap. The baby. Dust and perspiration. Her hair blown by the hot wind, her white shoes grey-brown. "How did you know I had gone into that place?"

He spun the wheel expertly, they leaped down the road. "Everybody knows everything anybody does around here, there's a saying you can't spit without she knows it."

Leslie decided that she must speak to Jordan about this oaf. He turned his head and stared at her with a quick bold glance.

"I watched you from the garage." He said gradge. "You ain't aiming to do much walking like that around here, are you?"

"Why not?"

"Right around the house it's all right, maybe, if you want to stir yourself afoot, but I wouldn't go to walking out on the road and cutting across prairie like you done."

"Why not?"

"Rattlers."

"Rattlers!" she repeated somewhat faintly.

"This time year it's beginning hot the rattlers start to stir around and come out when the sun is good and hot and they look for something good to eat hopping around. Shoes like yours," he glanced down at her soiled slippers and her silken ankles, "why they're liable to take a bite out of you by mistake."

"That's ridiculous!" she said. "You're trying to scare me."

"Might be. But anyway, you're too ganted to be loping around in the hot of the day, walking."

"Ganted ganted! What do you mean!" She had heard this word too often.

"Ganted. Thin."

"Whether I am thin or not is none of your business, boy."

162

"Sure ain't. But like I always say, the nearer the bone the sweeter the meat."

She was deciding whether to be really angry or merely amused at this cheeky lout when they approached the Big House and she saw a dozen cars clustered in the drive. Again she looked down at herself in dismay. The Girls.

"They mustn't see me. I look so awful. If I could change before they——"

He spun the wheel, he swung the car sharply around to the rear of the house. "You come on with me." They whirled past the kitchen and stopped at a blank wall that seemed part of the foundation. "Out." She climbed down, feeling like a conspirator and not liking it. Carefully, slowly he looked about him, then he reached high above his head and pressed at two corners the long bar that seemed part of the heavy ornamentation of this Spanish castle. She saw that the block was not wood but painted metal, and now part of the wall opened just enough to make entrance possible, and within she just glimpsed the outline of a spiral stairway and she heard the sound of water dripping ever so faintly.

He slid within, he held out his hard oil-stained hand.

"No!" she cried in panic, even while her reasoning mind told her that the whole situation was ridiculous was fantastic. She ran across the paved court, into the kitchen, leaving behind her a row of staring dark servants' faces, into the vast dining room. From the hall there came the high shrill chatter of many feminine voices and she smelled the ever present coffee and the scent of it sickened her a little now. Someone was playing the piano and with power and authority. Brahms. Well, that was better. It needed tuning. She must remember to have it tuned. Leslie turned and looked about her. There was, surely, a rear stairway hereabouts, somewhere. They mustn't see her looking like a drowned rat. Jordan Benedict's new wife.

From the doorway through which she had been peering came Luz Benedict's strident voice. "There she is now! Where're you getting to, Leslie? The Girls are here waiting on you."

Well, there's nothing you can do about it now, so face it and don't be silly. Stained silk, dusty shoes, flushed perspiring face, straggling hair, she advanced toward them smiling, toward the women who had been wondering about her these past weeks, whose topic of conversation and speculation she had almost exclusively been.

She smiled directly into the cluster of staring women's faces, she spread her hands in a little appealing gesture.

"Forgive me. I'm late. And I'm a sight. And I did so want to make a good first impression on all of you."

The staring faces relaxed, softened. The Girls moved toward her, she advanced toward them, her hands outstretched.

"Who was playing the Scherzo?"

"Adarene. That was Adarene Morey," the Girls said.

"Lovely. I'm going to have the piano——"

But Luz stepped between them and took over with the strict conventionality of the provincial mind.

"Meet Joella Beezer . . . Ila Rose Motten . . . Eula Jakes . . . Miz Wirt Tanner . . . Aurie Heldebrand . . . Fernie Kling . . . Miz Ray Jennings . . . Vashti Hake . . . Adarene Morey just married a month and come all the way down from Dallas just to meet you. Girls, this is Bick's wife—Leslie. That's a boy's name hereabouts, but she's Bick's legal wife just the same."

They clustered round her, their voices were high and shrill in welcome but there was, too, a genuineness about them, an eagerness and warmth. They were expensively and formally dressed in clothes that Leslie would consider city clothes. She wondered if she had expected a feminine version of the men's canvas and boots. Fringed antelope perhaps, and beadwork. They took her hand very formally, they said, for the most part, Howdy or Pleased to Meet You and she loved it. She behaved as though she were wearing the freshest of toilettes, the least shiny of noses. Of the group, two faces impressed themselves on her mind. There was Adarene Morey the Dallas bride—a plain quiet girl with intelligent understanding eyes and a queer knobby forehead and skimpy mouse-colored hair. It was she who had been playing the piano. Adarene. One of those names that sounded made up.

The other girl had come forward almost timidly—the Girls had, in fact, given her a little push toward Leslie. A very fat girl with an alarmingly red face. She bulged above her clothes, her blue eyes were fixed on Leslie with something like anguish. The young woman grasped Leslie's hand in a terrible grip, she looked deep into Leslie's eyes with a look of pain and questioning.

"And your name—forgive me—I want to be sure I have you all clear in my memory——" Leslie said.

"I'm Vashti Hake—your nearest neighbor—our place meets Bick's—yours——"

So this was the girl—this trembling mound of hurt pride and emotion.

"I hope we're going to be friends as well as neighbors." What a speech, Leslie! that inner voice said. Being mistress of the manor again, are you?

Above the chatter Luz Benedict's voice called to her. "Look what the Girls brought you!" She pointed to the great hall table on which stood bowls and platters and baskets. Mystified, Leslie stared at the offerings. A great bowl of chicken salad plastered with bright yellow mayonnaise. A plateau of chocolate cake. A saddle of venison. Jars of preserves. A ham. Homemade wine.

Dazed, Leslie surveyed these assorted edibles and wondered what she was supposed to do with them. Eat them, but how, when, why? The barbecue. The barbecue of course.

"How friendly of you! We'll take them to the picnic, shall we?"

They appeared shocked at this. "It's a barbecue. You can't eat that at a barbecue."

Luz Benedict's voice again. "And time to start, too. Come on."

"But Luz, I've got to change my clothes. I look simply terrible."

"We haven't got time," Luz said firmly.

Serenely Leslie moved toward the stairway. "You girls look so fresh and crisp. I can't go like this. I'd disgrace you."

"We're going," said Luz.

"I went for a walk," Leslie continued, as though she had not heard. She was ascending the stairs, smiling down on the others as she went.

"A walk!" they echoed incredulously as everyone else had done. She noted for the first time the feminine regional habit of making two syllables out of a one-syllable word. "A wo-uk!" they drawled.

"And I visited the school and when I came out I sort of got lost and then I heard a baby crying in one of the cabins and I went in to ask the way and the mother was sick and the baby was so wet and wretched and it was so hot and while I was changing it——" Ruefully she glanced down at herself. "I'll only be a minute. Does anyone want to come up to keep me company?"

In one concerted movement they surged up the stairs.

"Could we see your things? Could we?"

"Of course. But I didn't get much. Jordan and I were married in such a hurry."

The procession slowed, the heads turned as though moved on a single pivot to stare at Vashti Hake. The red anguished face became a rich purple. Equably Leslie went on, "Maybe my clothes aren't right for Texas. You've all got to tell me the right thing to do and the right thing to wear. Will you?" And she looked at Vashti Hake and she looked at Adarene Morey and she thought, Well, they will, at least. And impartially she smiled at all the rest. She was, in fact, rather fancying herself by now.

Though they were well dressed, if somewhat too elaborately for a noonday barbecue on the plains, it was obvious that East Coast fashions had not yet penetrated the Southwest. They watched her while she changed from the stained blue silk to a cream silk with a border of two shades of green. The skirt came to her knees, the neckline was known as the bateau, the whole as a sports costume. It was hideous to the point of being deforming but it was high fashion and over it the representatives of Dallas, Fort Worth, Hermoso, Vientecito, Corpus Christi, Kingsville, Houston and Benedict cooed and ohed and ahed. They rummaged clothes closets and held fragile garments up against their own ampler bosoms.

"Look, Joella! This would be perfect on you with your hair and all. Black chiffon with bead things. What do you call those, Miz Benedict?"

"They're paillettes. And I'm called Leslie."

"Oh my! Lookit!" Her Virginia riding habit, the breeches of beige Bedford cord, the coat of tweed, the canary waistcoat. The silks. The pink jersey sweater blouse. The pajama negligee of satin and lamé. The blue-green chiffon over chartreuse yellow for evening.

"They're all too dressy, aren't they? For ranch life?"

"You'd be surprised," Adarene Morey reassured her. "We all dress like mad, we've got nothing else to do."

Luz's voice rasped her dissent. "You don't see me worrying where I'm going to wear chiffon and paillettes and fancy riding pants. I got plenty to do."

The Girls laughed tolerantly at that as at a family joke. "Oh, you, Luz. Everybody in Texas knows you'd rather work cattle than make love."

Leslie adjusted the cloche hat of green grosgrain ribbon, she gathered up the fresh white gloves. From her new white buckskin shoes to her brushed and shining hair she was immaculate again and eager for the day ahead. She faced the Girls, smiling and friendly. "It was dear of you to wait while I changed."

She had changed more than she knew, in their eyes. Downstairs, seeing her for the first time, they had thought, Well, he'd have done a heap better to take Vashti Hake, fat and all, instead of going way up to Virginia to bring him home a ganted cockeyed wife.

They were off now in a haze of dust, a clatter of talk, a procession of cars down the long road, then across the prairie itself, into draws, down rutted lanes, through sandy loam, the mesquite branches switching and clawing the cars as they lurched past.

The talk was of people Leslie did not know, of events and customs and ways of which she was ignorant. She listened and smiled and nodded. I like the plain one with the knobby forehead, she thought, and the fat one with the touching look in her eyes.

Jordan. I'll see him at the barbecue, I can't wait to see him I've
scarcely seen him at all since yesterday, it's ridiculous.

"I love picnics," she said aloud. "We used to have them at
home in Virginia, the very first warm spring day." She thought
of the great hampers covered with white starched cloths; the
delicate chicken, the salad of lobster, the bottles of wine, the fruit,
Caroline's delectable cakes and perhaps a very special cheese that
some epicurean patient had sent Doctor Lynnton from Baltimore
or New York.

Sociably she turned to the girl seated next her. Eula, they
called her. "Do you live near here?"

"Eighty miles?" said Eula, and her voice took the rising inflection, as though asking a question rather than answering it.

"And you came all that distance? What's the name of your
town?"

"Forraje?" Eula ventured again with the rising inflection,
tentatively, as though she would be the first to retract the name
if her hearer did not approve.

Leslie began to speculate about the high shrill feminine voices,
about the tentativeness, about the vague air of insecurity that
touched these women. It was very hot, but she was having a fine
time, it was all new and strange, she felt light and free and very
very hungry after that early coffee and the emotional hours since
then. Quietly, she listened to the talk. Horses, children, clothes,
cooking, barbecues, bridge, coffee parties. Well, what's wrong
with that, she demanded of herself.

Miraculously, as though divining her thoughts, Adarene Morey
said, very low, beneath the crackle of high voices, "That's the
way it is. You'll never hear a word of talk about books or music
or sculpture or painting in Texas."

"But why?"

Adarene shrugged, helplessly. "I honestly don't know. Maybe
it's the climate. Or the distances. Or the money. Or something.
They never speak of these things. They have a kind of contempt
for them."

"Then what about you?"

"Oh, I'm considered odd. But it's all right because the Moreys are old Texas cotton."

"What you two buzzing about, looking so sneaky!" bawled Ila Rose Motten.

They were stopping before another gate. There had been gates and gates and gates. There were miles of fence—hundreds of miles of fence it seemed to Leslie. They were forever stopping and someone was forever clambering out of the car, opening a gate, closing it after the procession of cars had passed, climbing in again.

"Let me do it," Leslie volunteered finally. "I'll have to learn sometime." But she was clumsy at it, there was a trick about it, the women laughed good-naturedly and Leslie joined them. "Well, you can't say I'm not trying to learn to be a Texan." Luz was in one of the other cars. Leslie wondered if it was that which made her feel gayer, younger, more free. There was a high-humored air about the whole jaunt as they bumped their way over the dusty roads, across what seemed to be endless prairie. And now a long low cluster of buildings squatted against the horizon.

"There we are," said Adarene Morey, and turned to smile at Leslie. "That's headquarters bunkhouse, in case you don't know. I guess you aren't really acquainted yet, are you? Reata's so big, even for Texas."

Vashti Hake in the front seat beside the driver had been markedly silent. "You certainly have got your best company manners on today," Eula Jakes called to her, "for a girl who generally never stops talking."

Vashti Hake turned in the seat and the anguished blue eyes fixed themselves on Leslie. "Some of the boys are going to be there," she announced.

This Leslie had taken for granted until now. "I hope Jordan will be, at any rate. I haven't seen him since—well, I haven't seen him today," she confessed.

This appeared to cheer Miss Hake. "There'll be others too," she announced mysteriously.

Eula caught this challenge. "Vashti Hake, you got a new beau and haven't told any of us!"

"Old Eusebio?" Adarene inquired, laughing. Then, at Leslie's failure to comprehend, "Old Eusebio's the cook, he always does the barbecue at Reata, it's been going all night."

"I can hardly wait, I'm starved."

Now they drew up in the bare dusty space surrounding the bunkhouse. The sun glared upon the group standing near the long wooden table. Hopefully Leslie saw a little clump of mesquite pale green and cool-seeming but it was soon to prove deceptive. She was to learn there was little comfort or shade beneath this thin-leaved prairie shrub.

There was Jordan, not only in the boots and spurs and tans and Stetson but in chaps like a movie hero. As this leather god came toward her Leslie found herself running toward him, she had no other single thought in her mind but to be near him again. The Girls, Luz, the half dozen men who had hailed them as they drove up, the figure squatted in front of a red-hot fire on the ground, the Mexicans bent over a steaming hole near by—all vanished in a hot haze and she heard, unheeding, only a thin echo of their indulgent laughter as she stood on tiptoe to meet his kiss, her arms about his neck.

"You left without even good-bye."

"How do you know? You were sleeping in a tight little bunch as though nothing could wake you."

"I know, dearest. I was exhausted."

"I want you to meet some of the boys. I want to show you off, first chance I've had."

"I'm so happy. Stay near me."

He led her forward. "Boys, this is my wife Leslie. Leslie, Lucius Morey down from Dallas—you met Adarene. . . . Bale Clinch —you want to watch out for him he's running for Sheriff. . . . Ollie Whiteside . . . smartest lawyer around. Keeps us out of jail. . . . Pinky Snyth from the Hakes' place—say, Vashti, I hear your pa's sick and couldn't come."

Vashti Hake looked at Jordan Benedict without replying. The

plump rosy face flushed deeper, then paled ominously. Deliberately, and with a kind of awful dignity, this fat girl walked to the side of Pinky Snyth the little cow hand, so diminutive beside her, even in his high-heeled boots and towering Stetson. She took his hand in hers and as she spoke she abandoned the patois of of the Texan.

"Pa isn't sick. He's sulking. But he'll get over it. There's more than one bride and bridegroom here at this barbecue. Mott Snyth and I were married yesterday in Hermoso."

A final glare at Jordan Benedict, a look that was a tragic mixture of wounded pride and pitiful defeat. The triumphant bride burst into tears, bent to bury her face in the bridegroom's inadequate shoulder.

A hubbub of cries and squeals, of guffaws and backslappings, of congratulations uttered too loudly and disapproval muttered sotto voce.

Vashti Hake had made her point, attention was centered on her now, Bick had kissed the bride's wet cheek and wrung the little man's surprisingly steel-strong hand. Together, happily unnoticed, he and Leslie were free to move about unhampered. Only Luz Benedict bustled up to them as they turned away from the shrill group. She glared at Leslie, she jerked her gaze toward Bick.

"You're the cause of this!"

"Fine," said Bick equably and patted Luz's shoulder. "Vashti should have been married five years ago, big bouncing girl like that."

But nothing could disturb Leslie now. Here was Jordan, here was a day crowded with new sights, new sounds, fresh experiences. Vashti Hake and her little blue-eyed cowboy—they were part of the picture, touching, a little ridiculous. And this sinister spinster, this Luz Benedict with her plans and her frustrations— she was ridiculous too, and not to be taken seriously for a moment.

Leslie tucked her arm through Bick's. "Show me the bunkhouse. I've read about them all my life."

He pressed her arm close. "Nothing much to see." It turned out that he was right. Cots, each covered with a thin grey-brown blanket. A bit of mirror stuck on the wall and their meager belongings ranged on shelves—a razor, a broken-toothed comb, a battered clock. Dust-caked boots on the floor, a saddle, a bit of rope, a leather strap. A guitar on an upended wooden box.

At the look on her face Bick laughed indulgently. "What did you expect to see?"

"Pistols. Poker chips. Silk garters. Silver spurs."

"Serves you right for reading so much. Our boys aren't allowed to carry guns unless they're out on the range, and sometimes not even then. Or hunting, of course."

She threw a final look over her shoulder at the bare, hot gritty little room. "Another girlish dream gone. Tell me, darling, how much are they paid, your vaqueros?"

"Oh, twenty a month—some of them thirty. The top hands. Plus mounts and found, of course."

She stared in unbelief, she started to protest, thought better of it, was silent. It was high noon now, as they came again into the clearing the heat struck like a blow. Other than the bunkhouse the sole shelter was an open shed attached to the house. From the rafters hung strings of dried peppers and onions and herbs. There were strips of something dark and thick toward which she turned puzzled eyes until she realized that these were long hanks of beef drying in the sun and wind and dust while over them flowed a solid mass of flies. She turned her eyes away. She detained him, her hand on his arm.

"Jordan, was it pique? That sounds like a novel. I mean did that poor girl marry that little man because of you—and me?"

"I suppose so. But it had to be somebody. Think no more of it."

"Jordan, if you hadn't met me—if you hadn't happened to come out with Papa that evening to look at My Mistake—where is she, by the way?"

"She's in pasture, under a canopy for shade, and she asked for you this morning. We'll go see her this evening when this thing is over."

Having started she must go on. "But would you? Would you have married her even if you couldn't possibly have—I mean she is ever so nice but she isn't very attractive." She couldn't say, Would that sister of yours actually have deviled you into it, finally.

"Well, now, honey, while we're asking questions, would you have married that fellow in the pink coat?"

"Him—or someone. But you——"

"The girls are looking for you. The barbecue's about cooked, I guess."

She gave it up. As they walked toward the others she saw that the company had separated into two groups, male and female. The Girls were clustered near the table talking all together in high shrill voices. The men stood apart, bunched, low-voiced. Leslie thought the men looked strangely alike. Little Pinky Snyth was a miniature copy of the giants who towered above him. They all wore wide-brimmed hats of the same dust color, rolled at the brim; they wore the same khaki clothes, the same high-heeled boots, their strangely boyish faces were russet from sun and wind, their voices were soft and rather musical. Her arm through Bick's, she strolled with him toward the men's group. He disengaged his arm. "The girls are over there."

The dark shadowy figures of the Mexicans came and went. Some of these wore sombreros made of plaited straw and there was a strap of leather under the chin, very foreign-looking and somehow dramatic.

One of the women called to the grouped men, petulantly. "Now you boys come over and talk to us, I bet you're telling Pinky stories and they ain't fit to hear and we'd like to hear them. You come on, now, or we'll be real mad!" May-ud.

And when the men replied, speaking to the women, it seemed to Leslie that they changed their tone, it was as adults change when they speak to little children, coming down to their mental level.

The women were fair-skinned, without a trace of sun or wind-burn. She never had seen women so unrelaxed out of doors. She decided they must spend their days indoors, in the dim rooms. It was as though they regarded Nature as their enemy rather than as their fragrant soft-bosomed mother. Perhaps with good reason, Leslie reflected. There was no lolling on the cool fresh-smelling grass, for grass there was none. There was no lifting one's face to let the cool breeze blow gratefully over one, for the wind was the hot noonday Gulf wind.

Now the preparations for the meal were accelerated and she came forward interestedly to see and to learn.

In the center of the cleared circle, its perimeter neatly swept, was the red-hot bed of live wood coals on the ground. This was no ordinary picnic bonfire, this was a hard-shaped mound that must surely have been going for many hours. Leslie put the thought of the beef strips out of her mind and joined the women chirping and fluttering about the long wooden table.

Old Eusebio, squatting on his haunches before the fierce heat of the fire, was manipulating four cooking vessels at once. First, of course, there was the five-gallon pot of steaming coffee. Near by, on a crude tripod, was the vast skillet of beans. As Leslie watched, fascinated, Eusebio lifted the top off a still larger skillet and gave a stir to the mass of rice and tomato bubbling around chunks of beef. Chunks of beef. Leslie thought of the hanging strips with their crawling burden and decided against that luncheon dish. She was hungry in spite of the heat and the dust.

"Starving," she said sociably to Adarene Morey.

Adarene pointed to the pit near by about which three vaqueros were stooped. They were lifting something out of the hole in the ground and a delicious steam permeated the air. "They're taking out the barbecue. Here, have a piece of this. Have you ever eaten Mexican bread, it's delicious." They were all nibbling wedges of something crisp and stiff.

On the table were stacked disks a foot in circumference and thin-edged, they were piled a foot high and now Leslie saw the last of these being taken out of the third skillet and placed neatly on top of the stack. Adarene broke off a generous wedge from one of the crisp disks—the last one, still hot from the skillet—and

Leslie munched it and found it rather flat-tasting and said it was delicious.

Adarene Morey moved closer, her voice was low in Leslie's ear. "Talk to Vashti Hake, go over and talk to her, will you?"

Leslie looked into the kind intelligent eyes. "Thank you, Adarene."

Adarene Morey's voice went on, very low. "The Hakes are old ranch family. Texas ranch girls don't marry cow hands much, no matter what the storybooks say."

Casually Leslie strolled over to where Vashti Hake stood smiling defiantly, surrounded by a little group of the Girls. They were drinking coffee again, before dinner, steaming tin cups of the hot brew. They wandered about in their pretty shoes and their delicate summer dresses.

"Now Pinky! You, Bick! It's a scandal the way you're neglecting your brides, I'm surprised they stay with you."

The little knot loosened somewhat to disclose a bottle and the tin cups. "We're drinking a toast to the brides. Any you girls like a splash of bourbon?"

Leslie slipped her hand into that of the moist and rumpled Vashti, she searched in her bewildered mind for the right thing to say—she, one of the quick-witted Lynnton girls. "Uh—it's wonderful to come to Texas a brand-new bride and find there's a bride even newer living on the next ranch."

The big bosom heaved. "Oh, I guess you and Bick won't have much time for me—and Mott."

"Oh, but we will. We brides must stick together, you know."

"I noticed you call Bick by his right name, Jordan. I do that too. I call my husband by his right name, Mott. Everybody else calls him Pinky but I think the way you do, it's more dignified to call your husband by a name isn't just a nickname everybody uses. A wife is something special."

"Oh, very special," Leslie said, "I couldn't agree more with ____"

Floundering for an end to this speech Leslie was saved by the shout that went up as two vaqueros bore the steaming succulent treasure that had emerged from the hole in the ground. Leslie came forward with the group round the table. Tin plates. A clatter of steel cutlery. Leslie had known the fish dinners and clambakes of the Atlantic shore—the steaming pits from which emerged the juicy lobsters and clams and crabs and the sweet corn, all drenched with hot butter sprinkled with salt and pepper, the whole melting on the tongue, sweet and succulent beyond description.

These men were carrying a large sack, dark, wet, and steaming. This outer sack they deftly slit with sharp bright knives. Beneath it was another cloth, lighter and stained with juices. Still thus encased, the burden was carried to the table and placed on a great flat wooden board. They were crowded all round the table now, and in each hand was a wedge of the crisp thin bread.

The feast dish. Cloths that covered it were unrolled carefully, there floated from the juice-stained mound a mouth-watering aroma of rich roast meat. Leslie thought of her school days when the class had read Lamb's essay on roast pig, and how all the children's mouths—certainly her own—had watered at the description of the crackling savory meat.

The final layer of wrapping was removed. A little Vesuvius of steam wafted upward on the hot noonday air. There on the table was the mammoth head of an animal. It was the head complete. The hide—hair and the outer skin—had been removed, but all the parts remained, the eyes sunken somewhat in the sockets but still staring blindly out at the admiring world. The tongue lolled out of the open mouth and the teeth grinned at the Texans who were smiling down in anticipation. Collops of roast meat hung from cheeks and jowls.

"M-m-m-m!" cried the Girls.

"There's another down in the pit where this came from," shouted Pinky Snyth jovially. "Can't fool me. I saw it."

"We'll sure enough need it," Bale Clinch bellowed. "Appetites these girls have they're liable to leave us boys with nothing but the ears."

Curiously enough they stood as they ate. Deftly Eusebio jerked the tongue out, he sliced off the crown of the head, someone began to peel the smoking tongue and to cut it neatly on the wooden board. The hot spicy tidbits were placed on the pieces of thin crisp bread held out so eagerly and there arose little cries of gustatory pleasure.

"Here," Vashti said, and hospitably extended to her erstwhile rival a moist slice on a wedge of bread. "If you don't say this is about the best barbecue you ever ate."

"It's been eighteen hours cooking," Ollie Whiteside explained in his slow pontifical voice that was to stand him in such good stead when years later he attained his judgeship.

"How interesting," Leslie murmured faintly.

"Needs a sprinkle of salt," Vashti cautioned her.

Bick was regarding her with some anxiety and, she thought, a shade disapprovingly. Through her mind, as she smiled and accepted the food held out to her, went an argument founded on clear reasoning against instinct. You're being silly and narrow-minded. You've eaten cold sliced tongue, where did you think it came from—did you think it was born on a silver platter bordered with sprigs of watercress? After all, perhaps Texans wouldn't like the idea of lobsters and oysters and crabs, they're not very attractive either when they come up from the baking pit, with all those claws and tails and whiskers.

Bick was talking, he was explaining something to her. His low charming voice flowed over her soothingly. "This is the real Spanish-Mexican barbecue, Leslie. They despise what we Americans call a barbecue—meat roasted over coals. This pit-cooking is the real Mexican barbacoa. That's where we get the word."

"How fascinating," Leslie managed to murmur again. "Barbacoa."

"You see, we take a fresh calf's head and skin it and place it in a deep pit dug in the ground on a bed of hot mesquite coals. We wrap the head in clean white cloths and then tightly in canvas and down it goes the night before, and it cooks down there for eighteen hours——"

Now spoons were being used. With glad cries the Girls were

dipping into the top of the head and removing spoonfuls of the soft gelid brains and placing them on fresh pieces of bread with a bit of salt sprinkled on top. Joella Beezer, a hearty matron, brought up an eye with her spoonful. Leslie turned away, she felt she was going to be very sick, she steeled herself, she turned back, she smiled, she felt a little cold dew on her upper lip and the lip itself was strangely stiff.

"Eat while it's hot!" Miz Wirt Tanner urged her. "They's plenty more."

"I'm not very hungry, really. Perhaps if I just had a little of the rice and some coffee. I'm not accustomed to the—the heat—yet."

"My gosh, this ain't hot. Wait till July!"

She ate. She drank. She talked. She laughed. She said delicious how do they make it the rice is so yes indeed we eat it in the East though we usually think of Virginia as the South but of course it must seem East to you there is a dish we sometimes calves' brains with a black butter sauce.

The second head was brought up from the pit, was eaten though perhaps without the gusto of the first. Replete, then, the little company wandered off and left the littered table to the vaqueros and to old Eusebio. "It was wonderful," Leslie said to him. Her new word came to mind. "Delicioso. Gracias." The old mummy face with the live-coal eyes bowed statelily, accepting his due as a culinary artist.

She had not disgraced herself, she had not disgraced Jordan, she drew a long breath of achievement. She laughed and chatted, seated on a tree stump, feeling strangely lightheaded and cool in the blinding sun. One of the vaqueros at the table so recently deserted was pouring a full measure of molasses into a tin cup and now he sat spooning it up with relish, as though it were ice cream. In a corner under the open shed another of the Mexicans had got hold of the calf's head from which the company had so recently eaten. As she watched him he took a piece of bread and plunged his hand into the open top of the empty skull, he wiped the interior briskly round and round with the bit of bread, he brought the morsel up, dripping, and popped it into his eager open mouth.

Someone asked her a question, she turned her face up to the questioner, she smiled a stiff contortion of the mouth, she even arranged a reply of sorts in her mind, but it never was uttered. At that moment the bunkhouse tipped toward her, the sky rolled with it and the ground rose up in front of her and rapped her smartly on the head.

For the first time in her healthy twenty-odd years Leslie Lynnton had fainted dead away.

12

"NO," the doctor (hurriedly summoned from Benedict) said. "No, no sign of it I can see. Sun got to her, I'd say." The doctor from Benedict had worn boots and a Stetson and this had outraged Leslie's deep feeling for the medical profession, though she did not express her protest. She had shut her eyes and her mind against him, she had refused to answer his questions. "I feel perfectly well, really. I feel quite wonderful. It was just—Jordan—if you'll just——" She whispered in Bick's ear. "Make him go away. Please."

Very white she lay then in the big bare bedroom at Reata

and Bick had sent for Doctor Tom Walker at Vientecito. When he came in Leslie knew it was all right. He was a small slight man, his suit his shoes his hat were the clothes she had been accustomed to see worn by middle-aged men in Virginia's hot weather—by her father. Rather rumpled linen stuff, pale in color, with neat white or blue shirt and small bow tie and easy comfortable black or tan oxfords. He placed the soft straw hat and the scuffed black bag on a table and came over to the bed. He did not take her hand he did not feel her pulse, he did not say "Well, how are we?" heartily. He just stood there, dabbing his forehead a little with a white handkerchief.

"How nice," said Leslie to her own astonishment. She had not in the least meant to say it, it had blurted itself out.

"I never will get used to this damned heat," Doctor Walker said. "I'll just go in and wash my hands. How are you, Bick? I heard you'd married. High time."

She heard the water and his hearty splashing and then he stood in the bathroom doorway wiping his hands briskly and talking casually.

"This climate's new to you, h'm?"

"Yes."

"It takes a while. I was saying to Bick downstairs. I'm from Tennessee myself but this is different. I wouldn't want to live anywhere else now, this is wonderful country but you have to get used to it and look at it the long view. Fifty years from now."

"Fifty years!" She did a simple problem in arithmetic. "I'll be seventy-three! Seventy-three!"

"That's a nice age. You'll see wonderful things in Texas when you're seventy-three."

"I won't care then."

"Yes you will. Especially if you've been part of it."

"You sound like my father," she said then.

He had finished wiping his hands, he folded the towel neatly, he came again to the bedside, relaxed and easy. Now he picked up her hand as it lay there so inert on the coverlet.

"And who is he?"

She watched his face intently. If he didn't know when she said it he was no good either, just like the other one. He was intent on her pulse. "His name is Lynnton. Doctor Horace Lynnton."

There was one sign only, and she noted this because her eyes were so intent on his face. His eyes had widened, then the lids had dropped again over them. His hand was cool and steady on her wrist. He placed her hand gently on the coverlet, he smiled a little. The routine. The chest, the lungs, the back, the stomach, the heart, the belly.

"She'll be all right I think," he said turning to Bick Benedict standing so tensely at the bedside. "I'd say a temporary fatigue and a sort of—have you had a shock?"

"No."

"She's been fine," Bick said. "She's been wonderful until just today. When she fainted we thought—some of the women thought maybe——"

"Maybe next week you'll drive to my office where I can really examine you properly. You do that, will you?"

Doctor Tom Walker took out his pad and fountain pen, he began to write a prescription in a neat hand. He finished it, he capped the pen and he snapped his shabby black bag. He looked up at Bick, his glance went about the stark room with its incongruous drifts of silk and flashes of silver and crystal that bespoke her occupancy there. His eyes came to rest on her face.

"Horace Lynnton's daughter."

"Do you know him?"

"Do I know Horace Lynnton. It's like asking a private in the infantry if he knows the General of the Army."

She felt the tears, hot and stinging, in her eyes. "Thank you," she said inadequately. Then, "I'll write him you said that. No I won't. He'll think I'm ill."

"You're not," Doctor Walker said.

"What about it, Tom?" Bick asked. "What about it then? What made her faint and stay that way so long? She just wouldn't come to. I don't know how long. I guess I went kind of crazy I was so scared."

"Unconscious a long time, h'm?"

"The heat I suppose, eh, Tom? It wasn't a really hot day but maybe if you're not used to it, and in the morning I hear she ran around a lot in the sun."

Luz, Leslie said to herself. She told him—she or someone. Told him what? It doesn't matter. I went for a walk.

Doctor Tom Walker was silent. Then he stood up and he had the air of one who has made a decision. "Fainting is a way of shutting out of your consciousness something you find repellent. In the old days ladies used to do it quite a bit. It was a kind of weapon. They don't use it so much nowadays because they're more free to rebel against what they don't like. This young lady doesn't look like the fainting kind to me."

Bick brushed this aside with some impatience. "Yes. Sure. But what do you advise now? What's the thing to do for Leslie?"

Tom Walker seemed to ponder this a moment. "Well, Bick, if I were married to this girl I guess I'd spend the rest of my life cherishing her—no, I'll give you the advice of a man of medicine, not a romantic. You see, all this is new to Mrs. Benedict."

"Leslie," she murmured rather drowsily from the bed. She was feeling strangely relaxed, suddenly, and lighthearted and understood.

"New to Leslie. Beginning marriage is an adjustment under the most simple of circumstances. But when you have to adjust to marriage and Texas at the same time! Well, that's quite a feat."

"Now Tom! You're talking to an old Texian, just aiming to rile me."

Doctor Walker shook his head then, hopelessly; he turned to Leslie. "Tell me, if you could do whatever you liked here what would you want to do?"

She sat up vigorously and pushed her hair back from her forehead. Her face was sparkling, animated. "I feel better. I feel wonderful. Do you mean exactly whatever I'd want to do forever—or for a week, perhaps?"

Doctor Walker, neatly packing his stethoscope, looked at Bick Benedict. "Let's start with a week."

Bick had been standing at the foot of the bed, his eyes intent on her. Now he came to the side of the bed and sat down and took Leslie's hand. Absent-mindedly he ran his thumb over the narrow band that was her wedding ring. "Hardly anybody in the world can do exactly as they please for a week."

"Why not! If no one else is hurt by it."

Then, simultaneously, as though rehearsed, the two men asked, "What do you want to do?"

The three laughed, tension snapped, the doctor's visit took on an air of coziness. Leslie smoothed the coverlet with her free hand, her face serious and thoughtful. She raised her eyes to the window and the brazen sky, she glanced at Doctor Tom Walker and then her eyes came to rest in Jordan Benedict's eyes.

"I want to go into the kitchen and cook two chickens—pan-roast them—a quick broil first to brown and then a slow oven. Delicious. In butter and a strip or two of bacon for flavor. I want to whip up a meringue. With strawberries on top. Are there strawberries in Texas? . . . I want to go to Benedict and walk in the town and look in the store windows and I want to see the side streets where people live in their houses. . . . I want to have the piano tuned. . . . I want to see the Alamo at San Antonio. . . . I want to learn to speak Spanish. . . . But most of all I want to go with you, Jordan—I want that more than anything— to go with you and see what you do. I promise not to bother you —just to have someone show me and let me see and learn about the ranch. . . . And I'd like to talk—I mean good talk with all kinds of people at dinner and after dinner . . . and books . . . and flowers in the house . . ."

Bick's brow was furrowed. "Look, Leslie honey. You'll do all these things in time. But why not just relax for a while and take things as they are. Don't you think so, Doc?"

The slight figure in the rumpled linen suit stood looking down at the two seated there on the bed, hand in hand and miles apart. Slowly he tore into small scraps the prescription he had so recently written, he gathered the bits neatly in his palm and, walking over to the desk, he let them sift slowly out of his fingers into the wastebasket. "I think Leslie's prescription is better than this one. I'd advise you to try it. . . . Well, I'll be getting along." He stooped for his bag. Then, without glancing over his shoulder he said, "Come on in, Miss Luz. The diagnosis has been made, there's nothing wrong. Just a rush of ambition to the ego."

And there was Luz Benedict, not at all embarrassed at being caught. Doctor Tom looked at her, he quirked one eyebrow. "You weren't eavesdropping, were you, Madama?"

"There's no call to get personal, Tom Walker. I've got a right to know in my own house——"

"What a word—eavesdropping," Doctor Walker continued ruminatively. "Eaves. Dropping. Hanging over the roof to the eaves' edge, to listen at the window. Or perhaps beneath the window where the eaves used to drip. Eaves dripping, perhaps it used to be. A word caught here and there, drip drip . . ."

"What in the world are you taking the stump about?" Luz demanded.

But now the three seemed again as unconscious of her presence as when she had been lurking, unseen, in the hall. "What do you think, Doc?" Bick Benedict asked again, worriedly.

"I'm a man of medicine. Are you asking me as a physician or as an average intelligent man with a wife and three children?"

"Both."

Tom Walker leaned against the doorway, his bag in his hand. "I'd say, as a man and a doctor, there's nothing Leslie wants to do that isn't good and proper and even mighty helpful and shows the right spirit in a young wife. She wants to go into her kitchen and cook. Well what's wrong with that! She wants to learn about her new home. She wants to see the sort of work her husband does, and how he does it. She wants to acquaint herself with the town in which her husband has lived all his life and in which she will spend the rest of her days. She wants to play the piano and talk about things of the mind and the emotions. She wants— what was that other thing?—oh, yes, she wants to learn something of the history of the most colorful and dramatic and ornery state in the United States of America. If there were more wives like that——"

"I run this house." Luz Benedict's voice was high and shrill. "Her house! Her kitchen! I should think anybody'd be glad to have all that responsibility taken off them. She can't even speak Spanish——"

"I forgot that one," Tom Walker put in, but she went on, unheeding.

"—they would make out that they don't understand English the way they do when they don't want to understand or do something. Whyn't you just relax," she demanded, turning directly to the girl, her voice taking on a wheedling note. "Bick and me, we just want for Leslie here to have a good time." She apparently was addressing Doctor Tom Walker but her eyes were on Leslie. "She ain't real strong, you can see that. And look at what happened at the barbecue, just toppling over like a person dropped dead." This last with a certain relish. "Poor delicate child, so ganted."

Leslie, sitting up in bed, seemed now to tower as she sat. She flung the bedclothes aside and swung her long legs in a decorous arc so that in one swooping movement she had got out of bed, was standing in her nightgown, had thrust her arms into her robe and was wrapping it about her with the air of one who buckles on a coat of mail.

"Luz Benedict," she said, very distinctly, "I'm not going to behave like Dora in *David Copperfield,* I'm not the crushed little bride in a Victorian novel, and you're not going to behave like a fantastic combination of Rosa Dartle and Aunt Betsey Trotwood——"

"We don't read Dickens in Texas," Doctor Tom interrupted.

"I don't want to take your place, Luz Benedict, but I won't have you take mine, either. I know I can't take over this huge house twenty-four hours after I've come into it. I don't want to, yet. But I won't be a guest in my husband's house, I won't pretend I've just dropped in for a meal like those people at breakfast yesterday—or was it today—I'm all mixed up, it seems days ago."

187

"You see," said Luz.

Bick came to Leslie, he held her to him. "Leslie honey, you're tired and upset and you don't seem awfully strong——"

"Look here. Listen a minute." Tom Walker had an edge to his speech now, very unlike the soft casual tone of a few minutes earlier. "What are you trying to do? Break her down! Let me tell you something. This girl is as wiry as a steel spring and as indestructible. She's sound and strong and she'll bounce back when you two big high-blood-pressured people are wondering why you feel so tired after eating all that beef. You let her do as she rightly pleases." He picked up his bag again and turned toward the door, then he wheeled and turned back, his mouth smiling but his eyes serious. "And Luz, I've known you long enough to be sure that when you go in for that Texas homesy folksy lingo you sure got your kettle on fur somebody to git scalded. Honey." He made for the door, one hand held high in farewell. "Call me if you need me, any hour of the day or night." He was gone. Bick was after him. "Tom! How about a drink or a cup of coffee?"

And Tom Walker's voice from the stair well. "Next time, Bick. Lot of people to see, they think they'll feel better if I look at them, it's all in the mind." You heard the snort of his car in the drive.

The two women in the bedroom looked at each other. "That's all right," Luz said meaninglessly. Her usual high color was drained away now and Leslie found herself startled by this aspect, there seemed something sinister in the new white face.

Leslie said, "Let's have everything clear and open, Luz, and then there won't be these dreadful hidings and listening and little insinuations. I'm sorry if that sounds rude. I'm just trying to be honest."

"That's all right," Luz said again.

"I'm going to dress now. I feel just fine. It must be nearly dinner time. I'm going down to see what there is in that great enormous ice chest in that great enormous pantry and the one in the kitchen too, and wherever else there is one." At the look in Luz's face, "I think I'll go down right now, in my wrapper, and settle it. No steak."

13

BICK HAD SAID that night, "How about riding out with me after breakfast? Horses, I mean." Then, at her look of pure joy, "Yes, I know. But I start before daylight and it's a far piece down there. Dusty and noisy and hotter than today. Roundup."

"Roundup!" She repeated the word as though he had said Venice—lagoons—gondolas—music—love in the moonlight.

"It's tough going and you haven't felt so—yes, I know what Tom Walker said, you're all set to outlive me in a lot of coquettish black from Bergdorf's or Neiman's. But just the same today was a bad time."

"The barbecue," she murmured. "Not wishing to seem ungrateful, sir, but the barbecue."

"We'll eat from the chuck wagon. Rosendo's a good cook, I've ordered a special—no, I won't tell you. Anyway, no barbecued calves' heads. Jett'll drive you home when it gets too hot, I don't want you to ride back in the sun. He'll call for you with the car."

"Oh, Jordan, it sounds heavenly!"

"It isn't like the movies. Don't expect romance. What you'll see is rough."

She was happy. Even next morning when she wakened to the scent of strong coffee in the blackness and heard the murmur of faraway talk belowstairs she dismissed from her mind the sure knowledge that she was the subject of the conversation over the pre-breakfast coffee in the vast kitchen. Luz and Jordan. Luz talking, talking, Jordan placating. Buzzbuzzbuzz. Mumblemumblemumble. On and on. Defiantly she put on robe and slippers and slip-slapped down to the source of the sound. It led to the kitchen. There they sat at the kitchen table, Luz and Bick, elbows on the table, drinking their coffee before the first fingers of dawn had tapped at the windows. Through the years it continued to madden her that everyone in Texas rose before dawn, reason or no reason. Up early, to bed late, a vestigial custom left over from pioneer days, as useless now as the appendix.

"Good morning!" she cried and then thought, I sound like Mama. "Can I have—uh—I'm having a cup of coffee, too, before I dress."

Bick was in boots, canvas, shirt. "I was going to wake you when I got up. But I smelled Luz's coffee so I beat it downstairs first."

Leslie looked at Luz. She was dressed for riding. "I'll be dressed in a minute. Jordan and I are riding out to the roundup."

"I know."

"I thought we'd better begin to get acquainted. Honeymoons don't count, you're on your good behavior. Mm, lovely!" as she sipped her coffee. The Mexican servants were slipping into the kitchen, they made their morning greetings formally and respectfully, first to Jordan Benedict, the mighty male. Buenos días, señor. Buenos días, señora. Buenos días, madama. "Are my riding clothes going to be right?"

"You'd better let me give you a brush jacket," Bick said. "We go through mesquite some of the way. What's your hat?"

"Very informal. Just a little round-brimmed riding hat."

"That's no good. You'll be burned alive. Your face and the back of your neck. Luz, find her a jacket and a hat. . . . You know, all this stuff we wear in Texas isn't because it looks good in the movies."

So she rode in a haphazard costume made up of her own pants with glittering Eastern riding boots and high-necked shirt, a Texas brush jacket and a ten-gallon hat. The moon was still in the sky as the sun came up. Moonlight and starlight and sunlight, and the dawn air cool and a little moist and the Gulf wind stirring only gently. "This is the best time of day," Leslie found herself saying. "That's why they get up early. Now I know. Just give me time and I'll learn."

"That's why. That, and habit, and a few million head of cattle in these parts to see to."

The Mexican boys stood with the horses in the dim cool morning. No sound as they came down the steps but the stamp of the waiting horses' hoofs. "I wish one of them would neigh."

"Why?"

"No reason. Except that it would make the whole thing perfect."

Luz did not see them off. As they rode away Leslie found herself going over in her mind anything she might have left in her room in the way of letters, notes, memoranda. Then she was ashamed of having allowed this suspicion to enter her mind.

It was hard riding, she was unaccustomed to this broad Western saddle, the mesquite was a hazard, their talk was disjointed. Leslie felt free and gay and new. To ride again was exhilarating after days of trains and hotels and automobiles. She was to see the purpose of these millions of acres, she was to be part of the everyday work of Reata Ranch and of every ranch in this gargantuan commonwealth. She began to sing out of sheer high spirits, whereupon her horse stopped.

"Why did he do that?"

"He's a cow pony. When the cattle were restless the boys used to sing to them. Just sitting in the saddle, singing sort of slow and gentle. It quieted them. They don't do it much any more. That was in the old days—my grandfather's day—when they drove the big herds overland. One of the old hands must have broken in that pony of yours."

"It's enough just to feel like singing. This is what I hoped it would be. I shan't do any fainting today, Jordan. My very own Jordan. That sounds silly to you but it doesn't to me."

"I didn't say it sounded silly."

"A whole new life, brand new, for me. Imagine!"

"Girls do have, don't they, when they marry?"

"Leigh didn't. My sister Leigh."

"She married Karfrey, didn't she? And went to England to live? And he's a member of the English nobility. I should think that would have been——"

"But it wasn't. They live in Kent. In a house in the country in Kent. And people who live in a big comfortable house in Virginia have spent the last three hundred years trying to live like their English ancestors. When I visited her three years ago it was so much like Virginia, except that the English take their houses and gardens and clothes and horses more for granted. The cream was thicker, and the tweeds; and the carpets a little shabbier and the manners nicer and the women's voices higher—— Heh, wait a minute!"

"What?"

"The English women's voices. They're rather high and shrill. And the Texas women's voices are higher and shriller. English women have been regarded as sort of second-rate citizens for centuries. And Texas women seem to live in a kind of purdah. So they both talk in a high shrill way in order to get male attention."

"You're getting too much male attention at the moment, Mrs. Benedict. We'll get there by noon, at this rate."

"It's so wonderful to be talking to you alone like this. I thought I'd never have a chance to talk to you again."

They rode side by side now. "Have to be careful of gopher holes here. Your horse step into one of those he can throw you— or he can break a leg."

"Can't I wait for you so that we can ride back together when you're finished?"

"No, it'll be too hot then. And no telling when I'll be through. You'll see why after you've sat out in the sun for a few hours. Yesterday they nooned at the creek but today there'll be no shade. Jett will call for you and drive you home after lunch."

"Tell me about this Jett Rink."

"Jett's all right when he behaves himself. When he drinks he goes kind of crazy. I've fired him a dozen times but he always seems to turn up back at the ranch, one way or another. He's a kind of genius, Jett is."

"He is! Why, he just seemed to me a sullen loutish kind of boy. And sort of savage, too. I don't know. What do you mean, genius?"

"Oh, lots of ways. Machinery. Mechanics. There's nothing he can't fix, nothing he can't run that has an engine in it. That's invaluable around a modern ranch this size."

"You mean he's the only one?"

"One! There are dozens all over the place. But not like that locoed Rink. He's a wizard—when he's sober. But drunk or sober he doesn't belong on a ranch because you can't trust him with animals."

"How do you mean—trust him?"

"He's naturally mean with them. He abuses them. Kicks horses. Hits them over the head. I've seen him slam a calf right——"

"Don't! Don't tell me. I don't want to hear it. But why? That's what I want to know."

"He's got a grudge against the world."

"He sounds an exquisite escort for your bride."

"Don't you worry. I wouldn't let you drive back with him if I didn't know. He knows his place when it comes to the family.

A funny thing, the girls are hot for him, even the Mexican girls and you know how strict their parents are with them."

"No, I don't know."

"That's so, you don't. Well, they are. Regular old Spanish stuff, even the poorest of them. The girls don't go out alone with boys, sometimes they hardly have a chance to speak to the man they marry until after they're married. At the Mexican dances their mothers sit on the side lines like the old Boston and New York dowagers before the stag line came in. You've got to see it. Not a peso to their names, the fathers are cotton pickers if they're lucky, and you'd think the girls were just out of some finishing school. Of course our boys—the Reata vaqueros—they wouldn't let Jett come within a mile of their girls."

They had long ago ceased really to ride. They were sitting on their horses and the horses were walking as sedately as though they were not descended from the Arab horses brought into the country by the Spaniards centuries earlier; as though they had never been broken and trained with a hackamore, a snaffle bit or a rope.

"He sounds irresponsible and sadistic," she said.

"He'll probably end up a billionaire—or in the electric chair," Bick predicted.

The nearer the bone the sweeter the meat. It floated to the surface of her consciousness, she thrust it back. "I suppose ranches are sadistic sort of places, aren't they? I mean they make you——"

"Ranches are full of life and death and birth, if that's what you mean. A couple of hundred thousand of any living thing and you're likely to see some pretty fundamental stuff going on."

"I know. Give me time, darling. It's going to take me a while."

In silence they rode for a moment. Only the creak of leather, the faint jingle of metal. Horses' hoofs on sun-baked earth. Texas sounds.

"Leslie, since we came home I've been up to my ears in work. Maybe you've felt left out of things. Look, it's like this. I'm pulling one way—I think it's the right way—and Luz and Maudie

GIANT

and Bowie and Roady and the rest of them they're all pulling
another. They want the money—all the money they can get out
of the ranch. And I want to put money back into the ranch. It
takes a lot. I want to raise and breed the best beef cattle in the
world, I want to experiment with new breeds and new grasses,
I'm interested in the same sort of thing that Kleberg's interested
in on the big King ranch. Years ago those fellows on the old XIT
ranch had an inkling of the future but of course they hadn't much
technical knowledge, they didn't really know modern breeding
or range rehabilitation. Neither did the old Matador crowd. All
the big operators. They used up the range and shipped the cattle
and finished them in the East and bred the old Longhorns to
Herefords, Angus, Jersey, Swiss—anything that didn't die right
off from the ticks and the worms and the heat. The only one of
the family who's with me on the program I've mapped out is
Uncle Bawley up at the Holgado Division. Say, I've an idea you'll
be crazy about old Uncle Bawley. He's a character. Nearly seventy
but full of beans. We'll have to take a trip out there, you'll love
it. It's high country, the mountains——"

"Mountains! In Texas!"

"Sure mountains. There's everything in Texas. Mountains and
forest and rivers and desert and plains and valleys and heat and
cold."

"I know. You're in love with it."

He reined his horse, he looked at her, his eyes full of pain.
"Maybe it's going to be hell for you down here. Maybe I shouldn't
have brought you to Texas."

"It's a little late now. We're in it, darling. You didn't marry a
Texas belle."

"You're on that again, h'm? I will say Luz tried to shoo off
most of them but she was hell-bent on my marrying Vashti and
the reason was that one end of the Hake ranch touches ours, it's
like the old plot in the mellerdrama."

"Jordan, did it ever strike you that Luz is a little—melodramatic herself?"

"Luz! She's just a bossy old maid who wants to be everybody's

195

mother. She feeds the world—or would if it came near her kitchen, she knows everybody's business and thinks she runs Reata."

"And you."

"Funny thing, you know years ago she was supposed to marry old Cliff Hake. He wasn't old then, he was a handsome young heller, they tell me, big beefy fellow, but she didn't want to go to the Double B to live, she wanted to combine the two ranches and bring the whole thing under Reata. Of course Cliff wouldn't hear of it and they split up. Would you believe it!"

"Yes, I'd believe it. And so you were to marry Vashti in her place, all these years and years later. And now Vashti is married to that little pink man all because of you. Or really because of Luz."

"I meant to marry. Not Vashti, but I meant to marry, God knows there were plenty of girls around. I'm saying that without meaning to be a stinker. But I wasn't in love with any of them. Maybe you're right. Maybe I was in love with cattle."

"And power."

"How do you mean—power?"

"Papa says——"

"You set great store by your father, don't you?"

"I suppose I was in love with him in my own way just as you——"

"I don't like that kind of talk. It's ugly."

"Why no, dear. I'm just talking—uh—scientifically."

"Women have no call to be scientific."

"Not even Madame Curie?"

"What the hell has she got to do with it!"

"Nothing. Everything."

"Half the time I don't know what you're talking about. I don't believe you do either."

"I do this time. I don't think Texas is free at all. Free, the way you said it was. I've been here two days and every natural thing I've said and done has been forbidden. I'm not reproaching you. I'm just stating a fact that astonishes me. Speaking to the em-

ployees as if they were human beings like myself. Wanting to wear
pretty clothes in my home. Not liking to eat out of skulls. There
are—I'm warning you—certain things I'm going to do, Luz or no
Luz."

"Such as what?"

"I told you yesterday."

"I don't know that I can see my way clear to prettifying the
house. Pa spent enough on that big pile and Ma never even
lived to enjoy it. Anyway, the ranch comes first, every time,
always. I put all the money I can scrape together into new proj-
ects. We're working on a new dozer for clearing the mesquite. If
it works it's a human monster. We're setting up a testing station
for grasses. Gill Dace and I are working on the new breed of
cattle. The Herefords can't take this climate, they get the pinkeye
and worms, and the fleas and worms together eat the calves alive.
It cost me plenty to learn that. You should have heard the family
at the last yearly meeting! You'd think I was embezzling the
funds."

"Then why don't you let them do it?"

"It's for me to do. They're just a lot of money-eaters. Maudie
Lou and that husband of hers, they like yachts. Yachts! For a
girl born and brought up in Texas."

She gazed about her at the flat endless burning plain.

"Rebellion," she said.

But he went on, he seemed not to have heard. "If we can breed
up just one animal that will start a new race of cows. The tough
old Longhorns could stand the heat and the tick but their meat
was like rawhide."

Still is, she thought privately.

"Wait till you see the Kashmirs! Humped like camels,
grey-greenish velvet coats, there's an oil in their skins that repels
the fleas. If we can combine the Hereford meat and the Short-
horn strength and the Kashmir resistance! I'm willing to spend
the next twenty years of my life in bringing the perfect Kashmir
bull to the perfect Hereford-Shorthorn cow and if I do it's going
to be the most important mating, by God, since Adam and Eve."

"If that's what you want to do more than anything in the world why do you need millions of acres to do it in? A few thousand would do, wouldn't they? We could live in a six-room house and one car and no minions and be free. Free!" She stared about her. "How did you get all these millions of acres, anyway?"

"Never mind how we got it."

"I'm going to read up on it. There must be a book about it somewhere. In the Public Library at Benedict."

"There isn't a public library."

"Why not?"

"Oh, I don't know why not. You're worse than a kid—why why whywhy! All the time. We bought the land. We got it through purchase—my grandfather did. A hundred years ago. We swapped for it. We got it through Spanish land grants. And using our brains. It was my father's and my grandfather's and it's going to be my son's——"

"No one in the whole United States has the right to own millions of acres of American land, I don't care how they came by it."

"You're completely ignorant of what you're talking about. In my grandfather's day there was enough range grass to support a steer on two acres of land. In another five years you did mighty well if you could feed a steer on six acres. Now there are whole sections—hundreds of miles of Texas range—that won't support even one steer to every sixty-five acres. Even on what we call good range it takes a full twenty acres to feed a steer. It's gone to desert. And the ranchers just spend their time hoping at the sky."

"What made it that way, if it was all right years ago? Where did the grass go?"

"I never saw any woman ask so many damn questions!"

"I just want to know, darling. How else am I going to learn about Texas?"

"Come on," he said abruptly. "Let's get riding. We're headed for a roundup. Remember? That's my business. That's the way I earn my living."

"Living! How about life! You just look upon life as an annoying interruption to ranching. I stole that. It was first said in another way by a French writer named Gide—or maybe it was Proust. Pretty soon I'll forget how to read."

"I told you what it was like down here. The first time I met you. Now you've seen the setup. You know what it is. Like it or not, this is it."

"Jordan, let's not—Jordan, I'm going to love it. It's just that——"

"Reata takes all my time. It always will. You'll be a neglected wife. Everything's against you—climate—people—family—customs. I know. I warned you." He looked at her, his eyes agonized, pleading. "I love you. I love you. I love you."

The two horses stood close, side by side, leather creaking on leather. They stood like good Texas cow horses while the man and woman strained toward each other there in the saddles, his knee against hers, his thigh against hers, his shoulder his lips on hers there in the brilliant wild endless Texas plain, in the early morning scent of the desert spring and the false coolness and the faint false green of the unavailing mesquite.

She looked at him as they drew apart slowly. At no time in her life, before or after this moment, was Leslie Lynnton so nearly beautiful. They sat a moment, withdrawn, like two figures on a too highly colored Remington calendar print.

"It's going to be wonderful," she said finally, "and terrible. I suppose we're in for a stormy future. I'm going to try to change you and you're going to be impatient when I don't melt into all this." She swept the vastness with her arm.

"I'll try not to be."

"Whoever said love conquers all was a fool. Because almost everything conquers love—or tries to."

The sun was up, full blast. Already it was growing hot. Bick gathered up his reins. "Yippee!" he yelled like a character in a Western movie. Without another word they streaked across the prairie mile on mile, they galloped into Number Two Camp to find it a welter of dust, thudding hoofs, color, bellowing, clamor.

"Stay here. Just here. This is Tomaso. He'll take care of you.

If you get tired you can sit on top of the high fence there. You may be better there anyway. Too bad you didn't wear Texas boots, the heels hook in better. A million pairs at the house. Tomaso will look after you. I'll be back. Here, take this. You'll need it. Across your face."

He tossed her his handkerchief and was off into the melee, a figure of steel and iron and muscle.

Cattle. So close-packed that it seemed you could walk on their backs for a mile—for miles as far as the eye could see. From the little sand hills, from the mesquite motts and the cactus came the living streams, a river here a river there, a river of moving flesh wherever the eye rested, and these sluggish lines were added to the great central pool until it became a Mississippi of cattle fed by its smaller tributaries. Little figures on horseback guided the course of these streams. Now Leslie understood, she saw now what Bick had meant when he had said, "She's been the point so long she can't get used to being the drag." These little figures on horseback formed a triangle, and there in front was the point and there at the rear ends the drag. To the east the west and the south these tiny dots on horseback moved the rivers of red and white Herefords, the torrents of cattle with the white clown faces and the pink-rimmed eyes. The bawling of the calves, the bellowing of the cows was earsplitting. Now it was almost impossible to see through the dense clouds of dust. The men wore handkerchiefs tied in a triangle before their faces so that only their eyes were free. Leslie took the big handkerchief that Jordan had tossed to her, she tied it so that her nose and mouth were covered, a Moslem woman in riding clothes. The animals moved close-packed. Curtain on curtain of dust, the men on horseback the men running about on foot were ghostly figures in a fog of dust. Their faces were stern and intent, the riders seemed not riders at all but centaurs part horse part man, swaying with the animals as though they were one body.

They rode headlong into the herd, they seemed not even to touch the reins, they swung slightly in the saddle as the horse wove in and out like a fluid thing. You saw how this weaving movement of man and horse separated the bawling calf from its mother, the high plaintive blatting becoming more anguished as the animal sought frantically to return to the seething mass. Wide-eyed, breathless, Leslie watched this ancient process, unchanged for centuries. These men leaped off their horses, threw the struggling calf and roped him, were on the horse again in a swift single leap and off into the surging herd. As they rode you heard them calling softly, tenderly, quieting the milling frantic sea of cattle. Woo woo woo vaca! Woo woo woo novillo. Woo vaca. Woo woo woo! Like a mother humming to her restless child.

To Leslie it was a legendary scene, incredibly remote from the world she had always known. A welter of noise, confusion; the stench of singeing hair and burned flesh. Perched on the corral fence with Tomaso as bodyguard, her heels hooked on a lower rail, she began slowly to comprehend that in this gigantic melee of rounding-up, separating, branding, castrating there was order; and in that order exquisite timing and actually a kind of art. Here, working with what seemed to her unbelievable courage and expertness, were men riding running leaping; wrestling with huge animals ten times their size; men slim heavy tall short young old bronze copper tan lemon black white. Here was a craft that had in it comedy and tragedy; that had endured for centuries and changed but little in those centuries.

Bick had said, just before he left her with Tomaso, "This is going to be pretty rough, Leslie. I don't want to see you keeling off that fence."

"I promise you I won't do that again. I'm a big girl now."

She saw Bick Benedict—her own husband Jordan Benedict, she told herself with mixed feelings of pride and resentment as she watched him—working in this inferno of heaving flesh and choking dust and noise and movement and daring and danger and brutal beauty. Working like any one of the vaqueros amidst hoofs and flanks and horns.

A ballet, she said to herself. A violent beautiful ballet of America.

Idiotically she turned to Tomaso. "Couldn't it be done some

other way? Without all this danger and I mean not so many—thousands and thousands——"

"Yo no comprendo, señora," said Tomaso, sorrowfully.

She thought she recognized two or three of the men as among those who had been drawn up so proudly in line at the gates as she and Bick had entered Reata—when was it?—yesterday? The day before? A week a month ago? It seemed something far in the past. It was easy to recognize Polo with his air of authority, his unique elegance, the white teeth in that dark fine-boned face. This was, Leslie thought, a henchman such as a king would have. The night of their arrival she had happened to speak again of Polo and his dramatic vaqueros and Bick had said, "Old Polo's practically part of the family. When he was a boy he used to sleep outside my father's door."

Startled, she had said, "How do you mean—outside his door?"

"On the floor in the hall."

"Good heavens, why!"

"I don't know. They do. His son slept outside my door when I was a kid. For that matter, they still do, I suppose. Tomaso or one of the boys around the house."

"Now!" She was aghast.

"They're not there when I come in and they're gone when I get up. It's been going on for a century. I think it's pretty damned foolish, myself."

"Foolish! It's feudal! It's uncivi——"

"Now, now, honey!"

"Sorry."

"You should see the look on your face. I'd give anything to know what you're thinking, Yanqui."

"I was just reassuring myself by thinking of awfully American things. Like pork and beans. And Fourth of July. And Vermont. And pumpkin pie. And Fords. And Sunday school. And cocky Midwestern hired girls in Ohio, when I was a child."

"This is what I call American," he had said.

In a far corner out of the dust of battle old Rosendo had set up a tarpaulin, the chuck wagon was backed handily at its edge.

The wind wafted the scent of his cooking to the scene of feverish activity but it was lost in the stench of the branding. Calves bawled, cows bellowed, men yelled, hoofs pounded, gates slammed, flesh burned, irons clanged, dust swirled, sun glared. Leslie Benedict clung to the fence rail and knew why Texans paid fifty dollars for great cool sheltering ten-gallon Stetson hats.

Up clattered Bick, his teeth gleaming startlingly white in his dust-grimed scarlet face.

"All right, honey?"

"Fine. I want to ask questions."

"I was afraid of that." He pulled his horse up beside her there at the fence. "Hungry?"

She wrinkled her nose. "No."

"You will be when you get to the camp. Old Rosendo's part Mexican part Negro part Indian, he's a real cook, we'd have him up at the house kitchen but he won't work indoors."

"What can he cook under that little pocket handkerchief of a tent?"

"You wait. You'll see."

"Everybody talks Spanish. Tell me, that's Polo, isn't it, who was so splendid and dressy to welcome us."

"Yes. Polo's caporal. Foreman."

"What's he doing? He and the others. It looks cruel but I suppose it isn't."

"Not if America wants to eat. They're roping. And branding. Only the foreman and the bosses and the best of the ropers do that. The others—the men who are throwing the calves—they're called tumbadores. It's a great trick, throwing a calf, there's less to it than meets the eye, really. It looks like a feat of strength but they're not really lifting those calves. You squeeze the calf's ear, it jumps, you pull him sideways and he falls flat on his right side with his left side up, ready for branding. Over there's the branding fire. And those fellows who run the brands, they're really specialists. Marcadores, they're called."

"Marcadores. A lovely word. For such a nasty job. What's it mean?"

"Figure it for yourself, really. Marcar means to mark—to stamp —to brand. Marcadores—markers, branders. It's tricky work. Those irons are red-hot. It's the Reata brand, of course. If they press too hard the calves get a burn sore. If they don't press hard enough the brand won't be clear. They're dehorning too, those other fellows."

"It seems horrible but perhaps it isn't. What are those boys doing? The ones with the sticks and the buckets?"

"They're atoleros. Atole—well, mush. They've got a kind of lime paste in those buckets, they have rags wrapped around those sticks and they smear the lime on the fresh burns to heal them. . . . Well, you wanted to come."

"Don't you worry about me. I'm tougher than I was yesterday. I'm a tough Texan. Go on."

He grinned. "Well, brace yourself. You won't like what comes next."

"The one who's doing something to their ears and——"

"And castrating the male calves. He's the capador. He castrates the males and that makes them steers. And he nicks a piece off the end of the left ear of male and female and sticks it in his pocket, and he marks the right ear with a hole and a slit, for identification. At the end of the day he adds up, and the number of pieces of ear in his pocket shows the number of calves we've branded."

"Jordan Benedict, I'll never eat roast beef again as long as I live."

"Oh, yes you will."

"Don't tell me that's what you've planned for lunch!"

"No. Rest easy. It's chicken and Rosendo's apple pie."

"It just may be I'll never eat *any*thing again. . . . Look, there's a darling little boy putting something in a bucket. Gathering up and putting—why, he can't be more than ten years old. What's he bringing to the fire in the bucket?"

Matter-of-factly Bick said, "That's little Bobby Dietz, his father is ranch boss on Number One."

204

"But what's he doing?"

"Well, you might as well have it straight, you'll be here the rest of your life. He's picking up the testicles of the castrated calves. The tumbadores roast them on the coals, they burst open and they eat them as you'd eat a roast oyster, they're very tasty really and the vaqueros think they make you potent and strong as a bull. They're considered quite a dainty. . . . Come on, honey, it's time for lunch. Here's Tomaso with your horse. And listen—there's Rosendo's bell."

"Why don't the men stop working? I should think they'd be famished."

"They'll eat after we've finished."

On their way to the dinner camp they passed the fire of hot embers and she averted her eyes and then forced herself to look, and to smile. And at Bick's call the little lad came running to their horses, he came shyly, a handsome boy with very blue eyes bluer in contrast with the sun-browned face.

"Hello, Bobby!"

"Howdy, Mr. Bick."

"Where's your father?"

"He went back there in the draw, he says there's a bunch there the boys missed."

"Does, eh?" Bick looked at Leslie. "This kid comes of good stuff. He'll make a wonderful hand when he grows up. What are you going to be when you get to be a man, Bobby? A cowboy?"

"I'm going to be a Ranger, and shoot people."

"Not me!"

"No. Bad people."

"Bobby, this is Mrs. Benedict. This is the new señora."

The deep blue eyes were turned on her like searchlights. "What she wearing them funny clothes for?"

Bick grinned. "She hasn't had time to get some Texas clothes."

And away they cantered from the little boy and his macabre task, but not so far after all, they were to discover twenty-five years later.

Though ten minutes before she had been repelled by the thought of any sort of food under any circumstances, Leslie now found herself eating Rosendo's food with relish, not to say gusto. Having polished off chicken, string beans, apple pie and half a disk of skillet bread she inspected the chuck wagon with its orderly compartments for spices, flour, beans, rice, cutlery, tinware. She complimented the gifted Rosendo and was enchanted with the benign and wrinkled face beneath the vast straw sombrero. She felt well and buoyant of spirits.

"Let me stay this afternoon and come home with you. I'm not tired."

"Two more hours of sun and you'd wish you hadn't."

"I could steal a nap here under the canvas."

"Even a Mexican couldn't sleep under this canvas at noon."

In the burning sun the men were sitting on the ground scooping up their beans and red rice, spooning up molasses and wiping their plates with hunks of bread torn from the great disks stacked on the tent table. Certainly they seemed much less dramatic now squatting before their food, eating wordlessly and concentratedly like the animals they tended.

Sitting there with her husband under the scrap of unavailing canvas the gently bred girl was trying to arrange in her mind a pattern that would bring order into the kaleidoscope of these past three days.

Gropingly, as though thinking aloud, she said, "In Washington and in New York and in Chicago and Detroit and Columbus men get up and take a streetcar or a bus or an automobile and go to work in offices and shops and factories, they write things down, they push a lever, they go to a restaurant and eat lunch and come back to work and weigh something or add up something or sell something or dictate something, and they go home. And that is a day's work. But this!"

"Now what? What's the matter with this?"

"It's incredible, that's all. I can't believe that men earn their living this way. It's too difficult. Why, just look at Polo!"

"Where! What's the matter with him!"

"Nothing, darling. I just mean—look at him on his horse, he looks like a Spanish grandee. I've never seen a Spanish grandee but did Polo do all these circus stunts when he was a young man?"

"He sure enough did. Top hand. That's how he got to be caporal. He can still do them, and better than men half his age."

"How old is he?"

"Nobody knows. I doubt that he does himself. But he's getting too old for this job. And too old-fashioned. Would you believe he keeps his accounts in his head! Hours, wages, stock counts. They always tally, he's never been wrong, no one's ever been able to solve his system of mathematics, but it's infallible. It can't go on, though. I'll have to retire him and put in a modern system like that in the other divisions. I've humored him long enough. You ought to hear Maudie Lou and Bowie and the others on the subject!"

"Why don't they run the ranch, then?"

His head came up, his jaw set, his whole aspect changed as though he had been challenged. "I run this ranch. Don't make any mistake about that."

She looked at old Polo, seated so lightly on his beautiful horse. The vaqueros had finished their noonday meal, they were stretching and yawning, one of them took a mouthful of water from a tin cup and spat it out on the ground in some sort of primitive ablution.

"What will he do then?"

Bick was silent a moment. When he spoke he did not answer her question. "Polo put me on a horse when I was three. He taught us all to ride like the vaqueros, they're the best horsemen in the world, the Mexican cowboys, they're better than those Hungarians that used to show off in all that glitter at the Horse Show in New York. I used to hear my father say that by the time Luz was eight she could ride like a charro."

Charro. Charro? I can't ask questions every minute, I'll buy a Spanish dictionary.

"Dearest, do you work like this every day?"

"Well—no. No, I don't."

"I mean it's wonderful that you can do it, but it's ghastly rough and tough."

He actually blushed a little then beneath the russet burn, and he laughed rather sheepishly, like a boy. "Tell you the truth, honey, I was just showing off today in front of my girl. Like a kid chinning himself on the apple tree."

The men were mounting their horses, fresh horses she saw, from a great cluster of them she had not noticed until now, grazing against the horizon.

"New horses? Are they going to start all over again?"

"Sure, new horses. Or fresh, we'd say. Every Benedict vaquero has got at least ten horses. They've been changing right along, you just haven't noticed. They'll be riding about five different horses each, today. See that bunch of horses over there? That's called a remuda. They're what we call cutting horses. They're used to cut out certain animals from the herd. Trained for it. You don't even have to touch the reins half the time. Just sway your body and your horse will turn with your weight this way or that."

"Jordan! I forgot all about My Mistake. These two or three days have been so new and strange—different I mean. I forgot about My Mistake. Is she here? Where is she? Do you think she'll know me? My girl friend from home in Virginny. She brought us together. She introduced us. I'd never have met you without her. I love her."

"She's out in pasture. Very queenly, with a canvas shade on poles in one corner if she finds Texas too hot. A six-mile pasture, if you want to know. One of the boys has been exercising her a little every day to keep her in shape after the long trip down. I meant to tell you. Obregon there—over there, that tall fellow in the straw hat—had her out yesterday he says she's the finest little——"

"Oh, let me talk to him, will you? I'm homesick for her. Tonight when you get back let's visit her. Or surely tomorrow. Will you? I'll have to write Lacey all about her."

Summoned, the man came toward them. He was noticeably

taller than the average and very slim, with broad shoulders like the American cowboys Leslie had seen in Western motion pictures. His skin was a deep copper color and yet under the skin were freckles, an extraordinary thing. A chin strap held the crimped straw sombrero. His hair was cut in little dandified sideburns along his ears.

"Angel," Bick said as the man came toward them. "Angel Obregon."

"That's the husband of the woman with the baby! Tell him I know his wife. Is he the one? If he has a new baby he is. Yesterday—but then you don't know about it."

The man stood before them. Bick acknowledged his presence with his charming smile and an openhanded gesture as he said, "Un minuto, Angel." He went on speaking to Leslie, his manner leisurely. "The Mexican Obregons stem from some long-ago Irishman named O'Brien. That's the story, anyway. The Irish came in here in 1845, you know, section hands working on the new railroad, and a lot of them married Mexican Indian girls. Look at those shoulders. He inherited those from some pick-and-shovel grandfather named O'Brien. Three generations in Mexico made him an Obregon. Look at the Irish freckles under the copper skin."

"Jordan, he can't like it—standing there while you talk about him as if he were a—a—one of your bulls."

"He doesn't speak English. Look, Leslie, I'm not Simon Legree, you know." He turned to the man. "The little filly you exercised yesterday," he said in Spanish, "is a great favorite of the señora. The horse is her own. She has great feeling for the horse."

The man's face flashed into sudden radiance, he began to speak, the words rolling out with a great drumming of Spanish Rs. "He says she is a miracle of a horse, that she is swifter than any horse in Texas but she is not happy, he says perhaps she longs for her home."

A little involuntary cry came from Leslie. "Oh, Jordan, I must see her. She's homesick for Virginia. I want to put my arms around her neck and comfort her."

"Yes," said Bick stiffly. Obregon was speaking again, his hat was in his hand, he was speaking directly to Leslie in a flood of Spanish, the dark eyes glowing down upon her.

Helplessly she smiled up at the ardent face, then she recalled the words with which Tomaso had expressed his own inability to understand her, "No comprendo," she said triumphantly.

Bick stood up. "He is thanking you for being so kind to his wife yesterday. He says you have worked a miracle, his wife is much improved, his infant son—say what is all this, anyway! I can't have you messing around with——"

But she sprang up, impulsively she laid her hand on the man's arm. "Oh, I'm so glad. Tell her I'll be in to see her again, I'll bring her some delicious things and something for the baby."

"The hell you will! . . . That is all, Obregon. To work now." The man turned away, was off, he mounted his horse for the afternoon's work with the others. The siesta was finished.

The man and woman stared at each other. "Not again," Leslie said.

He came close to her. "You just don't understand. There isn't a ranch in the whole Southwest looks after its people better than we do. But you don't know these people. They're full of superstitions and legends. They believe in the evil eye and witchcraft and every damn thing."

"But he didn't say my eye was evil."

"It was just luck he didn't. If the child or the girl had turned sicker instead of better it would have been because you looked at them. They've got a whole lingo about pregnant women and newborn babies and all that Mexican stuff. You just don't know, honey. Look, the Hake ranch uses some vaqueros. Ask Vashti next time you see her, if you think Luz and I are—feudal, wasn't it?"

A dot had been scurrying like a bug across the prairie. Now it came closer, it spun around in a spiral of dust, it stopped with a yip and a grinding of brakes. The calves ran bleating and scattering. The cattle leaped in terror, the horses reared, the vaqueros muttered imprecations.

"Damn that lout!" Bick said. "If he ever runs down one of those calves I'll beat him up myself."

Jett Rink leaped out and yelled to the world in general, "You et?"

"Sí."

"I ain't."

He heaped a plate with beans stew rice bread and squatting on his haunches he ate the boiling-hot mess in the boiling-hot sun.

"You're late," Bick said.

"It ain't me. I had to catch that horse for Madama."

"What horse?"

"That new one. My Mistake. She wanted to ride her."

"She can't," Leslie cried, and there was outrage in her voice. "She can't! My Mistake's a race horse."

"She's riding her," Jett said coolly, and heaped his plate again with the steaming stew. "She sure hated to put on that Western saddle, that little filly did. Took two of us to get it on her. But Madama, she could ride a bat outa hell."

A trifle worriedly Bick said, "It's all right, Leslie. Luz can ride any four-legged thing." Abruptly he turned to Rink. "Eat your dinner and get going. I want Mrs. Benedict out of this heat."

Jett shoveled the food into his mouth, he gulped and swallowed and wiped his face with his sleeve. He coughed and choked a little. He burst into laughter. "Wait till you see her."

Bick turned back, stared. "See her! See who?"

"Madama. She's riding My Mistake way here. She darned near kept up with me in the car, there for a stretch."

"You're crazy!"

"I ain't the one." Jett laughed again. "You know what else she done? She rigged herself out in a old hoop skirt she got out of the attic, she said her grammaw could ride and rope in a hoop skirt and by God she's got herself rigged out in that outfit, rope and all, and she's riding hell-bent this way, last I saw of her. I'm surprised she ain't here aready. Said not to tell you. Said she'd show you. Acted like she was mad at something, the way she does."

Bick took off his hat and ran his hand over his hot wet forehead. His eyes searched the endless plain.

"Jordan, I want to stay. I want to wait till she comes. My Mistake isn't used to this terrible—to the sun and the brush and that heavy Western saddle. I want to see if she's all right."

Almost harshly he said, "You'll go along with Jett. I'll tend to Luz. Alone. I'll have Angel ride My Mistake home."

"But she'll have to rest first. My Mistake will have to rest. She isn't just a riding horse. A mile—two miles—three—but not this."

"I know a little about horses, honey. It'll be all right, I tell you. I'll send over to a line house—Dietz's place—and get some of Mrs. Dietz's riding stuff for Luz, take that damn masquerade off her. I'll send her home on a horse out of the remuda there. No, I'll put her on the horse you rode here. Gentle as a cow. That'll teach her."

"And when will you be home, Jordan?"

"Oh, God, how do I know! When my work's done."

Two million acres. He works like a cow hand. I've turned into a nagging wife asking her husband when he'll be home. But this is all crazy. Nobody can say it isn't crazy as a nightmare. Hoop skirts and race horses and old-maid sisters with twisted souls.

Her eyes followed Jordan's gaze out across the miles of open range, past the heaving backs of milling cattle and the figures of mounted horsemen. No moving thing dotted the landscape beyond.

Fifty feet away Jett Rink got up, tossed his empty tin plate and cup into the heap, wiped his mouth with the back of his hand.

Quietly Leslie said, "All right, Jordan." She came close to him, she saw the sharp white ridge of the jaw muscle beneath the sunburned skin. The blue eyes were flint-grey.

14

ALMOST GRATEFULLY she had sunk into the hot dusty front seat of the car. "I want to sit up front," she had said to Bick, "so that I can see everything on the way home."

Bick on his horse at the side of the car had leaned over and touched her hand. "We'll make a real Texian of you yet, honey. At that, I don't know any Texas woman who could take the heat and ruckus better than you did. Unless it's Luz."

"Nothing to see, up front, or back," Jett Rink said. But they were oblivious of him.

"I've had a marvelous morning. This was just what I meant. Yesterday, when that nice Doctor Tom asked me."

"You haven't seen anything. It'll take you years."

"I know. And we've got years. Isn't it lucky!"

Bick threw a quick glance around. He leaned far off his horse so that he was standing in one stirrup, his left hand on her shoulder, she leaned toward him he bent far forward into the car, and kissed her hard on the mouth. Instinctively she sensed or saw out of the corner of her eye that Jett Rink's foot moved to press the accelerator, then stopped, poised. She knew that he had suppressed a sudden murderous impulse to start the car with a swift leap while Jordan hung perilously half on the horse, half in the car.

Bick straightened, he turned in his saddle to look back at her as he rode away, his hand held high in farewell. He looked handsome and vital. Suddenly Jett pressed the accelerator hard and caught up with him.

"Look, Bick, can I take her around by the other way, the long back road? If she wants to see things, different things."

Bick looked down at them, hesitating. "Oh yes, Jordan," Leslie said. "If it's a different way."

Reluctantly he said, "Well, all right. But you, Jett, don't you get any big touring notions in that empty sheepherder's head of yours." He grinned. "Put him in a car and he goes road-crazy. Last December he started out to take Cora Dart—that's the schoolteacher—to the fiesta in Viento. Ended up at the Cowboy Christmas Ball at Anson in Jones County, better than two thirds the way up across Texas."

Jett's grin was sour. "Sure. Vamos por la casa. That's me."

They stared hard at each other. It was, Leslie thought, as though they hated one another and yet there was a kind of understanding—almost a bond—between them.

Now they shot off at terrific speed over the vast bare terrain. But once the camp had dwindled in the distance they slowed down, Jett was driving at the merest horse-and-buggy jog.

GIANT

"You want to go round Benedict way, seeing you didn't make it walking yesterday?"

"How did you know I started to walk to town?"

"Like I told you, everybody knows everything anybody does around here."

Enough of that. "Where is the road—the highway? You said you were taking the long road back."

"This here is it."

"But this is just a little wider than the one we took this morning with the horses. It isn't really a public road, is it?"

"No road. No road like that. I guess you don't know how big this outfit is. The roads around Reata are Reata. Anybody tries to cut across here that don't belong, why, they turn up missing. Anybody wants to drive from here to yonder, why they damn well got to go about a hundred miles out of their way to get there."

"Who says they must?"

"Bick Benedict, that's who says."

She decided not to pursue the subject with this strangely angry young man. His eyes actually were bulging a little and his mouth muscles were drawn back in a snarl like that of the stuffed catamount's head on the wall in the great hall. She began to regret the drive, she decided to ask no questions of this boor, since every utterance seemed to send him into a rage. They went along in silence, their speed now was frightening. He began to speak again, he spat out the words.

"How'd they come by it! Millions of acres. Who gets hold of millions of acres without they took it off somebody!"

Here at last was Leslie's chance to make use of that knowledge gained from books of Southwest lore over which she had so eagerly pored. She darted about in her mind for remembered facts, statistics.

"In those days Spanish land grants could be bought by anyone who had the money. It was just like a deal in real estate. The settlers bought it from——"

"Bought it—hell! Took it off a ignorant bunch of Mexicans didn't have the brains or guts to hang onto it. Lawyers come in

215

and finagled around and lawsuits lasted a hundred years and by the time they got through the Americans had the land and the greasers was out on their ears."

"That's not true—at least, not always," Leslie retorted, a trifle surprised to find herself suddenly on the other side of the argument. "They often bought it and paid for it."

"Yeah. Five cents an acre. Say, you're Bick's wife, you ain't supposed to go against a Benedict."

"I would if I thought they were wrong."

"Look, someday I'm going to have more money than any Benedict ever laid hands on. Everybody in Texas is going to hear about me. I ain't sitting here sleeping with my eyes open. I'm going to be a millionaire and I ain't kidding. I'm going to have a million dollars. I'm going to have a billion. I'm going to have a zillion."

"That'll be nice," Leslie said soothingly. She really must talk to Jordan about him. He was dangerous. That movement of his foot toward the accelerator. But perhaps she had only imagined it.

"You're not exactly loyal to your employer, are you, Jett?" She saw his head turn on that thick pugnacious neck as he stared at her. She went on, lightly, conversationally, a polite half-smile of interest on her lips. "You talk so interestingly about other people's background. Tell me a little about your own, will you? Your childhood and your father and mother. Unless you'd rather not."

"Why wouldn't I!" he yelled belligerently. "They was here in Texas enough years ago to be rich, too, only they wasn't foxy. It sure tells good. Ma, she's been dead since I was about two years old, I don't remember her even, they was seven of us kids, I don't know where they're at, most of 'em. Pa, he went in one day around here with his gun to get him some birds for us kids to eat, I guess. Strictly not allowed. Private, those birds, and the air they fly in is private. He never come out. He never turned up again after he went in there with his gun."

"Maybe he went away. Sometimes people do that—they don't

mean to but the responsibility is too much for them, their minds just——"

Now he turned squarely to look at her, his laugh was a short sharp yelp. "You sure got a lot to learn about Texas."

"I want to learn. I want to know about you and all the others on Reata."

"Yeh, well, we're all doing great. Me and all the others and the Mexicans specially. If they don't like it they can go back to Mexico and starve. I'm real petted. Bick, he give me a few acres out Viento way. Real lovely. You couldn't feed a three-legged calf off it."

"Jett, I find I'm more tired than I thought. I'd like to go straight home."

"You said you wanted to go see Benedict."

"I've changed my mind."

"Say, I didn't go for to make you mad. You asked me and I told you straight out. If you didn't want to know you got no call to ask me. You want everything prettified up, that's what's the matter with you."

Stunned, the impact of this truth silenced her. They tore along the landscape, it seemed to Leslie that movement was reversed in some nightmarish way and that it was the car that stood still, the flat glaring plain that whirled past them like a monotonous changeless cyclorama.

Far, far in the distance against the flat tin sky was etched the outline of Reata. "No!" she said to her own astonishment. "No, let's not go home just yet."

"The town?"

"Yes."

"The other side of Benedict—that's why I come this way—is Nopal."

"What's that?"

"Nothing. Only Mexicans. It's Benedict only they call it Nopal like it's another town. It's like real Mexico, I don't guess there's two white people living there."

"White. You mean—but the Mexicans aren't——"

GIANT

"They sure ain't white, for my money. Two Americans then. Maybe you like that better.

"Jordan told me—my husband told me that some of the Mexicans had been there—their families, I mean—hundreds of years. Haven't you read your Texas history! They were here long before you, or the Benedicts, or Reata, or anything that's here now. They belong here. They're more American than you are!"

"God damn it to hell!" he yelled. "You—if you was a man I'd kill you for that." His foot jammed down hard on the floorboard, they were tearing crazily along the ribbon of road. We are going to be killed, she thought. We must surely be killed. She sat quietly while the past day—the past week—this past strange changeful month of her life marched in orderly array through her mind. It was like reviewing some sort of noisy over-colorful and crowded party from which she was about to take leave as decently as possible. I must go, she said to an imaginary hostess. It's been so interesting. Thanks for letting me come.

They entered a down-at-heel little town, they had flashed past a broken road sign that said NOPAL. The car slid and bumped to a jolting halt in front of the dusty little plaza. Leslie lurched forward, slammed back, brakes screeched, tires squealed. The boy looked at her. Blandly he said, "Nopal means a prickly-pear tree, it's a kind of cactus."

She began to laugh a little hysterically. Then she stopped abruptly and sat silent a moment, her hands covering her eyes. When she brought her hands down they were fists. She pretended to look about her, she was conquering an almost overwhelming impulse to hit hard that heavy-jowled young face with the hard blue eyes set so close together.

"Ain't you feeling good, ma'am? You like a drink or something, Miz Benedict?"

Furious, she said, "You drove like a maniac. If my husband knew you drove like that! You're out of your senses!"

"I didn't go for to scare you. That's the way we drive in Texas. Everybody."

"I'm going to get out and walk," she said.

218

"Sure," he said, humbly for him. "But whyn't you wait and drive around a little first, it's just a dump of a town, nothing to see. Anyway, you don't want to walk, do you, in them clothes? What you always wanting to walk for?"

She glanced down at herself. Riding pants made by a Washington tailor. She looked about her. The plaza, the streets were deserted except for a woman in black ascending the church steps, a black rebozo covering her head.

"I want to telephone."

"I bet they ain't a telephone in town only the priest's house and maybe one two places you wouldn't go into." He hesitated a moment. "Say, don't be sore, Miz Benedict. I get mad easy. Uh—don't get sore."

For a moment she thought he was going to blubber. Well, the boy was a lout and something of a brute, but here she was and being here it was silly not to see something of this bit of Mexico in the United States. Here was another civilization, a strange land within her own familiar land. Streets of shanties on stumps, or flat on the dirt ground. The dwellings pitted and seared and scoured by wind and sand and heat and sudden northers. Dusty oleanders like weeds by the roadside. Broken sidewalks, crazily leaning balconies, sagging porches.

They were moving now, slowly, inching their way around the little bare plaza with the paintless bandstand in the center. Yet there was something about the town—a kind of decayed beauty. The church stood richly facing the plaza, its limestone and brick and stained-glass windows in startling contrast to the rest of the dilapidated little town.

"That there's the church, they call it a cathedral, I got to laugh." Jett Rink had assumed the air of official—though scornful—guide. "They don't do anything different from what they did a hundred years ago. Sundays you know what they do? They walk. And Saturday night. The band plays and they act like they never heard of America. The girls walk up on one side of the walk in the park here, and the boys they walk down on the other side and they ain't allowed to talk to each other. They just look

at each other, they can't talk alone, they say it's just like in Spain.
. . . American! I got to laugh."

A priest in his black strode across the plaza and disappeared
within the neat limestone house beside the church. A little velvet-
eyed girl ran through the quiet street, she glanced shyly at the
car parked there at the plaza's edge. A rickety cart trundled by,
a cask on wheels, it was the cart that sold water to the Mexican
households in this dry land. . . . Dim wineshops. The C.O.D.
café. Garza's Place . . . Rutted roads of white shell . . . Dusty
footpaths leading to the church.

"They ain't changed, those dopes, the way they eat and live
and all. They make their cinches of horse manes, by hand, like
they did a hundred years ago, and reatas of rawhide and they
got their own way of tanning buckskin. They stick together and
can't even talk English, half of 'em. Go around solemn-looking
on the outside, but boy! when they get together! Dancing and
singing their corridos telling about everything they do, like a
bunch of kids."

"People do that, you know. They cling together when they feel
frightened or unsafe."

Emilio Hawkins said a sign tacked crazily outside a grocery.
"There! Is that one of your two Americans?"

"Half-and-half."

A dapper figure emerged from Garza's Place. Glistening black
hair, sideburns, a roving wet eye, brilliant yellow boots, an incongruous dark cloth suit such as a businessman might wear in the
North. His Stetson was smooth and pale and fine.

"Hi, Fidel!" yelled Jett. "Hi, Coyote!"

The man bared his teeth and spat on the ground. Then he saw
Leslie, he stared and wet his lips and his great hat came off as he
bent in a low bow on the dusty street. He made as though to come
toward them but Jett stepped on the accelerator, they darted forward, Jett laughed a high sardonic laugh of triumph.

"He seen you, he knew who you was, all right."

"What of it?"

"Nothing."

"What did you call him? Coyote? Is that his name? How queer."

"Ha, that's good—coyote a name! They call him Coyote, his name is Fidel Gomez, he runs the Mexicans he's the richest man in town. He's got a nice house—I'll show it to you—no 'dobe stuff but concrete whitewashed and a tree in front and a bathroom and a dining-room set and a bedroom set and a parlor set and a Chevy and he married the swellest-looking Mexican girl in town, she was brought up real strict, she can't speak a word of English, he keeps her dumb all right. Everybody in the county knows Gomez. He makes out like he's the poor Mexicans' friend."

She glanced back. The man was still standing there gazing after them. "I want you to turn around," she said. "I want to speak to him."

"Say, you can't do that."

"Turn around, boy."

"Bick'd give me hell if he found out. I ain't going to turn."

Suddenly she was trembling with anger. "You'll do as I say. You'll take me back to where that man is standing. Don't you dare to tell me what I can or can't do!"

He looked at her, a sidewise almost comical look of surprise.

"Okay. Está bien." He spun the wheel, he turned with a shrieking of rubber on shell and brought up before the man at the edge of the dusty footpath. Astonishment was plain on the man's face, his eyes his mouth were ovals of apprehension.

"How do you do, Mr. Gomez," said Leslie with a formality which the man did not seem to find absurd. "I am Mrs. Jordan Benedict."

Again the man's hat was swept off with a gesture that belonged to another century. He bowed elaborately from the waist.

"La señora es muy simpática."

"I am sorry. I don't speak Spanish."

A gesture of his hand made nothing of this. "You need no language. Ma'am." The dark eyes rolled. "I say you are very charming."

Well, perhaps Jett Rink had been right, after all. "Uh—I—

I'm told you are a very important citizen here in Nopal. I am just having a look at your interesting little town."

His glance at Jett Rink was pure venom. His mouth was smiling.

". . . muy bondadosa," he murmured.

"I will tell my husband we met." She sounded, she thought, like an exercise in a child's copybook. "Good-bye."

Again the business with the hat. The bow. The baffled look. As before he stood looking after them as they drove off.

"But why do they call him Coyote?" She had to know.

"That's a name for hombres like him, it's a name the Mexicans call a chiseler, a crook. He lives off of them he sneaks them across the border from Mexico to work as pickers and then when they're here time he's through with them they don't have nothing left when they get through working in the Valley crops. And he rounds up the Mexican voters and does a lot of dirty jobs."

"I can't listen to talk like that."

"There you go again. You ask me, and then when I tell you you get sore."

Primly she said only, "It's getting rather late. Drive me home now, please—but not as fast as you drove here." Suddenly she was tired with an overpowering weariness.

"What's the hurry?" She did not reply. "You're grown up, ain't you? Your ma won't whup you when you get back, will she?" As she still disdained to answer, "We're only about fifteen minutes from Benedict, you said you wanted to walk around there and there's something there I wanted to show you, you'll be mighty interested."

"Some other time."

He rounds up the voters and does a lot of dirty jobs. In silence they drove into the town of Benedict. She wondered now why she had found it so fascinating that day of her arrival. Three days ago. Perhaps now it seemed commonplace in contrast with the old-world town she had just glimpsed. She saw it now as a neat enough little Southwest town squatting there in the sun and dust of a late spring afternoon; living in its little heat-baked

houses and selling its groceries over its decent counters and hand-
ing its tidily stacked bills out of the bank teller's window. Drinking its soda pop and Coca-Cola and eating its chili and enchiladas at the lunch counter and riding in its Ford.

"It's good and hot. You want to get out and walk, like you
said?"

"No."

"Nothing to see in Benedict. Viento, that's different, that's a
town. Or Hermoso. You ever been to Hermoso?"

"No."

"Corpus Christi?"

"No."

"Houston? They got stores there bigger than New York."

Bigger. Biggest ranch. Biggest steer. Biggest houses. Biggest hat.
Biggest state. A mania for bigness. What littleness did it hide?
Her eyes were lacklustre as she now surveyed the main street and
the side streets that ended in the open prairie. There were neat
street signs here and she saw that the names had been nostalgically
bestowed by people who long ago had crossed the endless plains
all the weary way from the green moist Atlantic seaboard, from
the woods and streams and fields of the Middle West. Ohio
Street. Connecticut Avenue. Indiana Street. Iowa Street. Somewhere in their background, far back among the family photographs, was the inherited memory of Northern sounds and sights;
the crunch of wagon wheels on snow, the crack of clapboards in
sudden frost, rocking chairs on shady front porches, ancient wine
glass elms dappling August streets.

Now they still lived like Northerners with the blood of the
North in their veins. They lived against the climate in unconscious defiance of this tropical land. They built their houses with
front porches on which they never could sit, with front yards
forever grassless, they planted Northern trees that perished under
the sun and drought, they planted lilacs and peonies and larkspur
and roses and stock and lilies-of-the-valley and these died at birth.
Arrogantly, in defiance of their Mexican compatriots, they wore
Northern clothes, these good solid citizens, the men sweating in

223

good cloth pants and coats, the women corseted, high-heeled, marcelled, hatted. We're the white Americans, we're the big men, we eat the beef and drink the bourbon, we don't take siestas, we don't feel the sun, the heat or the cold, the wind or the rain, we're Texans. So they drank gallons of coffee and stayed awake while the Mexican Americans quietly rested in the shade, their hats pulled down over their eyes; and the Negroes vanished from the streets.

So the big men strode the streets, red of face, shirt-sleeved, determined. Their kind had sprung from the Iowa farms, the barren New England fields, from Tennessee. Their ancestors had found the land too big, too lonely, it had filled them with a nameless fear and a sense of apartness, so they set out to conquer it and the people whose land it was. And these, too, they must overcome and keep conquered, they were a constant menace, they kept surging back to it. All right, let them work for us, let them work for a quarter a day till the work is done, then kick them back across the border where they belong.

"Hiya, Murch!"

"Howdy, Dub!"

So there it was, the neat little town, squatting in the sun and dust and trying to look like Emporia Kansas and Lucas Ohio. And Leslie Lynnton, with the romantic and terrible and gallant and bloody pages of a score of Texas history books fresh in her mind, thought of its violent past; it marched before her eyes. The Spanish conquistadores in their plumes and coats of mail marching through this wilderness. The savage Karankawa Indians. Coronado, seeking the fabulous Gran Quivira. Sieur de La Salle in the tiny ship *Amiable* wrecked in Matagorda Bay. Fort St. Louis on Garcitas Creek, a rude stockade with six little huts clustered about it. The Jesuit priests; the Spanish Missions, with their brown-robed sandaled monks living their orderly routine in this desert wilderness, and the bells in the chapel towers ringing across a thousand miles of nothing . . . Moses Austin, the middle-aged St. Louis banker who, by trying to establish three hundred American families in the Texas wilderness, thought to retrieve his fortune lost in the panic of 1819 . . . Stephen Austin, his son, the calm, the dignified, the elegant, and what was he doing in Texas, he sadly asked himself as he wrestled with his dead father's gigantic problem. . . . Sam Houston, the mysterious swashbuckling hero of a thousand tales . . . Santa Anna the glib and tough and crooked little Mexican general . . . Bowie the lion-hearted . . . Travis the war-minded . . . Davy Crockett the great fellow from Tennessee . . . the magnificent hopeless defense of the Alamo . . . Texas the Spanish . . . Texas the French . . . Texas the Mexican . . . Texas the Republic . . . Texas the Confederate . . . Texas the Commonwealth of the United States of America . . . Commonwealth . . . common wealth . . .

"Say, I bet you'd like to see what Ildefonso's making for you in there."

She stared at Jett. "What? What did you say?"

"That there's Ildefonso's place, he makes leather stuff for Reata—boots and saddles and straps and every kind of leather on the place, he gets fifty dollars for a pair of boots and more. And he can get any amount for one of his real tooled saddles and that's what he doing for you. Want to see it? Looka these boots I got on, I saved up ten months for them."

The smell of leather, rich and oily, came to you even before you entered the shop of Ildefonso Mezo. And there in the front of the shop was the ancient Mexican saddle tooled over all in an intricate pattern of flowers and serpents, the classic scrolls and leaves and patterns of ancient Spain and Mexico. Not an inch of it that was not embossed or embroidered, and stirrups pommel bridle reins shining with silver engraved in a hundred designs.

Jett Rink swaggered in, there was no one to be seen, he walked behind the glass case that held the boots of every size and degree of ornamentation—boots for a child of three, boots for a six-foot man, stitched and scrolled, high-heeled, pointed of toe. A whirring and a tapping and a clinking came from the long dim back room. "Hi, Ildefonso! Here's Miz Benedict come to see her new ridin' riggin'."

And here was Ildefonso Mezo, as much an artist of the leather of the Southwest as Cellini had been master of the silver-worker's craft in Italy. A little brown-faced man with bright black eyes and grizzled hair, and hands that might have been made of the leather which he artificed.

Standing before Leslie, the man bowed with the utmost formality. "Buenas tardes, señora. Entre. Ildefonso Mezo at your orders. I am honored."

What could she do, what could she say? "Gracias—uh—muchas gracias."

Then she laughed a little helplessly and Ildefonso laughed to keep her company and because he thought she was not so bad-looking and because she was Señora Benedict.

"Show us the saddle," yelled Jett Rink. "And the boots and the belt and the whole outfit."

"It is still in the work. I must ask Señora Benedict to come to the workshop."

Leslie, standing before the sumptuous old Spanish saddle, was tracing its design with her forefinger, feeling the great weight of the leather encrusted with embossed silver. It seemed enough to weigh down a stalwart horse to say nothing of his burden of rider and accoutrements.

"But this one—first tell me about this one. Did they actually use this!"

"How else!" Ildefonso assured her. He was plainly enchanted by her interest. "I could show the señora silver horseshoes that were used, silver was nothing it was everywhere. The Spaniards came to Mexico and they found silver in the mines and they covered everything with silver—their clothes and their furnishings and their saddles and harnesses. Until the Spaniards came there were no horses in Mexico but soon the Mexicans became the most daring riders—more daring even than the Spaniards. And so they still are."

"Come on! Come on!" bawled Jett. "Okay, the Mexicans are big shots, show us that saddle you're cutting will you!"

Still smiling, but not mirthfully, Ildefonso shook his head.

226

"Gato montés. Wildcat," he said. He led the way to the work-room doorway, he stood aside then so that Leslie should enter before him. Jett Rink swaggered after him. And now Ildefonso was the artist in his studio. Along the wall beneath the windows were the worktables and the dark heads were bent over these and the keen little tools made delicate intricate marks on leather yel-low and brown and cream and tan and black. Wooden horses held saddles in every state of construction and ornamentation. Leather straps and belts hung in rows like curtains, there were boots in the making, reatas, hatbands, bridles, every manner of leather thing needed on the vast ranch.

Ildefonso led the way to his own worktable. And there were Leslie's saddle and her boots and her belt and her reata and her bridle and her hatband together with straps and thongs and coils of leather whose use she did not even know.

"Weeks!" Ildefonso assured her earnestly. "Weeks ago they were commanded. But work such as this needs many weeks. A pair of such boots alone they need many days. From Virginia weeks ago the señora's shoes was sent to me. You did not know."

So that was where the old brown boots had got to. Leslie looked at all this artfully tooled trousseau of leather, stamped and pat-terned so intricately by hand with the coils and twists of the Bene-dict brand. And between these twisted coils were her initials—her new initials squirming over everything: L L B. She looked at the heavy ornate saddle and she loathed it. In a museum, yes. Beau-tiful to look at. But to use? No. She liked all things neat and reticent. A well-made English saddle, so clean-cut and econom-ical in its lines, had always seemed to her as lovely as a sonnet. She thought how shocked her sister Leigh Karfrey would be if ever she saw this; and Lacey, who looked upon a horse and a saddle as other girls regard a jewel of exquisite depth and cut. And My Mistake, that fleet and lovely lady, she must never be forced to carry this ornate waffle on her slim back.

Ildefonso Mezo looked at her, triumph in his eyes. Waiting.

Leslie overdid it. "It's—it's wonderful. It's magnificent. I've never seen anything like it." She decided to think of all the poly-

syllabic adjectives she knew and add an O at the end of them.
"Magnifico! Uh—marvelouso! Extraordinario!"

Ildefonso, under extreme emotion, then gratefully expressed
himself in Spanish. "What you say is true, señora. This is no common work of art this is art of the highest kind in leather, in all of
Texas there is no one who can do this work to equal Ildefonso."

She understood not a word but his meaning was unmistak-
able. She found herself falling into his own pattern of stilted
English. "Sí," she agreed genially. "Sí sí sí. I shall go home
now and thank my husband for all this. He told me nothing
about it."

A look of horror transformed Ildefonso's beaming face.

"It was to be a surprise for the señora. How did you know if
he did not tell you? I thought when you came in——"

She looked at Jett Rink.

Under her accusing gaze and Ildefonso's Jett's expression was
one of utterly unconvincing innocence. "He don't tell me what
he's doing, does he! Anybody can come into this here shop, can't
they, and look around!"

Abruptly Leslie turned away.

"Thank you for letting me see the beautiful saddle, Ildefonso,
and all the other—I must go now, I am very late."

Ildefonso bowed, his expression his manner were correct. But
as she turned he managed to catch Jett's sleeve for just a second
and his swarthy face was close to the ruddy hard-featured one.
A whisper only. "Cochino. Piojo!"

"Spig," said Jett Rink briefly. And clattered out to the car on
those high-heeled boots for which he had paid fifty dollars.

Leslie was already seated in the car, she was rather bored now
with the whole business, she thought, Well, I suppose I've done
something again that I shouldn't have. But what? Sight-seeing,
driven by a kind of oafish hired man. What's wrong with that!

"Look," he began truculently, "I didn't know he was buying
them like a surprise for you, how would I——"

"It doesn't concern you at all," Leslie said in her best Lynnton
manner. "I am rather tired. It has been a long day. Thank you

for showing me the little Mexican town. I would like to sit quietly now, and not talk."

Across the little town then, past the mournful steer in his glass case, out to where Reata could be seen hazily like a mirage shimmering in the heat against the flat Texan plain and the searing Texas sky.

I just drove around with this boy—around and around—because I didn't want to go back to the house. And to Luz. I didn't want to go back to my home. But that's terrible, not to want to go home even when you're as tired and hot and thirsty and stiff as I am. You can't go on behaving like this, you know, Leslie my girl, she told herself.

". . . girl like you before."

Jett Rink was saying something. She hadn't quite heard. He seemed to be driving very slowly, for him. "What? What did you say?"

The knuckles of his hands on the wheel showed white. "I says ——" He cleared his throat. "—I says I never seen a girl—a woman—like you before. You sure are different."

She was rigid with resentment. Then she relaxed. Now don't be silly, this is an ignorant ranch hand, poor kid he's never been taught anything, he's never known anything but poverty. So now she laughed a prim little artificial laugh and said, "Yes, the East and the West are different here in the United States, even though we say we are one big family."

He faced straight ahead. "I ain't talking about no United States geography. I'm talking about you. I never seen a girl like you. You ain't afraid of nothing. I've seen a lot of women. I been going with Cora Dart—the teacher—since she give up hoping she could hook Bick. She's got education and all, but I never seen anybody like you, that's for sure."

They were nearing the gates now. She'd never need to be with him again. "Well, that's a very nice compliment, Jett. I'll tell my husband you said so."

Boldly, deliberately, he turned to face her. "No you won't," he jibed.

229

She turned her head away in disgust. How could Jordan have dreamed of letting her go about with this dirty little boy. If Jordan didn't know someone should tell him. She would.

There was quite a cluster of cars parked in the drive as she came up. She had not yet learned to distinguish the Reata cars from others. Horses, too. She wished that one of these could be Jordan's and that he might be home to greet her. But that was impossible. Still, it was after five, surprisingly enough. Late, really. She had been up and about twelve hours. Tired. She opened the car door, stepped out without a word or a backward glance. Slowly she ascended the steps. This was the first time she had walked alone up these imposing front steps. She enjoyed it, it gave her a sense of belonging. She glanced about her with a spacious feeling. She was after all coming home; tired and hot, she was coming home. Now she noticed a glass-doored gun cabinet just inside the doorway, vaguely she recalled having seen it before out of the tail of her eye and having perhaps subconsciously dismissed it as improbable. But there it was, a neat row of guns hanging handily behind the glass doors of the case, long-barreled and shining and ominous. One, curiously enough, was outside the case, leaning negligently against a panel.

This somehow annoyed her. Guns. Whoever heard of a woman having to enter her house past a row of guns! These weren't Indian days—pioneer scalping days. Don't forget to ask Jordan. Anyway, it was a relief to be back after the long difficult day. A bath and a change. And after all, guns in the hall are kind of romantic. They're probably the Texas version of front hall clutter, like our tennis racquets and golf clubs and fishing rods back home.

Quite a hubbub of voices from the big room. Jordan's voice. "Yoo-hoo!" she called and felt a great surge of happiness. He was there, he would be waiting for her.

Bick came swiftly toward her across the great hall, the light from the doorway was on him, she thought, Why, he looks sort of strange and wild.

"Where the hell have you been!"

"Been?" she echoed foolishly.

"Where the hell did you get to!"

"Why, darling, you look all hot and haggard. Is anything wrong?"

Now it was he who repeated. "Wrong!" he yelled.

"I had a lovely time seeing Texas, we went to Nopal, it's unbelievable, isn't it, it's like a foreign village——"

But he was shouting again. "Nopal! Nopal! That locoed drunken bum took you to Nopal! Leslie, Leslie!"

"But it's all right, Jordan. What's so terrible about that!"

There in the big living-room doorway she saw Vashti Snyth and Cora Dart, they became part of a confused and bewildering picture. "Why hello! How nice to see you," she began, very socially, and moved toward them. Over her shoulder she added, in the direction of the purpling Bick, "It was your idea to have him call for me."

She was embarrassed, she was angry, she was mystified. So she erred rather on the stately side. Her code condemned family exhibitions of temper. She went smiling to the two women in the doorway, she took Vashti's hand in greeting, she had to pick up the limp and unresponsive hand of the schoolteacher but she managed it well enough. "D'you know, there's really more protocol in Texas than there is in Washington—or at the Court of St. James's for that matter. But I'll learn." She thought they were looking at her too strangely. "How nice to find you here. Uh, Miss Dart, I've had a wonderful idea; could you give me Spanish lessons—out of your school hours I mean—if you could——"

Then she saw Luz. She was lying on the big couch in a curious stuffed-doll fashion, her mouth was open, her eyes were shut and her breathing was a snore, but more horrible than a snore.

Leslie turned her head then to stare at the two women watching her so intently. "What?"

"The horse," Vashti said inadequately.

Bick came up behind her, his face was a curious grey beneath the russet now, and rigid. "It's our fault. She wanted to go with

us. My Mistake. She can ride anything. The Western saddle—
the horse stepped in a gopher hole, deep."

"What is it?"

"Concussion. Or worse. Fracture, maybe."

"Doctor Tom. Doctor Tom Walker."

"He's here. He's telephoning."

"Hospital in Benedict."

"There is no hospital in Benedict."

"That other—that Viento place."

"No hospital in Viento."

Cora Dart spoke for the first time. "She's dying." As though
she found satisfaction in saying it she repeated it. "Dying."

Hurriedly then Vashti became conversational. "He broke his
leg, the horse. When he stumbled and threw her. Luz's head came
up against a mesquite stump. They had to shoot him. Bick had to
shoot him."

Crazily Leslie thought, My Mistake will never have to wear
that silly saddle. That will teach you not to ride in hoop skirts,
Luz Benedict.

"Look out!" yelled Vashti Snyth. "She's going to faint again.
Bick!"

With a tremendous effort of will Leslie Benedict pulled the
swirling world into steadiness. "Oh, no I'm not," she said. "I'm
never going to faint again."

15

EVERYBODY CAME to the funeral. Fortunately the actual basic Benedict family was small. A closed corporation. But Texas converged from every point of the compass. Friends, enemies, employees, business connections; ranchers, governors, vaqueros, merchants, senators, cowboys, millionaires, politicians, housewives. The President of the United States sent a message of condolence. There had been no such Texas funeral since the death of Jordan Benedict Second.

Luz Benedict had become a legendary figure though no one actually knew her in her deepest darkest depths except, oddly

enough, outsiders such as Jett Rink and Cora Dart and Leslie
Lynnton Benedict. Perhaps Doctor Tom Walker. Bick Benedict,
her baby brother, knew her least of all; or if he knew, refused to
face the knowledge. Bick Benedict, whom she had deviled and
ruled and loved, whose life she had twisted and so nearly ruined;
toward whom she had behaved like an adoring and possessive
mother wife sister combined in one frustrated human being. The
world of Texas knew her as the Benedict family matriarch. Sometimes they wondered why a patriarch, in the person of Uncle
Bawley Benedict, ruler of the vast Holgado Division, and older
than his niece by fifteen years, did not head the clan. To this
the wise ones made answer.

"Bawley! Why, say, he wouldn't have it a gift. That ol'
Bawley, he's a maverick. If he had his druthers he wouldn't see
a Benedict one year's end to the next. He's smarter than any of
'em; than Bick, even. If he put his mind to it he could make the
whole passel come up to the lick log. But he sets back like he's
done for years, smiling and hushed, and lets Bick run Reata
and Luz run Bick."

Everybody who was anybody in Texas came to the funeral.
They came, not to mourn the violent exit of Miss Luz Benedict,
spinster, aged fifty, but to pay tribute to a Texas institution
known as the Benedicts of Reata Ranch. Almost a century of
Texas was contained in the small and resentful arrangement of
human clay now so strangely passive in the bronze and silver box.

Mortuary artifice had been powerless to erase entirely the furious frown that furrowed her brow. The lips were unresigned, the
jaw pugnacious. Luz Benedict, tricked by sly and sudden death,
could almost be said to bristle in her coffin. You, Death! You
can't do this to me! This is Luz Benedict of Reata, this is my
house this is my ranch this is my Texas this is my world.

Familiar faces, bent over her for a last good-bye, could well
say that she looked natural. Power was depicted there, arrogance,
and the Benedict will to rule and triumph. You can't do this to
me, I do as I please, all the Benedicts do as they please, I am a
Benedict of Reata I am Texas.

234

Every bedroom in the Big House was filled, guests were sleeping in the bookless library, in the mute music room. Even the old unused adobe Main House of family tradition—the house in which Bick Benedict and the Benedicts before him had been born—was opened now and aired and made habitable for the funeral guests who swarmed from every corner of the vast commonwealth and from most of the forty-seven other comparatively negligible states of the United States of America.

Privately the family thought how like Luz to inconvenience everyone in the Benedict world and to make them do her bidding against their own plans and inclinations. Here it was late spring and Maudie Lou Placer and her polo-playing husband had been just about to sail for a summer in England and Scotland and France. Roady Benedict had secretly sneaked a holiday from his Washington job of looking after Texas interests and was game-fishing in the luxurious wilds of the Benedict Canadian camp. Mr. and Mrs. Bowie Benedict were knee-deep in the blue grass of their Kentucky racing stables. Uncle Bawley was, as always, a lone eagle in his eyrie at the Holgado Division spread amongst the mountains of the Trans-Pecos.

Assorted cousins of the first second and third degree were snatched from their oysters Rockefeller at Antoine's in New Orleans, from their suites at the Mark Hopkins in San Francisco, from their tennis in Long Island, from the golf links of White Sulphur, and summoned to pay last homage to their kinswoman.

Leslie moved from group to group, from room to room, from crowd to crowd. Sometimes she did not try to identify herself, sometimes she said, "I am Mrs. Benedict."

"Which Mrs. Benedict?"

"Jordan. Mrs. Jordan Benedict."

Mystified for a moment, they would stare. Then, "Oh, Bick! Bick's wife. Well, say! I heard. Sure pleased to meet you."

"Do you live near here?"

"Milt K. Masters."

"Oh. Yes. I just wondered if you lived near Reata, Mr. Masters."

"Mr. Masters! Say, that's a good one. My name ain't Masters. My name's Decker—Vern Decker."

"I thought you said——"

"That's the name of the town I live in, town of Milt K. Masters. Named after the fella started it."

But she had no time then to ponder on what manner of man this Milt K. Masters had been to wish to perpetuate himself by stamping his undistinguished name on a little Texas town.

"How interesting. Of course. Named after a man. Like Houston or Kingsville or—or Benedict, for that matter."

"Well, now, it's just a little cow town but we think it's just about the best little town in the whole state of Texas. Quite a piece from here, four five hundred miles. You want to come down, pay a visit. How come you ain't been, you and Bick? I take it real unfriendly."

"I've only been a few days in Texas."

A few days. It was with a feeling of unbelief that she heard herself saying this. A few days since she had stepped off the train at Vientecito.

"Well, ma'am, you sure got a treat coming to you. You're going to get acquainted with the greatest state in the country. Yes ma'am, and I don't mean only size. I mean greatest everything. Crops. Cotton. Cattle. Horses. Folks."

"Do excuse me a moment, won't you? I think my husband is beckoning to me. He's just over there."

"Sure. Run right along. Say, it's pretty lucky Bick's got you now, keep him from being low-spirited. He's sure going to feel Miss Luz being gone. She was more like a mother to Bick than a sister."

She had telegraphed to Virginia the news of this family tragedy. Her father had offered to come to her, as she knew he would. Do you want us to come, his telegram had said, Mother and I can start immediately. Don't come, she had replied. It's such a journey the funeral is day after tomorrow I am well Jordan is well enough but terribly shocked how strange and terrible that it should have been My Mistake.

Her husband was a stranger whom she could not reach. She was someone living in his house. It seemed to her that there was no cousin so remote but he or she yet seemed closer to Jordan Benedict than his wife. He was sodden with grief and remorse. In his stunned mind was a confusion in which Luz and Leslie and My Mistake and the morning of the roundup and his years of deep and hidden resentment against this dominating woman were inextricably blended. Leslie tried to comfort him with her arms about him, with her intelligence, with her sympathy her love her understanding of this emotional shock whose impact he himself did not grasp.

For the hundredth time. "She just wanted to ride out to the roundup with us," he would say. "Why didn't she? Why didn't she come with us?" He wanted her to say it.

"We wanted to be alone. And that was right."

"If I hadn't bought My Mistake she'd be alive today."

Leslie decided on stern measures. "Yes, if you hadn't bought My Mistake your sister Luz would be alive today. And if Papa hadn't cured the ulcers of the horse's original owner he wouldn't have wanted to show his gratitude by giving Papa the horse. And if Wind Wings hadn't wandered into the wrong paddock, My Mistake never would have been born. If you want me to go on with this, if Papa hadn't been a surgeon, and if he hadn't married Mama and if I hadn't been their daughter—well, you can go back as far as you like, Jordan darling, if you really want to torture yourself."

She was shocked, she was in a way frightened, when she learned that by Jordan's orders Luz Benedict's saddle, her boots, her Stetson, her riding clothes and even the tragic hoop skirts of family tradition were to be left untouched in her bedroom as a shrine. How he must have hated her, Leslie thought. Guilt is an awful thing, it can destroy him, I won't let it.

So she went from group to group, from room to room, always with an eye on Bick. To anyone who had known her in the past it would have been amazing to see how she took charge of this vast household. The obsequies had assumed the proportions of a grim public ceremonial.

"We can put up another bed in this little sewing room. They can use the bath across the hall. . . . I know he will want to see you, he is resting just now he had no sleep last night. . . . A cake! How good of you I know it will be appreciated they are so busy in the kitchen. . . . You are Jordan's cousin Zora? Of course of course he often speaks of . . ."

The Girls were wonderful; and of the Girls Vashti Snyth and Adarene Morey were twin towers of strength and efficiency. They knew their Texas, they knew their Benedicts, they were the daughters and granddaughters and great-granddaughters of men and women who had wrestled and coped with every native manifestation from drought and rattlesnakes to Neiman-Marcus and bridge.

"I'll do it, Leslie. Just you sit down."

"I don't want to sit down. I can't."

"I know it. I don't mean really sit down. I mean let me do this and you make out like you're listening to all these people keep bawling at you, it'll take all the strength you got." This from the salty Vashti.

Adarene and Lucius Morey had arrived the day after Luz's death. They must have driven at ninety miles an hour, hour on hour, to make the distance. They entered the Big House, they took over. Servants. Food. Telegrams. Telephones. In a bedlam of big boots and big hats and big men and a cacophony of voices male and female these two seemed pure peace—Lucius Morey of the neat dark un-Texan suit and the neat dark un-Texan shoes and the shrewd blue eyes in the bland banker's face; Adarene of the plain countenance and the knobby forehead and the correct clothes and the direct gaze and the debunked mind.

The crowds streamed up the steps of the great front entrance, solemnly they Viewed the Remains, they swarmed in the dining room, the grounds, the drive, the outer road, the town of Benedict, the roads for miles around were alive with them. Arcadio at the gatehouse entrance could not limp fast enough to encompass the steady stream of visitors flowing through his portals. Three Mexican helpers were delegated as assistants. Besieged though they were, no one passed the gates who was not known to one or all of them, whether white black brown, from Fidel Gomez the Coyote of Nopal to the Governor with his aides, come all the way from Austin.

Bick met them all, his bloodshot eyes mutely questioning each mournful face as though hoping to find there the comforting answer to his self-reproach.

". . . Well say, Bick, I sure was throwed when I heard the news . . ."

". . . As representative of the Great Commonwealth of Texas I wish to extend in the name of my fellow citizens . . ."

". . . Mi estimado amigo, lo siento mucho . . ."

Leslie, with a scant week of Texas experience to guide her, moved among the mourners trying hard to remember Texas names, Texas faces, Texas customs. The Placers, that was easy; and Bowie and his wife and Roady and his wife and even a niece or two and a couple of nephews. But the others, millions of others. Let me remember . . . Uh, Mrs. Jennings . . . Somebody Beezer . . . Ila Something Motten . . . Mrs. Jakes . . . Kling.

Vashti Snyth insisted that food was the panacea for grief. She kept plucking at Bick's sleeve, she grasped Leslie's arm, she motioned in the direction of the dining room from which came a sustained clatter accompanied by rich and heavy scents.

"You got to eat if you're going to keep your strength up. How you going to expect to go through tomorrow if you don't eat! Leslie, Bick looks terrible. Bick, Leslie looks real ganted. Pa tried to get over and couldn't. He'll be next, mark my words. He's down sick, I ought to be there right now looking after him, he don't even beller at Mott any more, just lays there so pitiful, course he ain't been real rugged for a year and more, yesterday he said to me, Vashti, he said, it won't be long now, and when it comes you promise to put me away like I want to be put, no tie and my leather brush jacket. . . . Bick, whyn't you eat something, you look real peaked. Leslie, come on have a cup of coffee and a cake."

Adarene Morey came close to Leslie, her voice low in the midst of the clamor. "Relax. Bick's all right. It's good for him to have all these people around. Don't work so hard. Let them do the work. They're curious about you, you know. Even more than they are about seeing Luz, and how Bick behaves."

"Why?"

"The Queen is dead. Long live the Queen! If she can take it."

"I can take it."

There was a stir at the doorway, there was an acceleration of sound. "What's that? Who's that?"

Uncle Bawley's arrival was something of an event. Uncle Bawley who kinged it alone in splendid squalor at the Holgado Division, Uncle Bawley who had ignored Bick's wedding except for the sending of a monolithic silver edifice that resembled a cenotaph. Its purpose, whether for use or ornament, Leslie—and even Mrs. Lynnton—never had been able to fathom.

Now, as he strode through the welter of relatives, guests, neighbors and officials, Leslie was shocked. His eyes were streaming with tears, they washed down his cheeks and dropped off his chin. This was all the more startling because Uncle Bawley towered even above these Texas men who seemed to fill the rooms to bursting with their great shoulders, their pyramidal necks, their leather-colored faces, their leather-colored clothes, their enormous hats, their high-heeled boots, their overpowering maleness.

Yet there was about this gigantic man a grace, an air of elegance. He was wearing a dark suit and black boots and Leslie's knowing eye was quick to see that these garments had been born of the needle and shears of a New York tailor or even perhaps of a London magician of men's clothes. They almost hid the slight bulge that, at nearly seventy, was just beginning to mar his waistline.

Leslie felt she could not bear to face this giant with the streaming eyes. Those eyes were a faded blue, and the lids crinkled so that lines, etched by the sun and the wind, radiated from them fanwise at the temples. She knew he had been a Ranger in his youth, with gun notches and all the rest of the fabulous fanfare that went with stories of pioneer Texas times. Even now, in spite of his city suit, he was startlingly like a figure in the romantic fables of the region.

He came across the room, threading his way toward Bick, making slow progress because of the outstretched hands and the spoken greetings, muted but hearty with affection. She knew that he had arrived and that he had refused to stay at the Big House or at the old Main House. He was quartered in one of the nearby line houses. Later, when she knew him better, she had remonstrated at his uncomfortable quarters. "You should be staying here, in the Big House."

"Me here! Like to choke to death living in this pile. Just as soon sleep in the Egyptian pyramids."

At a gesture from Bick he turned to face Leslie. His eyes narrowed, then widened.

There was no escaping him, his gaze was upon her and now as he came toward her Leslie was dismayed to see that he mopped his eyes with his handkerchief and she marveled that his features were so composed under this fountain of tears. He stood beside her, he took her hand in his and looked down at her from his towering height.

Inadequately Leslie murmured, "I know what she must have meant to you—your eldest niece. I am so terribly sorry for you and for Jordan and for——"

He dabbed at his eyes with his free hand. "Don't pay this no mind," he said, and his voice was gentle and low and almost caressing. "I ain't bawling. This is what they call an allergy. Took me better than forty years to find out about it."

"Allergy!" she repeated after him, stunned.

"That's right. I'm allergic to cattle. Makes my eyes water quarts."

She smiled wanly and dutifully, scenting one of these regional jokes she did not understand. She played up to it. "Tell me the rest."

"The smart new doctors found it out after I'd been snuffling and bawling around for forty years and better. All my life a cowman and the whole Benedict family first and last for a hundred years or nearly. And then a kid at Johns Hopkins finds out I'm allergic to cows."

Leslie was utterly fascinated. She forgot about Luz and mourning etiquette and bereaved relatives-by-marriage. Temporarily she even forgot about Jordan. With a hand tucked in Uncle Bawley's arm she maneuvered him toward a quiet corner of the vast room, away from the tight groups that seemed to prefer to stand in the center of the room, talking talking talking. A huge couch whose overstuffed arms were the size of an average chair was angled away from the room proper, by some mistaken whim of a decorator—or perhaps of Luz. One corner of this engulfed Leslie though she sat with one leg crossed under her.

"This is wonderful," she said, and looked up, up at his towering height. "I'm—well—I know now what my mother meant when she used to say I-haven't-sat-down-today."

"Nothing can beat you out quicker than a houseful of people come for a funeral, especially if they're choused up like this. And you're new to it here. Bad enough if you're a Texian." His shoulders relaxed against the back of the vast couch, his long legs sprawled across the polished floor, his feet turned toes up, slim and arched in the beautifully hand-tooled high-heeled black boots. Leslie regarded him with anticipatory relish.

"I must tell my father all about you. He'll be enchanted."

"Enchanted with me?"

"He's a doctor."

"He here?"

"No. No, he's home. I mean he's in Virginia where we—where he lives. He'll be so interested. Please tell me a little more about it. The allergy, I mean. And about you. Do you mind if I call you Uncle Bawley—though I must say it doesn't suit you."

"I'd just purely love for you to do that. Leslie? I don't know as that suits you either. Usual thing I go slow with Yankees using their given names. They're touchy."

"That's funny. I think Texans are touchy."

"They're just vain," Uncle Bawley said in his soft almost musing voice. "Vain as peacocks and always making out like they're modest. Acting all the time, most of them. Playing Texas."

She stared at him, fascinated, she broke into a laugh, then checked herself, horrified. She inched her way across the hummocks of the couch so that she sat now just beside him and facing him, her back to the room. "How refreshing you are! I hope you don't mind my saying that, Uncle Bawley. Jordan told me about you, but not enough. Why didn't you come to our wedding?"

"I never go to weddings. Waste of time. Person can get married a dozen times. Lots of folks do. Family like ours, know everybody in the state of Texas and around outside, why, you could spend your life going to weddings, white and Mexican. But a funeral, that's different. You only die once."

She lied politely. "You sent us a magnificent wedding present, even though you didn't come."

"Was it? I never did rightly know what they sent. I just wrote to Tiffany's and I said for them to send a silver piece looked like a wedding present ought to look."

"They did," Leslie murmured, wondering when the packing boxes containing all those wedding gifts would arrive from Virginia, and where she could possibly place Uncle Bawley's cenotaph even in this gargantuan house with its outsize rooms. Mischievously she decided to try a Texasism. "They sure did." Gently she led him back to the original fascinating subject. "You must find it very trying—the allergy I mean. In your—uh—business."

"It's mean as all hell, pardon me, but up in the high country where I live, mountainous and the air clear, why sometimes I hardly notice it. It all but stops except for a few weeks maybe in the hot of summer if we don't get the seasonal rains we should. Down here, though, in the brush, the minute I set foot it starts like a fountain. The dust and the wind and the cow claps and the hair hides all together they set these springs to working. If the folks around here was smart they'd pay me just to walk around sprinkling this brush country. Course the dust's the worst down here. That and the wind."

"The wind," she repeated after him. "The wind the wind. Doesn't it ever stop? Don't tell Jordan—but the wind makes me nervous. Blowing blowing day and night."

"Don't pay it no mind," he said soothingly. "Texas folks are all nervous and jumpy. Don't appear to be, being so big and high-powered, but they are. You notice they laugh a lot? Nervous people do, as a general rule. Easy laughers, but yet not what you'd call real gay by nature. Up in the Panhandle they're even jumpier than they are down here in the brush. Up there the wind blows all the time, never stops blowing, even the cattle are kind of loco up there. But where I live, in the Davis Mountains, it's just about perfect."

He took from his coat pocket a folded handkerchief, white and fine, and as he wiped his brimming lids Leslie caught the pricking scent of eau de cologne. She sniffed the tangy scent now and beamed upon her new-found relative. This giant of the leathery skin, the gentle voice, the fine linen, the glove-fitting boots, was something of a dandy.

Now he glanced at her, a sharp sidewise look. "Maybe you think it's funny, a cowman getting himself all smelled up pretty."

"No, I like it. I like fastidious men."

"It's made me a heap of trouble. First off, my real name's Baldwin—Baldwin Benedict—that's what they named me. Then along come this crying and that cinched it. I was Bawley Benedict."

"Oh, Uncle Bawley, I'm so sorry. What would you like me to call you?"

"That's all right, I'm used to it. But I had to fist-fight my way through school and college. The Mexicans hereabouts call me Ilorono—The Weepy. At Harvard I was fullback and heavyweight boxer just in self-defense. I was a heavier build then. Puppy fat. I like to wore out my knuckles proving I wasn't a sissy. I have to laugh when I think of it now."

"Harvard?"

"We all go a couple of years, didn't Bick tell you? And a trip to Europe young. The girls go to some school in the East." His tone, his diction took on a complete change. "Just to prove to the world and ourselves that we aren't provincial."

She leaned toward him. "Please don't think I'm rude. But you talk—I mean Harvard and Europe and everything—and just now you—but most of the time you talk—well, the only ones who don't are Jordan, and Maudie Lou. And now you—when you weren't looking."

"I know. Sometimes we forget to talk Texas."

"But Uncle Bawley, it's regional, isn't it? A kind of dialect just as the Boston people speak one way and the deep South another and the Middle Westerners another."

He had not mopped his eyes for a full five minutes, the tears had ceased to flow. "Partly. That's right. Down here it's a mixture of Spanish and Mexican and Nigrahs and French and German and folks from all over the whole country. It settled into a kind of jargon, but we play it up. Like when I was a young squirt visiting New York there was a girl named Anna Held a French actress. She was all the rage, milk baths and pearls and so on, by that time she could speak English as good as you and me, but there she was a-zissin' and a-zattin' because it was good publicity and cute. That's us. Mostly, we know better. But we talk Texas because it's good publicity and cute."

"Uncle Bawley," she said earnestly, "I love talking to you."

He blushed like a girl. "That's funny."

"Why?"

"I hardly ever talk to a woman. I got out of the habit. No women up to the Holgado Division, hardly, except two three of the section bosses live in the line houses with their wives and kids. But most of the cow hands are single, we don't use vaqueros up there, too near to the border. Course there's all the Mexican families in Montaraz, that's the town just outside the ranch."

The town outside the ranch. She smiled.

"What you smiling at?" he demanded. "What'd I say made you smile like that and kind of shake your head?"

245

"I just thought how very Texan. The town outside the ranch. Most people would say, the ranch outside the town, wouldn't they?"

"Maybe so. If it wasn't for Holgado there wouldn't be any town. Handful of Mexicans, maybe."

She hesitated a moment, but only a moment. The habit of wanting to know was too strong. "But didn't you ever marry? Why?"

"What girl would have a man who stands there bawling with tears running down his face while he's asking her to marry him!"

Leslie was staring at him, she was scurrying about in her mind, putting together bits and pieces as her years with her father had taught her to do. "Cows!"

"How's that?"

"Allergic to cows."

"That's right."

She was looking into his face with the most utter concentration. "Uncle Bawley, did you want to be a cowman? Did you want to be head of Holgado and a big Benedict rancher and all that?"

"Hell no, honey."

"What did you want to be?"

"Funny you should ask me that. I haven't thought about it in years. What I wanted to be was, I wanted to be a musician. Pianist." Leslie's head turned toward him as if it had been jerked on wires. But the big pink face was bland, almost dreamy. "There's always been music in the family, one way or another, but the minute it shows its head it gets stepped on."

"Uncle Bawley, do you mean you wanted the piano to be your career?"

"Well, I don't know's I looked at it square in the face, like that. But when I got to Europe I studied there with Levenov till they made me come home. Big rumpus, there was. The whole family. You'd thought I wanted to run a faro wheel or marry a Mexican. Young men were younger then, I guess, than they

GIANT

are now when they're young. Pa got after me. Bick's Pa too. My
brother, named like Bick. Jordan. They got me out roping and
branding and one thing another. Nothing spoils your hands
quicker than that. For piano, I mean. Time they got through
with me I was lucky if I could play chopsticks. About that time
Brahms was just beginning to catch on, I was crazy about his—
well, you know, you can't fool around with anything like that,
I sat there at the piano looking at my fingers, it was like they were
tied on with wires. That was when I quit."

"Oh, Uncle Bawley dear!" She was terribly afraid she was
going to cry. She looked down at his great sunburned hands,
splotched with the vague brown spots of the aging.

He looked at her and smiled, his teeth were brownish and
somewhat broken, the great round face was beginning to be a bit
crumpled, he was a monumental structure he was almost three
times Leslie's age, she wanted to take his hands in hers and press
her lips to them as a mother comforts a child who has been hurt.
He must have sensed something of this as he looked at her. Apologetically he hurried on. "How'd we get onto that! Well, there
was Holgado to run and I was picked to run it. Now when I
look back on it, it's kind of crazy. Benedicts and big Texas ranch
folks, they act like they were royalty or something. Old-fashioned
stuff." He leaned toward her. "Let me tell you something, Leslie.
If your kids get a real notion they want to do something, you see
to it they do it."

"I will, Uncle Bawley. I promise I will."

"You get Bick to bring you out to Holgado for a nice visit. In
the spring it's real pretty. When the Spanish dagger is out. And
summers, after the seasonal rains it's right green, places."

"Is it a success? Does Jordan—do you and Jordan think it's
successful?"

"Holgado! Why, say, it's the money-maker of the whole outfit.
Even Maudie Lou and Placer and Bowie don't complain about
its being unfinancial. Course I don't stock all the newfangled
stuff Bick goes in for here at Reata. Not that I don't think Bick's
a smart boy. There's nothing he don't know about a ranch—horn

247

hide and hair." He smiled at her, a singularly sweet and childlike smile. "I ain't talked this much to a woman in years."

"You're just fascinating," Leslie said. "You're wonderful. I love you."

From behind her shoulder came Maudie Lou Placer's high hard voice, she was leaning a little over the back of the huge couch.

"There are people coming in all the time, they are asking for you, naturally. Elly Mae and I are doing all we can, and Roady and Lira of course, but Bick is worn out and it seems to me that you and Uncle Bawley—well———"

Leslie sprang up. "Oh, Maudie Lou, I am so sorry. I wasn't thinking."

"Rilly!" said Maudie Lou in her best borrowed Eastern accent.

The big room was now so densely packed that just to elbow a way through it was a physical effort. Nowhere in all this vast desert could one find an oasis of peace and quiet. A clamor of talk here, a rumble of sound from the adjoining rooms and the great hall. The huge dining room was all too small. The modest twenty places habitually laid had swollen to sixty—seventy—and now there were three rows of tables and there was never a gap in the places. People drifted in as though it were a restaurant, they sat and ate and left and others took their places, the food flowed out of the kitchen an avalanche borne on a flood of coffee. The air was heavy with the odors of cooking, grey with cigarette smoke. A dozen—twenty—Mexicans manned the cooking and serving. Steaming plates platters bowls. Back and forth back and forth. Siéntese, señor . . . Traígame el café solo. . . . Crema. . . . Heh, Domingo! Traígame otro . . . Sí señor, sí señora.

The driveway swarmed with cars and horses, they stretched down the road and spilled over into the weed-grown space in front of the old Main House half a mile distant. There was, for the accommodation of house guests, quite a fleet of cars shuttling back and forth between the Big House and the Main House, like a bus service.

It was midafternoon, Leslie had eaten almost nothing that day.

She looked at the great double doors of the parlor beyond—the doors so constantly opening and closing to admit the intimate hundreds to the room they called the parlor where the little angry woman lay in state. And she tried not to think of the heat and of the night and of the next day. And she wished with all her heart that the huge house and the well-meaning hordes that swarmed within it and without it, and the hundreds who served it, would vanish into the desert distance and that she could be alone with that Jordan Benedict she had met in Virginia, away from the noise and clamor and uproar of the endless spaces of Texas.

She made her way to Bick standing there near the doorway with a group of men. She slid her arm through his; she thought, He looks ghastly it's as if he had shrunk in his clothes.

"I've been talking to Uncle Bawley. He's marvelous."

"Yes. Uncle Bawley's great guy."

"Jordan, have you eaten anything?"

"Yes. I had some coffee."

"Coffee! You can't live on coffee. I haven't had anything either. Won't you come with me?"

Gently he took her hand from his arm, he shook his head. "One of the girls—Maudie Lou will go with you—Adarene—here's Adarene, right here." He turned back to the men.

And here was Adarene. "You look kind of funny," said Adarene. "Are you all right?"

Leslie clutched her arm. "Adarene, would they think it was queer if I just went up to rest in my own room a few minutes?"

"Of course not."

"Will you come with me?"

Guiltily they wormed their way through the crowded room, through the hall to the stairway up and down which people she never before had seen were purposefully tramping. It was like being in a museum on a free exhibition day. When she opened her own bedroom door would she find a score of strangers there, sprawled on chairs and bed?

"Here we are," said Adarene, and turned the doorknob. The door was locked. The two women stared at each other.

"Who?" demanded Leslie fiercely. "Who is in there?" She pounded on the door with her fist, her feeling of outrage was the accumulation of days. There was no sound from within.

"Shall I peek through the keyhole?" asked Adarene.

"Keyhole! My own room!"

"It's an enormous keyhole."

"Well——" Leslie faltered, and glanced apprehensively over her shoulder down the length of the long hall. There was Lupe coming swiftly and soundlessly toward them. In her hand was the cumbersome key that fitted the massive door. Her dark eyes were lively and understanding, she jerked her head meaningfully toward the swarming crowd. The key grated in the lock, she flung the door open, her eyes darted about the room as though someone might have crept through the keyhole.

"Entre, señora." She handed the key to Leslie and made a quick motion of the hand that advised locking the door from the inside. With another jerk of the head toward the babel below she vanished, closing the door behind her. The two women sensed that she waited a moment there outside until she heard the turn of the key.

"They're the ones who'll really mourn Luz," Adarene said. "Did you hear them last night?"

"No. Hear what?"

"The Mexicans will have their own mourning ceremonies for her. Lew and I could hear them last night, long after midnight down in the barrios, playing the guitar and singing her favorite songs. For weeks they'll be saying rosarios—evening prayers. And a lot of other mourning customs that are kind of weird, some of them."

"Because she was a Benedict? A kind of feudal custom?"

"No, not altogether. She was hard on them but she understood them—the older generation anyway—they respected her. She was the leading mare—the madrina. Of course they never called her that, but they knew. They always know. . . . Why don't you lie down and shut your eyes, rest a while? Maybe you can sleep."

250

"Adarene, dear good Adarene."

"Do you want Lupe to bring you a cup of tea?"

"Not now. Just to sit here away from the crowd."

Briskly Adarene said, "Anyway, it's given you a chance to meet the State of Texas. Ordinarily it would have taken a newcomer weeks and months and years. They're all here—large and small. Old Texas and new Texas. The cotton rich and the rotten rich and the big rich. Cattle, and the new oil crowd, and wheat and the Hermoso and Houston and Dallas big business bunch."

"I wish I knew half of what you know," Leslie said. "It would be better for Jordan."

"You were pretty vivacious over there talking to Uncle Bawley, weren't you?"

"I didn't realize."

"You're on exhibition. Uncle Bawley's never been known to talk as long as that to any woman. He's woman-shy."

"I didn't mean to be disrespectful to—to Luz. He was enormously interesting."

"Luz was a bitch and a holy terror and kind of crazy, too. Everybody knows that. But she was Luz Benedict. Madama."

"There's so much I don't understand."

"You'd have to be born here—around 1836."

"Adarene, are you happy here?"

"I wouldn't be happy living anywhere else. I've tried it. Texas is in my blood. I don't rightly know what it is—a kind of terrific vitality and movement."

"I get the feeling that they're playing wild West like kids in the back yard."

"Maybe. Some of the time. But it really still is the wild West—a good deal of it, with an overlay of automobiles and Bar-B-Que shacks and new houses with Greek columns and those new skyscrapers that my Lucius and Gabe Target and his crowd are running up. Skyscrapers out on the prairie where there's a million miles to spread out."

Leslie walked to the window and glanced out between the jalousies and closed her eyes and came back and sat at the edge of the bed. She smoothed the coverlet a bit with her hand, a little aimless gesture. Then she lay back and pressed her forearm over her eyes.

"I'm kind of scared."

"No wonder. You've had quite a week. But you'll get used to it. It's the ranch that's got you scared. I don't know why Bick keeps on living here the year round. I won't do it. We're ranchers too, you know. Everybody's got a ranch, big or little. But I won't live on it. It's all different. Or maybe I am. Even the cows are different. I'm not thirty but I can remember the Longhorns. Not many, but some. Now they're stocking grey velvet oriental monsters with slanting eyes and humps on their backs. Scare you. Scare anybody."

"Oh, Adarene——" Leslie began. There was a smart knock at the door. A series of them with determined knuckles. Leslie sat up, she smoothed her hair. The two women exchanged glances, Adarene's finger went to her lips.

Leslie stood up. "Maybe it's Jordan. . . . Who is it?" Aloud.

"Girls! Girls, can I come in?" Vashti.

"Damn!" said Adarene, under her breath; her eyebrows went up in rueful inquiry. Leslie nodded. And there, when the great key had been turned, was Vashti bouncing in with the over-eager uncertain look of a little girl who tags along unwanted by her playmates. Round red eager she glanced from Leslie to Adarene. "I saw you go up and then when you didn't come down I thought, well, they didn't just go to the lou all this while maybe there's something the matter is anything the matter?"

"Thank you, Vashti," Leslie said. "Nothing's wrong. I just felt I had to rest a minute."

Vashti threw her washed-blue eyes ceilingward in an effort at mental concentration. "Let's see now. How long is it since you and Bick were married? Wedding trip and all. Month, anyway— isn't it?"

"No," Leslie said. "I mean, yes, it's a month. But I'm tired because of what's happened, and so many people to meet."

"I guess," Vashti offered then, "you'll be glad when this is all over."

Adarene Morey took charge. "Vashti, stop talking like a dope. Do people usually like to keep a funeral going on around the house!"

Vashti moved about the room humming gently to herself which was a habit she had—Leslie was later to learn—when she had a bit of gossip to impart. She meandered to the broad expanse of the dresser with its silver and crystal and scent and silk. She sniffed at the stopper of a fragrant flask of perfume, her head on one side like a wary plump bird, her eyes glancing corner-wise at Leslie.

"I guess Jett Rink will be too," she observed airily. "Glad."

Adarene Morey stood up. "Let's go down now, girls. If you feel rested, Leslie."

"What has Jett Rink to do with it?" Leslie asked, though instinct told her not to.

Vashti now assumed the air of an aggrieved little girl. "Well, I just meant what they're saying downstairs, the men and all."

"Vashti Hake!" Adarene said in sharp warning.

"Snyth," retorted Vashti in correction.

"All right. Hake or Snyth," Adarene went on, dropping into Texas patois in her indignation, "you've got no call to go eye-balling around picking up gossip don't concern you."

"I didn't pick it up. Mott told me." She melted in a fatuous smile. "That's the nicest thing about being married to Mott Snyth. He knows all the talk around, first off."

"I'll bet!" said Adarene with vigor.

"Adarene Morey, if you mean because Mott used to be a cow hand before he married me and cow hands are the talkingest men there is——"

"No, Vashti, I didn't mean anything like that. Pinky Snyth is no worse than all the other Texas men when it comes to gossiping."

Leslie felt there had been enough of this. "Will you two please tell me what you're talking about!"

253

"We-e-e-ll," Vashti began, with dreadful relish, "they're saying around it was Jett got Miss Luz to try riding My Mistake in the first place and it was him said he bet she could put on a hoop skirt like her grammaw and rope anything running in a roundup, and why didn't she do it and ride out just to show you——"

"Me!"

"Well, I'm just saying what they said he said, I don't know. So sure enough what does Luz do but go up to the attic trunks and get out that hoop skirt and a big old Western saddle with a horn like a hitching post. And the minute that horse felt that saddle and glimpsed that hoop skirt he was like possessed it took three to hold him and she hardly'd climbed on Mott said when he was off like a bat out of hell—that's what Mott said—and they're saying around that after Bick shot the horse that killed Luz, why, Gill noticed there was a kind of funny-looking spit, like, around the horse's mouth——"

"Gill?"

"The vet. The head vet. Gill Dace."

"Oh yes. Yes."

"So he noticed there was a funny-looking spit, like, around his mouth and so he made some tests in the lab and sure enough somebody must have given him something hopped him up, Gill said it was enough to hop up a whole herd of drought-starved Longhorns, let alone one horse."

Adarene Morey attempted to stay the flood. "That's just a lot of stable talk, I don't believe a word of it, anyway Jett Rink wouldn't dare."

She thought Leslie looked very odd, feeling around like that for the edge of the chair behind her before sinking down on it.

"He would so. He and Luz hated each other like poison and then when Cora told Luz about her and Jett, why, Luz said she'd turn them both off the ranch, you know the way she wanted to run everybody's business her own way and seemed she couldn't bear for anyone to get married, even if they had to, like Cora, look at the way she behaved about you and Bick——"

Leslie stood up very tall and straight. "Thanks so much for coming up with me, it was sweet of you. I'm going down now. Are you coming?"

"Sure," Vashti agreed briskly. "I just came up to see if I could help. The boys are saying Bick gave Jett ten minutes to get off the ranch and they say he's going to take that piece of land away from him he gave him that time old Rink turned up missing, but he can't do that because Jett was smart, he's got it down on paper it's his. They started a terrible fist fight only if Gill and those hadn't pulled them apart."

Leslie was moving toward the door, she proceeded rather grandly, giving the effect of wearing a long train which definitely was not in evidence. The key turned with a great clunk. She opened the door, "Petra!" she called above the din below. "Lupe!" She felt very strange and light in this new world of sound and movement and violence. It's because I've eaten nothing I suppose, she thought.

Aloud she said, "Vashti, when you were a little girl did they ever smack you good and hard?"

"My yes."

"Not hard enough," said Leslie.

Innocently, quite unruffled, Vashti prattled on. "Even now, sick as he is, times I think Pa'd like to slap me if he could, Pa's always bossing everybody around, he's always after Mott, saying Pinky do this way, Pinky do that way, just like Luz does—used to do. . . . It's sure going to be nice for you, Leslie, having the run of this big house and nobody to boss you around. . . . Ooh, look, they's hardly anybody in the dining room now, it must be getting late, I'm kind of hungry myself. It's funny, funerals make you hungry, I guess it's feeling so bad and worked up and all . . ."

But Leslie was not listening. She put her hand on Adarene Morey's arm. "Listen. Get hold of Lupe, will you? She'll be here in a minute, she's always materializing here in the upper hall. Tell her—here's the key—to bring here to my bedroom some cold chicken and a bowl of fresh fruit and a pot of hot coffee and some bourbon and ice and a quart of champagne—and if they haven't any champagne in this big damned arsenal I'll scream my head off."

"They have, honey."

"I'll be back. I'm going to get Jordan."

Downstairs she found him exactly as she had left him, a strangely shrunken giant surrounded by other giants who seemed to have gained in height and breadth in the half hour that had elapsed since last she saw them.

As always the men now assumed different faces as they turned toward her, a woman; the faces they would put on for conversation with a child.

"Well, Miz Benedict, you're holding up mighty well and so is old Bick here. It's sad occasions like this and how you stand up to 'em shows what a person's made of. . . ."

She heard them, she replied only with that agreeable grimace which, very early in her Washington and Virginia social life, she had learned would pass for conversation in a pinch. She came close to Bick, she spoke very low in his ear. "Come with me, dear."

He shook his head. "No. I'm all right."

She faced the men. "Jordan is exhausted. He hasn't slept or eaten. I'm trying to have him rest before the evening—uh—" she had almost said the evening session—"before the evening." Appealingly she looked up into those big tan faces. "I feel quite faint myself—but that doesn't matter."

They rallied with a boom. "That's right, Bick, you go 'long. . . . You got to think of yourself and the little girl here. . . . Times like this it's the ones are left behind got to keep up their stren'th and carry on. Now you mind the Missuz and go 'long, now."

Toward the hall, toward the stairway, her hand on his arm. In the hall melee they encountered Uncle Bawley battling his way toward the open outer door. "Uncle Bawley! Where are you going?"

"See you all tomorrow." He dabbed at his eyes.

"But dinner. Have you had dinner?"

"I'm eating with Dietz over to the line house."

"Jordan's going upstairs to rest just a little while. You'll be back this evening?" She wished Jordan would say something.

Uncle Bawley shook his head, the teardrops flew right and left. "Crowds aggravate it. Anyway, I turn in at eight."

"Eight!"

"Up at four. See you tomorrow, Bick." He strode off. They were ascending the stairs when he came up behind them, he grasped Bick's arm, he jerked a thumb toward Leslie, he looked into Bick's face. "This girl is an unexceptional," he said earnestly. Was off down the stairs and out of the door.

Lupe had been partially efficient for once; the bowl of fruit was there, the bourbon, a bottle of champagne in a nest of ice.

"What's this?" Bick asked testily.

"This, darling, is what's known as food and drink, and the rest of it will be along in a minute. I hope."

The great brass sun was descending now in the vast tin sky, she opened the jalousies a little, she wished she could open the door so that the Gulf wind would meet the draft that funneled through the house, and at least move the air with a semblance of coolness.

Bick stumbled into the bathroom as Petra flung open the bedroom door without knocking, a habit that from the first moment Leslie had found maddening. Petra and Lupe carried trays, there was no table laid, Leslie cleared a space on the desk-table. She saw with utter dismay that the chicken she had envisaged as a platter of delicate cold slices in a nest of crisp green was a vast hot boiled fowl with gobbets of yellow fat marbling its skin, its huge thighs turned upward, steaming. There was a bowl of hot mashed potatoes and a wet greenish mass that looked like boiled beet tops. These bowls she picked up, one in each hand, and gave them to Petra and Lupe. "Take them. Take them away."

But they shook their heads, they placed the bowls again on the tray, Lupe, the older, spoke in Spanish as always, her voice low but vibrant with insistence. Leslie caught a familiar word or two —"patata . . . con carne . . . señor . . ." The señor likes potatoes always with his meat. All right. I'm being quite a clever girl, she thought, with my new Spanish. She smiled, she nodded, she urged them from the room. She busied herself with the trays.

The bathroom splashings and puffings had ceased. He emerged, his face seemed clearer, younger, the sagging lines were partly erased.

"What's this?" he asked as before, viewing the table with distaste.

"It's chicken," she said briskly. "I ordered it cold and they brought it hot. This is potato, I can't imagine why, and that's some sort of dreadful greens. And this is your wife. Remember?"

She came to him, she stood before him, she placed her cool slim hands on his cheeks. He bent his head and kissed her perfunctorily and walked away from her and seated himself in a chair by the window away from the food.

"A drink," she said. "You can have bourbon or you can have champagne, one or the other. You can't have both because one is grain and one is grape and they say you mustn't mix them. The French say so."

He looked down at his hands, he turned them over and inspected his palms as though expecting to find there something fresh and interesting. "The French, huh? They sure ought to know. You're hell-bent on civilizing me, aren't you?"

"Champagne I think," she said, and plunked ice into the glasses to cool them and gave the bottle a twirl. "Bourbon lasts longer but champagne's quicker. Open this, will you, dear?"

"Celebrating, aren't you?" he said, his eyes ugly.

I'm going to take over now, she told herself. I'm going to go right straight through, I'm going to jolt him out of this.

"No. I just wanted to make you eat a little and rest a little because if you don't you'll be ill. And because I love you. I wasn't thinking of Luz at the moment."

He passed his hand over his forehead and brought the hand down and wiped its palm on his handkerchief. "I didn't mean—I'm all mixed up today."

"But now you've brought it up, the truth is that it was Luz or us. And it is better that it was Luz."

He brought his head down to his two clasped hands. She came

258

to him and knelt on the floor and put her hand on his shoulder.

"Jordan, after this is over and everything is quiet, Jordan darling, couldn't we close this house or just use it for guests or something—there are so many here all the time—couldn't we open the old house—the little Main House—and live in that, you and I?"

"Why? What for?" He had raised his head. He was listening.

"I like it. It's a house. I'd love to live in it."

He looked around the room now, she saw that his mind was looking at the rooms and rooms and rooms that made up this fantastic pile rearing its bulk on the plains. "What's the matter with this house?"

"It's like living in a big public institution. It's got everything but high stone walls and sentries. It's Alcatraz—without charm. And then those miserable shanties down there where the Mexicans live."

"I noticed your nigger cabins in the dear old South weren't so sumptuous."

"I know. But neither are the sumptuous old mansions sumptuous any more. The South has been busted for almost a century. And Texas is booming. Papa says that twenty-five years from now the cabins and the mansions will disappear in a new industrial——"

"Forget what Papa says."

"All right. Your father built this house. Do you feel sentimental about it?"

At last he was jolted out of his numbness. He stood up as though jerked to his feet. "I hate it. I've always hated it. Ma hated it too. The only person who likes it is—was—Luz." His head drooped again.

Now! she thought. "I want our son to be born in the little old house."

"Son!" he shouted.

"It's just bound to be a son. No real Benedict would consider anything but a male first child. And I want him to be born in the house where his father was born."

16

THE GIRLS said she ought to get away. "It's fierce here July and August, even for us Texians, and we're raised on it." Proudly they quoted astronomical Fahrenheit figures. "Your condition and all, Leslie."

"My condition's fine. Fine and normal. My adrenal glands are working like a pumping station, Doctor Tom says. I'm a mass of energy."

"Yes, but just you wait," they predicted darkly.

"I'll have to. Unless they've modernized that old nine months' schedule. It's odd, isn't it? but the heat seems to stimulate me in

261

some crazy way. Jordan says I whirl so fast that he has to go out in the pasture and look at the big windmills to rest his eyes."

The Girls fancied the local custom of dropping in for coffee and conversation at ten or eleven in the morning. They arrived with their hair in pins, they sat they talked they drank gallons of coffee. Or they telephoned in the morning. They sat at the telephone and talked and drank coffee. These time-wasting habits drove Leslie to quiet desperation.

Mr. and Mrs. Jordan Benedict were moving out of the Big House and into the old Main House. The County rocked with the news. Together Bick and Leslie were supervising the reconstruction of the ancient dwelling. But it was Leslie who majored in the project. Leslie had plans to redecorate and refurnish from eaves to root cellar. She whisked about all day with rainbow-hued swatches of cloth in wool silk canvas felt denim linen chintz dangling from her fingers, stuffing her handbags, pinned crazy-quilt-fashion to the front of her dress. She knew exactly what she wanted, her decisions were almost instantaneous, her taste unerring, but no one was safe from her happy plans. It was as though she were giving a huge party and wanted everyone to share in the entertainment.

"Do you think this blue is too deep? Too Mediterranean? I want it to be the color of the Texas sky. That washed grey-blue. . . . This pale yellow is just right against it, don't you think? The lemon-yellow of the huisache in the spring. . . . What a time I had finding this pale green, just the shade of the mesquite. Jordan says he's spent billions trying to blast the mesquite off Reata and now I'm bringing it into the house. . . . Is this the color of mountain pinks? I've never seen them but if Jordan takes me up to Holgado later perhaps they'll still . . ."

Bits of paper flapped in the wind. Daubs of paint waited for approval on newly plastered walls. Chairs chests tables beds appeared remained or vanished. Leslie carried notebooks and a six-foot metal measuring tape that sprang out at you like a snake, whirring and rattling. Her supercharged energies encompassed Spanish lessons as well. She had discovered in the town of Benedict a sad-eyed professorial man of middle age who worked in some obscure capacity at the Ranchers and Drovers Bank.

"Pure Spanish," Bick assured Leslie. "Oñate's got no Mexican in him. He's as Spanish as Alfonso and darned near dates back like a Habsburg, too. His people have been in Texas practically ever since North America cooled off."

Fascinated, Leslie asked, "How many millions of acres does he own? He looks so defeated, though."

"Not an acre."

"But why!"

"Oh, you're still that Why Girl. Uh, the Oñates sold their Spanish land grants a century ago."

"Mhm," she said musingly. She supplemented the Oñate hours with alternate lessons in the more colloquial Mexican-Spanish lessons given her by the new schoolteacher who now ruled in Cora Dart's place. "Señor Oñate's Castilian Spanish is all very nice in Madrid court circles but I notice that when I go lisping around the Mexicans don't know what I'm talking about. Though all you need to do, really, is to speak Texan."

"What d'you mean, Texan?"

"Even if you don't know a word of Spanish you can't talk to anyone on Reata—to anyone in Texas, for that matter—five minutes without using words borrowed from the Spanish. Or Mexican. How about Reata! Retama. Remuda. Corral. Ranchero. Stampede. Mesa. Canyon. Rodeo. Corral. Sombrero. Pinto. Bronco. Thousands of words."

"Well, naturally. Everybody knows that." He regarded her fondly. "You really feeling all right, Leslie?"

"Simply superb. And so do you." Yes, you, she thought. We're happy, normally naturally happy, because a woman named Luz Benedict is dead, and it's much healthier to admit it, but he won't or can't yet.

He laughed. "Me! Well, that's different. I'm not exactly uh——"

"Yes you are, in a way. Because you're in love with me and I'm in love with you. We're one. We're three in one, really. What you feel I feel, what I feel you feel, you're really as pregnant as I am."

"Say, honey, for a girl brought up the way you were you're pretty rough-talking, aren't you?"

"Rough? It's a biological fact that two people in love———"

"All right all right all right! Suits me fine. Say no more." His arms about her, his vital being engulfing her.

Leslie and Vashti now had a common bond. These first weeks of pregnancy were not, however, flattering to Vashti. The Hake glands did not adjust as skillfully as did the Lynnton. Panting and uncomfortable, Vashti eyed her enceinte neighbor with an expression as near resentment as her naturally placid features could convey.

"Lookit the way you look, and then me. It's made you pretty, almost, your complexion and eyes and all. I got spots and my hair is stringy no matter what I do with it, and you don't even show. I look seven months instead of seven weeks. Pa doesn't even believe that Pinky and I behaved right before we were married, he says."

"It's because I'm tall and skinny," Leslie assured her. "What you all call ganted. Never mind. We'll both look worse before we're better."

But Vashti, moist and lumpy, was a disconsolate heap in one of Leslie's bedroom chairs. She sipped her ubiquitous coffee. "It's all I can do to sit up, let alone run around the way you do. Run run run with all those samples and stuff. What do you want to go and live in the little Main House for anyway, honey? It looks like a bad old mill. All these lovely rooms here in the Big House, it's a palace. Compared to it that old Main House is a Mexican shack."

"Palaces have gone out. Like the people who used to live in them."

Jordan the erstwhile glum bridegroom, Jordan of the knotted brow and the tense jaw, relaxed in this atmosphere of bustle and change and anticipation. He laughed at her, fondly. "You're trying to make Texas over into Virginia, honey. Next thing you'll have me riding in one of those red coats and some big old bull will come along and tromp me to death."

"Why are you Texans so afraid of anything that's beautiful or moving! You're all still stamping around with a gun in one hand and a skillet in the other. You're still fighting Indians and Mexicans and orange soufflés. Give up. Adapt yourselves. They're here to stay."

He shook his head, hopelessly. "I should have known. That very first morning up there in Virginia when you came down to breakfast blinking like a lighthouse pretending you were wide awake and used to getting up early. Talking a streak about Texas. You'd never heard of it until you reached out and grabbed me."

"My knight in shining armor! Shining, that is, if I use enough Brillo."

Grinning he regarded her and his smile faded. "Do you know what? I think you need to get away. How would it be if you took a breather somewhere cool with Adarene, maybe, or Vashti?"

"Darling, you don't know very much about wives, do you? I don't want to go anywhere until I've finished the house. And when I do go I want to go with you."

"I'm up to here in work."

"You always will be. Me too—I hope. But I'd like to see lots of places. San Antonio and the Alamo that they're always talking about."

"I know. But hot there now."

"Just a day or two. And then we could go up to Uncle Bawley's in the lovely mountains. Mountains!"

"Girls aren't invited to Uncle Bawley's."

"This one is."

"No!"

"Yes! Remember he left two minutes after the funeral? He came over to me with his eyes streaming and said, 'Along about July you get Bick to bring you up to Holgado. No women as a general thing, but you're different.' I've never been so flattered. And some of those Washington boys weren't bad at it."

265

GIANT

"In July it's likely to rain up there in Jeff Davis County."
"Oh, it's *that* Davis!"
"High up there at Holgado, a mile high some places, the nights are cool."
"It sounds heavenly! Jordan, can't we plan to go perhaps by midsummer? The house will be set and the ranch can run itself for a little while—all these millions of people on it, somebody must have some sense besides yourself. Anyway, I'm supposed to have whims now, and be humored."

Chip-chip clink-clink hammer-hammer went the tools of the workmen as they pierced the rocklike clay walls of the old Main House, transforming small dark rooms into luxurious bathrooms, adding servants' quarters, devising closet space, building the wide veranda that Leslie stubbornly insisted would be like an outdoor dwelling added to the house itself. "I won't sit indoors all day, like a cave dweller. And it will be cool, with this everlasting breeze, if we shade it and plant a sun-shield of trees, and lots of vines and have everything cool canvas in pale greens and pinks and blues. They do it in the tropics. Why not Texas!"

The old house had originally been built by slow hand labor, its stone and adobe walls were two feet thick, its window embrasures were cavernous, even the fierce shafts of the brush-country summer sun could not pierce this century-old fastness. It was cooler than the Big House ever had been.

Luz Benedict gone. Jett Rink gone. Cora Dart gone. Harmony. Peace. Home. The Big House became to Leslie as impersonal as the Vientecito depot. Guests came, went, it was like an hotel without a room clerk or a cashier's window. Sometimes—not often—Leslie found herself watching a doorway, listening for the quick tap-tap of scurrying boot heels, dreading to see the small vigorous figure, to hear the strident domineering voice dictating plans to the carpenters and painters. Leslie sensed that Bick, too, sometimes listened and held his breath. At such moments she would come to him and slip her arm through his and look up into his face. And she would say, as she had on her honeymoon, "I'm having a lovely time."

266

Almost fearfully he would bend his head to her lips. "Me too, honey."

"I feel as creative as Leonardo da Vinci, what with the baby going on inside and the house going up outside."

Her letters home were chatty and high-spirited. . . . I don't want to come back home for a visit now with my figure like a grampus and it's no good your coming here at this season it's howling roaring hot but somehow I don't mind I feel so very vital that I'm scared the baby will turn out to be an acrobat. . . . No Mama dearie don't send a complete layette from Best's there are really good shops here in Houston and Dallas and Hermoso though I haven't seen them yet, and even in Vientecito near by. . . . Besides, they have showers here, I don't mean Rain Showers I mean Baby Showers, the Girls give you Baby Showers and bring bootees and bibs and rattles and knitted gips. . . . Everything is different here you must see it. I am beginning to understand it a little. Some of it is wonderful and some of it is horrible, but perhaps that is true of any place—San Francisco California, or Chicago Illinois, or New York New York. But this isn't only an outer difference. You know how these things interest me, Papa. Your fault, I'm afraid. It's a difference that has to do with the spirit. Goodness, that looks awful on paper. So smug. . . . Doctor Tom says I can ride and walk and exercise as usual but no one walks. . . . We are going to a great Fiesta in Vientecito it's an annual thing, they never have bazaars or fairs or exhibitions in Texas it's always a Fiesta and everything's very Spanish or very Mexican or both and yet the real Mexicans aren't allowed to . . .

Not gradually, but quite suddenly, she felt that she belonged. She was part of the community. Her unabated curiosity about every aspect of Reata ranch life and the life of the town and the county and the far-flung state itself was a source of mingled amusement and irritation to Bick. He would greet her with a groan and, "Here's that Why Girl again," when she appeared at unexpected moments in unlikely places; when he and Gill Dace, the chief vet, were deep in some bovine experiment at the ranch lab; or in the midst of one of the rare sales of choice Benedict breeding bulls, attended by only the most serious and solvent stockbreeders within a radius of five hundred miles.

In the evening Bick would say, "Look, honey, what did you want to come down to the tent for! Hot and all that dust and yelling around. That's no place for a woman. In your condition."

"My condition's simply elegant and I don't even look out of drawing yet. Anyway, Luz used to take part in all that, didn't she?"

A muscle in his cheek twitched. "That was different."

"I'll never huddle in the harem and nibble poppy seed and sew a fine seam. You knew I was a nosy girl when you married me. I didn't deceive you, sir. From the first moment we met I couldn't have been more unpleasant."

"True, true," he murmured. "I only married you because I hoped I could slap you around and bully you into being my ideal little woman."

"Your mistake. You're stuck with it. Anyway, you know you're crazy about me."

Half in earnest, "Only your grosser side. That fine mind you inherited from your father is pretty damn repulsive. In a woman, that is."

"It'll come in handy when we're old gaffer and gammer."

Up and down the ranch. In and out of Benedict. The tradesmen and the townspeople recognized her and greeted her in open friendly Texas fashion. She drove her own car now, for short distances. The workings of the little town, the pattern of its life, of the county life, of the Texas way of living and thinking, began to open up before her observant eye and her keen absorbent mind.

"Jordan, what are those streams and streams of old broken-down trucks and Fords that go through town with loads of Mexicans? Men and women and boys and girls and even little children. Swarms of them."

"Workers."

"Workers at what?"

"Oh, depends on the time of year. Cotton pickers. And vegetables and fruit. In the Valley."

268

"Where do they come from?"

"If they're Mexicans they come from Mexico. Even a bright girl like you can figure that out."

"And when everything's picked where do they go?"

"Back to Mexico, most of them. A few sometimes hide out and stay, but they're usually rooted out and tossed back."

She tidied this in her orderly mind. Little bits and pieces marched obediently out of her memory's ranks and fell into proper place. *Coyote. Gomez. Fidel Gomez. Coyote. That's a name the Mexicans call a chiseler a crook. He lives off of them he sneaks them across the border from Mexico to work as pickers. . . . Time he's through with them they don't have nothing left when they get through working in the Valley crops. . . . And he rounds up the Mexican voters and does a lot of dirty jobs. . . .*

"Where do they live while they're here, with all those children and everything? What are they paid?"

"Leslie, for God's sake!"

"I just want to know, darling. This is all an everyday bore to you but I'm brand new, everything's different and strange to me. I can't help it. I am that way."

"I don't know. Very little. Couple of dollars. Whatever they're paid it's more than they'd get home in Mexico starving to death."

"Where do they live?"

"Camps. And don't you go near, they're a mass of dysentery and t.b. and every damn thing. You stay away. Hear me!"

"But if you know that why don't you stop it! Why don't you make them change it!"

"I'm no vegetable farmer, I'm no cotton grower. I'm a cowman. Remember?"

"What's that got to do with it! You're a Texan. You've been a great big rich powerful Texan for a hundred years. You're the one to fix it."

He shook his head. "No, thank you very much."

"Then I will."

"Leslie." His face was ominous, his eyes stared at her cold with actual dislike. "If you ever go near one of those dumps—if I ever hear of your mixing into this migratory mess——"

"What'll you do?"

"I swear to God I'll leave you."

"You can't leave Reata. And to get me out you'd have to tie me up and put me in a trunk or something. And I wouldn't stay put. I'd come back. I'll never leave you. I love you. Even when you glare at me like Simon Legree."

"And you'd look like Carrie Nation, barging around stuff that's none of your business. Fixing the world. We'll be the laughing-stock of Texas if this keeps on. I've heard that women in your condition sometimes go kind of haywire but I never thought my wife would be one of them."

He clumped out of the room, she heard the high-heeled boots clattering down the hall, the slam of the door, horse's hoofs on sun-baked earth.

He's gone. Where? Not far. Gill Dace. The Dietzes'. Old Polo. Anyone who is part of this kingdom. If Luz were alive he'd be rushing to her, his mother-sister. And she'd tell him he's right, he's always right. Should I do that? You're a wife your uh individuality should be submerged in the I don't believe it I can't I must be myself or I am nothing and better dead. Now sit quietly here in the chair and think. What started this squabble that is one of a hundred we're always having and then we make up in bed. Then in a day or two or three we are bickering again. Bick bickering now pull yourself together don't be cute. What started this one? You wanted to know about those thousands of Mexicans piled into trucks like cattle where do they live while they are picking what do they earn but you must not know this is a state secret so many things are state secrets all the things I am interested in perhaps I am becoming a worthy bore like those Madam Chairmen Madams Chairman anyway those large ladies in uncompromising hats at Meetings with gavels and pitchers of ice water. Jett Rink. He's the boy who could whirl me out to one of those camps and tell me all about the pickers. Put that out of your mind. Well then who else because I've made up my mind I'm not going to sit home and drink coffee and talktalktalk and play bridge in a Southwest harem the rest of my life Jordan was really furious this time I suppose I really am a kind of nuisance to him my darling Jordan. It is still early morning who will drive with me? Vashti? No. The new schoolteacher that Miss Minty, no. Besides, she has to teach school don't be silly. Señor Oñate at the bank, no. I wish Adarene were here instead of way up in Dallas it would be wonderful with Adarene. Dimodeo could drive me or one of the men in the garage or the stables.

"I'll go alone," she said aloud. "Why not! Don't be a sissy. After all, the Valley lies just the other side of Nopal, it won't take more than two or three hours, the whole thing, I'll be back in time for lunch."

In her shining little car in her neat silk dress, exhilarated and slightly short of breath from excitement, she tooled along the wide bright road in the wide bright morning. Through Benedict, familiar now, past the fences and fences and fences that were still Reata, into the grey-white somnolent little town of Nopal. The office of Fidel Gomez. That was the thing. He was the one to take her to a camp. He brought them in in droves. Let him explain what it was that Jordan didn't want her to see.

In her smart white kid handbag she had her little pocket Spanish-English dictionary. *Spanish and English used in the Western Hemisphere,* the cover read. Then neatly, *Español e inglés* (why the small *i,* she wondered always) *del Hemisferio Occidental.* Fair enough, she said to herself happily. She was enjoying herself immensely, full of success.

The streets were strangely empty, as before. A woman in a black rebozo came toward her. The street boasted no sidewalk, there was only a dirt path. Leslie stopped her car, she waited, she leaned out and called in her stumbling Spanish, "Oficina Señor Fidel Gomez. Favor de—uh—decirme."

The woman looked at her she looked away she muttered Yo no comprendo, she walked on. A man then. A small dark man with a resigned suffering face and greying hair in the black. Favor de decirme Oficina Señor Fidel Gomez? The man stopped dead, his eyes swiveled past her, he shrugged, he hurried swiftly on.

Well. What was the matter with everybody! Or what was the matter with her Spanish, more likely, she decided. Perhaps he didn't have an office. He had been hanging around outside that wineshop or whatever it was, that last time. Maybe that was the place. But Jordan wouldn't like that, her going there. She would just park outside and blow the horn. Up one dusty little street and down another. Bodega. There, that was it.

At the second blast of the horn, as though this were an accustomed form of summons, a figure leaned far out of the doorway and it was magically Fidel Gomez. Leslie decided not to try a lot of favor de this time.

"Come here, Mr. Gomez." Three faces appeared in the doorway peering behind Gomez' shoulder. With a nervous backward glance he came forward, removing his great Stetson passing his jeweled brown hand over his hair, placing the hat again on his head and again removing it as he stood at the door of the car. And as before she noted that his eyes were wide with apprehension.

No nonsense. "I am Mrs. Jordan Benedict. Remember?"

"Señora, can you ask——"

"Yes, well, I was talking to my husband this morning and I told him I wanted to see one of the camps—you know—where the Mexicans work—the pickers I mean. Where they live. So I drove over. Will you get in and we'll drive to one. You'll have to show me the way."

He shook his head, smiling a little patiently as one would gently chide a child. "No, señora, you would not want to go there."

"But I do. If you don't take me I'll go alone."

"You cannot do that."

"Don't tell me what I can or can't do! Is this the United States or isn't it!"

"Oh yes, señora," he assured her earnestly.

"Well, then, get in the car and we'll go."

272

"I will first telephone. I will call your husband."

Briskly, "He isn't home. He's—he's way out on the range or whatever you call it, somewhere. He left early this morning. Get in the car, Mr. Gomez."

Fidel Gomez pointed to a large bright scarlet automobile blazing proudly under the rays of the Southwest sun. "My automobile is there."

"Oh. Well?"

"If you will permit I will drive before you and you will please to follow me. We will stop at my house if you will honor me and my wife. We will drink coffee."

"No! Really no. I can't. I don't drink much coffee——"

Very gravely, "It is ten o'clock. My wife will be honored. She will, of course, come with us."

She looked at him standing there, so bland so obsequious so immovable so—I never knew how to pronounce it, she thought, but the word is imperturbable. He bowed now, he entered his car and preceded her, a small solemn procession, down the street.

The Gomez house was a neat square white box. Mrs. Fidel Gomez was a neat square dark box. Mrs. Gomez spoke absolutely no English, the Coyote informed Leslie when she tried to assure Mrs. Gomez that coffee was not necessary and that Mrs. Gomez' presence on this expedition was not necessary.

"My wife is happy to accompany us," Fidel Gomez assured Leslie. "She is honored. She will come with us. First we will have coffee."

In Mrs. Gomez' round olive Latin-American face and in Mrs. Gomez' round black eyes Leslie detected a faint flash of Anglo-American wifely resentment. She then vanished briefly while Leslie, in a quiet fury, and the Coyote in a pattern of correct Mexican etiquette sat on the edges of their chairs and conversed. A parlor set in a large-patterned combination of plush and flowered stuff. A large bridal photograph, gold-framed. And in a corner the household altar with its gaily colored images and its paper flowers, its candles and incense burners and the cross.

"I am interested in everything that is Texas," Leslie babbled, feeling foolish. "And Mexican, of course. Whole families in those trucks. Even babies and old men and women. They can't work, can they? Children of seven or eight, they seemed. And quite old old people?"

"Excuse me," said the Coyote. "One moment only."

"It's no use your telephoning my husband. He's not there."

"Excuse me. One moment only."

When he returned, "What are they paid?" she asked, relentlessly.

Mrs. Gomez appeared, carrying a tray. She had changed from her neat house dress to a tight and formal black. The ritual proceeded. They drank the strong black sweet coffee eying one another over the cup's edge, crooking their little fingers, fuming and smiling. He is being correct, Leslie realized. He is following an absolutely correct plan of conduct for a coyote toward a Benedict. Click-click cup on saucer, sip-sip coffee on tongue, quackquack voice on air. He is just trying to take up time for some reason. Jordan.

Abruptly she rose. "I am going now. If you wish to come with me, come. But you needn't. I can find a camp alone."

At a word from him Mrs. Gomez gathered the cups and in stately silence carried them away. A moment later the three stood facing the two cars by the roadside.

"Would you and Mrs. Gomez like to ride with me? Or . . . ?" She sensed there was some sort of protocol here.

The stiff and unconvincing smile still on his face. "It will be more comfortable for you if my wife and I we drive in my car to show the way. You will follow in your car. In that way——"

Uh-huh, she thought. He is not to be seen driving with the wife of Jordan Benedict. "Lovely," she said, matching smile for smile. "But I want to see a camp. No nonsense."

"Mrs. Benedict," he said. At least he's dropped the señora stuff, she noted.

Each in the burning-hot front seat of a car. Off. A mile, two three four. There was the Gomez hand flipping a stop signal at the left of the red car. And there was a desolate trampled piece of land by the roadside. And there were the broken camp shacks and the sheds; there were the crazy outhouses. A low-slung crawling dog, lean as a snake. No human thing moved in the camp.

Fidel Gomez came around the back of his car and stood at the door of Leslie's car as it stopped. He leaned an arm against the sill and smiled. "It is not worth to get out," he said. "There is no person there."

"Why not?"

"What is here is working, picking. The season here is near the end."

She looked at the barren field. No shade from the cruel sun.

"But I saw little children in those trucks and those old broken cars with the mattresses and the pots and pans. And old people."

"They are picking."

Sharply she jerked the brake, locked the car, dropped the keys neatly into her handbag. "I'm going to get out and see the place."

Her challenging eyes met his flat depthless black ones and in that instant she saw two little red points leap at the center of his pupils. Two little red devils, she told herself. How strange. I've never seen that before. She stepped out, shook her rumpled skirts, adjusted her hat. "Mrs. Gomez?"

She was almost relieved to notice that he no longer wore the smile. "My wife will sit in the automobile. She will wait."

She walked down into the roadside ditch and up the other side and into the smothering dust of the bare field. Now she saw that there were ragged small tents beyond the sagging sheds. She walked swiftly toward the nearest shed. She heard his footsteps just behind her. She peered into the splintered shelter. Empty. A mattress or two on the floor; blankets, too, spread there as though the sleepers had risen from them and left them as they were; some sagging collapsible beds. No one. Two or three rusty stoves, open and unlighted, stood incongruously in the open field. Here and there on the ground you saw the ashes of what had been an open fire.

"You see," came the voice of Fidel Gomez, always just behind her, "there is no one, they are all busily at work in their jobs. A good thing."

Now she heard a low murmur of talk. Gingerly, and feeling somehow embarrassed, she peered into one of the ragged pup tents. A woman lay on a mattress on the ground. Squatting on her haunches at the side of the mattress was an old woman. The two looked wordlessly, without a sign of resentment, at the chic silken figure that held aside the open tent flap.

"Oh, I'm so sorry. Please excuse me," Leslie murmured idiotically. And stood there, staring. Then, over her shoulder to Gomez, "There's someone here. Please tell them in Spanish I'm sorry to have—I mean intruding like this——" as if she had blundered, unbidden, into a formal dwelling.

"I speak English," said the girl on the mattress.

"Oh, how nice!" Leslie said. "Are you ill?"

"I have had a baby," the girl said.

"How lovely!" Leslie said.

"He is dead," the girl said.

Leslie took a step forward and let the tent flap fall, so that she stood within and Gomez outside. The heat under the canvas was stifling. "When?"

"Last night." Then, at the look in Leslie's eyes: "They took him away this morning, early, before my husband went to work, and the others."

"Let me help you. Let me—— Where is your home? Are you Mexican?"

"I am American," the girl said. Now Leslie, accustomed to the half-light of the tent, saw that the pinched and greyish face was that of a girl not more than seventeen. She felt her own face flaming scarlet. There! she said to herself. Take that!

"I have my car here. If you're able—could I somehow take you home? I'd be glad to help. You and your—mother?"

"My home is Rayo. Near the border. There is no one there. We are all here, working. This"—with a little gesture of formality—"is the mother of my husband."

"Working," Leslie repeated dully. She began to feel strange and unreal. Then, to her own horror, "Who?"

"All of us. Tomorrow I will work, or the next day. My husband and my brother and my husband's brother and my sister and my husband's mother."

She had to know. "How much? What do they pay you?" She heard a little stir outside the tent.

The girl did not seem to find the question offensive or even unusual, she answered with the docility of one who never has known privacy. "Together it is six dollars a week."

"Six!"

"Sometimes seven. Sometimes five."

"All?"

"Sure all."

Leslie opened her smart white handbag. Sick with shame at what she was doing. A crumpled little roll of bills there—ten—twenty—she didn't know. Miserably she stepped forward, she stooped and placed it on the mattress. "Please," she said in a small wretched voice. "For the baby. I—please don't mind."

The girl said nothing. The old woman said nothing. They looked at the money, their faces expressionless. Abruptly Leslie turned and stumbled through the tent flap into the blinding sunshine, she bumped into the man standing so close to the flap but she went on unheeding until a stench that was like a physical blow made her recoil. She opened her eyes. There were the open latrines, fly-covered, an abomination beneath the noonday sun.

The early morning quarrel, the drive, the hot sweet coffee, the shock, the heat, the stench now gathered themselves tightly together like a massive clenched fist to deal Mrs. Jordan Benedict an effective blow to the diaphragm. She was violently sick on the dust-covered scabland.

Delicately Fidel Gomez turned away.

17

NO, HE HAD NOT come in at midday, they told her. But then, he rarely did. White and shaking she put herself to bed. No, no coffee, she said in her halting Spanish to Lupe; and put her hand quickly to her mouth. She lay there in the heat of the day, quivering a little now and then with an inexplicable chill. The sounds of the great house and of the outdoors came to her with curious remoteness as though filtered through a muffled transmitter. The hammering and clinking of tools wielded by the workmen busy with the remodeling of the Main House. Far-off voices from the Mexican quarters. Cars coming, going. As always there were guests here at the Big House, half the time she scarcely knew who they were, or what their purpose there. Hoofbeats. It was one of the sounds she loved. She dozed a little. Words drifted through a mist. I have had a baby. How lovely! He is dead. Leslie turned over on her elbow and began to cry, ceased to cry and fell asleep.

She awoke refreshed, she bathed, she dressed herself in one of her trousseau tea gowns, tried a dab of rouge, regarded herself critically in the mirror, decided that pallor was more effective for her purpose, even if less flattering, wiped off the rouge. She read and listened. She wrote a letter and listened. The crude clangor of the dinner gong. The voices of guests in the hall, the tap-tap of high-heeled boots. He had not come up and when she went downstairs, her head high her spirits low, he was not there. How do you do? Good evening. Howdy. Have you had an interesting day? Oklahoma! No, I haven't but of course I've heard so much about it. Yes, he usually is but he is so very busy at this time of year.

They sat at dinner, eleven in all, she could see the doorway and the great hall beyond but he did not come and she ate quite a surprising dinner and talked and listened and said I hope you will excuse me I have been a little not really ill but under the Texas weather. With a society laugh.

Back in her room she took up some sewing. She sat near the lamp and made small stitches. The Little Mother To Be. She hated sewing. She wadded up the stuff and tossed it aside, she took up her book but a slow hard hot kernel of anger was forming in her vitals. I really hate him, she said. I hate all of it. I loathe and despise it. She leaned back and looked straight ahead at nothing, her eyes wide and staring. She relaxed, slowly. She slept again, worn out by emotion and the heat.

When she awoke Bick was seated across the room. He was looking at her, his arms hanging loosely on either side, his legs sprawled. She was wide awake. In silence they stared at each other. Hammer hammer hammer. But the workmen had gone. It was her heart. She stood up. He stood up. They came together, they were not conscious of having walked or run or even moved.

They were together. She could not be near enough. "Closer," she demanded insistently. "Closer closer."

Flushed and disheveled then she lay in his arms.

"That Gomez telephoned?"

"Yes."

"What's so terrible about it! What's so terrible about going to look at a Mexican work camp?"

"Sh! Never mind. I talked to Adarene."

"Here?"

"No, Dallas. I called her. She thinks you're due for a change. So do I. Let's go up to Holgado for a few days."

"Oh, Jordan! When?"

"Right away. Adarene said they could start tomorrow, if we can. But I said day after tomorrow."

Her disappointment was like a knife thrust. "Can't we go alone, just you and I? It would be so wonderful if we could go alone."

"It would. I know. But there are a lot of things I've got to talk to Lew about. Luz's will and a lot of things. He knows the whole family setup. And Vashti and Pinky are——"

"No no no! Please! Not the Snyths too!"

"It's ranch business, honey."

"I can't see why that's a reason for traveling in bunches, like a safari."

"Texans always do. It's a hangover, I reckon, from the old days when if they didn't stick together they'd be scalped by Indians or lose their way or get bitten by rattlesnakes."

"How are we going? A string of automobiles? Or perhaps all of us in big hats on palominos with old Polo in the lead like a Buffalo Bill Wild West parade."

"My bittersweet bride. I thought we'd drive as far as San Antonio—if you still insist on a day there, in the heat. The Moreys will come down from Dallas and meet us there. I don't want you to take a long trip by automobile. From there we'll go by train, a private car, San Antonio to Holgado."

"Like royalty."

"In the last fifty years that road has made enough off us to give us private parlor cars for shipping beef cattle, if we want it."

Before they slept she told him of her day at Nopal. It was cleansing to her, like a confessional, until he said, "But it's got nothing to do with us."

"But it has! It *is* us!"

Sadly, almost desperately, he said, "Are you going to keep on being like that? Are you always going to be like that?"

"Always," she said.

Bick at the wheel, Pinky and Vashti following in the car behind them, they started Texas fashion two days later in the dim starlit dawn. Into the hot old romantic city of San Antonio with its hot new commercial streets like the streets of any modern American city, North or South East or West. Leslie made no comment, she was crushed by disappointment. They passed the Plaza with its towering office buildings its busy bus station its crowds milling up and down the streets.

"Alamo," Bick said briefly, and pointed to a dust-colored building with its dust-colored wall.

"That." Her voice flat.

Ignoring the modern St. Anthony Hotel they went to the Menger because the Benedicts always stayed at the Menger. It was old Texas with its patio and its red plush and its double beds; its smell of bourbon and bay rum and old carpets and fried food and ancient dust; its tiled floor sounding to the tap of high-heeled boots and the clink of spurs.

"Well, that's more like it!" Leslie exclaimed, heartily. "I love it."

"You're pleased by the damnedest things," Bick said. "You turn up your nose at the Big House and here's this hotel filled like a museum with the same kind of Texas stuff——"

"That's different," she argued airily. "Who wants to live in a museum! Jordan, when we really move into the Main House let's not have a visitor stay overnight there, ever. It will be our house. They can stay at the Big House, I don't care who they are.

Royalty or even Papa and Mama or Maudie Lou or any other Benedict."

"I've always heard about this Virginia hospitality," he jibed.

Vashti knocked at their door, you could hear her eager small-girl voice chattering with Pinky like a child at a party. In they bounced. Ten minutes later the Moreys arrived from Dallas. The bourbon emerged from suitcases, ice and glasses came tinkling down the corridor, Adarene, as quietly executive as a professional guide, took the plans in hand. Immediately the three men went into a small huddle. Bick made a large gesture. "Anything you girls say is all right with us."

"You look simply lovely, Leslie," Adarene said. Then, hurriedly, "You too, Vashti. Now girls, we've only got this one day and part of tomorrow, and it's awfully hot, even for San Antonio. Let's get organized. Though I don't think you two are ideally fixed for sight-seeing just now, I must say."

"Nonsense. We're full of demon energy," Leslie said. "The Alamo. That's the first thing."

But Adarene had made her plans more dramatically. "No, you've got to work up to the Alamo. The Missions come first."

"Now just a minute," Bick objected, emerging from the huddle. "Those Mission stairs. Leslie can't go climbing those. Every step is a foot high, they twist like a rope, it gets you in the thighs and the knees and the calf of the leg. I'm not going to have my son born with corkscrew legs."

"That's right," Vashti agreed. "I never will forget the first time I visited San Antonio, Pa brought me, I was fifteen. Everything in one day. I did all the Missions, one right after another. Concepción wasn't so hard, and then that cute little San Francisco de la—something—Espada I think. Anyway, couple others, and by the time I got to San José Mission I was beat, I didn't know about those twenty-three stairs built like a fan so you kind of meet yourself climbing up to the tower. Next day I was like somebody had their legs cut off and pinned back on with safety pins. They wouldn't hold me up. Crippled."

"I won't do them all," Leslie pleaded. "But I've got to see them and climb just one stairway. The San José one, Jordan?"

"Not the San José," firmly.

"It's sort of a novelty, being considered fragile."

Adarene eyed her thoughtfully. "I was just thinking. Maybe we should have gone right on up to Holgado."

"Stop hovering, dearies. Yes, it's hot. And I'm having a lovely time."

Lucius Morey, that strange mixture of Vermont and Texas, Lew the unloquacious, in his dark business suit and his plain black shoes and neat white shirt and the incongruous Stetson hat, had sat silent while the talk eddied about him. The bland face, the keen light blue eyes now turned toward Leslie. He spoke in that nasal dry tone that they termed his Coolidge voice. "Leslie, you're a real fine girl," he said gravely.

Leslie did not share in the laugh that greeted this pronouncement. Just as gravely she said, "Thank you, Lucius. For the first time I feel sort of Texan, here in San Antonio."

"No wonder. This is where the whole thing began," Bick explained. "I don't mean the Spanish Missions and all that. This is the real beginning of Texas. This is where two old boys, flat broke and in their fifties, met up on the Plaza. One of them was the Baron de Bastrop and the other was old Moses Austin. This was San Antonio de Bexar in those days. And Americans were about as welcome in Texas then as——"

"As Mexicans are now," Leslie said.

"Texas history is real interesting," Vashti offered. "Only nobody knows anything about it only Texans. Easterners always yapping about Bunker Hill and Valley Forge and places like that, you'd think the Alamo and San Jacinto were some little fracas happened in Europe or someplace. Look how important they were! If it hadn't been for Sam Houston, and Bowie with that knife of his, and Davy Crockett and Travis, why, there wouldn't of been any Texas in the United States, can you imagine! No Texas!"

"Vashti, don't give any Texas lectures when Leslie's around,"

284

Bick advised her. "She began to bone up on Texas ten minutes after she met me. By now she knows so much Texas history she makes old Frank Dobie look like a damyankee."

"Let's get going," Pinky cautioned them. "Maybe Leslie knows more but Vash can outtalk any historian living *or* dead. Say, Bick, you ever tell Leslie about how Texas has got the right to split up if it has a mind to?"

"No," Leslie said, mystified. "Split up? How?"

"Oh, all right," Bick groaned. "They put it in the state constitution when Texas joined the Union. She wouldn't join otherwise. It says Texas has the right to split itself into five separate states any time it wants to."

Leslie stared, unbelieving. "Like one of those bugs," she murmured, not very tactfully, "that reproduces by breaking off pieces of itself."

"If we ever do it," Lucius Morey reflected, "we'll have enough United States senators down here in the Southwest to run the whole damn country."

"Never will though," Adarene announced with definiteness. "Texas'll never split itself because if it did it wouldn't be able to say it was the biggest state, and being biggest is what we yell about most."

"Anyway, all five pieces would want to claim the Alamo for itself," Pinky concluded, "so I guess we're yoked for life."

"San Antonio's rigged for the tourist," Lucius Morey said, "but back of the bunco it's the real thing anyway, somehow. It's an old Spanish city real enough, with a flower in its hair and a guitar handy."

The narrow river meandered through the town like the stream of tourists, doubling on itself, turning up at unexpected places. Here in this ancient American city the brush-country Texan momentarily forgot about the miles of mesquite and the endless plain. Hermoso hadn't this look, or Houston or Dallas or Vientecito or Austin. Adobe huts two hundred years old crouched in the shadow of skyscrapers. Blood and bravery and beauty and terror and the glory of the human spirit were written in the history of these winding streets. They had been trails stamped out by the feet of conquistadores and of padres and the early Spanish settlers. And by the hoofs of the Castilian cattle brought in by the Spaniards in 1690. Their wild offspring, caught and bred again and again through the centuries to Longhorns Shorthorns Angus Hereford Brahmans Kashmirs, were to become the monolithic monsters who fed on the nutritious grasses of Reata Ranch.

Leslie bought a guidebook and a concise history of the city, modern and debunked. She walked about reading from these, one finger between the pages, her gaze going from book to object in approved tourist fashion.

"You can't do that!" the Texans protested, outraged.

"Mmm—San Antonio," mumbled Leslie. "Who named it San Antonio?"

The Texans stared at one another. "Uh——"

Her forefinger traced down the page. "Let's see . . . Don Domingo Teran de los Rios, with Father Damian Massanet and an escort of fifty soldiers . . . June 1691 . . . came upon ranchería of Payayas . . . What's a Payaya?"

"Indian tribe," Bick replied briskly.

"Wonderful word, isn't it?—all those ya-yas in it. I never heard of them."

Emboldened by Bick's success, "A branch of the Comanches, I believe," Lucius Morey ventured. "Mean-acting Indians, the Comanches were."

"Look, Leslie," Vashti objected. "This way we'll never get to show you anything. Why can't you just see things and not have to know about how they got there and everything."

But Leslie was reading again in a rather maddening mumble. ". . . The Indians called the village Yanaguana . . ."

She looked up, speculatively.

"Nobody knows nobody knows!" Adarene assured her.

". . . uh . . . Father Massanet set up a cross . . . christened the place San Antonio in honor of St. Anthony of Padua. . . . In 1718 Don Martín de Alarcón and Fray Antonio de San Buenaventura Olivares with settlers monks and soldiers . . ."

286

She looked up from the book, her face alight. "Don Domingo de los Rios. Fray Antonio de San Buenaventura Oli—— I don't know why it makes me happy just to say all those words and to know about Payayas and those poor little fifty soldiers. But it does."

"It reads real pretty," Pinky agreed. "If there's one thing about San Antonio, it's history."

"Who's showing who Texas, that's what I want to know!" Vashti demanded, somewhat sulkily for her. "Indians. Who cares about Indians and soldiers and stuff! The Mexican quarter is real picturesque, they wear charro outfits and play guitars."

Leslie tucked the guidebook under her arm and turned to a passage she had marked in the modern volume. "Uh, San Antonio is the pecan-shelling center of the Southwest. The industry employs about twelve thousand Mexican workers in the Mexican Quarter . . . uh . . . average piecework wage for a 54-hour week is $1.56. . . ."

Gently Bick Benedict took the book from her hands and closed it. "How would you have liked it if I'd told you how Virginia——"

"But we stumble all around Europe with our noses in Baedekers. I don't see why we shouldn't know about our own sights." The tactful Adarene to the rescue.

Pinky settled it. "The Benedicts have been in these parts for about a hundred years now. Anybody around here see Bick Benedict with his face in a guidebook, he's liable to be run out of the state of Texas."

"Oh, my land let's get going." Vashti again.

So off they went to visit the musty little Missions with their tortuous stairs and Leslie produced her book again with its dry terse accounts of incredible deeds in which padres and Indians and Spanish grandees, slaughter and agriculture and sculpture and frescoes were fantastically mingled.

"The walls of Mission Concepción are forty-five inches thick," Leslie read. "Think of it! The Indians built them with almost no tools. And the monks." She read on. "Acanthus leaves . . . front façade . . . Renaissance influence of the Churrigueresque school of Spanish Baroque . . ."

"Oh, for heaven's sake, Leslie!"

They ate Mexican food to the strumming of the Mexicans' guitars on the Plaza. Spicy burning food. Tortillas. Enchiladas. Mole de guajolote.

"What's that?" Leslie asked.

"Terrific turkey thing," Bick explained. "It's the top Mexican dish. Turkey with a sauce made of—oh—chiles and ground almonds and all kinds of spices and chocolate——"

"Chocolate!"

The musicians in their charro clothes. Shadowy figures in and out of the dim arcades. A vendor's soft persuasive cry. Strange exotic smells. Leslie fell silent.

Bick touched her hand. "Come on back to us, honey. What are you thinking about way off there?"

She turned toward him gravely. "I was thinking of Boston."

"Boston!"

"I mean—it's a kind of wonderful country, isn't it? I mean—I was thinking about how it all hangs together somehow even when it's as different as—I was thinking about Boston because San Antonio and Boston are absolutely the most different—the Ritz Hotel in Boston. That cool green dining room with the long windows looking out on the Common. Those big elm-tree branches make a pattern against the glass. And those dowdy Boston women and the agreeable Boston men with their long English heads. And the lobster so sweet and fresh and tender and the heavy white linen and the waiters' beautiful clean white fingernails. And old Faneuil Hall." She stopped, she looked into their disapproving faces. Lamely, "I haven't explained very well. I just meant it's just a kind of wonderful country altogether I mean——" Her voice trailed off into nothing.

She was noticeably silent in the Alamo. "I guess maybe you were oversold on it in the first place," Lucius Morey said. "All Yankees are. Anyway, the Alamo is a feeling, not a place."

All around the adobe walls swirled the life of a modern city.

Big business streamed in and out of the department stores, in and out of the new post office, in and out of the bus station. The old tragic Alamo with its history of blood and bravery was a new Alamo, reconstructed within an inch of its life.

Picture postcards. Souvenirs. At a desk in the great grey stone hall sat a schoolteacherly woman in spectacles who eyed the visitor with detached severity. The figures moving about the dim room tiptoed as in a cathedral and their voices dropped to a whisper.

In the glass cases were the mementos. Proof of the mad glorious courage of a handful of men against a horde—men who had come to this Texas wilderness from Massachusetts and Tennessee, from Virginia and Louisiana and Connecticut. In the glass cases under lock and key were the famed long-rifles that had barked so hopelessly against the oncoming enemy. Neat and cold and quaint in their glass caskets the long-rifles lay now, with their ornamental brass eagles and their six-foot unavailing barrels. And there was the slashing knife of Bowie. Bowie, on his cot in the crumbling Alamo fortress, Bowie already dying of typhoid and pneumonia and exposure and alcohol, wielding the pistols and the knife from his cot bed until they ran him through with their bayonets and it was finished.

The letters under glass too—stiff formal letters written in extremity by desperate men. ". . . Your favour of the 11 Inst came safe to hand by the last mail and I will hasten to answer the contents."

He must indeed hasten, this Davy Crockett who wrote so politely, for he was soon to die for Texas—for this strange and vast and brutal land that he and the drunken ruined brave Bowie of the terrible knife and the glory-seeking Travis all fought for and died for, though they had perhaps little legal right to do either.

Tourists trailed through the garden, through the chapel, through the museum, whispering and pointing and staring. Young bridal couples, honeymooning. Middle-aged ranchers, their high-heeled boots clicking on the stone floors, their wives plumply corseted in city clothes. Leslie watched a stout dark-skinned Mexican with his wife and three small children. Their faces were impassive as they looked at the knives, the guns, the flags. They were neatly dressed in their best. The woman trailed a little behind the man, and stared and quieted the restless infant in her arms.

There at the far end of the dim room were the six flags that had flown in sovereign authority over this violent and capricious state. Draped and festooned, they made a brilliant splash of color against the grey stone wall. The flag of ancient Spain. Of France. Of Mexico. Of the Republic of Texas. The Southern Confederacy. The United States of America. Two hundred and fifty years of violence of struggle, of unrest.

Leslie Benedict stood in the shadows of the great vaulted room, her head averted. "Don't mind me. Pretend you're not with me. I cry at parades, too, so don't mind me."

She stood there in the room that had become a sort of shrine to the arrogant swaggering giant—Texas. Texas. Jett Rink. Jordan Benedict. Adarene Morey. Doctor Tom Walker. Angel Obregon. Pinky Snyth. Uncle Bawley. Vashti Hake. She stared at the festooned flags and the colors misted and became faces and the faces faded and the folds of the flags began to ripple strangely.

"Heh, you feeling funny, Leslie?" Bick, his arm around her shoulder, his eyes searching her face with concern.

"No. I'm feeling fine. The flags. I suppose I stared at them so long the colors made me dizzy."

"You've just about seen it all. How about going back to the hotel and getting a rest? Before we make the train."

"In just a little while. I want to see the pictures. Just the pictures, and then we'll go."

Oil paintings made vivid splashes of scarlet and blue and gold against the walls. Men in buckskin breeches. Men in battle. Men dying. Men attacking. Invariably there were the brave white Americans rising superior over the dark-skinned Mexicans. Even if they were about to die they fought on, facing their adversaries with fortitude and an expression of civilized superiority.

The Mexican and his wife and children had finished gazing at the old guns and knives and battered mementos in the glass cases, and puzzling over the faded ink of Travis' desperate letters:

Commandancy of Bexar,
Feb. 23d. 3 o'clock P.M. 1836
To Andrew Ponton, Judge, and Citizens of Gonzales:
The enemy in large force is in sight. We want men and provisions. Send them to us. We have 150 men and are determined to defend the Alamo to the last. Give us assistance.
W. B. Travis-Col, Commanding.

They were standing just beside Leslie now staring at the paintings in oil of those to whom the men and the provisions never came. Here in crude glowing colors were depicted the dark-skinned men in natty bright uniforms and the white-skinned men in the bloodstained shirts and the buckskins of the storied pioneer, and the dark men were hacking with knives and shooting with guns at the valiant white-faced men, and the faces of the one were ferocious and of the other agonized and brave. And which was right and which was wrong? Leslie asked herself. And which was aggressor and which defender?

Beside her the Mexican and his wife with the child in her arms and the two wide-eyed children gazed at the pictures and the oldest child—the boy—pointed and asked a question, puzzlement in his eyes and in his voice. And the man replied in Spanish, low-voiced.

"Better watch out, Bick!" Pinky said. "Your wife's got that look in her eye can't tear herself away from Bill Travis. Or is it Sam Houston?"

Bick laughed as he took Leslie's arm. "They were both great boys with the ladies. Which is it, Leslie? They're good and dead, so I don't have to mind too much."

Leslie turned as though she had not heard. "You were right about sight-seeing. I am rather tired."

"You take things too hard," said the practical Vashti. "What was it you were so upset about in there?"

"It could be so wonderful."

"What could? What could be so wonderful?"

"Texas."

"Texas! Listen at her! Texas *is* wonderful. Honestly, Leslie, sometimes I think you're real horrid, the way you talk."

Bick's arm was about his wife's shoulder. "It used to rile me too, Vashti, until I caught on. It's what they call impersonal observation."

Briskly Adarene Morey said, "Anyway, we've all had enough of Missions and Mexicans and mole de guajolote. I'll be glad to get on that train."

"When we're all settled on the train let's order something wonderful for supper," Vashti suggested as they walked down the Alamo garden path.

"Steaks," Pinky said.

"No!" the women shrieked.

Vashti's plump pink face took on the look of a misty-eyed dreamer. "What I'd love is regular train food you never get anywhere else, hardly. Chicken potpie with teensy onions in the cream gravy, and corn muffins and that salad with Roquefort cheese dressing and for dessert blueberry pie à la mode with chocolate ice cream."

"You all right, Leslie?" Adarene inquired anxiously, as her friend turned noticeably pale.

"I'm all right," said Leslie. "Holgado. Is it really cool?"

18

THE SPECIAL CAR had been docilely waiting for them on the siding at San Antonio, ready to be picked up by the crack express that hurtled across the continent to the Mexican border and beyond into Mexico itself. There was the porter welcoming them like an old family servitor. He knew who took charged water, who took branch water, who took it straight; the Benedicts and the Moreys and the Hakes apparently had been part of his railroad life for years. He greeted them like long-lost benefactors.

"Well, this is mighty nice," Lucius Morey said and sank into one of the great plushy seats with the air of one who has come home after a hard day's work.

Pinky tossed his big Stetson with an expert twirl so that it landed neatly in the overhead rack at a distance of twenty feet. "I haven't done so much walking since one time my horse died on me middle of the desert. I had to lug my old kack twenty miles afoot. Nothing beats you out like sight-seeing."

"That's right," Bick agreed. "I'd rather do a day's roundup than one more Mission."

The jaunt took on a holiday air. Everyone felt relaxed. Vashti bubbled. "Ooh, look, it's a brand-new car they've got it uphol-stered in blue isn't that cute I never saw blue before on a train it's always green . . ."

"George, we'll want a setup right away, plenty of ice . . ."

"That goes there and this goes here—no, the Benedict draw-ing room . . ."

"A menu from the dining car we'll eat right here . . ."

The three men then said "Phew!" and glanced toward the little pantry from which came the tinkle of ice and glass. A waiter in a cardboard-stiff white apron and jacket appeared with menus. "Tengo hambre," Pinky yelled. "Come on, amigos, let's get to-gether on this. Vash! Girls!"

The three women emerged from their rooms along the corridor at the far end of the car. In some miraculous way heat and weari-ness had vanished. They were fresh and fragrant as peppermint patties.

Solemnly they sipped their highballs and scanned the list of dinner dishes "Six dinners to haul in from the galley back in the dining car," Pinky said. "So don't let's go hog-wild and order the works, it'll take from here to breakfast to get it."

There was a gate—a little crossbarred iron gate—that stretched across their car platform and separated it from the other cars. It was not locked, it folded back on itself like an accordion. Their private porter, full of his own importance, closed it opened it as he went back and forth on his errands. Now and then a stray passenger would drift in past the folding gate, thinking this was a public lounge car, he would see six people seated there talking and drinking and laughing, he would sink into one of the luxurious seats and look about him with an air of relief and calm. Slowly an uncertain look would come into his face, then puzzlement, then embarrassment. No one said anything, the deferential colored porter did not approach these people. They vanished, red-faced. One man came in, boots, Stetson, city clothes. He seated himself, then his face beamed with a smile of recognition. "Well, say, Bick, you old sonofagun! Pinky! Howdy, Pinky!"

"Hi!" the men said. "Howdy, Mel!"

He rose, he came toward them, then a certain something seemed to strike him, an apprehensive look came into the frank blue eyes. Deliberately he stood. Those crinkled eyes that had stared so many years across the endless plain now slowly encompassed the luxurious room on wheels, the strangely empty seats, the porter eying him with amused hostility from the far doorway; the neatness, the lack of piled-up luggage.

"Have a drink, Mel?" Bick called to him. "How about supper with us? Had your supper?"

"Well, say," Mel stammered, blushing like a boy. "I didn't go for to stomp in on your party. Excuse me!" He shook his head and raised his hand in a rather touching gesture of apology and farewell as he walked out of the car. You heard the little folding gate outside go clink and clank as it opened and closed.

Leslie felt guilty and embarrassed but no one else seemed to attach any importance to the coming and going of Mel or his fellow travelers.

Pinky said, "Mel still got that little bitty place up to San Angelo? About fifteen sections, ain't it?"

"Thereabouts. Ten twelve thousand-acre piece," Bick said. "Over-used his grass, and over-stocked. Going under, I'd say."

Pinky disposed of him. "That's the trouble with those little fellows. Feeders. They let the grassland run down and have to feed their young stock cake and then they wonder where the money goes."

"Cake!" said Leslie, scenting a Texas joke.

They laughed tolerantly, Bick laid a fond possessive hand on her knee. "Cake, Yankee, is feed—cottonseed cake. Concentrated cow feed and good and damned expensive."

"That's right," Pinky agreed virtuously—Pinky the erstwhile cow hand newly come into the prospect of two million acres. "Abuse the rangeland and what's happened to Texas the last half century! Couple inches of topsoil lost from millions of acres, that's what. Like to've wrecked the state."

"Why don't they make them put it back?" Leslie inquired.

A roar went up. Vashti Hake's shrill defense came to her through the uproar. "Never you mind, Leslie."

She could laugh with them, but she persisted. "Well, but why?"

Thoughtfully Bick stared out of the window at the hundreds—thousands—millions of acres of semi-arid land.

"Because man hasn't the trick of making earth—or maybe he just hasn't got the time. To build back a couple of inches of topsoil in Texas would take nature from eight hundred to four thousand years."

Fascinated, Leslie persisted. "Then why doesn't somebody teach them not to neglect the grassland in the first place?"

Vashti had been rummaging in a huge box of chocolates with which she had fortified herself against the rigors of the journey. She was eating a fondant-filled sweet and drinking a bourbon highball, a unique gustatory feat of which even Pinky disapproved. He offered mild protest. "Vash, chocolates and liquor don't go together, they don't set right. Anyway, all that supper'll be along any minute."

Vashti ignored this epicurean counsel. Through a mouthful of creamy fondant and a sip of the highball she still sounded brisk and emphatic.

"Teach hell! They got no right to go ranching on a little bitty old piece you couldn't run a goat on. They'd do better go to work for folks know how to run a real ranch. Like Pa. Or Bick. Or even the Moreys though they only run two three hundred thousand acres since they got to be city folks."

"No!" said Leslie, to her own surprise. "That isn't the way. That isn't a good way."

Vashti hooted good-naturedly. "Isn't the way! Listen at the Texian talking!"

It was not until twenty years later that Bob Dietz the agronomist spoke the words which Leslie now was too inexperienced to phrase.

"Reata," he said two decades later, "and the Hake ranch and all those overgrown giants are dated. A man who knows modern methods can make a success of four sections and not feed his stock a pound of hay or cake even in a drought season. But success or failure, a man who's running his own ranch is a man. But on a place like Reata he's a piece of machinery. And anyway, no man in a democracy should have the right to own millions of acres of land. That's foolish old feudal stuff."

Now, falteringly, Leslie tried to express her own half-formed observations. "I just mean I think it's better for a million men to own their own little farms than for one man to own a million——"

"Heh, hold on there!" Bick laughed. "You're talking about the husband of the woman I love."

"That's right, you want to watch out with that kind of talk," Vashti said. "Every single thing you say is repeated all over Texas inside of twenty-four hours."

Leslie smiled politely. "Now Vashti. I've been in Texas long enough to know you mean all over Reata."

"I mean all over Texas."

"Why?"

"Because you're Mrs. Bick Benedict. And a Yankee. And different. And Texas is like that. Next thing you know they'll be saying you're one of those Socialists."

"Pooh, you're just trying to scare me. I won't scare."

Bick leaned toward her, smiling, his eyes serious. "Texas," he said, "is a village—of about three hundred thousand square miles. There's more cattle in Texas than there are people. And Texas people are kind of lonesome people, they like a piece of news to chew on. You're news."

"In Ohio," Leslie said equably, "we three Lynnton girls always were considered slightly crazy, and even Virginia thinks we're odd. But Papa brought us up to think for ourselves and say what we thought."

"He sure did!" Bick said in full round tones.

"Papa!" Vashti yelled. "That's funny. My pa raised me up too."

"Well, they don't come any crazier than you do, Vash," Pinky stated reasonably.

"Of course Texas," Leslie went on, "is really very conventional, so that anyone who varies from the——"

"Conventional!" shouted the Texans in chorus.

Lew Morey, the mild-faced, raised a placating hand. "It's too hot to be arguing whether Texas is conventional or not."

"I kind of know what she means," Adarene Morey said. "I honestly do. But didn't you mean provincial instead of conventional, Leslie?"

"Never mind who means what," Bick interrupted irritably. "People have been wrangling about what Texas is and isn't for a hundred years and more. Let's talk about something else, will you!"

Smoothly Lucius Morey poured a conversational oil slick. "I'll bet anybody that in another ten years, the way the airplane business is booming since the war, you'll be flying up to Holgado inside an hour, instead of having to eat and sleep on a long train trip this way."

Pinky took a thoughtful sip of bourbon. "I don't know's I'd relish flying up to Holgado in all that mountain country. Too many hard clouds up around there, as the fellas used to say in the war."

Adarene Morey regarded her undramatic Lucius. "Lucius flew in the war," she said to Leslie. "You wouldn't think it to look at him, but he was an ace."

"Why wouldn't you think it to look at me!" her husband challenged her. "Mars kind of changed his face these last couple of wars. Used to be a big hairy fellow with whiskers. Now he's mostly a kid just about managed to have his first shave."

Leslie regarded the bland Morey with new interest. She was silent a moment. Then she swung her chair around away from the window view of the flat land skimming by in the early evening light. "You won't believe it! I've never asked Jordan what he was up to in the war. We've all wanted to forget it, I suppose. Jordan, did you win the Battle of the Marne single-handed?"

Vashti spoke quickly. Even Luz could not have sprung more alertly to his defense. "Some had to stay home and raise beef cattle so the soldiers could eat."

Thoughtlessly Leslie said, "Old men can raise beef cattle." Immediately she regretted it.

"If it hadn't of been for Texas," Vashti went on, "we probably wouldn't even have won the war."

"Well, now, Vash," Pinky drawled in mild remonstrance, "maybe that's a little bitty overspoken. But did seem every second one who got a medal was a Texan."

Leslie tried to cover the hurt. "I didn't mean—Jordan, I didn't mean——"

"That's all right," Bick said stiffly. "My father was a sick man. I was twenty-two. He died just a little after. I guess he figured it might be better in the end to raise a few hundred thousand head of beef cattle to feed the world than for me to kill a couple of Germans. Maybe he was wrong."

"Practically he was right," Leslie said quietly. "But for you he was wrong."

Now it was Adarene Morey who tried to guide the talk into impersonal paths. "Everything's changed since the war. I don't know. As if something was lost. Even old San Antonio is all changed."

"It'll be just one big flying field, the whole town, the way they're headed," Pinky predicted morosely. "We thought it was something big, time they put down Kelly Field. Now they're starting in on this new Randolph Field, they say it's going to set us back better than ten million dollars, just to lay it down. Keep on, pretty soon San Antonio can't see the sky for the wings."

"That's all right," Lew Morey said. "That's just Texas making sure they can't ever start another World War on us."

"Who'd be fool enough to start it!" scoffed Bick.

Clink-clank went the little iron gate. Quite a parade of starched white aprons and starched white coats and alert black faces beneath precarious trays. At the head of this procession, like a commanding officer, marched the dining-car steward (white). Well, Mr. Benedict, it's mighty nice to have you traveling with us again. . . . Haven't seen you this way in a long time, Mr. Morey. . . . Miss Hake . . . uh . . .

"I'm Mrs. Mott Snyth now. This is my husband Mr. Mott Snyth."

Hope everything's going to suit you all right I tended to it myself personally if you find anything wrong why just send word, why, thanks now if you folks going to want breakfast it might be a good idea give us your order now, well, coffee anyway, I always say a cup of coffee first off and you can face anything. . . .

It was not a gay meal. The little side tables had been hooked ingeniously into the wall, the couples sat two by two before the over-abundant food. Pitchers of cream, mounds of rolls, bowls of iced butter in the true tradition of North American waste. The repast finished, the six sat replete, somewhat uncomfortable, and silent. Even Vashti was strangely quiet.

"We're due in at daybreak," Bick said.

"Everything in Texas starts at daybreak," Adarene Morey complained. "Pioneer stuff." Leslie smiled at her across the aisle. Dear Adarene. Dear oasis.

Bick stood up, yawned, stretched, peered through a window at the Texas night. "I don't know how the rest of you folks feel but I'm all for letting the scenery go by until morning."

The Benedicts had the drawing room, the Moreys and the Snyths a compartment each. "Just roughing it," Pinky grinned. "But anyway it's better than on the ground like I've done a million times, with my saddle for a pillow."

Mumblemumble whisperwhisper! They all knew better than to talk aloud in those connecting cubicles.

"Jordan darling, I didn't mean it that way. I just remembered that we'd never talked about the war, I suddenly thought——"

Vashti expressed herself in whispers to Pinky. "Sometimes she says the meanest things and doesn't mean them, that I ever heard spoken."

Lucius Morey ran an investigating thumb over his chin as he stared at his reflection in the mirror of the little bedroom. "She'll be all right as soon as she gets the hang of Texas."

"She's all right now," Adarene retorted very sotto voce from the depths of her lower berth. "It's just Bick that never will be really in love with anything but Reata."

Next morning at dawn Leslie saw in the distance something that broke at last the limitless horizon. There, blue against the golden plain, were the mountains. She felt a lift, a lightness in the air. And there at the little station was Uncle Bawley towering yet blending into the landscape like the mountains themselves.

Leslie walked toward Uncle Bawley, she did not extend her hand to him she kept on walking and quite naturally walked into his arms and stayed there a moment with a feeling of having come home to someone she had known for a long long time.

"Well, there's something Holgado never saw before," Bick said.

"You better look alive, Bick!" Pinky yelled. "Uncle Bawley's going to cut you out!"

Bick grinned. "I've seen history made. Uncle Bawley with his arms around a girl."

"If I'd knowed it was so easy," Uncle Bawley said ruefully, "I'd of started earlier."

They piled into the waiting car, a glittering costly thing, elegant and sleek as Uncle Bawley's boots, but even the women recognized it as a model of vintage make.

Bick surveyed this conveyance, opulent and stuffy as a dowager in black satin. "You still pushing this ice wagon, Uncle Bawley!"

"I never drive the thing myself, I keep it for visiting royalty, like you folks. Nothing the matter with it, it sits there in the garage, the boys have to take it out and exercise it every week to keep it from going stale on me, like a horse."

Over the roads at a fearsome Texas speed. The air seemed a visible opalescent shimmer, there was about it a heady coolness, dry and bracing as a martini.

Leslie gazed about her. "I don't wish to seem too annoying, but I am going to take a number of very deep breaths." In the middle of one of these she stopped and pointed dramatically as they sped along. "They're real mountains!"

"What did you think they were? Cream puffs?" Bick said.

"I mean they're high. They're really mountains."

Bick produced statistics. "Baldy's over seven thousand feet. Sawtooth's almost eight. That right, Uncle Bawley?"

"Seven thousand nine hundred and ninety-eight," Uncle Bawley said. "Only reason I remember is I always wondered why the fella that measured it couldn't have throwed in the extra two feet, made it an even eight. Sounds higher that way. But no, he had to go and be honest."

Seen from the road as they approached it from a far distance Holgado seemed a village in itself, a collection of adobe houses, whitewashed, squatting on the plain. But presently the main house took on dimensions, sprawling like the old Main House at Benedict in a series of rooms and patios. Here were the offices, the bedrooms, the dining room, the big living room whose waxed and shining tiles were strewn with Mexican rugs and the skins of mountain lions.

Though here, as at Benedict, stuffed animal heads complete with horns manes fangs and ferocious eyes glared down from the walls upon the beholder, Leslie could regard them impersonally. They seemed to suit this house and region. They made a proper background for this giant in the canvas working clothes of a rancher.

"You have some coffee on the train?" Uncle Bawley asked. "Breakfast is ready any time you are. You folks probably want to go to your rooms first—you girls specially."

The thick-walled house was incredibly cool, no sunlight penetrated the deep window embrasures. Neat white bedrooms opened off a neat white gallery; neat white bathrooms, a haphazard

Mexican chambermaid a precarious Mexican waitress, a neat black male cook in a very starched white apron and towering chef's cap.

"Well!" Leslie exclaimed coming into the cool dining room and feeling strangely fresh and gay considering the journey and the hour. "You pioneer Benedicts certainly rough it. What's that heavenly smell?"

"Ham and eggs and biscuits and steak and fried potatoes is my guess," Bick said, "if I know Uncle Bawley. And probably sausage and pancakes and maybe chicken."

"No, I mean an outside smell. I got it as I came along the veranda. A lovely scent, fresh and sweet."

"We had mountain showers," Uncle Bawley said. "That's the smell of wet greasewood and piñón and grass, it's a nicer smell than any French perfume."

In came the steaming breakfast dishes in fantastic profusion, they were ranged on the long side table against the dining-room wall.

"Oh, how lovely and lavish!" Leslie said. "That's the way we serve breakfast at home."

Vashti looked up from her plate. "You do! For just you and Bick!"

"Oh. I meant at home in Virginia." A little too brightly she turned in confusion to meet Uncle Bawley's eyes. "Do you think it's the altitude makes me feel so gay?"

"Let's say it's that and the company," Bick suggested. "And maybe Uncle Bawley's coffee, it's notorious, they say a pound to a cup is his rule."

"No such thing, it only tastes like that because up here folks are already pepped up with the air," Uncle Bawley said. "Down in the brush country you got to hop yourself up with coffee every few minutes to keep going."

"By now, Leslie," Adarene Morey explained, "you've probably noticed that West Texans look down on East Texans, and South Texans think nothing of the Panhandle crowd up north. Central Texas snoots the whole four corners, and the only time they all get together is when an outsider belittles the entire darned state."

"That's right," Pinky agreed. "Take like my maw, she used to pick on all us kids, big and little, and we picked on each other, but let anybody outside say a word against any of us, why we were one and indivisible."

Blandly Lew Morey inquired, "Bawley, you're going to show Leslie and the girls your house, aren't you?"

"You well know I ain't."

"But isn't this your house?" Leslie asked.

"It's my house. But I don't live in it. I only visit here when I have company."

"But where . . . ?" Startled, she stared at him.

He pointed past the veranda to an adobe house perched on a little rise a hundred feet back from the main house. A rather shabby old structure, its veranda slightly off plumb, its windows curtainless.

"That's the house I live in."

"Oh, Uncle Bawley, do let me see it. You must have wonderful things in it."

A shout went up. Bewildered, Leslie looked from one to the other. "Jordan, have I said something?"

"No, honey. I thought I'd told you that no woman has ever set foot in Uncle Bawley's house, even to clean it."

"Especially not to clean it," Uncle Bawley corrected.

"But I never saw a man who looked more spick-and-span than you, Uncle Bawley," Leslie argued.

"Only from head to foot. Not underfoot."

She looked at the old man, she marveled at the pain which old wounds could continue to inflict.

It was more than five years later that Leslie finally saw this retreat in which old Bawley Benedict nursed his loneliness and unfulfillment; this welter of newspapers, saddles, boots, saddle soap, pipes, gourds, trophies, pans, massive silver punch bowls, empty peach tins, time-stained copies of the *Breeder's Gazette*. Five years later, when Jordy was four and Luz three a female entered this sanctum. Leslie had taken the two children up to Holgado for the cool air and the altitude. The three-year-old Luz was missing one frantic afternoon. There was a galloping here and there by cowboys, a calling and a searching before they came upon her. She had trotted off in the absence of her Mexican nurse, she had made her way up the little hill to Uncle Bawley's house, and there they found her fluttering and rummaging ecstatically amongst the heaped-up scraps and piles of waste like a sparrow in the dust of the road.

Now Leslie was never to forget these first ten days at Holgado. The clear lightness of the air exhilarated her after the humid heat of the Gulf coast country. The mountain showers seemed to bring up from the earth a sweet freshness, reticent but haunting.

"It smells like white freesias," Leslie said. "People are always making a fuss about honeysuckle and roses and magnolias. Freesias have the most exquisite scent of all."

"None of those around here," Uncle Bawley said, "and I don't know's I'm familiar with that brand of flower. But we've got a blossom up here comes out in the spring. It's called the Spanish dagger on account of the sharp spikes of the plant, they can go into you like a stiletto. It's too late now, they've gone by, but the flower is white-petaled and mighty sweet. To my notion it's about the prettiest flower there is anywhere." He paused a moment. "If you can liken a person to a flower, why, I'd say that's the one you're most like."

This compliment delighted her, she repeated it to Bick that first evening when, red-eyed and yawning, he came to their room where she already was sitting up in bed, reading. The house was bookless except for a shelf of technical volumes. These were ranged in the grim room that contained the big glass-doored gun cabinets. Shining and sinister in their racks, these slim black-barreled items of ranch household equipment did not appear anachronistic to anyone but Leslie.

The books turned out to be gnawed-looking volumes on Spanish land grants in Texas. Intended as a baldly stated record of early land transactions in the region, they actually were, quite unconsciously, a cloak-and-dagger account of such skullduggery,

adventure, and acquisitive ruthlessness as to make the reader
reject the whole as mythical. Settlers, pioneers, frontiersmen used
cupidity against ignorance, turned land into cash and live men
into dead men with blithe ferocity. Leslie devoured them, fascinated, horrified.

"Jordan, what do you think? Uncle Bawley is turning into a
ladies' man. He told me about the Spanish dagger flower and he
said he thought it was the loveliest flower in the world. And then
—pardon my pointing—he said I was like the flower. How's that
for a misogynist!"

"Uh-huh. He meant spikes and all, I suppose?"

Spiritedly she said, "I hope so. Who wants to be merely white
and sweet, like a blanc mange!"

The first evening after the very good dinner, and on each
succeeding evening, the four men gathered into the tightest of
knots in one corner of the great living room. Their talk was low-
voiced but their tone had the timbre of intensity. Occasionally
a word wafted itself over to the somewhat looser knot formed by
the three semi-deserted women. Election . . . Commissioner
. . . tax . . . district . . . oil . . . Congress . . . Gomez
. . . precinct . . .

Vashti sometimes played a defeated game of solitaire through
which she chattered unceasingly. "Jack on the queen ten on the
jack I hope it's a girl because they're so cute to fix up with pink
and hair ribbons where's that nine for goodness' sakes but a
course Pa and Mott they're yelling it's got to be a boy whee
there's that ol' nine——"

Adarene was doing a gros point chair tapestry, her basket of
brilliant-hued wools made a gay splash of color in the firelighted
room. After three evenings of this Leslie drifted casually across
the room and sat down on the couch beside Bick.

Conversation ceased.

"Aren't you men being a bit too cozy?"

Bick's left ear, she noticed, was a brighter pink than usual.
"This is ranch stuff, Leslie. Business."

"How fascinating! I'll listen. And learn a lot."

Lew Morey leaned toward her, he patted her knee in a strangely paternal gesture for a man of his years. "Now now you don't want to fret your head about such talk."

Suddenly she saw him clear. The bland almost expressionless face, unlined, quiet. There leaped into her mind a line she had read in a newspaper story about a frightfully rich oil man from the East. He had come to Oklahoma in the early oil days of that fantastic commonwealth, he had made his brisk millions, he had lost them almost as briskly. "They cleaned me," he had said in the newspaper account. "The still-faced men. They got to me."

The still-faced men. Bland. Nerveless. Quietly genial. Lucius Morey.

"We're fixing it so that you girls can have all those doodads you're always buying," Pinky Snyth explained, his rosy face creasing into a placating smile—a smile such as one would bestow upon an annoying and meddlesome brat. "All that stuff you're getting for that new house of yours. How d'you think poor ol' Bick's going to pay up for all that unless we figger out!"

The cow hand. The shrewd pink-cheeked curly-headed little gimlet. Turned cattle king.

Leslie settled back as for a long stay. "How right you are! I ought to know. Here I am, spending all that money without real-izing how Jordan has to plan and—and devise—to get it. So now you just go on talking and I'll listen as quiet as a mouse—though I must say I think mice are awfully noisy, squeaking and scuttering around——"

Bick's voice was flat and hard. "This isn't only business. It's politics. Men's stuff."

"But darling, I was brought up on politics. You lads talk as if you hadn't heard that women have the vote. To us Washington was as next-door as Benedict is here. We were in and out like whippets. And Jordan, you know our house was crammed with political talk and career men and striped trousers and national and international what not. Go on. Talk. I love it."

They were absolutely dumb. Uncle Bawley broke the silence. "My, that's a pretty dress you're wearing, Leslie."

In disappointment she looked at him. "You too, Uncle Bawley!"

The gaze of the handsome old wreck of a giant met hers and to her amazement his faded blue eyes suddenly were deeply blue-black with the burning intensity of a young male in love.

Leslie stood up. She was furious she was confused. "You men ought to be wearing leopard skins and carrying clubs and living in caves. You date back a hundred thousand years. Politics! What's so dirty about your politics that I can't hear it! Gomez! Jett Rink! Gill Dace! And all of you. Smiling and conniving——"

Bick Benedict rose, he seemed to tower above her. "Leslie, you're not well——"

"I am well! I'm well in body and I'm well in mind. But mildew is going to set in. I can feel it. That slimy white sticky stuff that creeps into all the corners and closets down there unless you open the doors and windows and let the sun in."

Feeling rather triumphant though strangely shaky she walked across the room to where the two women sat like figures, she thought, in the fairy tale of the Sleeping Beauty. Vashti's right hand was suspended in mid-air, a playing card held in her fingers. Her mouth was open, her eyes very round. Adarene's needle was poised motionless above her embroidery frame.

"Boo!" said Leslie.

Uncle Bawley called across the room. "What do you girls say we have a sunrise breakfast tomorrow, ride up into the hills? And I'll cook."

Vashti's childlike squeal. "Ooh! I'd love it! Let's."

"Well, then, you girls better get your beauty sleep," Pinky said. "Or we won't be able to rout you out come daybreak."

Shrewishly Leslie called to him over her shoulder, "Yes, send the idiot children to bed so that you massive brains can talk in peace."

The men managed a tolerant laugh but Leslie hoped she detected in it a touch of malaise.

Adarene again began to ply her needle, in and out, in and

out. She did not look up. "If you think anything you can say will make a dent in the tough hide of Texas."

"I'd like to crack their skulls together like coconut shells."

"I'm going to get me a snack before I go to bed," Vashti said.

Automatically Leslie rejected this. "After all that dinner!"

"I'm eating for two." Virtuously.

"At least," Adarene agreed. "Look, Leslie, just pay them no mind. It's the elections coming up this autumn. With Luz dead and Jett Rink off the place and that Fidel Gomez getting uppity they say, there are lots of important things to straighten out. I heard that Jett Rink was trying to make trouble with the ranch hands."

"What's that got to do with elections?"

Adarene took three or four careful stitches, the big needle went through the coarse stiff web of the material, pop pop pop. "You've never seen one of our elections, have you?"

"No. What about them?"

"Well, sometimes it gets sort of—uh—dramatic. The Mexican vote is pretty important."

"Isn't any vote important?"

"I suppose so. There are about four million whites in Texas. And about a million Mexicans."

"Whites. Mexicans. I never thought of Mexicans as—but if they vote they're citizens, aren't they?"

"Yes. Yes, of course. But——"

Vashti, slapping down the cards with the vehemence of one who is playing a losing game, was still mumbling maddeningly as she played. ". . . There! There's the deuce. . . . Come on now you ace. . . . Oh, damn!" Scrabbling the unobliging cards together she looked up, defeated. "It's real exciting at election. Regular old times, guns and all. They lock the gates and guard the fences, nobody can get out."

"Who can't?"

"Everybody. The Mexicans. The ranch hands."

"Vashti. Uh—look, Adarene. You two girls forget sometimes that I'm new to Texas. I love to know about things. Now. They

GIANT

lock the gates so that people can't get out at election time. Why?"

In a tone of elaborate patience, as one would speak to a backward child, Vashti said, "So they'll vote right of course, honey. So they won't go out and get mixed up with somebody'll tell 'em wrong. This way they vote like they're told to vote."

"Told by—who tells them?"

"Depends. Our place it's Pa and two three behind him. And now Pinky too, of course."

"Of course. And at Reata, who?"

Adarene rolled up her embroidery, her voice cut this interrogation. "How about a three-handed game of bridge if those mean men won't talk to us or play?"

But Leslie leaned toward Vashti in utter concentration. "Who at Reata?"

"Oh goodness, I don't know, I don't pay much attention to men's stuff like elections and so on. Luz, she used to be the real boss. She sure was the point when it came to rounding up the Mexicans. Then there was Jett Rink, of course, drunk as a sheep election time but that always made him tougher and they were scared of him. And then Fidel Gomez around Nopal and Benedict, all the Mexicans there."

Adarene Morey stood up. "Girls, I think I'll go to bed, get my beauty sleep if we're going to get up before dawn. How about you, Vashti?"

"I ain't really sleepy. We slept so late this morning. Pinky never batted an eye till seven. I thought he was dead. It's this mountain air and all, I guess."

"Listen a minute, Vashti. What offices do they vote for? Local? State? National?"

"H'm? Oh. I don't know, rightly. Do you, Adarene? I don't pay any attention. Commissioners, I guess. Anyway, for around here. Of course everybody is tied up with the ranches, miles and miles around. Why, they wouldn't be alive if it wasn't for us, it's their living, hauling cattle, working cattle, supplies and stuff and all that goes with it. I don't know, don't ask *me*, Pinky says I'm a nitwit about stuff like that. Whyn't you ask Bick? Bick'll explain to you all about it. I'd like a sandwich or something, wouldn't you, girls? And a glass of milk and maybe some of that pie left over if there is any. Let's raid the icebox, maybe the boys will too."

Leslie glanced toward the four men at the far end of the room. Their heads were close together, their voices low, their shoulders hunched.

"No, I think I'll take Adarene's advice and go to bed. And read."

"You can take my movie magazine I bought in San Antonio, I'm through with it."

Adarene laid a hand lightly on Leslie's arm. "Stop looking like Lady Macbeth, honey. Take Texas the way Texas takes bourbon. Straight. It goes down easier."

"All I know is," Vashti now was prattling on, "Mott says less'n ten years from now about six men'll be running the whole of Texas. Gabe Target he says, and Ollie Whiteside if he gets Judge, and Lew and a course Bick and Pinky—Mott, I mean."

At ten o'clock Leslie, reading in bed, smelled the aroma of coffee, the state nightcap. The strong smell of the brew made her slightly queasy, she wished Bick would come in and open another window. She took deep grateful breaths of the cool sweet air. There was no sound. The men must be in the kitchen at the far end of the house. She resumed her reading of the naïve volume on Spanish land grants. She must have dozed a bit for suddenly Bick was in the room, he was pulling off his boots with a little grunt.

"Jordan! I must have dropped off like a dozy old lady. It's this heavenly air."

Bick Benedict did not reply. He regarded his bride with a hard and hostile eye. She looked very plain. Her habit of reading in bed through long night hours had made spectacles advisable and these were of the owlish horn-rimmed variety. The bare electric light bulb was glaring down on her face. As always, when emotionally disturbed or when reading absorbedly, she had wound and unwound tendrils of her hair so that now she presented a Medusa aspect. There was a small highlight of cold cream on one cheek. Finally, the slight cast that usually made more piquant the beauty of her eyes now was exaggerated under the strain of reading beneath the glaring white light.

Harsh unspoken words formed in Bick Benedict's mind as he went about the business of preparing for bed. So this was Leslie Lynnton the Virginia belle and beauty that he had split a gut to get. No Texas girl good enough, huh? Oh no!

She now removed her glasses and regarded him thoughtfully, tapping her teeth with her spectacle bows. She had closed her book, one finger inserted to keep her place. He's angry, she told herself, because I wanted to hear the talk. And I suppose I wasn't very polite. That cave-man stuff.

"This old book is fascinating, it's about Spanish land grants. It says in those days they measured by varas. Do you know what a vara is?"

He did not reply.

Mm. So you won't talk, eh? She went on then, equably. "They cut a switch off a tree—about a yard long, it says—and that's what they measured the land with. A vara's length. A switch's length. And then sometimes they measured by the wagon wheel, it says. They tied a red rag to a wheel spoke and walked behind the wagon and every time the red rag flashed round it was roughly fifteen feet. Isn't that sweet! No wonder people could have million-acre ranches—I mean——"

In his pajamas he was standing before the wall mirror running an investigating hand over his cheek. He regarded his own image intently. "Why, thanks," he said. "Can you tell me more about Texas? It's all so fascinating."

"Sorry about my cave-man speech, darling. I'll apologize tomorrow to the others, first thing."

"That's big of you." He came to the foot of the bed and stood glaring at her in anger. His diction was pure Harvard and hard-bitten. "You certainly distinguished yourself this evening."

"Sh! Jordan! They can hear every word in every room along this veranda."

"That's fine. And we heard every word you said in there too, tonight. Dirty politics! And we date back a hundred thousand years! Who the hell do you think you are! Joan of Arc or something!"

She held her breath as the words rang through the little stark white bedroom. They were holding their breath too, she thought, and hearing all this, there in those other little stark white bedrooms along the gallery. "I said I'm sorry about the name-calling. It was impolite. But in principle I was right."

"You come down here and try to tell us how to run the ranch! And the town! And the state! I swear to God I think you're crazy! Insulting my friends. I've stood it because of your—the way you feel just now. I'm through with that. You're my wife, you're Mrs. Jordan Benedict. When the hell are you going to settle down and behave like everybody else!"

She got out of bed then and stood facing him, the book still in her hand, pressed against the laces at her breast. "Never."

They stood glaring at each other. Automatically his hand came up. He stared down at it. Dropped it to his side.

"I almost hit you."

"I know. My darling."

"You're running around in your bare feet. Cold."

"It doesn't matter."

"Get back into bed."

Shivering she crept between the covers. He turned out the light.

Silence in the little room, silence in all the little rooms, silence in the dark fragrant Texas night so full of turmoil and unrest and conflict.

"Oh, Jordan, I wish we could live up here in the mountains. I wish we could stay up here and Uncle Bawley could run Reata. Couldn't he? Couldn't he?"

"Get this. If you can understand anything that isn't Virginia and pink coats and hunt dinners and Washington tea parties. Just get this. I run Reata. I run Holgado. I run the damn wet Humedo Division and Los Gatos too and a lot you've never heard of. Everything in them and on them is run by me. I run everything and everyone that has the Reata brand on it."

"Does that include me?"

"Dramatizing yourself, like a cheap movie." Silence again. He spoke, his resentment hung almost a palpable thing in the darkness. "Tired. The hardest kind of day's work doesn't wear me down like ten minutes of this god-damned wrangling. I'm not used to it."

"You're not used to marriage. . . . Jordan, who was it said that thing about power?"

"Oh, Christ! I don't know who said anything about power."

"Papa used to quote it. He said——"

"Papa Papa! Forget Papa, will you!"

She lay very still, concentrating. The cool still fragrant mountain night. Suddenly she sat bolt upright. Her low vibrant voice hung in the darkness. "Power corrupts. That's it. I can't remember who said it. An English statesman I think. He said power corrupts. And absolute power corrupts absolutely. Jordan."

But he did not hear her. He was asleep.

19

IT WAS DARKER than night when the Mexican maid brought the morning coffee to their room. But all Holgado was astir. Hoofbeats. The deep reverberations of powerful motor vehicles, the sound intensified on the thin mountain air. The hiss and drum of Spanish spoken along the corridors. The tap-tap of men's boot heels, the clink of spurs. The scampering feet of Mexican servitude—a sound that Leslie found irksome. "They don't walk. They run. On their heels. I should think it would shatter their gizzards." But the other Texas morning sounds she loved. . . .

315

Sí sí señor . . . Momento señora . . . Las botas, sí . . . Hace mucho frío . . .

Bick emerged from the bathroom fully dressed. Tiptoeing. He peered toward her bed, the bathroom light behind him.

"I'm awake."

"Vashti's complaining about the cold."

"It's heaven."

Last night's quarrel was cast aside like a soiled garment discarded in the fresh new day. "If we're going to make that fool sunrise breakfast of Bawley's. Even you girls can't make the sun wait while you dress."

She threw aside the covers, sat a moment hugging her shoulders. "I'll be dressed in fifteen minutes. I must say I'd like sunrises just as well if they could run them later in the morning."

"I don't know—is this ride up the trail good for you now? How about you girls taking a car instead? We boys can get a head start riding."

"The first time I met you you bragged that your mother practically produced you on horseback."

"She was a Texan."

"Even for Texans the equipment is, I believe, standard."

He grinned. "See you later. I'm going down to the corral. I'll pick a gentled one for you."

She was still slim and almost boyish in her riding clothes. As she came along the veranda she could hear Uncle Bawley's voice from the direction of the dining room, there was a sharp edge to his usual tone of almost caressing gentleness. "No, I don't want any cook along, I'm going to do the cooking myself. How about a couple dozen those Mexican quail, I'll rig up an asador over the fire, they'll make good breakfast eating, with bacon."

Vashti and Adarene were not yet down. It was still dark, the lights shone everywhere about the place. In her hand she carried the book on Spanish land grants, she had finished it and now she would tuck it back into the sparse shelf in the gun room just off the patio. She opened the door, peered into the grim unlighted room, her hand groping for the electric switch. A sound, a little

316

quick startled sound. She hesitated. Waited. Silence. But there was a sense of presence there, of a something that held its breath and waited. Oh, pooh, a mouse. Her fingers found the light, flicked it on.

A boy, dark ragged shaking, was flattened against the white-washed wall, the palms of his hands were spread against it like one crucified, the emaciated body was trying to press into the wall itself. The black eyes, fixed in a frantic stare, became imploring as the eyelids relaxed a trifle and a caught breath lifted the rags on his breast. Before she darted out and shut the door, before she lifted her voice to call, in that split second her inner voice said, That was Fear you just saw that wasn't flesh and blood that was blind naked Fear in the form of a man. Then she called, a note of hysteria in her voice. "Uncle Bawley! Uncle Bawley! Uncle Bawley!"

He was there with incredible swiftness, speeded by the urgency in her voice, towering above her, his hands on her shoulders. "What's wrong! Leslie!"

"In there. There's a—there's somebody hiding in there."

He flung open the gun-room door. The boy was on the floor, a heap on the floor like a mop like a rag. Speaking in Spanish Uncle Bawley said, "Get up!" The boy did not move. Uncle Bawley picked him up as you would a wet dog, gingerly, by the neck and shoulders and half carried half dragged him along the floor to the patio.

"No," Leslie whispered. "No. Don't——"

"It's all right. Happens every day." Uncle Bawley looked enormous above the little heap of rags on the floor. "Nobody's going to hurt him. He's just a wetback."

"A what?"

"Wetback. Swum or waded the river between Mexico and here, must have walked a hundred miles and more."

Foolishly she stammered, "What river?"

"Now Leslie! Rio Grande of course. They do it all the time." Now he leaned over the boy, he spoke to him in Spanish, Leslie caught a word here and there. In Uncle Bawley's voice there was something that caused the bundle of rags to raise its head. Leslie's Spanish lessons bore fruit now. A familiar Spanish word, the inflection of Uncle Bawley's voice, her own instinct combined to give her the sense of what was being said. Come come, boy, stand up! You have waded the Rio Grande you have walked the long miles, that takes the courage of a man. Don't crouch there then like a dog. No one will hurt you. Stand up! You are a man! He stirred the bundle with the toe of his shining boot.

The rags moved, the thing got to its feet, the face was a mask of abject terror and glimmering hope mingled. Seventeen, perhaps. A skeleton.

"How long have you been in there?"

"This morning only. I walked all night and the night before and the night before and before. By day I lay where I could, hiding."

"Food?"

The shoulders came up, the bony hands spread.

"Have you seen Immigration Officers or Rangers these past nights?"

"Once men passed near me as I lay in a ditch. I prayed I pressed deep into the ground I pushed myself into the desert I was the desert I prayed to the Miraculous Christ and to the Señor de Chalma and to the Virgin of Guadalupe and they heard and my prayers were answered."

"I bet," said Uncle Bawley.

The boy was still talking, a stream of words poured out in relief and hysteria and hope.

"Tell me," Leslie said. "I only catch a word here and there."

"It's nothing, Leslie. Happens all the time I tell you. About fifty sixty thousand of these wetbacks slip out of Mexico every year, swim or wade the Rio Grande where it's shallow, travel by night and hole up by day. The Border Patrol and the Immigration boys and Rangers and all, they can't keep all of them out. Sometimes they make it, a lot of 'em are caught and thrown back. Sometimes they're shot by mistake, sometimes they wander around and starve. This skin-and-bones says he's been eating rats."

"No!" She was stiff with horror.

"But he ought've come in with the regular Mexican labor lot. Thousands of them brought across legally here to Texas. Pick the cotton and the crops, fruit and vegetables in the Valley, and so on. He says he tried to make it, they were full up."

"I'm going to call Jordan."

Instantly Uncle Bawley raised his hand. "Nope. Jordan's against it. He'd call the Immigration boys come and get him."

"He wouldn't!"

Uncle Bawley glanced over his shoulder. "If Bick comes along now and sees the boy he'll turn him in. He's set against it I tell you."

She stared at him. "If I don't call Jordan what will you do?"

"Feed him give him some decent rags turn him loose tonight."

She stared now at the boy, the black eyes were fixed on her, they shifted then to the great booted towering figure. "Do that," she said. "Do that." Her lips felt stiff.

Uncle Bawley turned to the boy. He spoke again in Spanish, he pointed to his own shabby house on the hillock behind the main ranch house. "Has anyone else seen you?" The boy shook his head. "That house. Run there now. No. Wait. I'll take you."

Leslie stood in the patio. She watched the two quickly ascend the little slope, Uncle Bawley's huge bulk just behind the shadowy figure, screening him. She stood there, waiting, peering into the dark. She was there, outlined against the patio light, when Uncle Bawley emerged and joined her.

"What you getting upset about, Leslie? Immigration fellas come along looking for hide-outs the way they sometimes do, why, they wouldn't dast go near my house up there, they well know nobody's allowed, I'd take their jobs away from them if they did."

She was completely bewildered. She thought, What a statement! "I'm so mixed up," she stammered.

"What you so upset about, Leslie?" In that soft strangely musical voice. "He's mostly Mexican Indian, that boy, he's used to traveling hundreds of miles afoot." A tiny door in a corner of her memory opened and a handful of words flashed out. Walk! You can't walk. Nobody walks in Texas, only the Mexicans. "Anyway," Uncle Bawley went on, "he'll have a regular fiesta today, sleep in a corner all day up there, I'll fetch him up coffee now and a lot of good grub, give him pants and a shirt and shoes —he'll sell the shoes first off——"

"How do you know Jordan would have turned him back! I don't believe it. He isn't like that. In the Valley . . . I saw . . . there's a horrid man called Gomez . . ."

He came to her, his great hand on her shoulder, he looked down at her. "Now now Leslie girl, nothing to go to bawling about, just another Mexican Indian coming back to Tejas, you might almost say. It's only that Bick's made a rule against it here at Holgado, so near the border, and all over Reata. And he's right. Texas can't take in all of Mexico's misfits. It's illegal, it makes big trouble. If they come in with the seasonal labor migration, that's different that's in the law. Haul 'em in, pay 'em a couple of dollars, haul 'em back, well and good. But a kid crawls in, starving like that one, I pay Bick no mind. Only let's keep this just between us, you and me. H'm?"

"Yes, Uncle Bawley. I wish I could get it all straight in my mind. They use them. Cheap. And then throw them back, like old rags. A century of it but it's never really worked out right, has it?"

Evasively, "Where's the rest of the boys and girls, I wonder, haven't heard a peep out of the Moreys or the——" His voice trailed off. He faced Leslie squarely. "Strictly speaking—which hardly anybody does—why, what with picking the cotton and the fruit and now the Valley is all planted with vegetables, a big new industry, and the old railroad building days and all, why you might say the whole of Texas was built on the backs of boys like that one. On the bent backs of Mexicans. Don't let on to Bick I said that."

Through her tears she looked up at him and the blur wiped the lines from the face, the little sag from the shoulders. With a gesture utterly unpremeditated, wanton, overpowering, she threw

her arms about his neck she brought the fine old head down to
hers, she kissed him full on the lips, long hard lasting.

Horrified. "Forgive me. What is the matter with me! Uncle
Bawley!"

He stood a moment, his arms hanging at his sides. "My, that
was nice," he said quietly. "But you ever get a notion to do that
again, Leslie, I'll turn you over my knee and spank you good.
Hear me."

"Yes, Uncle Bawley."

Vashti's voice high and shrill from the direction of the guest
rooms. "Adarene! Leslie! Where's everybody got to!"

Uncle Bawley turned and walked into the house.

Adarene's voice, "I'm coming. We overslept."

Pinky skipping along the gallery toward the patio. "Now Vash,
don't you go to eating before breakfast."

"Why don't we get going, then! I'm starved."

"All right. Cup of coffee."

Fifteen minutes later they clattered out in the cool scented
darkness, Bick keeping close to Leslie. Adarene sat very straight
in the saddle. "Rides like a Yankee," Lucius Morey commented.
"Adarene never got over that school she went to, up the Hudson."

Vashti, an imposing mound of flesh looming ahead in the first
faint dawn, rode cowboy fashion, one vast hip slipped to the side,
one arm hanging loose or waving in the air, she kept up with
the men and greeted the dawn like a Comanche on the warpath.
The hills loomed grey then brown then rose then burst into
scarlet. The plains, green and gold, ran to meet them.

"Oh, Jordan!"

"Not bad, huh?"

"The light, the curious light. Not like anything in America.
It's Egypt—with the Alps thrown in."

"Egypt and Alps hell! It's Texas."

A streak of gold-beige, like a flash of smoky sunlight, shot
across the nearby brush and vanished behind a hillock.

"Antelope," said Bick.

He was riding at Leslie's left, Uncle Bawley was at her right.

"Uncle Bawley, you told me that there are more cattle than people in Texas," Leslie said. "But I never see any. Look. Miles and miles and miles, but not a four-footed thing."

"They like the brush," Uncle Bawley explained. "And the quiet places away from the roads and highways. Maybe the old wild Longhorn strain ain't all bred out of them. Like me."

"And cowboys. Where do you keep them? I saw more cowboys in the movies at home. Those strong silent handsome males were all over the place—in the pictures. My sister Lacey writes and asks me——"

"Strong silent clabbermouths! Cow hands talk all the time, they're lonely people, they'll talk to anybody. If they can't talk they sing to themselves or to the cows."

"Movies!" scoffed Bick. "Movies and those rodeos at Madison Square Garden and around, they give people the impression that a cow hand goes out and throws a steer every morning before breakfast, just for exercise. It's a technique, like any other profession, you have to have a gift for it, you have to spend years learning it, it's something you have to have handed down from father to son. I did, and my father did, and my son's going to."

"That's right," said Uncle Bawley. "They write to Bick all the time, and they write to me and the big ranches around, college kids that want to be cowboys. They say they can ride a horse, they ride on the farm in Vermont or Kansas or someplace, and they ride in Central Park in New York, they say they want to learn to be cowboys. Well, say, I wouldn't have them free, they ain't worth picking up off the ground after the horse has threw them."

Suddenly, "Look, Leslie," Bick said, and pointed to a small herd gloomily regarding the riders from the range fence.

Leslie stared at the animals, they returned her stare glumly, hunched near the fence, their shaggy heads and bald faces, their humped backs and short-haired hides giving them the aspect of monsters in a nightmare. "What are they! They're frightening!"

"Now, Bick, don't you go making me out a fool, front of Leslie."

Bick was laughing, and the riders ahead were pointing and grinning back at Uncle Bawley. "They're called cattlo. Tell her, Bawley."

Ruefully Uncle Bawley eyed the weird creatures so mournfully returning his gaze as the little cavalcade rode by. "That's right—cattlo. It's a word made up out of cattle and buffalo and that's what those critters are, they're bred up out of cattle and buffalo, bred years back to see if we couldn't fetch something the heat and the ticks wouldn't get to."

"You got something sure enough," Bick grinned.

"I don't know's they're much meaner-looking than those critters you're talking so big about, Herefords bred to those old humpy sloe-eyed beasts you're always yapping about. Kashmirs! And Brahmans. Camels with an underslung chassis, that's what they are. Cows with humps on their backs. It ain't in nature!"

But Bick laughed as he rode along. "Just you wait, Bawley, you're going to see a breed that'll make cattle history before Gill Dace and I finish with them."

Pinky turned in his saddle to shout back to them. "I never heard so much talking a-horseback in my whole life. Who ever heard of talking riding!"

"It's me," Leslie called to him. "I have to talk to them riding because it's the only time they ever sit down."

"I'll go along ahead," Uncle Bawley said, "get a fire going and the skillet on." He was off with a clatter and a whoosh. The other horses tried to follow but the big man on the powerful horse outdistanced them.

"That horse of Bawley's," Bick explained, as he eyed Leslie with some concern after their spurt of sudden speed, "is the fastest thing in Jeff Davis County and maybe in Texas. For riding, that is. And look at the build of him! A regular galon for size."

"He'd have to be huge to carry around that mountain of a man. Uh, sorry, dear, but I feel a question coming on. Galon? What's a galon?"

As they jogged along with the rose of sunrise reflected in their faces, "Well, let's see. I just used the word unconsciously. The

Mexicans call a big horse a galon, it's a horse they used to have for hauling, not for riding. Before machinery did the work. They say that in the war for Texas Independence the Mexicans would hear the American teamsters yelling at those big square pudding-footed horses going through the Texas sand and mud and clay, hauling the heavy stuff of war. The teamsters would yell to the horses, 'G'long! G'long!' Get along, get along, see? So the Mexicans thought a heavy horse was a galon."

"True?"

"True enough. Anyway, it's fun telling you tall Texas tales. You always look like a little girl who's hearing Cinderella for the first time."

"Antelopes and galons and cattlos and sunrise and quail for breakfast——"

"And me."

"And you."

"And Vashti."

"Jordan, we're quite near the Mexican border, aren't we?"

"Not far."

"If we were to meet a wetback now—just one poor miserable Mexican wetback—what would you do?"

"Dear little Yankee, do you think wetbacks go dripping along the road in daylight carrying a printed sign that says I Am a Wetback?"

"No, but if you did see one, there in the ditch, hiding. What would you do? Would you pass him by, would you help him, would you turn him in?"

"You know what happens to little girls who play with matches, don't you? They get burned."

"Oh, Jordan, I'm just trying to get things straight in my mind. It's all so new to me and some of it's fascinating and some of it's horrible. Labor, almost like slaves, but that's legal. Wetbacks, but that isn't legal. You all use the Mexican vote in Benedict and the whole county——"

"Uh-huh. Like your Negro vote in the South."

"Yes, but that doesn't make it right."

"Honey, if I'd known you were going to turn into a Do-Gooder I'd have married any nice comfortable Texas girl and damned well let you wrestle with Red Coat and his dandy little Principality. I'll bet you'd have had a fine time straightening out the Labor Situation in the Schleppenhausen or wherever it is he rules. . . . Come on, they're all miles ahead of us. Let's really ride before they send back a search party for us."

Clattering down the main road, then off on a dirt side road and up the narrow trail with the smoke of Uncle Bawley's fire pointing the way and the scent of Uncle Bawley's coffee and quail and bacon. He was squatting Mexican fashion in front of the fire of mesquite, the plump quail were roasting on an improvised spit and the bacon was slowly sizzling in the pan. The others already were sipping burning-hot black coffee as they stood about the fire.

"Mm, smells divine!" Leslie said.

"Let me warn you, Yankee," Bick said. "Before you begin to complain. Texas quail are tough as golf balls."

"Let me help, Uncle Bawley," Leslie offered. "I'll baste them. That'll make them tender."

"He'll never let you," Vashti said. "Uncle Bawley is a real batch, he likes to do things his own way. Texas way."

"No different from anybody else," Uncle Bawley argued. "Cooking over an open fire is cooking over an open fire, no matter where." He was lifting the crisp strips of dripping bacon out of the pan as they curled and sizzled, he looked about him for an absorbent receptacle on which to place them to drain until the quail should be golden brown. His wandering gaze—the eye of the practiced rancher and camper—fell on a nearby clop of old sun-dried cow dung; porous, dehydrated as a sponge or a blotter. Delicately, methodically, he placed the first strip of bacon, and the second and third, on top of this natural draining surface. "No different from anybody else," Uncle Bawley repeated. "Texans aren't, only maybe some little ways."

Leslie began to laugh, peal after peal, helplessly. The others stared at her, surprised, vaguely resentful but scrupulously polite.

20

THE BOY was named Jordan. Jordan Benedict Fourth. Like royalty. Leslie had objected to no avail. It became Jordy for short in order not to confuse him with his father, Jordan Third.

"Yes, I know there's been a Jordan in the family for a century. Jordan First Second Third and now Fourth. But remember what happened to all those dynasty boys? Those Ptolemys and the Louis lads and the Charleses?"

"What would you call him?"

"David."

"David! What David?"

"The boy with the slingshot. The one who killed the giant Goliath."

"That's a nice bloodthirsty idea."

Bick Benedict's happiness was touching to see. "But he's no Benedict," Bick said, regarding the black-haired dark-eyed morsel. "He's his mother's son. I've been canceled out of the whole transaction."

"You're just disappointed because he didn't turn out to be that perfect Hereford-Kashmir bull calf you've been trying to produce."

A month later Vashti Hake Snyth presented Pinky with twin daughters. Mercifully, old Cliff Hake had died just before the birth of the twins. The mammoth matron made no secret of her disappointment. "In a way I'm glad Pa went before the twins came. He was mad enough when I was born. They say he wouldn't speak to Ma for a month after. He'd prolly have disinherited me, seeing these, or shot Mott for a Texas traitor."

She named the plump girl babies Yula Belle and Lula Belle. As they grew in length and width and attained young girlhood they were fated to be known to the undazzled swains for five hundred miles in every direction as the Cow Belles.

Vashti's plan for at least one of these stolid morsels was confided with her usual subtlety to Bick and Leslie.

"Your Jordy'll have to marry one of 'em, stands to reason. No crawling out of it this time, with two of them waiting."

"Both or nothing," Bick said.

To Bick Leslie said, not altogether humorously, "Vashti as my Jordy's mother-in-law! I'd send him to Tibet, rather, and have him brought up a lama in a lamasery."

"Don't you worry. Jordan Benedict Fourth is going to be a tough Texas cowman. Nobody'll have to tell him where to head in. He'll take care of himself."

Jordy Benedict was scarcely a month old when his father gave him his first reata, his boots, his Stetson his saddle, all initialed all stamped with the Reata Ranch brand. As he outgrew the tiny boots expressly made for him fresh ones were ordered, exquisitely soft bits of leather fashioned by the hands of the craftsman Ildefonso Mezo. When the boy was two years old Ildefonso had taken the baby foot in his brown sensitive hand. He saw that it was not high-arched like the feet of a century of booted Benedicts. Hesitantly, frowning a little, the boy's small foot in his palm, he looked up at Bick Benedict.

"Plana." He ran a finger over the instep. "Flat. This is more the foot of a dancer."

"Dancer!" yelled Bick.

"This is not the foot of a jinete. It is not a foot for the stirrup."

"It damned well will be."

At three, arrayed in full cowboy regalia, the boy had been lifted to the horse's back. Bick himself had set him there, had placed the reins in the baby fingers, had remained alongside, mounted on his own horse while Leslie stood by tense with fear. The child had sat a moment in frozen silence, his eyes wide, his mouth an open oval of terror. Suddenly he broke, he began to slip off the saddle, he screamed to be taken down. Down! Down!

Bick was disgusted. "I rode before I could walk."

"He's only a baby," Leslie said, her arms about the screaming child.

"When I was his age I yelled to be put on a horse, not taken off. If they didn't put me on I began to climb up his legs or tail or something. Ask anybody. Ask Polo."

"All right, that was very cute, but that was you. This is another person. Maybe he just doesn't like horses. Maybe he doesn't like riding. Maybe he's a walker like his mother."

"He's a Benedict and I'm going to make a horseman out of him if I have to tie him to do it."

"You've been playing God so long you think you run the world."

"I run the part of it that's mine."

"He's not yours. He's yours and mine. And not even ours. He's himself. Suppose he doesn't like sitting in the saddle from morning to night! If there's something else he wants to do I won't care if he can't tell a horse from a cow. There are important things in the world outside Reata. Outside Benedict. Even outside Texas!"

"Not to me."

"I think you actually mean that."

"Damn right I do."

But this came later. Just now the boy was seven months old. Leslie longed to have her father see him; to show him to her mother and her friends. She began to plan a Virginia visit. "It's been almost a year and a half. I can hardly believe it. Jordy'll be all grown up before they see him."

"Why don't they all come here for a visit?" Bick suggested.

"I wrote them. But Papa can't get away just now. Lacey's got a beau who isn't safe to leave she says. Mama alone . . . ?"

"You're right." Hastily.

"I feel so—I don't know—kind of listless and no appetite and this morning——" She stopped, struck by a sudden shattering suspicion.

Doctor Tom had made the suspicion a reality. "No!" Leslie, appalled, had rejected the diagnosis. "I can't! Jordy's only seven months old!"

"Everything grows fast in Texas."

"I won't! There'll be only—let's see—nine—sixteen months between them. I won't!"

"You're a healthy young woman. It'll be all right, Leslie. If this one's a girl you'll have a nice start toward a real family, all in about two years." Doctor Tom regarded her with keen kind eyes. "It's better this way. Something—two somethings—real and important to tie you to Texas."

Bick had been startled, then hilarious and definitely pleased with himself. "I'll consent to a girl this time, just to show you I'm no pasha."

Half laughing half crying, "I'm like one of the Mexican brides. I haven't even had a chance to wear my trousseau dresses. They'll be museum pieces."

"Give them to the Mexican girls around the house."

"Mama would sue." A terrible thought struck her. "Now I can't go home."

"Next year then, honey. In triumph. With two babies. Don't forget to show them to that duke or whatever he was, in the pink coat. I'll bet he couldn't have——"

"Oh, I wouldn't be so sure. He seemed to me quite a talented young man." She felt irritable, restless, trapped. "I wish I could dress up and sit at a restaurant table and hear some music. And even dance, perhaps. I look awful. My skin is like a crocodile's. I hear that dresses are longer and waistlines shorter and the boyish bob is out. I feel like a squaw."

"I can't get away for a long trip now. Anyway, you don't feel up to it. Tell you what, let's run down to Viento and stay at the Hake for a couple of days."

"Hake. If it's anything like——"

"It's quite a hotel. Music and the Seville Room and hostesses and a gold-and-marble lobby, all new. Didn't I ever tell you about the Hake? Besides, this is Fiesta week down there."

"Crowded."

"We'll be all right. We keep a big suite at the Hake the year round. It's quite a story. Old Cliff Hake built the hotel to spite the Jaggers outfit at the old Lone Star House. He was staying at the Lone Star and he got good and boiled one night and thought he was back in the old days fifty years ago. He ran out of his own liquor and forgot all about Texas being dry, began shooting up the Coffee Shoppe, poor old maverick, and then he shot his way into the lobby, there was a Baptist Bible Society Convention going on——"

"Oh, Jordan, you're making this up!"

"Ask Vashti. Ask anybody. After that they wouldn't give him a room at the Lone Star. Old Cliff was so mad he said he'd build a new modern hotel that would put the old Lone Star out of business and he sure did. The night of the opening he and Vashti led the grand march in the ballroom, you had to dress in Spanish costume, the invitations said Frontier Fiesta, Cliff was drunk as an owl and Vashti wasn't exactly cold sober. Well, guests began playing hide-and-seek behind those new marble pillars in the lobby, dodging bullets."

"Poor little man," said Leslie. "Living in a day that is gone."

Bick stared. "I wouldn't put it exactly that way. Cliff was modern as the next one."

The Vientecito trip was quite a success. Leslie was amazed at the natural beauty of the thriving little city, perched as it was on the high bluff overlooking Vientecito Bay and the Gulf of Mexico beyond.

"It's dazzling!" she exclaimed as she and Bick drove along the miles of waterfront. "In any other country in the world it would be a Riviera, with casinos and beaches and restaurants and all that dreadful stuff. Miles and miles and miles of waterfront! Jordan, let's get out and walk. Really walk."

"Walk! What for?"

"What does anybody walk for!"

"I never could figure out."

The long promenade was strangely deserted, even the Fiesta crowds only drove briskly by, staring at the brilliant expanse of rolling waters as at some strange and unapproachable phenomenon of nature. Boats bobbed at the piers, sails glinted against the horizon. The man and woman walked alone, two figures against the background of sky and water, no other living thing moved except the swooping gulls and an occasional Mexican fisherman sitting hunched over his crude pole at the edge of the breakwater. The wind blew, it whipped you along if you went with it or buffeted you if you went against it, there was none of the exhilarating salty tang of ocean air.

Leslie drew in a few experimental deep breaths. Nothing happened. "Had enough?" Bick asked.

"Why doesn't it make me feel terrific?"

"Uh—how would you like to go out in one of the boats? I always keep a boat here and so does Roady. And there's the speed boat too, if you want to hit it up."

"Boat. Oh, I think boats aren't the thing for me just now——"

The bright thriving city was in gala dress. Plump matrons in fringed silk shawls and high combs and mantillas, mahogany giants in costumes that were an impartial mixture of late Texas and early buccaneer thronged the streets, the Hake lobby. Mexican food was dispensed at street corners, signs worded in Spanish proclaimed this attraction or that, there was a gigantic parade which Bick and Leslie and an assortment of unexpected guests (true to the state custom) watched from the windows of the big Benedict suite. Float after float rumbled past, bunting-draped flower-festooned; Spanish costumes, Mexican costumes; charro costumes, vaquero costumes, señoritas, ruffled long-skirted dancers, grandees, pirates, conquistadores, toreros, Spanish music, Mexican music; Miss Charlene "Cookie" Tacker, voted Queen of this year's Fiesta, held royal court atop a vast moving platform transformed for the occasion from its prosaic everyday aspect as Baumer's Trucking and Hauling vehicle. Men and women in satins and sombreros astride creamy palominos. The horses, glinting in the sun, looked like mythical creatures in a child's fairy tale. Skittish quarter horses prancing and sidling. False ferocious mustaches and beards, grandees in goatees.

"You all right, Leslie?"

"I'm wonderful."

"You don't want to get all tired out. Maybe you'd better go in and rest for a while. Lie down. This'll be going on for hours."

"I love it. After it's finished—later—let's go down in the lobby. I want to look at all the people."

"An awful jam down there. We'd better have dinner served up here."

"Oh, no! No! I want to have it in the restaurant. It's—it's kind of stimulating to be in a crowd again. People, lots and lots of people."

"Pretty rough down there. . . . All right all right. I'll reserve a table. I hope. But it's late."

"Never too late for a Benedict," the dining-room telephone assured him.

The parade the music the clamor the crowds streamed and blared and shouted on and on in the street below. At last, baffled, Leslie asked her question. "But where are the Mexicans? It's all about Spain and Mexico and old Texas. Where are they? All the

333

people in the parade and even on the streets are what you call—well—Anglo."

"Uh—oh, they have a celebration of their own another day—a real Mexican Fiesta over in the Mexican part of town."

"Mexican Americans who live here in Vientecito?"

"Well, sure."

"I suppose Coronado and all those conquistadores you're always naming everything after were one hundred percent white Protestant Americans."

"You going to start all that again? Come on now, this is Fiesta, Yankee. No fair crabbing."

The hotel lobby fascinated her. Vast, marble-columned, it was, architecturally, a blend of Roman bath and Byzantine bordello. Gigantic men in boots and ten-gallon hats lolled in the stupendous leather chairs amongst the mottled marble and the potted palms. The Mexican bellboys, slim and elegant in their tight uniforms, agile as eels, were in startling contrast with the monolithic men whose bags they carried, whose errands they ran.

Clearing a path ahead of her, battling his way through the lobby mob . . . Hi, Bick! . . . Bick, you old maverick, where you been all these . . . Howdy, Bick! Say, I'd like for you to meet my wife she's right over there. . . . What you doing in this stampede! . . .

A corner in a far end of the room near a pillar and beneath a gigantic palm. The assistant manager magically produced a chair. Here you are, Mrs. Benedict, right in the middle of the roundup. You want to look out, Bick, she don't get tromped the way they're milling around today.

Bick was puzzled. "It doesn't seem like you, Leslie, wanting to get into the middle of a mob like this."

"I know. I suppose I'm hungry for people. Crowds of people. Once in a while it's sort of exhilarating."

"Will you be all right here for a minute? I'll just butter up those people in the dining room so we'll have a decent table. The Beezers are here, they're going to eat with us, and the Caldwells and Jim and Mamie Hatton—you met the Hattons, remember? At Len's?"

"Yes, of course." Brightly. Hattons?

The clamor was tremendous. She enjoyed it. She seemed to draw in through her skin and her senses a kind of vitality from the sheer strength and high spirits that flowed from these sun-soaked beef-fed people. Quietly she sat in her corner in her pretty trousseau dress, a bit snug for her now, and watched the surge and flow of these pseudo-Spanish and mock-Mexican Texans in their Fiesta finery.

"Howdy, Miz Benedict."

Jett Rink in his good Stetson and his good handmade boots and his clean canvas clothes. "Jett!"

"Yes ma'am. I watched for you to come down. I knew you had to, sometime. I heard you was here. And I was across the street watching the parade, I seen you—saw you—at the window."

Seen you saw you. The schoolteacher wife. "How are you, Jett?"

"Good."

"And your wife? I hear you married Miss Dart, the school-teacher."

"Not now we ain't. That's all busted up."

She glanced past him toward the dining-room doorway. Jordan would be furious if he found her talking to this boy. She turned her head away. But he stood there before her, staring at her.

"I'm running a rig now. Ain't you heard? I'm the works, driller and tool dresser and grease monkey all rolled in one."

"Grease monkey?" She couldn't resist the question.

"On the oil rig. We're drilling on my own piece, me and my uncle and little brother. Starting to, that is."

She rose. "That's splendid. Good-bye."

"Huh?" He glanced over his shoulder. "Say, I know Bick's got his kettle on for me, I ain't aiming to meet up with him—yet." He turned his hard relentless gaze upon her, those hot narrow eyes set so close together bored into her eyes. They traveled slowly down her face to her mouth and rested there a moment, then

335

down to her throat, her breast. "I been wanting to see you," he said, almost humbly.

She brushed past him, she began to push her way through the throng.

"I'll be seeing you again," Jett Rink said. It was not a casual farewell. It was a threat.

The crowd closed in on her. She was elbowed this way and that. A hand gripped her arm. "Leslie! I told you to stay till I came back for you." Jordan's dear face full of concern for her.

"I didn't like it there. Hot."

"The folks are waiting for us. Let's have dinner early, before the big mob."

The Seville Room maître d'hôtel turned out to be a head-waitress, brightly blonde and dressed as Carmen. Her kind care-worn face beamed a genuine welcome. "Hiyah! Right this way, honey." In the same breath she speeded a parting guest. "Come back quick!" Her flounced skirts bobbed energetically as she skipped ahead of Jordan and Leslie. And there were the Beezers and the Hattons and the Caldwells, brimming with friendship and warm hospitality. The men had brown paper parcels under their arms, and these they now somewhat sheepishly brought forth as bottles. Carmen hovered solicitously, she beckoned and a Mexican bus boy brought ice and glasses and water.

"Where at's your castanets, Carrie?" Ed Beezer inquired.

"Never you mind," Carmen retorted inadequately, her anxious eye on the doorway even as she bent over their table.

"Pay him no mind, Carrie," Joella Beezer said kindly. "How's your little girl?"

Carmen momentarily forgot the doorway guests. "Little! Say, you ought to see her! Taller than me, she's singing in the choir of the First Baptist now, and taking vocal."

"Well, you got a right to be real proud!"

Bick looked at Leslie. "Well, you asked for it." His hand sought hers. "I love it," she said. She dropped her voice. "I love you."

Carmen, guileless as milk, bustled off to greet the Fiesta diners that now thronged the doorway. Her voice rang above the blare of the big band on the platform at the far end of the room. "Hiyah! Howdy! Sure nice to see you. Right this way, honey!"

Well, Mexican food is the thing tonight, sure enough, they decided. Not as good here as it is in a real Mexican joint, but good enough. What d'you say we start with enchiladas? . . .

Heartburn. "I think a steak for Leslie here," Bick said. "Steak all right, Leslie?"

"Fine," Leslie said. "Perfect."

The band broke into the measured beat of a tango. Gourds chattered, drums pounded. The little dancing floor in the center of the dining room suddenly was asquirm with posturing figures in mantillas and silks and boleros. Handsome Texas males. Blooming Texas matrons. Dazzlingly pretty Texas girls with their strangely boyish six-foot beaux. The aroma of coffee, the smell of hot spicy food. No dark faces other than those of the Mexican bus boys moving silently from table to table.

Ed Beezer challenged Leslie's wide-eyed interest in the colorful clamorous room. "I bet you never saw anything like this up North, Miz Benedict. You'd never believe you were in the United States, would you?"

"Never," Leslie said. "Never."

21

EVEN BICK CONCEDED that the girl, from the moment of her birth, was completely a Benedict. She was fair as her brother Jordy was dark, sunny as he was somber. "Well, that's more like it!" Bick exulted. "Too bad we can't switch them around, but anyway now we're really coming through with the strain." With a cautious caressing forefinger he traced a path down the fragile pink face from brow to chin.

"Luz. H'm? We'll call her Luz."

"No!" Leslie cried. "We've never even mentioned that among the names we've——"

339

"Yes, but she looks it, though. All that yellow hair and blue eyes and look at that skin! Luz Benedict. Luz. It means light."

"Not Luz. Not that."

"What then?"

"You'd think I was some sort of prize cow that has her calf taken away from her after she's produced it."

"Wrong. Cows feed their calves."

"Oh, all right, if that's the only language you understand. And if it's light you want we'll name her Claire. Not Luz. Never Luz."

"Nothing to get so upset about, honey. You just don't like Benedict names, that's all. You were dead against Jordan too, remember?"

"This is different. I can't bear it."

"All right. I'll be big about it." His arms about the woman and the child, his cheek against Leslie's. He laughed a short grudging laugh of confession. "I guess I'm so set up about these two kids—two new Benedicts for Reata—I won't admit anybody else has a right to them. Even their mother. My darling girl. My two darling girls. . . . All right then. Your turn this time. If Claire is what you want then it'll be Claire."

But he fell into the habit of calling her Luz. Just a kind of nickname, he said. And in time the child and everyone who knew her forgot that she ever had had another name. Only Leslie remembered. Even she, in time, became accustomed to the use of the name she hated. The child was Luz to the hundreds on Reata, Luz at school, Luz to her friends. She herself forgot the name of Claire and signed herself Luz Benedict. At school in the East she explained, "I was named for my aunt, Luz Benedict. You ought to hear the stories about her! A real Grade B Western movie type."

The County began to approve of Leslie. In a limited way. Mrs. Jordan Benedict—you know—Bick Benedict's wife. Yes, she took to Texas like a heifer to cake. You wouldn't hardly know she wasn't a Texian born, only a little ways. Two children, boy and girl.

Now she longed for a glimpse of her family; for Virginia, for a taste of the easy graceful life of her girlhood. "This is your home. But you talk as if you were homesick," Bick said.

"I suppose I am. I suppose I will be until I see it again."

"It's going to feel mighty funny to me, end of the day, no kids no wife."

"It will be fine for both of us. We've been together every day every night since the day we were married."

"Isn't that good?"

"It'll be better after a few weeks apart."

"All right, all right. Tell you what, I'll come up and call for you. I'll have to go to Washington anyway about that time. That's what I'll do. Otherwise you'd probably never come back to this poor old beat-up cow hand."

Though they spoke lightly they were both terribly in earnest. This was more than a little visit with the family back home in Virginia. This was a long look around. This was a separation in spirit as well as body. These two terribly dissimilar people would not admit even to themselves that they were about to take a cool detached look at the brief tale of their married years, and a long speculative look at the years that stretched ahead.

In the spring she made the trip to Virginia, traveling true to Benedict tradition in a private car with two Mexican nursemaids; Petra her own maid; a welter of trunks, boxes, bags, small luggage; and gifts ranging from a complete Western riding outfit for Lacey including saddle boots hat, to crates of Valley grapefruit and bushels of paper-shell pecans.

Leslie was in a state of chills and fever as the Southwest receded, then the Midwest was left behind and the train approached the Eastern seaboard. Her father. The lovely rambling old shabby house. Lacey. Apple trees in bloom. Rich green grass in the meadows. Her mother. In exactly that order of her longing. Jordy and Luz were dressed within an inch of their lives hours before they reached their destination, managed to ruin this effect, were undressed, dressed again. The safari wound its way out of the train to the station platform in such a brouhaha of squeals shrieks chatter laughter tears Spanish English and Southern sweet talk that Leslie only tardily became aware of the actual presence of her sister Leigh, Lady Karfrey, here in the flesh in Virginia instead of being a voice on the overseas telephone from England.

"Leigh!" Her surprise was less than completely joyous. She looked about her. "Is Alfred with you?" She hoped not, she wanted only her own dear family for this homecoming.

"He's joining me in a few weeks. Leslie, he's mad to see Texas."

"To see Texas!" Leslie repeated with sinking heart. Then, hastily, "He wouldn't like it."

But there was no time now to go into this. Jordy and Luz were being kissed, exclaimed over, thoroughly disorganized. Howling, they were carried off by their Mexican nurses who conversed in a torrent of Spanish to the Lynntons' Negro servants. With the miraculous rapport of the minorities they understood each other.

Mrs. Lynnton said, "Leslie! Your skin!" She said, "Leslie! Your hair!" She said, "Leslie Lynnton, that's one of your old trousseau dresses. Well, I should think the wife of a husband with three million acres would be able——"

"Only two and a half, Mama."

Lady Karfrey said, "You travel like an East Indian maharanee. I thought Texas was a republic or a democracy or something. Do all Texans travel with a retinue?"

"Only a few."

Lacey looked at her gift of the massive Western saddle, the hand-tooled boots, belt, reata, as one would gaze upon an exhibit of prehistoric tribal utensils. The saddle especially fascinated her. "It looks like a rocking chair. And all that carving! It weighs tons, doesn't it? . . . What a pommel! Goodness, look at it miles high, what do they use it for—flying the Texas flag?"

Doctor Horace Lynnton said, "Well, Leslie."

It was she who threw her arms about him and held him close as if he were a child. "Oh, Papa!" He looked so much older than she had remembered him, so much frailer, so much paler and more stooped. "Oh, Papa, you aren't—have you been well?"

"You've been looking at seven-foot beef eaters for two years, all Eastern men will look like albino dwarfs to you."

GIANT

He held her off and regarded her with the eyes of a loving father and a great physician. Then he nodded his head as at the conclusion of a satisfactory diagnosis. "You've come through it all right. Some scar tissue. But in the main a triumph."

"Through what?" snapped Lady Karfrey. "One would think she'd been to the wars and back." Leigh Lynnton Karfrey of the tart tongue had always been tinged with the jealousy of the first-born for the next in years. "What has your darling daughter been through that's so terrible!"

"Through the first years of marriage. Two children in two years. And Texas. It makes any mere warrior look like a sissy." Doctor Horace rolled a non-existent pill between thumb and forefinger, an elderly habit that Leslie had never heretofore noticed in him.

In a haze of sentimental remembrance Leslie walked through the lovely and beloved old house. The drawing room. How faded the curtains were. Her old bedroom so tidy now, with the bed head pushed against the wall. It all looked shabbier than she had so longingly pictured it in these past nostalgic years. And smaller. There was the apple orchard in bloom. With the new vision of one who has seen a vast domain equipped with every modern mechanical device she noted that the trees badly needed spraying and pruning and mulching. There in Virginia and Washington and Maryland were the boys and girls—men and women now—with whom she had spent her carefree girlhood and the more serious years of young womanhood during the war. Now they welcomed her with all manner of festivities. Cocktail parties. Hunt balls. Dinner parties. Teas. Receptions. Luncheons. Presidential, ambassadorial, senatorial affairs, quite splendid and formal. Local society affairs, quite the opposite.

"But Leslie, you can't go to all these things in those clothes!" Even Lacey, of the erstwhile overalls, was scornful of Leslie's dated gowns. "The new things are way below the knees, and some evening dresses are almost to the floor."

Mrs. Lynnton took her daughter in hand. "It's bad enough to have Leigh home for the first time in ten years looking like a

343

frump. But she does it purposely. She tries to out-English the English. They've always been dowdy, God knows, but since the war they've made a religion of it. Leigh's brought along enough scratchy old tweeds for daytime and moth-eaten old portieres for evening to make a British county wardrobe."

"But Mama, you know perfectly well Jordy was born almost on the dot of nine months. I had hardly time to change from my traveling suit to a negligee when I found I was pregnant."

"Don't be common, Leslie."

"Well—uh——" Leslie indulged in a noncommittal grin. "Then just as I'd got myself pulled together and thought I'd go to Hermoso or Dallas on a dress-buying spree——"

"Dallas!"

"You'd be surprised. So then it was Luz. And here I am."

"Well, Washington's no place for shopping, heaven knows, but it will have to do. You can't go to Washington dinners looking as if you were dressed for a hoe-down."

There was a great deal of talk about a catastrophe called the Crash, and a long-lasting condition known as the Depression. This, it seemed, was an emotional as well as a financial condition. People dated things from it as they once used the war as a basis for time computation. Before the war. During the war. After the war. Now they said, "No, we haven't had one since the Depression. . . . I used to but that was before the Depression. . . . He's been like that ever since the Depression."

She was having a dazzling time of it. Old friends, new clothes, delicious food; gaiety, amusing talk; girlhood beaux who had not found consolation in her absence. Surprisingly, they all seemed to have learned quite a lot about Texas. Modern Texas.

"How did you know that!" Leslie would exclaim when someone referred airily to the vast Hake or Beezer or Waggoner or King or Benedict ranches; or to Neiman-Marcus in Dallas or the newest skyscraper in Houston.

"Everybody knows about Texas," they said. "It's getting to be the fashion. Pretty soon Texans won't even have to brag any more."

A newly met acquaintance at a Washington dinner might say, "I know you're from Texas, Mrs. Benedict. Well, of course we've all heard of the fabulous goings-on down there. Exaggerated, I suppose?"

"No. Understated."

If he happened to be a somewhat stuffy newcomer he would smile uncertainly, scenting a note of sarcasm. Reassured by Leslie's earnest gaze, he would go on. "But I suppose the Depression has hit you folks down there just as it has everyone else. Wall Street has a long reach."

"No one ever complains about the Depression down there. I don't think it has touched them. Us. When I left Texas everything seemed as booming as always. If anything, a little more so."

Her warm and charming smile took some of the edge off this. But the man would glare and then sigh as he drank a mouthful of pleasant dinner wine. "If I were twenty years younger I'd go down there and start all over again."

After the first two weeks her nostalgic longing was satisfied. She took to visiting Caroline in the kitchen in quest of that gifted woman's somewhat haphazard recipes. "Yes, but just how much sugar, Caroline?" Or flour or baking powder or butter or lemon. "It's delicious when you make it, but what are the quantities?"

"A body cain't be so businessified about how much this and how much that, Miss Leslie. I just th'ow in."

Mrs. Lynnton said, "You didn't come up here to fuss around in the kitchen. If your cook isn't suitable why don't you send her away?"

"My cook is a he. Not bad. I've tried to teach him a lot of Virginia recipes. But the Mexicans aren't very gifted with our kind of cooking."

"A Mexican cook! No wonder your skin looks blotchy. Chili and red peppers and all sorts of strange hot spices. Deathly!"

"Reata food is now considered epicurean. Most of Texas prefers beef cut hot off the steer and flung into the frying pan."

When at last she encountered Nicky Rorik the conversation and the emotions in which they became involved were something

345

of a shock to both of them. Safely Mrs. Jordan Benedict, mother of two. The Pink Coat was at the point of marrying an attractive rather prim girl of Pittsburgh derivation whose grandfather (not at all hale at the moment) possessed one of the four greatest fortunes in the Western Hemisphere.

Leslie and Nicky relaxed comfortably and had a real talk.

"According to the storybooks," Leslie said, "I ought to find you pallid and what-did-I-see-in-him. But my goodness you're attractive, Nicky!"

"If I were to tell you what I feel about you this minute you would leave me sitting here. Leslie."

"It's pleasant to know that we both had such good taste. We were almost in love in a nice—or maybe not so nice—kind of way."

"And then along came that enormous Texan."

"Not so enormous, really, when he's stacked up against his native state. Anyway, it wouldn't have done. No money in the Lynnton family—if you don't mind my putting it crudely. Is she terribly rich?"

"Fantastic."

"And very nice, I hear."

"She is a little like you. A carbon copy, fourth perhaps and not sharp and clear like the original. But like."

"Your country will be grateful to you. And to her."

It was all very reassuring. She wondered if she could possibly tell Jordan. No, of course not. Still, it would be pleasant to think about later, perhaps, when she was older and the children had the measles and Jordan was even more matter-of-fact than usual.

Lady Karfrey was proving something of a problem. As the time for Sir Alfred's arrival was now a matter of days she attacked the business at hand with her usual ferocity, possessed as she was of a drive equal to Leslie's but with none of Leslie's charm.

"I've been studying up on your Texas, Leslie. I must say you don't seem to talk much about it."

"I didn't think you'd be particularly interested," Leslie countered faintly.

GIANT

"Of course I am—as we're going down I hope. Now tell me, what do you do down there? For society, I mean. I know it's a ranch, and millions of miles. But what do you *do?* I mean—concerts plays clubs gardening politics committees? House guests?"

"Uh, no gardening, dearie. Don't confuse the Texas climate with Kent, England. But house guests, yes. Hordes of house guests."

"That will be stimulating. But what do you *do?* All that land and all those cows. You don't just sit and look at it."

"Well—uh—people visit, sort of. And everybody drinks a lot of coffee."

"Coffee!"

"Oh, my poor darling girl!" moaned Mrs. Lynnton, who was sitting over the breakfast crumbs with her two daughters.

"Poor me eye!" Leslie said briskly, to her own surprise.

Lady Karfrey now moved in for the kill. "Alfred always has been fascinated by Texas, he's mad to have a look at it. His grandfather, you know, had an interest in that vast thing that went bust in the 1870s, wasn't it? Called the T. and P. Whatever that means."

"Texas and Pacific Railroad." Horace Lynnton now spoke from the corner of the veranda off the dining room where he had been smoking his pipe, viewing the Virginia sky through the falling apple blossoms, and listening to the acquired English accent of his least favorite and eldest daughter. "It went bust through Jay Cooke and those big Wall Street boys in the panic of 1873. A lot of English had money in it. The railroad was to service the big ranches that the English were supposed to buy."

Speculatively Leslie surveyed her formidable sister. "Just imagine if it hadn't failed, Leigh. You'd have been the Texan in the Lynnton family. Though I don't know how you'd have met Alfred."

"Let's talk about our visit. When would it be convenient for you?"

"Leigh, we'd love to have you, of course. But I don't know that

347

you'd like it, really. Alfred isn't used to—he'd find it too terribly hot after the cool English———"

"Nothing's too hot for the English," Leigh Karfrey stated with great definiteness. "Or too cold. Remember India. And Hudson's Bay. And all that. They just put on a topee or long woolen underwear as the case may be, and thrive. They always have."

"But you can be frying under the sun at noon and freezing an hour later in a sudden norther. Texas is like that."

"It sounds absolutely Alfred's cup of tea," said Lady Karfrey.

Leslie tried to imagine Sir Alfred at Reata. A chubby little Englishman with a somewhat falsetto speaking voice and a mottled magenta coloring. He doted on good food, had a name as a collector of antiques and bibelots. Christie's and Fortnum and Mason's were always sending him special notices.

"Besides," Leslie said deliberately, "I don't know when I'm going back."

There was the silence that follows indrawn breaths. When she had recovered, "Just what does that mean!" demanded Mrs. Lynnton.

"Benedict's in Washington, isn't he, next week, that is?" Lady Karfrey marshaled her facts. "He's calling for you, isn't he? To take you and the children back? You said."

"That was the plan."

"Was!" shrilled Mrs. Lynnton.

Doctor Horace Lynnton stood framed in the veranda doorway. "Want to take a little walk with your old pa, Leslie? I've hardly seen you or talked to you since you came. Really, I mean. And now this talk of going back home." Wordlessly she joined him, she tucked her hand in his arm, close, as they descended the broad shallow steps to the garden. Horace Lynnton's voice, louder than necessary, came clearly to the undeceived ears of his wife and eldest daughter. "I've been at the hospital every day, you're at some party every night. Next thing I know you'll be gone. Why don't you stay until you're really ready to———"

"Well!" said Leigh Karfrey to her mother. "What do you make of that!"

The somewhat stooped elderly man and the blooming young woman walked close together through the garden, through the orchard, across the meadow and into the woods as lovers would have walked, seeing nothing with the conscious eye. Silent.

When Doctor Lynnton broke the silence it was as though he were continuing a spoken conversation. "Of course it's something no one can decide for you. But if you feel like talking about it a little."

"Oh, Papa. I'm so confused."

"You don't love him?"

"That's the terrible part of it. I do. Not only that, I'm in love with him. More than when I married him."

"But he seems to me to have a first-rate mind, too. Not only smart but aware and civilized. And amusing, too, I thought. Amusing is very important after the first years."

She thought of her mother. Not amusing. She pressed his arm. "Yes, he's all those things. But he's got that blind spot. Papa, he and I don't see alike about a single thing—except unimportant things. Handsome intelligent sexy ambitious successful vital amusing tender tough. Everything."

"But——"

"Power-mad. Dictator. His thoughts and energies and emotions are bounded by the farthest fence on the remotest inch of Reata Ranch. He's not unkind to people. Around, I mean. But to him they're only important in relation to the ranch, his life, Texas. He'll never change."

"No, we don't change."

"We?"

"Dedicated men. Men primarily in love with their work. Like Bick. And me." As she stared at him, peered into his face open-mouthed, like a child: "Leslie, your mother talked the same way. Poor girl, she's had a thin enough time of it too all these years while I've been pouring myself into the laboratories and hospitals. She's had what was left, and it wasn't much. It was unreasonable of me to expect her to understand. So I took it out on you girls.

349

I tried to make you conscious of the world. Your mother never changed. But neither did I."

"Jordan will never change. I know that now."

"No. But you're forgetting something."

"What?"

"The world will. It's changing at a rate that takes my breath away. Everything has speeded up like those terrific engines they've invented these past few years. Faster and faster, nearer and nearer. Your Bick won't change—nor you—but your children will take another big step. Enormous step, probably. Some call it revolution but it's evolution, really. Sometimes slow sometimes fast, horrible to be caught in it helpless. But no matter how appalled you are by what you see down there in that strange chunk of the United States, still, you're interested. Aren't you?"

"Fascinated. But rebelling most of the time."

"What could be more exciting! As long as you're fascinated and as long as you keep on fighting the things you think are wrong, you're living. It isn't the evil people in the world who do the most harm. It's the sweet do-nothings that can destroy us. Dolce far niente. That's the thing to avoid in this terrible and wonderful world. Gangrene. The sweet sickening smell of rotting flesh."

Bick Benedict, when he arrived, seemed by his very buoyance to make all this talk mere academic babble. He was a mass of charm and high spirits. Virile handsome actually boyish, Leslie thought she never had seen him so pleased with himself and the world. His arms about her, Jordy and Luz flung themselves at him. In the first flush of their reunion she thought it was herself and the children that gave him this vibrating aura of well-being and elation. But she began to detect something within himself that was the source of this bubbling.

Surveying him with a wifely gaze, "What makes you so full of beans? This glitter in your eye can't be just wife and children."

"Purely spiritual, honey. It's just the result of all that high-minded talk down there in Washington. They've voted to continue the twenty-seven percent tax allowance on oil. Clear."

"But you haven't any oil. Have you? You've always said you hated the stinking oil wells."

"That's right."

"I don't understand."

"But I'm right petted on oil—off my land. I don't mind others having it because from now on the whole world is going to be yelling for oil. Texas is booming. The rest of the country is flat."

"Is that good?"

"Only good enough to make us the richest state in the whole country. We're a country within a country."

"Again!"

"Oil and beef and cotton. You can't stop it, you can't top it." He breathed deeply, for a moment she thought she saw a strained look in his eye. He gazed around and about the Virginia landscape and he laughed.

"God, it looks little! The fields. And the sky. Are you ready to come back with your old man, honey?"

"Jordan, I'm no different from what I was when I left."

"I don't want you different. We Texians like a little vinegar on our greens. Gives it flavor. Come on, let's go home."

22

ON THE JOURNEY homeward Leslie said, "If you had told me, on our honeymoon, that the next time we made this trip I'd be traveling with you and masses of our children and hundreds of nurses and millions of bags and bottles and toys and stuff!"

"You'd have made it anyway."

"You're so pleased with yourself I think this is the time to tell you that Leigh meant it when she said she and Karfrey want to visit Reata."

"Why not!" Bick demanded, largely. "Penned up on that little island all their lives! Do 'em good to have to hunt for the horizon.

Anyway, it'll be worth it just to see Karfrey in a ten-gallon hat."

"I wish Papa and Mama would come down at the same time. And Lacey too. Just to take the curse off the Karfreys."

His well-being encompassed this without a sign of strain. "That's a fine idea. Folks down here are beginning to think you're an orphan. Look, I'm going to send them all a telegram at the next stop."

Down they came to Reata, the lot of them.

"Do you mean to tell me," demanded Mrs. Lynnton, "that I am not going to be allowed to sleep under the same roof with my daughter and my grandchildren!"

"Mama dear, you're staying in the Big House because there isn't room here in our house. You'd go simply crazy here, and I don't like to shush the children. Over there it's bigger and quieter and more restful for you."

"Restful! The place is full of utter strangers stamping and jingling through the halls all hours of the day and night. Nobody even knows who they are. I asked one of those Mexican girls. She just shook her head and jabbered something in Spanish. Spanish!"

"They're business acquaintances of Jordan. People he has to see. Or they come to see the ranch. They come from everywhere."

"What are you running? A hotel! God knows we're hospitable in Virginia. But this!"

"Mama, this isn't just a ranch. It's a scientific laboratory too. And a kind of show place for the whole ranching world. Reata and the King ranch and the Hakes' Double B and a few others are sort of famous, you know. People come to see and learn. Jordan loves it. He's breeding a new kind of cattle."

"If God had meant to have men create new cattle He'd have given them the job in the first place, with all He had to do."

The family visitors adapted themselves to the climate, the environment and the customs with astonishing ease. Lacey was off on a horse from morning until night, she was more at home in the stables than the house. The vaqueros adopted her as one of themselves, they explained in Spanish and she understood in English. Even old Polo demonstrated to her the value of the new breed of fleet-footed creatures whose swift quarter-mile spurting powers were invaluable in the roundup and on the range. Quarter horses, they were called.

Mrs. Lynnton took alarm. She sought out Bick. "Lacey spends all her time with those Mexican men, no one knows where she is the day through and half the night. I've spoken and spoken to Horace about it but he's as bad as she is."

Bick grinned, he pretended to misunderstand. "No! You mean the Doctor's galloping around on quarter horses!"

"You know perfectly well he's down at that laboratory of yours with that vet, or poking into the wretched shacks around here, looking for local diseases, they're worse than any slave quarters in the old Virginia days I can tell you."

He could not be angry with her, actually, though he thought privately that he would like nothing better than to drive her out to really good rattlesnake country some hot bright afternoon.

Reata was a country in itself to which each visitor could adapt according to his or her own taste. Luxury or hardship, leisure or work. Lacey ate her midday meal out on the range with the vaqueros. In the evening she reported on her day, to the horror of Mrs. Lynnton.

"For lunch we had some rather awful stuff looked like entrails. And beans of course. Don't they ever tire of beans!"

Mischievously Bick said, "I must ask the boys to fix you up with a tasty dish of magueys."

"Magueys?"

"It's quite a Mexican delicacy. White maguey worms fried crisp. Elegant eating."

A squawking sound from Mrs. Lynnton. Sir Alfred took a more world-wise view. "Why not? All foreigners eat certain beastly messes. Look at the French with their snails!"

"True, true," agreed Horace Lynnton. "And is there anything more repulsive-looking than a succulent Baltimore soft-shell crab?

Or, for that matter, a nicely aged English plover's egg or a properly disintegrated woodcock."

Lacey, full of her day's doings, rattled on. "I rode miles and miles today and ended up at the Dietzes' place, that little Bobby Dietz is the smartest little boy I ever saw. Not smarty smart like Eastern kids but wise smart. He knows about soil and cattle and feed and horses. The Dietzes say they're going to send him to Texas U., but he says he wants the husbandry course at Cornell. If he were ten years older I'd ditch my beau and marry him. What a kid! . . . Look, Bick, there was a fellow in the camp today he came rushing in sort of wild-looking and covered with grease and driving the worst broken-down Ford I ever saw. He gulped down his lunch red hot though I must say the Mexican boys didn't seem very glad to see him. When he found out who I was he was really rather nervy. I mean not like the cowboys and vaqueros I've met, I think he'd been drinking. He wanted to know all about you, Leslie."

Bick stopped her. "What was his name?"

"Something that sounded like Jeb——"

Bick pushed back his chair and stood up. "By God I've told them that if he ever sets foot on my land they're to shoot him."

Lacey giggled a little at this. "Yes, they told him—at least I gathered they told him—— Do you know I can understand quite a lot of Spanish now——"

"Oh, they told him."

"And he just said sort of 'pffft!' as if he were spitting through his teeth—he was, really—and jabbered something I couldn't get in Spanish, I must say it didn't sound too complimentary——"

"Now Jordan," Leslie said quietly. "Sit down and finish your dinner."

"I've finished. Excuse me, folks. I've got some business to tend to." You heard him a moment later talking on his office telephone, the Spanish words drumming.

Leslie pretended to make nothing of this. "Ranch business again. Oh dear! And we're having the most lovely dessert."

"I'm awfully sorry, Leslie," Lacey said. "I was just talking, I

356

didn't dream there was anything important about this really crummy-looking man."

Mrs. Lynnton eyed her youngest daughter disapprovingly. "Lacey, how many times have I told you not to chatter? Men don't like women who talk so much."

At the shout of laughter that went up she looked about her in vague surprise.

After dinner Doctor Horace took Leslie aside. "Tell me something about this fellow Lacey was talking about. I don't like to see a big full-blooded man like Bick go as white as that."

"When Jordan's sister died I didn't write you and Mama all the queer details because you'd have been upset. I was. Horribly. I don't yet quite understand the whole gruesome business."

She told him, speaking rapidly and very low, meanwhile smiling and nodding reassuringly across the room at her mother. "What are you two whispering about?" that lady demanded. As Leslie talked and her father listened she began to feel strangely relieved as from a burden. "You see, he's just an ignorant crude lout. But tough. He has some sort of crazy plan in his head, I suppose. But I can't understand," she concluded, "why Jordan takes him so seriously. He's nothing, really."

"Nobody's nothing," Doctor Lynnton said. "You can't cancel out any living human being. Sometimes they surprise you. This boy has a deep grudge. Not only against Bick, I'd say, but against the world. If he's strong enough and carries it long enough he might do quite a lot of damage."

"I don't see how. He never can touch us, that's sure."

Doctor Lynnton, during this visit, covered a great deal of scientific ground so unobtrusively that he seemed scarcely to move at all. He ambled. He spoke to everyone he encountered—vaqueros, merchants, servants, ranchers, any Mexicans within reach. He himself talked little, they seemed always to hold forth while he listened and nodded his head gently and said I see I see. His conduct was, in a more orderly and intensified way, based on the pattern his daughter had followed when first she had come, a stranger, to Texas.

"Well, Papa," Leslie said, at the end of the first week, "do you get the idea?"

"Somewhat. Somewhat. Very complicated, beneath the surface. But fascinating beyond my expectations. This is a civilization psychologically different from any other part of the United States. The South is a problem, certainly; and the Eastern seaboard. The West Coast is faced with its peculiar difficulties, and even the Middle West isn't as serene as it seems. But this! Bigness can be a curse, you know, too. Texas is very big. Reata is very big. Your Bick is very powerful. People in big empty places are likely to behave very much as the gods did on Olympus. There's a phrase for that—one of those nice descriptive American sayings. 'Throwing your weight around,' we say."

The visitors met and were entertained by the neighbors for hundreds of miles around. "Con Layditch telephoned," Bick would announce casually, "wants us all to come over, they've finished their new house, they're having a barbecue and square dance to celebrate." At an anguished look from Leslie, "No, honey. Steaks."

The visitors would find themselves whirled two hundred miles for dinner.

"All these foreigners," Sir Alfred remarked as they scudded through the little towns, as they watched the vaqueros at roundup, as they were served their food. "These Mexicans everywhere. I should think they'd be quite a problem, what?"

"Yes," Doctor Horace agreed. "And imagine the problem we were to them when we came swarming in a hundred years ago. We were the foreigners then."

"Room enough for everybody now, I must say," Mrs. Lynnton announced, looking about her largely. "Miles and miles and miles of nothing. Scares you. Makes me want to holler."

Doctor Horace pounced on this. "It does!" Thoughtfully.

Leslie had dreaded the inevitable meeting between Vashti Snyth and Lady Karfrey. They came together with a clashing of broadswords. After the first encounter Leslie found herself de-

fending the people and customs she herself had so recently criti-
cized.

"Vashti is a college graduate. She's traveled quite a lot in
Europe. They go East every year. She speaks French very well."

"It hasn't touched her," Lady Karfrey asserted. "She's a Texas
national monument like the Alamo or that cow you showed us in
the glass case in the village. Neither college nor Europe or time
or tide will ever change her. I hope."

Conversations between Vashti Snyth and Leigh Karfrey were
brisk and bristling.

"My, I should think it would feel wonderful for you to get
where you can really draw your breath," Vashti said with that
tactlessness which was, perversely enough, a rather endearing
quality in her. "That little bitty old England, you can't take a
good long walk without you fall over the cliffs into the ocean. I
liked to choke to death there in all that cramped-up fog. And
then the mutton. Mutton! My."

"You imported all our beautiful English Herefords. And immediately they arrived they fell heir to your cattle diseases—pinkeye, and ticks, and worms!"

"We're trying to breed out all the Hereford strain in our stock.
We don't really need to haul anything in here. We got everything.
We got cattle in plenty. And cotton. And wool and mules and
grapefruit and horses and wheat and turkeys. And Mott, my husband, says we got sulphur and coal and copper and lead and a
thing called helium—I don't rightly know what that is, but anyway it's good stuff to have around—and lumber he says and
limestone and vegetables in the Valley, and pecans. And a course
all this oil now. We got just everything in Texas."

Lady Karfrey cleared her throat.

"I have been gathering a few facts, dear Mrs. Snyth, since I
arrived in your state. Everything you say is true."

"Sure it's true," repeated the unsuspecting Vashti.

"As you say, of all the states Texas is first in cotton—but last
in pellagra control. First in beef—and forty-fifth in infant mor-
tality. First in wool—and thirty-eighth in its school system. First

in mules—and forty-seventh in library service. First in turkeys—
and its rural church facilities are deplorable. First in oil—and
your hospitals are practically non-exis——"

Magenta surged into Vashti's indignant face. "I been in England. I never saw such poor runty beat-up looking people in my
born days as you got in what you call the East End. And poor
teeth and bad complexions, drinking tea all the time and nobody
in the whole country gets milk and oranges and he says the roast
beef of old England is a non-existent, Mott says."

Strangely enough it was Karfrey, the Englishman, who said,
"How right you are, Mrs. Snyth. But then you must remember
that you could put all of England down in one corner of Texas
and never find it, really."

Mrs. Lynnton, in her own insecure way, struggled for a foot-
hold of understanding. The food, the storerooms, the swarms of
servants inside and out, the vastness, the lavish scale on which the
Big House and the Main House were run, bewildered and irritated her.

"When I get back home I'm going to send Mitty down. You
remember Mitty, Caroline's daughter? She's every bit as good a
cook now as Caroline and in some ways better."

"No, Mama. It wouldn't do."

"You owe it to your children. I saw Jordy yesterday with that
weird little Mexican girl he's always playing with, they were both
eating tortillas as if it were bread and butter."

"So it is, in a way."

The visiting Lynntons and Karfreys usually drove over from
the Big House before dinner there to lounge in comparative coolness on the Main House veranda. There were always tall iced
drinks, the Gulf breeze filtered through vines and screens, the
voices of the children came pleasantly from the far end of the
veranda. It was the most relaxed hour of the day, it was the time
Leslie liked best. Bick was always at his most charming. Lacey
was full of her day's doings. Her father and mother had learned
to accept for her this strange life of hardship and fantastic luxury.
The Karfreys were frankly having the time of their lives.

"Besides," Leslie now said, continuing her conversation with her mother, "that weird little Mexican girl isn't a girl at all. She's a boy."

Mrs. Lynnton turned to stare at the distant children.

"I don't believe it."

Bick called to them. "Jordy! Angel! Ven acá!"

The two came reluctantly, Jordy to stand at his mother's side, her hand on his shoulder; the other child stopping short of the group. Weird, Nancy Lynnton had said. Now the group of adults gazed at the dark small Mexican child and the child stared back at them poised lightly, like a tiny fawn, as though ready to dart off at a sound, a hostile glance. Fawnlike three-cornered eyes, due to a slight lift or pinch in the center of the upper eyelid. The little figure was bony of shank, flat of chest, the hands strong and big-boned sticking out of the stuff of the sleeves. A small boy's hands, a small boy's legs, a small boy's chest and eyes; and the bones of the alert face and the well-shaped head were those of a boy. But the dress with its Mexican ruffles and its petticoats and the red hair ribbons—all this was the garb of a girl. And the long black hair was neatly brushed and braided, it shone with brushing and with unguents, unlike the thick careless locks of other small Mexican ranch children.

"This is Angel Obregon," Leslie said, and smiled at the boy, "the son of Angel Obregon, who is a vaquero here at Reata." And she held out her hand to him as she spoke, as though to draw him to her side with Jordy, her own son. But the boy only looked at her and did not move.

In her halting Spanish Leslie said, "Won't you say good evening, Angel? Buenas tardes, señoras. Señores."

"Señores come first in Spanish, honey," Bick reminded her.

Now Angel's black eyes were strangely sparked with determination, the baby jaw was set with fierce effort. The lips opened, the whole face took on animation and purpose. "Good . . . even . . . ing . . . sirrrs . . . good . . . even . . . ing . . . madamas." In a triumph of stumbling English. Then, with a shriek of hysterical laughter he was off. Jordy, too, broke away,

361

the two could be heard down the veranda howling at the splendid joke.

"Well, if that don't take the rag off the bush!" Bick exclaimed. "The little muchacho has learned English off of Jordy!"

"Splendid!" observed Doctor Horace. "It's beginning to work."

It was obvious that Leigh Karfrey was busy taking mental notes on the Habits and Dress of the Mexican Child in Texas. Mrs. Lynnton was quivering with disapproval.

"Leslie Lynnton, will you tell me the reason for dressing a child like that! Day after day, playing with Jordy!"

"I suppose it does seem queer," Leslie agreed. "We're used to it."

"Tell them," Bick urged her. "It's quite a story."

Leslie took a little fortifying sip of the cool drink in her hand. "Mm, let's see. Well, that very first day after I arrived in Texas, a bride——"

"And what a bride!" Bick muttered, ambiguously.

"——I started out for a morning walk, in my youth and innocence. To see the sights."

"Dear me!" said Doctor Horace.

"Finally I began to feel like a wanderer dying of thirst in the desert and I stumbled into one of the Mexican houses. I'd heard a baby crying there. The woman was in bed, ill. It was her baby, crying. The baby was little Angel there. Not a word of English. But I understood her, sort of, just the same. We've become great friends since then. And later I learned about her and her baby. She'd been married almost three years and no baby which for a Mexican girl is practically a disgrace. She was ill a good deal but finally this child was expected. They knew what had caused all the trouble, of course. One night Angel had left his hat on the bed and everyone knows that is bad luck. So Deluvina, the wife, had paid for special masses and she had taken herb medicines and the midwife had massaged her and on the Tree of Petitions she had hung a little cradle made of bits of mesquite wood and in it she had put a tiny doll dressed as a girl baby because she thought they were being punished for wanting only a boy all these years. She prayed morning and night and in between. And she promised God that she would be humbly grateful for girl or boy, and that in either case its hair would be tended and brushed and anointed and when it was a foot long it would be cut off and given as a thank offering to God. You can't know what that means. Mexican girls don't cut their hair. It is their glory. The child's name was to be Angelina. And Angelina was born, and she was a boy. But the promise had been made to God by Deluvina and by Angel Obregon kneeling before the altar. They named him Angel after his father. They let his hair grow and Angel was dressed as a girl and his hair was always tied with a red ribbon as you've seen it and washed and brushed and anointed for it belonged to God. Other Mexican children might have piojos in their hair, but not Angel. His grandmother's chief duty is to keep it brushed and shining. And when it is a foot long there will be a great celebration and Angel's hair will be cut off by the priest and placed as an offering on the shrine. Then they will put Angel in pants and take away his skirts."

"Well I never!" exclaimed the outraged Mrs. Lynnton.

"Barbaric!" said Lady Karfrey.

"By that time," Doctor Horace mused, "he'll be so confused as to be incoherent. Or such a tough guy, in self-defense, that Reata Ranch can't hold him."

Sir Alfred was casting an eye toward the dining room. "Dinner any second now," Leslie assured him. "Will anyone have another drink?"

"Do you think," Nancy Lynnton demanded, "that this child is a fit playmate for Jordy!"

"Don't let those skirts worry you," Bick assured her. "This kid's a tough hombre. In fact, I wish Jordy had some of his stuff. His father Angel Obregon used to be my sidekick when I was a kid. And his father's father taught me roping—he and old Polo. Even today old Angel is the best mangana thrower on Reata. In Texas, for that matter."

"This could be wonderful," Doctor Horace mused aloud. "Maybe someday it will be."

But no one consciously heard him or heeded him, except Leslie.

"Mangana?" inquired Sir Alfred, abandoning hopes for immediate dinner.

"To throw the mangana you have to be a brush roper. And roping in the brush is trickier than roping in the open. For the mangana the animal is running and the roper is standing still. The loop turns over in the air and it catches the animal high around the front legs so's not to break the leg between the brisket——"

But now there was the sputter and cough of an engine in the drive. A grease-spattered Ford with flapping fenders came to a stop with a shrill squeal of old brakes and seared tires.

Jett Rink sprang out. His face was grotesque with smears of dark grease and his damp bacchanalian locks hung in tendrils over his forehead. He leaped from the car and began to run as he landed, without a pause, and he limped a little as he ran.

He came on, he opened the door of the screened veranda, he stood before the company in his dirt and grease, his eyes shining wildly. They stared at him in shocked suspense, relaxed as they were against the cushions, glasses in hand. Leslie thought, Now he is really crazy something terrible is going to happen. Jordan. The man stood, his legs wide apart as though braced against the world, the black calloused hands with the fingers curiously widespread as they hung, his teeth white in the grotesquely smeared face. He stared at Bick with those pale blue-white eyes and there was in them the glitter of terrible triumph.

Bick did not even rise from his chair. Very quietly, sitting there, he said, "Get out."

Jett Rink spoke four words only. His voice was low and husky with emotion.

"My well come in."

"Get out of here."

Now the words shot geyser-swift out of Jett Rink's mouth like the earth-pent oil his labors had just released.

"Everybody said I had a duster. You thought ol' Spindletop and Burkburnett and Mexia and those, they was all the oil there was. They ain't, I'm here to tell you. It's here. It's right here. I got the laugh on you."

Now it was plain the man was drunk, the eyes were bloodshot, you could smell the raw liquor on the heavy hot air of the shadowy veranda.

Bick leaned forward slightly his muscles tensed; and still the others sat staring at the man.

"My well come in big and there's more and bigger. They's oil under here. They's oil here on Reata and someday I'm going to pay you a million dollars or five million or ten and you'll take it because you'll need the money. I'm going to have more money than you ever saw—you and the rest of the stinkin' sons of bitches of Benedicts!"

Now, rather wearily, Bick stood up, he said, "Leslie, honey, you and the girls go along indoors."

Leslie stood up, neatly folding the bit of sewing in her hands. But she did not go.

"Go along home now, Jett," she said. "It's nice you've struck oil. Go along now." As she would have spoken to a stray that had run in on the place, man or animal.

He looked at her, lurching a little with weariness or drink or both, his legs wide apart like one who walks the deck of a ship. Then, with the swiftness with which he always moved, the man came over to her, he reached out and just jerked ever so lightly with a grimed hand one end of the soft little bow that finished the neckline of her silk dress. He tweaked the piece of silk with a gesture that would have been insolent even in an intimate and an equal.

"My, you look pretty, Leslie," he said. "You sure look good enough to eat."

Bick's first blow struck him squarely in the jaw but Jett Rink's monolithic head scarcely went back with it. Bick hit him again, Jett dodged slightly and the blow landed full on his mouth and a little blood trickled down his chin and he twisted his mouth as though he were eating and she thought he was going to spit out the blood full at Bick, but he laughed only and did not even lift his hand to wipe the blood away.

"My, you're techy, Bick," he said. "You're techy as a cook."

Karfrey came forward, and Horace Lynnton. And now Jett Rink turned as though to go, grinning, and Bick rushed to grapple with him. He had reached the screen door. Bick was on him. Jett Rink's knee went sharply back and then drove forward like a piston and struck Bick squarely on the groin. Bick grunted. Doubled. Even as they caught Bick and dragged him to a chair Doctor Horace's hands were moving expertly over him.

Jett Rink had leaped into the battered car, had spun it like a crazy toy, was off in a cloud of dust.

23

"NO!" Bick commanded, fuming among his pillows. "Keep Roady away and Bowie, too. Get Bawley on the telephone."

Uncle Bawley had come down from Holgado in a swift overnight journey. Now he sat in Bick's bedroom, and for once it was the Lynntons, not the Benedicts, who held conclave: Doctor Horace, Mrs. Lynnton, Leslie.

"Soft!" Uncle Bawley declared, his gentle voice soothing the sting of the words. "That's what's chousing up this world. Everybody's turned soft. Pulled your gun and shot him, Bick, you'd saved yourself a heap of trouble. But no, you let him give you the knee and stroll off."

"He didn't stroll. He ran." Leslie to her husband's defense. "Jordan hit him twice, hard enough to fell a steer. It was like hitting a stone wall."

"Drunk. No use hitting a fella who's crazy drunk. He don't feel a thing."

Doctor Horace nodded in agreement. "An anesthetic, alcohol."

Mildly chiding, Uncle Bawley went on. "Shot him, the whole state would have been beholden to you. A loco umbry like Rink gets hold of oil and money, why, he's liable to want to be Governor of Texas. Or worse. What started you wrassling with a polecat like Jett in the first place?"

Propped up against his pillows, his eyes flint-grey with fury, Bick's legs threshed between the sheets. "He came up to Leslie and put his filthy stinking hand on her."

"No!" shouted Uncle Bawley.

"Yes!" Bick yelled.

"Bick's first blow was pure reflex," Doctor Horace observed. "Straight to the jaw."

"Bick well knows Rink's got a jaw like a jackass and besides he don't fight fair. Belt him in the ba—I mean, hit him below the belt, and first. That's the only kind of fighting he understands. Now you can't do a thing. Not a thing."

"Why not!" Mrs. Lynnton demanded. "Why not, I'd like to know! We saw it, all of us. You can call Leigh and Alfred. They'll tell you. And Lacey."

"Bring 'em on!" Bick shouted, glaring. "Bring everybody! Call in the house help. Call in the county!"

Leslie, seated at the bedside, leaned toward him, gently she placed her hand on his waving arm. "Now darling, you know perfectly well no one saw except my own family."

"Mexican servants hear everything and see everything and know everything that goes on. They get it through their pores or something. And what about that skunk! I suppose he isn't talking."

368

"Psychopath," Doctor Horace murmured. "Actually, of course, this Rink should be confined for treatment. Potentially dangerous."

Uncle Bawley rose, a commanding figure in the room now so charged with conflicting emotions. "Look how it sounds. Rink's fired from the ranch a few years back, he marries the schoolteacher he's got into trouble—pardon me, Miz Lynnton ma'am—and he don't seem to hold a grudge he starts wildcatting for oil with no money and no crew and no sense on his own little piece of no-account land Bick gave him long ago, deeded. And by God, what does he do, he hits oil. So he jumps into his junkheap car to tell his old boss Bick about his good luck he's struck oil on the piece Bick gave him time his father turned up missing." At a growl from the man in the bed—"Well, now, Bick, I'm just telling it the way it would sound, told. And this young fella spills his good news and his old boss throws him out and wallops him in the jaw front of everybody. That'd go good in a court of law."

"I wasn't thinking of the law," Bick said, sullenly.

"Furthermore," Uncle Bawley went on, "look what I heard this morning. Just on the way from Viento to here. I heard Rink's got hold of leases on pieces around. No-account land that's prolly rotten with oil."

With a mighty gesture Bick threw the covers aside. "I'm going to get up. What am I! Du Barry! Vamoose, ladies, as they say in the Westerns, unless you want to see a really fine physique in the raw."

Leslie glanced quickly at her father but he only smiled approvingly. "That's fine, Bick. You're all right."

"Sure Bick's all right," Uncle Bawley agreed, but the eyes that searched Bick's face were doubtful. "He took worse than that many a time when he was Harvard tackle."

"That's right," Doctor Horace agreed, too genially.

"Where's the kids?" Uncle Bawley demanded. "I want to look at something fresh and pretty. No offense, ladies. But this kind of ruckus makes me sick, nothing clean-cut about it. The good old days we'd of——"

"These are the good new days, Uncle Bawley."

"Maybe. Say, Leslie, where at's Jordy and Luz? Kids kept separate from grownups nowdays, like they were a different kind of animal. Mix 'em up they learn quicker, it's good for them."

"They're waiting for you, dying to see you. I told them first thing this morning, it was a mistake, they were so excited they hardly ate a mouthful."

"I suppose old Polo's got Jordy up on a horse roping a steer every morning before breakfast."

Leslie tucked her arm through his as they walked toward the veranda. "Jordy doesn't like riding. He isn't even interested in horses, much."

"No!"

"I sometimes think perhaps he's a little like you—when you were a child, Uncle Bawley."

"Poor little maverick."

"Luz is the rancher and cowboy. Do you know what that baby did! She somehow got hold of Jordy's riding things—his boots and rope and hat and all—she wriggled into the outfit every which way and there she was wobbling around in high heels and the pants wrong side to, and the Stetson down over her ears. I've never heard Jordan laugh like that."

"Luz, h'm?" He glanced, a quick sidewise look, at Leslie. "She sounds like she's taking after—uh, she bossy too?"

"Well, independent."

"And Bick, he's hell-bent on breaking Jordy in already, I bet."

"Yes."

"There's a difference between breaking in and just plain breaking."

"Somebody will have to help me. Later."

"I'm good for another fifteen eighteen years—maybe twenty. Hard cash and a pretty good brain. Neither of 'em going to go soft on me even time I'm ninety unless the United States and me both are hit to hell."

"Uncle Bawley." She looked up at him. "Thanks, Uncle Bawley."

"Well, I guess I'll go hunt up the kids."

"I'll be with you in a minute. I want to talk to Papa."

"Yes," he said, as though in answer to an unspoken question. "I'd do that."

Alone with her father in Bick's office she put it to him squarely. "Why did you put him to bed?"

"Shock," Doctor Lynnton said, his manner very easy. "And it was the best place for a man as crazy mad as Bick was. Take away a man's pants and he can't go far."

"I don't think that was your real reason." They stood facing each other, the man benign, controlled; the woman determined to hear what she feared. Between them the resemblance was startling. "I don't believe you. If you don't tell me I'll send for Doctor Tom."

Horace Lynnton seated himself at Bick's desk, he motioned his daughter to a chair. Suddenly they were no longer merely father and daughter, they were physician and patient. Leslie's steady eyes did not leave his face.

"That young savage didn't do Bick any real physical harm. Uncomfortable, though, a terrific dirty blow like that." He was looking down at his own square blunt-fingered hands spread out on the desk top. "Later, after we'd brought him round and put him to bed, I thought I'd give him a real going over while I was about it. Of course I didn't have the proper equipment."

"Well?"

"Did he ever complain—that is, does he ever get short of breath?"

"No. At least I haven't noticed it if——"

Now he looked up and full into his daughter's eyes. "It's a thing that has to do with the heart. Now wait a minute. It isn't the heart itself. That's a perfectly sound muscle, I'd say. But the big artery that feeds it."

She looked down at her own hands gripped tightly in her lap. "What do we do now?"

"Nothing. And don't look so serious. I don't believe I'd even say anything to him, just now. Apprehension is sometimes worse than the disease. If you could manage to have him not quite so active, not galloping hundreds of miles on those horses, up before dawn, running this empire singlehanded."

"He loves it more than anything or anyone. It's his life."

"It's his life."

"He can't do things halfway. It's always extremes. A rage one minute, angelic the next."

"Rages are bad for him."

"He's only like that when he's crossed in something he wants to do."

"From what I've learned about your Bick these past days, roaming around this enormous place, I've gathered that Bick's father ruled him—and the ranch—like an emperor. Then this sister Luz took his father's place and his mother's too. She must have been a real top sergeant. Now I gather the rest of the family are at odds with him. He's interested in experiment and they're interested in income."

"He'll never change, Papa. You might as well ask the Gulf wind to be quiet, or a norther tearing in from the sky. What shall I do!"

"Twenty years from now, when he's pushing those middle fifties, make him rein in. Now it's a matter of not taking things so emotionally and not doing everything himself. Why doesn't he go out on the range occasionally in a car instead of on a horse? I see others doing it."

"Yes, he's modern about everything but himself. He's an engine. He's a power plant. He's a dynamo."

"So is the heart."

"I'll never know a moment's peace again."

"Yes you will. Human beings can adapt to almost anything. Just hold onto his coat sleeve now and then, if he's going too fast. Leslie, I'll tell him if you want me to."

"He'd only go faster, in defiance. He is like that."

When the family left Reata—the Lynntons and the Karfreys to the east, Uncle Bawley to the west—a new peace seemed to settle down upon the Main House, upon the ranch, even upon the town of Benedict. Nancy Lynnton, departing, had flung a final shower of admonition at her daughter. ". . . and watch that cook he'll poison you yet . . . hardly more than a baby and putting him on that huge horse . . . get a good rich skin cream and pat it in night and morning . . . children . . . Mexicans . . . sun . . . wind . . . dust . . ."

"Mama's marvelous," Leslie remarked, feeling strangely gay and released. "In those last ten minutes she covered everything in the heavens and the earth beneath."

"Families are fine," Bick announced. "But they should be exposed to each other one member at a time. That goes for my family too, so don't get your feathers up."

"But Jordan, I couldn't agree with you more. It was wonderful to have them and to see them here——"

"And to see them go."

For the first time since her coming to Texas she felt something that was almost contentment. She had seen her old home and her friends in Virginia; her family had seen her new home. There, she thought. That's that. Now then. Jordan. Jordy. Luz.

Suddenly, as she looked at herself in the mirror there in the intimate quiet of their room—the guests gone, the children asleep, the world their own—she had a disquieting thought. She turned to stare at her husband.

"Jordan! We're the older generation, aren't we? Suddenly."

"Not me," he said firmly. "Maybe you, old girl."

"No, but I mean it. Jordy and Luz are the next generation we're always talking about. How did that happen? What's become of ours? We were the next generation until just a minute ago."

"It's always the next generation. I never could understand why they were always the generation that mattered—the next generation. They're always supposed to be better or smarter or more important. And we're supposed to sacrifice for them. So perhaps you're right, we are the older generation all of a sudden. Gosh! And I was feeling right romantic a minute ago."

"Jordan, would you sacrifice for Jordy? And Luz?"

373

"Sacrifice what?"

"Anything. Beginning with life itself."

"Let's not get dramatic, honey. I've had a hard day in the salt mines."

"But I mean. Just suppose—for example, I mean—that Jordy should want to do something different, be something beside a Benedict of Reata. What would you say to that?"

"Jordy's going to be a cowman. I'm not going to live forever."

"Yes, but suppose when he's eighteen or twenty he says he wants to be—oh, an engineer or a poet or a doctor or President of the United States or an actor or a lawyer."

"Well, he won't be."

"You don't mean you'd try to stop him, like a father out of Samuel Butler!"

"Who?"

"*The Way of All Flesh*—oh, never mind that—I mean you wouldn't actually stop him!"

"The hell I wouldn't."

24

JORDY GREW tall and slim. Jordy grew handsome and shy. Jordy was possessed of quiet charm and looked like his mother and walked in the footsteps of his father and loathed the daily deadly grinding business of roping and branding and castrating and feeding and breeding and line-riding and fence-building and dipping and shipping.

"I want you to know everything," Bick said again and again. "A Benedict ought to be able to do anything on Reata that any hand can do, white or Mexican. I could, at your age. Maybe as a kid I wasn't as good as the older men. But good enough. That's the way I was brought up."

In the choking dust the boy learned to cut out a calf a cow a steer from the vast herd. He would ride in amongst the bellowing animals, he handled his cutting horse with dexterity, zigzagging this way that way in pursuit of the desired quarry. Bick, mounted on his own horse, would stand watching near by, immobile as an equestrian statue.

"Get that white-faced boneyard. How did an esqueleto like that get in . . . That runty red there . . ." Grudgingly, at the end of a long burning day of grinding work he might say, "You did pretty well, son."

"Thanks, Papa." The boy did not raise his eyelids to look at his father. Leslie always said those long silky lashes were wasted on a boy. "Thanks, Papa." He looked down at his leather-bitten hands.

Leslie called Bick's attention to a little defect in speech that somehow seemed more pronounced as the boy grew older. At first it had seemed a childish trick, rather endearing. "Jordan, have you noticed that Jordy stutters quite a lot? Especially when he's upset."

"He'll outgrow it."

"But it's worse than it was. A real stammer."

"Lots of kids do that. Their ideas come faster than they can talk."

"Jordy isn't really a little boy any more. And Luz wears lipstick as automatically as levis. Let's face it. They're almost grownups."

No one needed to say do-this do-that to Luz. She had taken to horses as other little girls demand dolls and lollipops. By the time she was twelve she could cling like a cat to an unsaddled horse's back. Riding low she could stay plastered to the side of a quarter horse running through the brush, a wilderness of thorns and branches, the twining arms of one mesquite interlocked with the arms of the next and the next so that they formed a bristling barrier.

Bick's admonitions to his daughter were the reverse of the orders he issued to his son. "You're not to ride alone in the brush. Hear me! . . . Keep away from that stallion, you crazy!"

Now her physical resemblance to her father was startling. The sunburned blonde hair, the blue eyes that gazed unsquinting almost straight into the glaring sun. She stood as he stood, she spoke with his inflections. Headstrong. Direct. Somewhat insensitive. When the Snyth twins, arrayed in identical pink, were bound for this or that festivity, Luz, in pants and shirt, would be down in the corral or sprawled, grease-grimed, over a balky Ford.

"Luz, the Snyth twins have been on the telephone for hours. They say you promised to pick them up. Scrape that grease off and hustle into your clothes. It's a seventy-mile drive it'll take you at least——"

"Why don't they take themselves! I'm tired of those cowbelles hanging around my neck."

The Reata vaqueros worshiped the girl. In the non-Mexican line-house families she was as accustomed as their own members, she was as likely to be found eating with them as at home. To the Dietz family she was as casual as one of their own sons or daughters. From Bob Dietz, eleven years her senior, she unconsciously received a fundamental education in the sciences embracing soil, seeding, feeding, breeding. During his summer vacations from Texas University and, later, from Cornell, he worked as a matter of course on Reata. Whenever he permitted her Luz rode with him or drove with him, a wide-eyed child in pigtails, her mind absorbent as a thirsty desert plant. She was twelve. Fourteen. Fifteen.

Leslie took this up with her husband. "Jordan, Luz spends all her time with that Dietz boy."

"I wish Jordy did. Bob Dietz knows more about modern ranching than any man on the place. Of course, some of his ideas are cuckoo. I'm all for modern methods but some of this stuff they give them at college!"

"Yes, but I mean Luz isn't a child any more. Bob's a nice boy, and smart——"

"I'll tell you how smart I think he is. Someday that kid's going to be General Manager of Reata unless Jordy pulls up his socks and gets going. That would be a fine thing, wouldn't it! A Benedict just a kind of figurehead on Reata."

"I'm talking about Luz. She's down at the corral or galloping around with Bob Dietz the minute he's home."

Bick waggled his head in admiration. "Gill Dace says she knows more about the stock than his boys do. He says the first time he used that fifty-thousand-dollar Kashmir bull on the new prize heifer Luz was down there telling him about the advantages of artificial insemination."

"Oh, Jordan!"

"This is Reata, honey. Luz knows by this time that the stork doesn't bring our calves."

"Oh well, she'll be going away to school next year."

Luz, the outspoken, ranging the countryside in the saddle or at the wheel, came home with bits and pieces of gossip and information which she dispensed perhaps not as artlessly as one might think. Mealtime frequently was enlivened by her free-association chatter.

"They say Aunt Luz was always trying to keep people from getting married, she couldn't bear the thought. . . . Papa, they say when you brought Mama home you were more scared than if you'd been a horse thief. They say Aunt Luz took to her bed with a fever so she wouldn't have to go to the wedding when you were married, and she actually did have a fever, isn't it wonderful! Of course in those days they didn't understand about psychosomatic illness. And they say——"

"Hold on! Who's this They?" Bick demanded.

"Oh, around. I forget who."

"Well, you just forget all the rest of it then, will you! The whole driveling pack of lies."

She would regard her father with the disconcerting gaze of the young and merciless. "Is it true, Bick honeh, that every woman in Texas tried to get you? They say there wasn't a prize catch like you since before Sam Houston got married."

"I'm sure it's true," Leslie agreed briskly. "It took me two whole days to land him. And in Virginia that's considered overtime."

"They say there was a schoolteacher named Cora Dart at the

GIANT

ranch school and there was some hanky-panky going on between
her and you, Papa, and then——"

Angrily, "Who's been telling you this stuff?"

"I don't remember. Somebody at the Beezers' barbecue. I wish
people were as romantic as that now. It sounds like a movie.
They said Cora Dart tried like everything to marry you. She's
the one that crazy Jett Rink married and divorced, isn't she? The
first one. And when Papa married you Cora Dart took up with
this horrible Jett—you should just hear the stories about *him!*—
and when Aunt Luz learned what was going on she said Cora
Dart would have to leave. And then she got killed. Aunt Luz, I
mean, and they say Aunt Luz was really in love with Jett Rink
herself even if she was old enough to be his mother, really it all
sounds so fascinating and uncouth I just wish——"

The hot red of fury suffused Bick's face.

"Now Jordan!" came Leslie's voice, cool and calm. "Now
Jordan, don't get upset over nonsense. You know it's not good
for—for anyone."

Like twin scenes in a somewhat clumsy comedy the boy and
the girl privately confided each in the parent who was sympathetic.

"Look, Mama," Jordy said, "I wish you'd speak to Papa."

"You're a big hulking boy now, Jordy. Isn't it time you did
your own speaking? And time you stopped this calling us Papa
and Mama?"

"He says that's what he called his parents. When it comes to
human beings everything has got to be done around here just as
it was a hundred years ago. Reata without end, amen! Of course
cattle that's different. It's no good my trying to talk to him. He
acts as if I were ten years old and feeble-minded."

Jordy's entire aspect changed when he talked to his mother. He
was a man, assertive, rebellious, almost confident. In his father's
company he dwindled to a timorous hesitant boy.

"What is it you want me to speak to him about?"

"Harvard. That's part of the old pattern. But it happens that
that's what I want to do more than anything in the world."

"You do!"

"Yes. But not for his reason. They've got the best pre-med course in the country. And after that I want Columbia University P. and S."

"Now wait a minute. Being a doctor's daughter I know pre-med means———"

"That's right. Pre-medical. Biology chemistry physics. And Columbia's Physicians and Surgeons has got it all over the others. Besides, the New York hospitals give you a better chance at material than any city in the world except maybe London."

She stared at him. "You want to be a doctor."

"I'm going to be."

"Oh, Jordy! Your grandpa will be so happy to know———"

"Yeh, that's fine, but I don't want to slide along on his reputation. He's in all the encyclopedias and medical books and everybody knows about him. Horace Lynnton's grandson, he'd better be good. I don't want that. When I'm through I want to work right here in Texas. A Mexican with tuberculosis here hasn't got a chance. There's a Doctor Guerra in Vientecito, he's got a clinic I'd give anything to———"

"Your father takes the most wonderful care of the people on Reata. You know that. Free medical attention and all that."

"Uh-huh. The cattle too."

"Your father probably will be delighted. You'll have use for all that medical knowledge right here on Reata."

"I don't want to use it here on Reata. I want to be free to work where I want to work."

She knew she must tell him. "Jordy, your father isn't as strong as he seems. It's a heart thing. The arteries that feed it———"

"Yes, I know."

"You do!"

"I've learned a lot about the human body down at the lab with Gill and out on the range doctoring the stock with him and the boys. It isn't the same, of course. But there are quite a few hearts and lungs and livers and lights in a Reata herd."

"Your father expects you to take his place someday." She must know if he was strong enough to reject this.

He stood up. "I'd die for Papa if it was a quick choice between his life and mine. But I won't live for him."

"He won't consent to it, Jordy. Even if we're both for it."

He saw, then, that she was with him. The boy's brooding face came alive. "I haven't any money, Jordy. You know how it is on Reata. Millions, but nobody's got ready cash."

"Don't I know it!" Jordy agreed ruefully.

Quietly she said, "Uncle Bawley will do it if your father won't."

"Old Bawley! What makes you think so?"

"He will. I know."

Luz used the more direct approach in her talk with her father. "I'm not going to Wellesley."

"What does your mother say to that?"

"She doesn't know."

"The Benedict girls always go to Wellesley."

"No girlie school for this one."

"Oh, I suppose Yale, huh? Or maybe Harvard with Jordy." He laughed at his own joke, not very heartily.

"You're warm. Cornell."

"You're crazy."

"You go to college to learn something. Cornell has got the really scientific husbandry course."

"You've got a little-girl crush on Bob Dietz. If he took a course in dressmaking in Paris that's probably what you'd want to do all of a sudden."

She faced him angrily. "You wouldn't say that to Jordy."

"Your mother says you've concentrated too much on cows already. She thinks a year or so in one of those schools in Switzerland."

Elaborately casual, Bick and Leslie approached the subject, each testing the other. Until almost eleven that night he had been working in his office that adjoined the Main House dining room. Now it was time for that last cup of coffee in the Texas coffee ritual. Leslie had brought the tray to him and she had said, "Jordan, all this coffee so late at night, it can't be good for you, anyway you don't get enough sleep, up at——" when she stopped. She put the tray down on his desk, he leaned back in his chair and looked up at her.

"What's the matter?"

"It just came to me that I was saying something I've said five thousand times. I must be getting old."

"If it weren't so late at night I'd make you a hell of a gallant speech about that, honey. But anyway I realized today we've got a couple of grown-up kids."

"Just today?"

"Know what Luz said? Of course she's too young to know what she really wants. But she said she won't go to Wellesley or even to that school in Switzerland you're so stuck on."

"What then?"

"Says—get this—says she wants to go to Cornell and take the husbandry course."

"No!" But even as she uttered this monosyllable of rejection she thought, Well, perhaps we can make a bargain. Perhaps now is the time to tell him.

"We've hatched a couple of odd fledglings, darling. Jordy says he wants to be a doctor."

Bick shrugged this off. "Over my dead body."

"I feel the same about Luz."

Almost warily they eyed each other like fighters in their corners.

"Anyway, Jordy's going to start his first year at Harvard, just as we always have."

"Don't you think that's a sort of outworn family tradition now? Unless he's going to learn something really valuable and practical? You Benedict boys were sent East for—what was it?—a polish. Jordy doesn't need it."

"He's going."

"It takes seven years of medical school to learn to be a doctor."

"Now look here, Leslie, I don't want to hear any more of that."

"It might be a good idea if Luz skipped Wellesley and went to

Switzerland right off. She could use a swipe of polish, if you ask me."

"They're both too young to know what they're doing. One thing's sure. Jordy's going to run Reata. He's got to learn."

Jordy learned. He rode magnificently. He spent days and nights and weeks and months out on the range with the vaqueros, sleeping as they slept, eating as they ate. Old Polo's family became as much a part of Jordy's life as his own. Old Polo taught him from his rich store of knowledge acquired through the centuries before the Anglo-Saxon had set foot on this hot brilliant land. Polo's wrinkled wife gave Jordy strange unguents and weird brews to use when he had a cold or a fever (Leslie threw these out); Polo's handsome daughter-in-law fed him hot spicy Mexican dishes; Polo's pretty little granddaughter, Juana, one of a brood of eight, gazed at him adoringly, managing demurely to convey with her eyes that which a proper young Mexican girl must not express in words.

Old Polo, the caporal, deposed now but refusing to admit his downfall, hovered over Jordy like a benevolent despot. He still sat his palomino, a storybook king of vaqueros. The Benedict vaqueros still addressed him as Caporal, though Angel Obregon now reigned in his place, and young Angel, seeming one with his horse like a centaur, galloped at his father's side.

Young Jordy in the saddle and Bick mounted near by, with Polo on his miraculous quarter horse that he had trained to work reinless, guided only by a pressure of the knee or by the weight of the rider's body thrown from this side to that. In the lean brown hands that looked so fragile and that yet were so strong was the rope that obeyed his every wish like a sentient thing, whirling, leaping, performing figures in mid-air.

"The media cabeza," Bick called to Jordy. "The half head. Now watch Polo. The loop will catch the bull behind one ear and horn and in front of the other and then under the jaw. All at once. That's a mean-acting bull."

Out would go the rope, snakelike, curving, looping. The huge animal was stopped dead in his tracks.

"Maravilloso! Rebueno!" Jordy shouted.

"Shut up, Jordy. You telling Polo he's good!"

"Yes, but did you notice his hands?"

"Hands! What do you suppose he uses——"

"I mean——" sotto voce—"the old boy's got a little tremor, see, in the right hand, but when it came to throwing the rope he controlled it. That's pretty terrific."

"This isn't a diagnosis, this is roping, for God's sake what's the matter with you!"

But Bick's heart lurched within him in pride as he saw the boy thus mounted; in his cream-white Stetson and the shirt and the buckskin chaps; the rather sallow pointed face, the dark eyes ardent beneath the great rolling hatbrim. Leslie's eyes.

The lazo remolineado. The piale. The mangana. These were tricks used for expert roping in the brush. "Keep close to the horse's mane when you ride in the brush," Polo counseled him. "Where his head can go you can go."

Roping in the open range was less hazardous. "Not so many motions," Polo would warn him. "Leave all that to the city cowboys, to the brave ones who rope the skinny cows in the rodeo in New York. The motions are pretty, but you scare the cattle."

Young Angel Obregon, shorn now of his long black braids, needed no such instruction. Of the two inevitable reactions to his childhood years of petticoat servitude he had chosen the tough one. He rode as one of his charro ancestors. At sixteen he was a swaggerer, a chain smoker, the despair of his father Angel and his mother Deluvina. At seventeen he spurned Reata with all its years of Obregon family loyalty. He took a job as bellboy at the Hake in Vientecito and on his visits to the ranch he swaggered the streets of Benedict in sideburns, fifty-dollar boots, silk shirt, his hair pomaded to the lustre of black oilcloth. He and his friends affected a bastard dialect made up of Mexican jargon, American slang, Spanish patois. His talk was of cars and girls. He did not speak of an automobile as a coche but as a carro. A battery was not an acumulador but a batería. A truck was Hispanicized as a troca. A girl was a güisa—a chick. The Reata vaqueros said of him, in Spanish, "He's trying to change the color of his eyes to blue." Young Angel ran with the bonche.

His father, Angel Obregon the Caporal, his mother Deluvina, were by turns furious and sad at this metamorphosis. He was a disgrace to the raza—the proud race of Mexican people. They were ashamed. They spoke to the padre about him. To old Polo. Even to the patrón, Bick Benedict.

Almost tearfully Angel Obregon said, "He is a good boy, Angel. It is as if some bruja, some evil witch, had him under a spell. He is without respect for the things of life."

Thoughtfully Bick agreed. "I don't know what's the matter with the kids today. They're all alike." He hesitated a moment. But it was a temptation to talk to someone who felt as he did— someone to whom Reata was life, was the world. "My son doesn't have the real feeling about Reata." They were speaking in Spanish. Bick looked at this man whose blood for generations had gone into Reata. He wanted Angel to dispute his statement, he wanted him to say, no, you are wrong, he is a sincere Benedict, the type genuino. But instead Angel now nodded in sorrowful agreement.

Curiously enough, the friendship of the two boys had endured. On Angel's rare visits home he and Jordy discarded the pretense they wore in the presence of their parents. They heard each other in understanding.

"Vaquero with twenny or twenny-five dollars a month," Angel said, and laughed scornfully. "Sometimes I earn that in two days at the Hake if there's a big poker game on in one of the rooms, or a drinking bunch, and I'm on duty. Vaquero like my father and his father and his father, not me! I want to marry with Marita Rivas, Dimodeo Rivas' daughter. But I don't want my kid to be vaquero, and his kid and his kid. Now who does that is a borlo."

Jordy said, "My father is always experimenting to get better beef. The perfect all meat all tenderloin heatproof tickproof beef animal. That's good, that's swell. But I want to do that with people, not animals. T.b.-proof Mexican-Americans, that would be even better."

385

On parting Angel no longer said, "Adiós!" He used the Mexican slang of the city. "Ay te watcho!" I'll be seeing you.

Bick Benedict decided that the time had come for action. He would have a talk with Bob Dietz, the kid was finished at Cornell, he'd speak to him now. He planned not to make a casual thing of it, a mere chat about a job if he happened to meet the boy out on the range or in the lab or the corral. This would be a serious talk. He called the Dietz telephone at supper time.

"Bob? . . . Bick Benedict. . . . Bob, I want to talk to you about something important. Jump into your car and come over here about eight."

But Bob Dietz, it seemed, was going to a Grange meeting. Somewhat nettled, Bick said oh, the hell with that, you can go to a Grange meeting another time, this is important.

"I'm sorry," Bob said, "but I'm the speaker there this evening. I'm scheduled to talk on soil and crop rotation. I'll be glad to come tomorrow if that's all right with you."

"You turned into a dirt farmer or something?" Bick jeered.

"Just about," Bob Dietz said genially. "Tomorrow okay then?"

Bob arrived before eight. Bick in his office heard his voice and Luz's laugh from the direction of the veranda, they seemed to have a lot to say to each other, though Luz did most of the talking, there was the slower deeper undercurrent of Bob's voice with a curiously vibrant tone in it. Frowning, Bick came to the door. "Bob! Come on in here. I'm waiting for you."

"Oh. I thought I was a little early."

Bick preceded him into the office, he motioned him to a chair, he sat back and looked at the young fellow, he thought, Golly that's a handsome hunk of kid. There was rather an elaborate silence during which Bob Dietz did not seem ill at ease.

"You wondering why I sent for you, I suppose."

"Why, no, Mr. Benedict. Not especially."

"You'd better be. I've got something pretty important to say to you." There was another silence. Bob Dietz did not squirm or shuffle his feet or cough. Bick thought he never had seen such clear eyes. The whites were blue, like a baby's. Healthy young bull. "I've been watching you pretty close these last few years. Ever since you were a little kid. It took me a while to get over the idea that you were ten years old, two front teeth out, the kid that used to run around fetching for the tumbadores at branding." He laughed.

Bob Dietz laughed too, politely. "I thought I was pretty smart," he said.

"Well, you were right. You are. Now I'm going to come to the point. Reata may have dropped a million acres or so in the last fifty years, but it's bigger than ever in more important ways. Our breeding and feeding program is something I needn't tell you about. You know. This isn't just a ranch any more, it's a great big industrial plant, and run like one. It takes experts. I know about you—well say, I ought to—and I've checked up on you at Cornell. And what they say there is pretty hot."

Bob Dietz looked mildly pleased. He said nothing.

"I'm not getting any younger—that's what my wife calls a cliché——" Bick was a trifle startled to see Bob Dietz grin at this. "Anyway ten years from now this is going to be too much for me even with Jordy taking over a lot of it. I want to start you in now. From what I know about you, I'm not making a mistake. Soil. Irrigation. Breeding. Feeding. Crops. You know the works. My plan is, you start in next spring. I've got a ten-year plan and then another ten-year plan, and so on. Say, the Russians haven't got anything on us at Reata, huh? At the end of ten years you'll be General Manager around here—under me and Jordy. At the end of another ten years—well, anyway, you're fixed for life. And good. Now don't tell me any more, when I call up, about how you have to go to a Grange meeting. Got it?"

"I think so, Mr. Benedict."

"You'll want to go home and talk this over with your folks. You ought to. So I don't expect you to say anything just now. You go along home and mull this over and we'll talk about it again, say, day after tomorrow, that's Wednesday."

"I know now," Bob Dietz said. "I couldn't do it."

"Couldn't do what?"

"A ten-year plan—a twenty-year plan—the rest of my life on Reata, like my father. I want a place of my own."

"You crazy kid! A place of your own. Do you imagine you'll ever have a ranch like Reata!"

"Oh, no sir! I wouldn't want it. I wouldn't have it for a gift. Heh, that doesn't sound good. I know the terrific stuff you've done here. I want a little piece of land of my own for experimentation. Never anything big. That's the whole point. Big stuff is old stuff now."

"Is that so!" Bick was stunned with anger, he could feel something pinching his chest, little pains like jabs. "So big is old-fashioned now, huh?"

"I didn't mean to be—I didn't go to make you mad, Mr. Benedict. I just mean that here in Texas maybe we've got into the habit of confusing bigness with greatness. They're not the same. Big. And great. Why at Cornell, in lab, they say there's a bunch of scientists here in the United States working on a thing so little you can't see it—a thing called the atom. It's a kind of secret but they say if they make it work—and I hope they can't— it could destroy the whole world, the whole big world just like that. Bang."

As he left Luz must have been waiting to see him go. Sitting in his office, stunned, furious, Bick heard them talking and laughing together again. Then their voices grew fainter. To his own surprise he rushed out to stop them like a father in a movie comedy.

They were just stepping into Bob Dietz's car.

"Luz! Where you going!" Bick yelled.

"Down to Smitty's for a Coke."

"You stay home!" But they were off down the drive in the cool darkness.

Leslie appeared from somewhere, she slipped her hand into his arm, she leaned against his shoulder. "Luz is almost a grown-up, darling. Girls of her age don't have to ask permission to go down to Smitty's for a Coke."

388

25

"SOMEDAY," Texas predicted, wagging its head in disapproval, but grinning, too, "someday that locoed Jett Rink is agoing to go too far. There's a limit to shenanigans, even his."

The Spanish conquistadores had searched in vain for the fabled Golden Cities of the New World. They had died on the plains, their bones had rotted deep in the desert and the cactus and the mesquite and the dagger flower grew green above them, their thorns like miniature swords commemorating the long-rusted steel of the dead men. And now here were the Golden Cities at last, magically sprung up like a mirage.

389

There were in these cities a thousand men like Jett Rink and yet unlike except for their sudden millions. Other men might conduct their lives outrageously but Jett Rink had become a living legend. Here was a twentieth-century Paul Bunyan striding the oil-soaked earth in hundred-dollar boots. His striding was done at the controls of an airplane or at the wheel of a Cadillac or on a golden palomino with tail and mane of silver.

A fabric made up of truth and myth was hung about his swaggering shoulders. Wherever men gathered to talk together there was a fresh tale to tell which they savored even while they resented it.

"Did you hear about that trip of his, hunting there back of Laredo? Seems him and that Yerb Packer were in that hunting shack Jett's got there. They were eating in the kitchen—you know Jett—drinking more than eating I reckon, and with this and that they got to quarreling and then to fighting. They was clawing and gouging like a couple of catamounts, blood running down their faces, their clothes half tore off. Well, Yerb clouts Jett a real sock and Jett he reaches out on the shelf there for a big bottle of some kind of fluid like it kills bugs and you pour it down the sink and plumbing and so on. It's got acid in it or something. Anyway, he fetches Yerb a crack over the head with it, the bottle busts and the stuff pours all over Yerb, liked to burned the hide right off him, they say he'll be months . . ."

". . . You know that hospital for old Vets of the World War, a bunch of them been sitting around there for years now, poor lunks, went in maybe when they were twenty after the war, thinking they'd be out cured, and now they're forty and more, some of them, and never will be out. Well, anyway, somebody sent over a bunch of free tickets for the football game. So the bus took some of them that was well enough to go to the game. But along about the middle of the game a mean norther blew up, rain and cold, and quite a few folks skedaddled for home. This one old fella he gets soaked, he wasn't feeling too good to begin with, a artificial leg and all. So he leaves, he starts heading down the road toward the car park, he figures somebody will sure pick him up and give him a lift back to the hospital. Well, along behind comes Jett in his Caddy he's got those strong-arm guys always riding with him. Jett's driving though, you know how he is, he'd been liquoring up to keep warm. You know the way he drives, even sober a hunderd miles is crawling to him. This lame old vet don't hear him coming or maybe Jett don't see him in the thick rain, he misses him by an inch. Well, the vet gives a quick jump, just barely saves himself and falls down a course with that leg and all, but he scrambles up and shakes his fist at Jett like a fella in a play and he lets out a line of language even Jett Rink couldn't do better. Jett gets an earful of this and what does he do he gets out with those guys with him and they beat up this old cripple, they hit him around the head and all, they say he's lost his hearing. I hear Jett paid out quite a hunk afterwards but just the same what I say is someday Jett Rink's agoing to go too far."

"What became of that first woman he married? Schoolteacher, wasn't she? Imagine!"

"Oh, that was a million years ago. He's had two others since then. Maybe three. I haven't kept track. Second one was a secretary of his, must have had something big on him."

"They say when he's really good and drunk he talks about that wife of Bick Benedict."

"He's a dirty liar! She's straight as they come. Too straight. They say a regular do-gooder. From up North, she is. But straight."

Sometimes he strode, very late, into one of the big city shops—Neiman's or Opper's or Gulick's—when they were about to close for the day. He liked to inconvenience them, he felt deep power-satisfaction in compelling the saleswomen or department heads to stay on after hours, serving him, Jett Rink. He liked his little joke, too. He would extend his hard paw to shake hands with a saleswoman of middle age, perhaps, with a soignée blue-grey coiffure and a disillusioned eye. As her thin hard-working hand met his she would recoil with a squawk of terror. In the great palm of his hand he had concealed a neat chunky steel-cold revolver.

As he lolled in the brocade bower that was a fitting room they would spread for his selection furs silks jewels.

"This looks like you, Mr. Rink," they would say, fluffing out the misty folds of a cobweb garment. Frequently they were summoned to bring their wares to one of his ranches and there these would be displayed for him, an oriental potentate in redface. A mink coat. A sapphire. A vicuña topcoat for himself or a special hunting rifle with a new trick.

SOCIETY
By Gloria Ann Wicker

Mrs. Jordan Benedict and daughter Luz are Hermoso visitors and shoppers this week. While in the city they are stopping at the Tejas Hotel. Miss Luz Benedict will spend a year or more at a select girls' school in Switzerland. There are other more interesting rumors which have not yet been confirmed.

Luz read this aloud to her mother as they sat at breakfast in their sitting room at the Tejas. "What rumors, I wonder. And just how interesting. It sounds so tantalizing. No girl ever had a duller summer."

"Reata's always good for a rumor," Leslie said, "when there's no news. Come on, dear, let's get started or we'll never cover this list."

"It's too hot, anyway. Why can't we wait and get it all in New York next month?"

"I like the idea of shopping for ski pants in Texas when the temperature's one hundred."

Gulick's opulent windows reflected the firm's disdain for such whims as temperature time or place. Hot or cold, autumn was just around the corner. Gulick's window displays were aimed at those Texans who early armed themselves for a holiday in New York in California in Florida Europe Chicago or even that Yankeetown Dallas. The lure of one window was too much even for shoppers like Leslie and Luz, bent on sterner stuffs. Wordlessly they stopped to gaze at it. Luxurious though every article was, each had the chaste quality of utter perfection.

The window held a woman's complete evening toilette. Nothing more. A fabulous fur wrap. A satin-and-tulle gown. Diamond necklace. A bracelet of clumped jewels. Long soft gloves flung carelessly on the floor like thick cream spilled on carpet. Cobwebs of lingerie. Wisps of chiffon hosiery. Fragile slippers. Jewel-encrusted handbag.

"Mm," said Luz.

"Nice," Leslie said.

As they stood there a hand slid through the arm of each, separating the two women. "Like it?" said a man's voice. "I'll buy the whole window for you, Leslie."

Leslie stared into Jett Rink's face.

Instinctively she jerked her arm to free it. His hand held it inescapably. He was scarcely taller than she, his eyes were level with hers, his face was close, the eyes intent, bloodshot. He was smiling. Now, still holding the arms of the two women locked beneath his arms, an iron hand pressed tightly against each hand on his shoulder, he turned his head slowly on that short thick neck to stare at the girl.

"You're Luz. I'm Jett Rink, Luz."

"Yes. I've seen pictures of you. Look, do you mind, you're just a little too hearty, you're hurting me."

"Luz. A hell of a thing to do to a pretty girl like you, name her after that old bitch."

The arms of both women jerked to be free. He held them. He turned again to Leslie. "Am I hurting you too, Leslie?"

She thought, clearly. On Sonoro Street in Hermoso in front of Gulick's. Nothing must happen. Nothing to disgrace Jordan and the children. She spoke quietly as she always had spoken in the past to the violent boy, now a more violent man.

"I'm not going to wrestle with you on the street. Take your hand away."

He swung them around as if in a dance, one on each side. "Would you wrestle in the car?" At the curb was an incredibly long bright blue car. A man sat at the wheel, another stood at the rear door. "Come on, girls. Let's take a ride."

It was unbelievable it was monstrous. For the first time she knew fear. He propelled them across the sidewalk.

"No!" Leslie cried. Faces of passers-by turned toward them, uncertainly.

Luz's free left hand was a fist. Now she actually twisted round to aim at his face but he jerked his head back, and he laughed a great roaring laugh and the passers-by, reassured, went on their way grinning at the little playful scuffle. "I'm not going to hurt you. Don't make such a fuss." He and the man standing at the car door half lifted half pulled them into the deep roomy rear seat, Jett between them. The door slammed, the man whirled into the front seat with the driver, the car shot into traffic.

Her voice rather high, like a little girl's, Luz said, "What is this, anyway! Let's get out, Mama."

Leslie looked at the monolithic faces of the two men in the front seat. "If you hurt Luz," Leslie said, her voice low and even, "you know perfectly well that no bodyguards can keep him from killing you." At the absurdity of this melodramatic statement she began to laugh somewhat hysterically.

"There you!" Jett turned triumphantly to Luz. "Your ma knows I was just fooling, I saw in the paper where you girls were in town and I been wanting to have a little talk with your ma. I been stuck on your ma for years. Did you know that?"

"I think you're a goon," Luz shouted.

Jett's voice took on an aggrieved tone. "There you go. Comes to a Benedict, no matter what I do, it's wrong. I was just kidding around. I watched for you to come out of the Tejas. And then over to Gulick's and standing there looking in the window like a couple of little stenographers or something. Say, you don't have to tell me," he went on, easily, conversationally. "I know Bick's pinched for money all the time, that big damn fool place he thinks he runs. I'd buy you the whole Gulick setup, Leslie, the whole ten floors and everything in it, if you say the word. I'm sick of buying stuff for myself. At first I got a bang out of it, but not any more. Look at this coat! I got a topcoat like it, too.

Vicuña. Feel! Soft as a baby's bottom. Looka this watch." He thrust out his great hairy wrist. "It does everything but bake a cake. This Caddy's a special body and armored, thirty thousand dollars."

"What are we going to do, Mama?" Luz said. Her voice now was as quiet as her mother's had been, but its undernote was tremulous.

"It's all right, dearest," Leslie said. "It's his idea of a joke."

"I ain't joking, Leslie. I got to talk to you. Like I said."

The man seated at the right, in front, picked up a sort of telephone receiver that was one of a battery of contrivances attached to the dashboard. He spoke into it with mechanical clarity and conciseness. "Passing corner of Viña and Caballero. . . . Three minutes. . . . Past corner Viña and Caballero. . . . Two and three quarter minutes."

Their speed never slowed, a huge building like a warehouse loomed ahead, a ten-foot metal fence enclosed it. The car approached this at terrific pace, in that instant before what seemed an inevitable crash the gates swung sharply open, the car tore through without diminishing speed, the gates swung shut, the huge car stopped with a shriek of brakes. The man in front got out. He stood at the car door. Jett Rink was scribbling a note, holding the pad up close to his chest as he wrote. He tore it off, the man at the door took it. "You call them yourself. And tell them it's got to be there within a half an hour or no dice. . . . Now then, girlies, I want to talk to your ma, Luz. Do you want to sit here in the car while we go and sit on the bench there in the shade? Or do you want to sit there and we'll stay in the car."

Curiously, it was Luz who now took over. "We'll both get out or we'll both stay in. Or I'll begin to scream and while it probably won't do any good in this place I'll scream and scream and scream until——"

"Oh, all right." Wearily, as though agreeing to the whim of an unreasonable child. "It's hot, no matter where you sit. You go on over there, other side of the entrance. Your ma and I'll sit

395

on that bench here, have our little talk. Either you girls want a Coke or something cold to drink?"

Leslie looked up at the blank windows of the building. "What is this place?"

"It's nothing only a warehouse where I keep stuff, valuable stuff. I got places like this all around. First I was going to drive you out to the ranch, I got a place about an hour out. But a lot of folks out there all the time, visiting and all, I figured you wouldn't like that. I wouldn't want to do anything you wouldn't like—you and the kid."

She glanced at him but his face was serious. "I thought you were drunk. But you're not, are you?"

"I ain't had a drop for two days. Minute I knew you was in town I quit, I knew I wanted a clear head and sometimes I get fuzzy when I take a couple. I'm stone cold sober."

Slim, almost boyish seated there beside her in his neat expensive clothes, a blue shirt, a polka-dotted tie.

"Such silly behavior. You've scared Luz to death, she didn't know you when you were a greasy kid on Reata. What is it? You want me to help you make friends again with Bick, or something like that, I suppose."

"You suppose. You suppose I don't know you're smarter than that! You're the only really smart girl I ever knew. And that ain't all. Not. Quite. All." He had been smoking a cigarette. Now he tossed it away. "Look. I been crazy about you all these years. You know that well and good." He was talking carefully and reasonably as one would present a business argument or a political credo. "I tried everything to get shut of it. I had all the kinds there is. I even been married three four times. Did you know that?"

"I've never thought about it at all."

"Why do you suppose I done that—did that?"

"Some men do. It's an unadult trait. It means they've never really grown up."

He dropped his tone of calm reasoning. The little twin dots of red flicked into the close-set hooded eyes. He leaned toward

396

her. "I got to get shut of it. It's making me sick. Look at this."
He held out his hand. "Look at that! Shakes like that all the
time."

"That's alcohol and shot nerves and fear."

"Leslie. Leslie. Come with me. Leslie."

Equably, and quite conversationally as though exchanging
chitchat with a friend. "I'm really quite an old lady now, you
know. You just think you're still talking to that rather attractive
girl who came, a bride, to Reata. . . . It's very hot here, Jett."

"Anything you'd want. Anything in the world. He wouldn't
care. He don't care about anything only Reata."

She stood up. "All right, Luz!" she called. "We're going
now."

He grasped her arm. "I'll go after Bick and you and your two
kids. I swear to God I will. I'll never let up on all of you."

"You've been seeing too many Western movies."

She moved toward the car. The man sat up at the wheel. The
second man came down the steps and toward the car.

"I ain't going," Jett said. "Luz, you sit up front there with
him. Leslie, you get in the back here. You too, Dent. You call
back here for me in ten minutes."

He stood there a moment in the brilliant sun.

"I'll do like I said," Jett called softly to Leslie, through the
window.

"Where to?" asked the driver.

"Gulick's," Leslie said airily. "We have a great deal of shopping to do."

"No. Please." Luz did not look round. "I'd like to go to the
hotel first. For a minute. I forgot something."

"Tejas," Leslie said then.

The gates opened.

Down the street. In traffic against traffic in and out in sickening suicidal zigzags. He has told them to kill us this way, Leslie
thought. Then, reasonably, No, they'd be killed too, so probably
not. They stopped at the Tejas entrance. They were in the lobby,
they were in the elevator, they were in their rooms.

"I'm going to call up Papa."

"I wouldn't," Leslie said. "Not until we've talked a little first."

Luz was crying, quietly, her eyes wide open and the tears sliding unwiped down her face. "I was scared. I kept thinking I'd do something terrific and brave, but I was scared."

"So was I, dear."

Luz wiped her face now, she stood staring at her mother as at some new arresting object. "I think it's the most romantic thing I ever heard of! And I think he's kind of cute."

"Don't say that."

"But I do. I've heard a lot about him and I never believed it, but it's true. He's a kind of modern version of the old buccaneer type like Grampa and Great-grampa Benedict. They were tough, too, in a different way, of course, land swiping and probably a lot of hanky-panky with the Mexican girls. I must say Jett Rink's windup was an anticlimax, though. I expected rape at the very least——"

"You're being silly, Luz. This man is a twisted——"

"The Snyth twins say he's the fashion now, he's so tough he's considered chic. I must say I'm impressed with you, Mama, being the secret passion of that hard-boiled . . ." She had gone into her bedroom, her voice trailed off, then came up sharply: ". . . what in the world is all this! Mom! Come here!"

Boxes. Boxes and boxes and boxes. Stacked on beds and chairs. The smart distinctive blue-and-white striped Gulick boxes.

Miss Luz Benedict, the address slips read. Miss Luz Benedict. Miss Luz Benedict. Miss Luz Benedict.

She yanked at the cords. She opened a box. Another. Another. The fabulous fur wrap. The satin and tulle evening dress. The necklace. The slippers . . . The window.

". . . Gulick?" Leslie at the telephone. "I want to talk to Mrs. Bakefield. Mrs. Bakefield's office. . . . This is Mrs. Jordan Benedict. . . . Mrs. Bakefield? Yes, Mrs. Jordan Benedict. There has been a mistake. We just came in—the Tejas—and there are a million packages that don't belong to us. It is just some terrible mistake. . . . Oh, Mrs. Bakefield! He must have seen some sort of mention in the newspaper. . . . No . . . Oh no, she doesn't even know him . . . I hear he is very—well—eccentric now and then. . . . Just send for them . . . yes . . . now . . ."

26

A BENEDICT family meeting—a Benedict Big Business Pow-wow—was in progress. But this was not the regular annual Benedict family business assemblage. This was an unscheduled meeting called by the outraged members of the clan. For the first time in a quarter of a century the Big House was cleared of all outside guests. Only the family occupied the bedrooms, clattered down the halls, ate at the long table in the dining room. But the house was well filled for they had come, down to the last and least voting member. The thick walls seemed bursting with the strain of temper and fury within.

They sat in the vast main living room that had been planned to accommodate formal occasions such as this—funerals, weddings, family conclaves. A handsome lot they were, too; tall, fit, their eyes clear their skins fresh with carefully planned exercise and expensive proteins and vitamins.

Uncle Bawley, oldest member of the clan, was presiding but no one paid the slightest attention to him. In appearance he was extraordinarily unchanged with the years except for the white shock of hair above the mahogany face. These meetings were ordinarily conducted with parliamentary exactitude, everyone polite and gruesomely patient in spite of the emotions always seething beneath the ceremonial behavior. But now the great chamber vibrated with heat and hate and contention. Parliamentary procedure was thrown to the Gulf winds. Uncle Bawley's gavel (mesquite, and too soft a wood for the quelling of Benedict brawls) rapped in vain for order.

Bick Benedict stood facing them all, and Bick Benedict shouted. "I won't have it. We're doing all right without oil. I won't have it stinking up my ranch."

"Your ranch!" yelled a dozen Benedicts. Then, variously, "That's good! Did you hear that! You're managing this place and getting your extra cut for it. Your ranch!" New York Chicago Buffalo California Florida Massachusetts Benedicts.

Leslie, sitting by, an outsider, thought, Oh dear this is so bad for him I wish they'd go home or why don't they stay here and try running it for a change, the Horrors.

One of the more arrogant of the Benedicts, who dwelt on the East Coast, now dropped all pretense of courtesy.

"Just come down off it, will you, Bick? And face it. You've got delusions of grandeur. You're big stuff, I know, among the local Texas boys. But we happen to have an interest in this concern. And we've got the right to say by vote whether we want or don't want a little matter of five or ten million a year—and probably a lot more—a whole lot more later—divided up amongst us. I don't know about the rest of you boys and girls, but me, I could use a little extra pin money like that."

Stubbornly facing the lot of them, his face white beneath the tan, and set in new deep lines, Bick repeated stubbornly the words he had used over and over again as though they presented a truth that made all argument useless.

"Reata is a cattle ranch. It's been a cattle ranch for a hundred years."

"That's just fine," drawled an unsentimental Benedict. "And there used to be thirteen states in the Union and the covered wagon was considered hot stuff."

The laugh that now went up encouraged Maudie Placer to sink a deft dart. "And please don't quote that story about old Pappy Waggoner when he was drilling for water and they brought in all that oil on his North Texas place. Quote. 'Damn it, cattle can't drink that stuff.' Unquote."

Now Leslie saw with a sinking heart that the grey-white in Bick's face was changing to scarlet. "Do you people know who wants the lease? Do you know who wants the rights?"

"Yes, Teacher, we do. It's the Azabache Oil Company and a mighty pretty little outfit it is, too. I'm real petted on it."

"I'll bet you are. You've been away from Texas so long you've forgotten your Spanish. D'you know what Azabache means! It's Spanish for jet, if you want to know. And it doesn't mean just jet for black oil. It's jet for Jett Rink. Jett—Azabache. He controls most of it. Well, by God, I won't have Jett Rink owning any piece of my country here on Reata——"

"Hold on there! Just—a—minute. You've got a pick on Jett Rink, you've had it for years. Some little personal feud. Who cares!"

"I tell you you'll all care if he gets a toe in here."

"All right all right. He's a mean umbry. Everybody knows that. We don't want to love him. We just want a nice thick slice of that billion he's got stashed away."

"He's got nothing but a lot of paper. He's in over his head. Everybody knows that Gabe Target could sell him down the river tomorrow if he wanted to."

Now Uncle Bawley forsook Rules of Order. "That's right,

Jurden!" he bellowed—he who never had called his nephew anything but Bick. "Don't you let 'em ride you!"

"The law!" shouted a Benedict.

"How about Pa's will!" Bick countered. "And Grampa's! You going to fight those too?"

"You bet we are. We're going to fight them for years if we have to. We don't care what the will says. There wasn't any oil on Reata or anywhere near it when Pa's will was made. We'll get every lawyer in New York and Chicago and Houston and Hermoso and Corpus Christi and Austin and Vientecito——"

Uncle Bawley threw his mesquite gavel across the room and brought his massive fist down on the table with a crash and a succession of crashes that silenced even the shouting Benedicts.

"Stop this bellering I say or I'll arrest the lot of you and I can do it. I'm a State Ranger and I'm supposed to keep law and order and I'm agoing to. . . . Sit down! . . . Now then. I'm sorry, Jurden, but we got to put this to a vote. And what the vote says, goes. That's the law. That's the rule of this family and always has been. . . . Roady, pass those slips. . . . Bowie, you'll collect. . . . You all get out your big gold fountain pens and I hope they leak all over you for a bunch of stampeding maverick Benedicts. Now vote!"

The vote stood two to twenty-five. That night Uncle Bawley took off for Holgado and the high clear mountain air. Within three days there was not one Benedict left in the cavernous walls of the Big House.

Leslie Benedict found herself in the fantastic position of a wife who tries to convince her husband that a few million dollars cannot injure him.

"You'll go on with your own work just the same. Better. It won't affect the actual ranch. You'll be free of their complaints now."

"Rink." Bitterness twisted his mouth as he spoke the name. "Jett Rink owning rights to Reata."

"He doesn't. He just holds a lease on a tiny bit of it. Besides you've told me yourself the Azabache Company isn't only Jett

Rink. It's a lot of other people. Some of them are people you know well."

"He controls it."

"You'll never need to deal with him. Think of the things you can do now!" She paused a moment. "I don't mean only the things you're interested in. They're wonderful but I mean—couldn't we use some of it maybe for things like—necessary things, I mean, like new houses for the ranch people and perhaps the start of a decent hospital and even a school where they're not separated—a school that isn't just Mexican or just—— Oh, Jordan, how exciting that would be!"

He was not listening, he did not even consciously hear her.

"Nobody's ever set foot on Benedict land except to produce better stock and more of it. You're not a Texan. You're not a Benedict. You don't understand."

"I'm not a Texan and I'm not a Benedict except by marriage. I do understand because I love you. It embarrasses you to hear me say that after all these years. I'm trying to tell you that if there's got to be all that crazy money then use some of it for the good of the world. And I don't mean only your world. Reata."

"Uh-huh. You won't be so smug when you see Benedict swarming with a pack of greasy tool dressers and drillers and swampers and truckers. It's going to be hell. Pinky Snyth was talking about it last night. Vashti's leased a piece of the Double B to Azabache."

"Well, there you are! You needn't feel so upset."

"The whole country's going to stink of oil. Do you know what else Pinky said! He and Vashti are talking of building in town—Viento or even Hermoso—moving to town and the family only coming out to the ranch week ends and holidays. Like some damned Long Island setup."

"Vashti might like that. I'm sure the twins would."

"Yes. Maybe you would too. H'm? Nice slick house in town? Azalea garden, nice little back yard, people in for cocktails and Patroness of the Hermoso Symphony and the Little Theatre in the Round—Square—Zigzag—or whatever the goddamned fashion is. We could use these two three million acres for picnic grounds and so on."

"Jordan my darling. Jordan. Don't be like that."

She hesitated a moment. She took a deep breath. Now for it. "You know, we don't exactly have to have millions of acres in order to live—you and the children and I. It's killing you—I mean it's too much. Why can't we have a few thousand acres— how Texas that sounds! But anyway—why can't we have a ranch of our own, smallish, where you could breed your own wonder-ful——"

The blue eyes were agate. "I've lived on Reata all my life. I'm going to live here till I die. Nothing on it is going to change."

"Everything in the world changes every minute."

"Reata's just going to improve. Not change."

So now the stink of oil hung heavy in the Texas air. It pene-trated the houses the gardens the motorcars the trains passing through towns and cities. It hung over the plains the desert the range; the Mexican shacks the Negro cabins. It haunted Reata. Giant rigs straddled the Gulf of Mexico waters. Platoons of metal and wood marched like Martians down the coast across the plateaus through the brush country. Only when you were soaring in an airplane fifteen thousand feet above the oil-soaked earth were your nostrils free of it. Azabache oil money poured into Reata. Reata produced two commodities for which the whole world was screaming. Beef. Oil. Beef. Oil. Only steel was lacking. Too bad we haven't got steel, Texas said. But then, after that Sunday morning in December even the voice of the most voracious was somewhat quieted.

With terrible suddenness young male faces vanished from the streets of Benedict. White faces black faces brown faces. Bob Dietz was off. The kids in the Red Front Market. The Beezer boys. High. Low. Rich. Poor. The Mexican boys around Garza's in Nopal and the slim sleek boys at the Hake in Viento and even the shifting population that moved with the crops and the seasons —all, all became units in a new world of canvas. Texas was used to khaki-colored clothes, but these garments were not the tan canvas and the high-heeled boots and the brush jackets of the range and plains. This was khaki with a difference.

Young Jordy Benedict at Harvard was summoned home to Reata.

"You're needed here on Reata," Bick said tersely. "Beef to feed the world. That's the important thing."

"I can't stay here now."

"Yes you will. Any one of ten million kids can sit at a desk in Washington. Or shoot a German. Producing beef here on Reata is the constructive patriotic thing for you to do. You're just being hysterical."

"I'll go back to school. Or I'll be drafted. I won't stay here."

"No draft board will take you. I can fix that all right anywhere. And I won't send you a cent if you go back to Harvard."

The two men were talking in Bick's office. The boy quiet, pale. The older man glaring, red-faced. Casually, Leslie strolled in and sat down.

Brusquely Bick said, "We're talking."

"I'm listening. I've been listening outside the door so I may as well come in." Jordy glanced at her and smiled a little. It made a startling change in the somber young face. "Jordy, you look more like your Grandpa Lynnton every day."

As if this were a cue Jordy relaxed in his chair, his eyes as he looked at his father now were steady. "When I'm through at Harvard I'm going on to Columbia P. and S."

"P. and S.?" Bick repeated dully.

"Physicians and Surgeons. School. We need doctors as much as beef. That's why I'm going on instead of in. I haven't used any of the money you've sent me all this time. And thanks, Papa. Your money is all in the bank there in Boston, waiting for you. I couldn't use it because you didn't know about me."

Bick Benedict turned with a curiously slow movement of his head to look at his wife. "Then you must have been sending him your money."

"Jordan dear, don't go on like a father in a melodrama. I

haven't any money. You know that. Everyone on Reata is short of money except the cows."

"Who then?" He stood up. "Who then!" A dreadful suspicion showed in his face. "Not . . . !"

She came to him. "It's Uncle Bawley. And I asked him. So don't blame him for it."

Slowly he said, "That old turtle." Then, "The three of you, huh?"

Jordy stood up. "Papa, you know I never was any good around here. I never will be. Any man on Reata can do the job better than I ever could."

"That's right," Jordan said. "You never were any good. You never will be. You're all alike, you kids today, white and Mexican, you or Angel Obregon. No damn good."

"Angel's fine," Leslie said matter-of-factly. "I saw him today in Benedict, he looked wonderful in his uniform. Jordy, Angel's going to be married Tuesday. Did you know that?"

"Yes. I'm staying for the wedding."

"Oh, you're staying for the wedding?" Bick repeated, cruelly mimicking his son just a little, even to the stammer. "Well, that's big of you! That's a concession to Reata, all right." He turned the cold contemptuous eyes on Leslie. "You've been years at this. Twenty years. Satisfied?"

Her tone her manner were as matter-of-fact and good-natured as his aspect was tragic. "Watch that arithmetic. Jordy going to be twenty-one pretty soon."

Bick had been standing. Now he sat again rather heavily at his desk. He did not look at them. "That's right. We were going to have a party. Big party."

"Not in wartime, Jordan."

He looked up at his son. "I hadn't forgotten, it just slipped my mind. You'll be coming into your Reata shares. You don't mind living off Reata even if you don't want to live on it, huh?"

Quietly Jordy said, "They'll see me through. I've thought about that. I've got as much right to them as Roady's kids, or Bowie's or Aunt Maudie's."

Bick Benedict picked up a sheaf of papers on his desk, shuffled them, put them down. "Doctor, h'm? New York, I suppose."

"Now Jordan!" Leslie protested. "You know Jordy loves Texas as much as you do. In another way, perhaps."

"You counting on putting old Doctor Tom out of business, maybe."

"I think I'm going to have a chance to work with Guerra in Vientecito when the war's over. If he's lucky enough to come back in one piece."

"Guerra! You don't mean—why, he's——"

"Rubén Guerra. His practice is all Mexican, of course. Uh— look. There's something else I'd like to talk to you and Mama about. I'm afraid you won't like this either."

"I've had about enough for just now," Bick said, and turned back to his desk and the aimless shuffling of papers. "Tell your life plans to your buddies, why don't you! Doctor Guerra——"

"He's busy in Europe just now."

"Well, Angel Obregon. Or Polo." He was racked with bitterness and disappointment.

"All right, Papa. I will."

27

YOUNG ANGEL OBREGON did indeed look fine in his uniform. Uniforms were nothing novel to Angel after his tenure in the skin-tight mess jacket and the slim pants, the braid and gold buttons of the Hake Hotel bellboy. But this uniform he wore with a difference. His movements about the vast marble columns of the Hake lobby had been devious and slithering as a seal's. Now, in the plain khaki of a private, he swaggered. Months of camp training had filled him out, he was broader in the shoulder, bigger across the chest. He always had had, like his forebears, the slim flanks and the small waist of the horseman.

411

"One of those Pacific places," he said. "I bet. That's where they're shipping all us Mex—all us Latin Americans, they say we're used to the hot climate, they're nuts. Vince Castenado came home with malaria, he says it's all jungle."

Half of Benedict and practically all of Nopal were invited to the wedding. Angel was marrying Marita Rivas, one of the daughters of Dimodeo. A middle-aged husband and father now, Dimodeo Rivas, head of the clipping, snipping, nurturing, spraying, watering, planting group of men who tended the flowers, the precarious lawns, the rare transplanted trees, the walks the roads, the new swimming pool—the whole of the landscaping around the Big House and the Main House.

Of course young Angel had furnished the trousseau according to custom. The importance of Marita's marriage would be gauged by the display of her gowns and her bridal dress, at the boda—the wedding feast.

"We'll have to go," Bick said heavily, grumpily. "Angel's son. It wouldn't look right if we didn't. I'm only going because of his father."

"Why Jordan, I wouldn't miss it! Angel! He was the first Reata baby I saw. The morning after I came here. He wet all over one of my trousseau dresses. And now we'll see the trousseau dresses he's got for his bride. I have to laugh when I think of those long black braids he used to wear."

"You don't see him wearing any hair ribbons now."

Everyone was there, from the Benedicts of Reata to Fidel Gomez the coyote from Nopal. Fidel was a personage now, he no longer needed to bother about exploiting his own people. Fidel Gomez, too, had been touched by the magic wand of the good fairy, Oil. His run-down patch of mesquite land outside Nopal now hummed and thumped with the activities of the men and machinery that brought the rich black liquid out of the earth.

There was the bridal ceremony, full of pomp and ritual, and the bride in white satin with pearl beads and wax orange blossoms. The dress was later to be hung properly in the best room for all to see, and never to be worn again. A high platform had been built outside Dimodeo's house. After the church ceremony the bride appeared on this in each of the seven dresses of her bridal trousseau, so that all should see what a fine and open-handed husband her Angel Obregon was. The girls eyed her with envy and the men looked at her and at the proud Angel and thought, Well, a lot of good those dresses and that pretty little chavala will do you when you are sweating in the islands of the South Pacific. What a tontería! But Marita walked proudly along the platform.

Leslie had seen all this before at many ranch weddings but she was as gay and exhilarated as though she never before had known the ceremony of the boda.

"This is the kind of thing I love about Texas. Everyone here and everyone happy and everyone neighbors. It's perfect." She squeezed Bick's arm, she smiled, she met a hundred outstretched hands.

"They'd be a hell of a lot better off if they'd save their dough and get married quietly now in wartime," Bick said. "But they're all the same. Marita'll be pregnant tomorrow and have her first in nine months flat."

"Like me," said Leslie, "darling. When we were married."

Young Angel had had a few drinks of tequila. "Fix 'em over there quick, and I come home to Marita and a little Angel—only we don't call him Angel, that is a no-good name for a man."

The tables were spread out of doors, long planks on wooden standards, and there was vast eating and drinking, and laughing and talking and the singing of corridos especially written for the occasion, telling of Angel's prowess and potency and Marita's beauty and accomplishments, and the blissful future that lay ahead of them. Luzita, away at school, would have loved it, Leslie reflected. She would write her all about it. Just look at Jordy. He seemed to be having a wonderful time, not shy and withheld as he so often was. She called Bick's attention to Jordy.

"Look at Jordy! He's having a high time. I was afraid he'd feel—uh—that he would be upset, seeing Angel in uniform. Going, I mean, so soon. But look at him!"

413

"Mm." Bick stared down the long table at his son seated next to a pretty young Mexican girl and looking into her eyes. "He's being a shade too gallant, isn't he, to that little what's-her-name —Polo's granddaughter isn't it?"

"Don't be feudal. She's a decent nice little girl and her name is Juana. Jordy's being polite and she loves it."

A fine feast. Barbecued beef and beans. The great wedding caque was the favorite feast cake called color de rosa. It was made of a dough tinted with pink vegetable coloring, or colored with red crepe paper soaked in water, the water mixed with the cake dough, very tasty. There was pan de polvo, little round cakes with a hole in the middle, shaped with the hand, delectably sugary and grainy. There were buñuelos, rolled paper-thin and big as the big frying pan in which they had hissed in deep fat. Delicious with the strong hot coffee. There was beer, there was tequila, there was mescal. A real boda, and no mistake.

So Angel and Marita looked deeply into each other's eyes, and danced, and behaved like proper young Mexicans newly married. Everyone drank to Angel's return, unharmed, to Benedict. No one knew that Angel would return from the South Pacific, sure enough, landing in California after the close of the great Second World War, and coming straight back to Benedict. But he came home as bits and shreds of cloth and bone in a box. He came home a hero, his picture was in the papers, he had proved himself a tough hombre sure enough there in those faraway sweating islands. So tough that they had given him the highest honor a tough hombre can have—the Congressional Medal of Honor. The citation had been quite interesting. Private First Class Angel Obregon . . . conspicuous gallantry and intrepidity, above and beyond the call of duty . . . undaunted . . . miraculously reaching the position . . . climbed to the top . . . heroic conduct . . . saved the lives of many comrades . . . overwhelming odds . . .

It made fine reading. And the widowed Marita and old Angel Obregon and his wife and his ancient grandmother all knew that there must be a funeral befitting the conduct of the bits that lay heaped in the flag-draped box. But the undertaker in Benedict—Funeral Director he now was called—said that naturally he could not handle the funeral of a Mexican. Old Angel, a man of spirit, said that his son was an American; and that there had been Mexicans in Texas when Christopher Columbus landed on the continent of North America. But the Funeral Director—Waldo Shute his name was—big fellow—said Angel should take the box to Nopal, why not? Someone—there were people who said it might have been Leslie Benedict—thought this was not quite right. Talk got around, it reached a busy man who was President of the United States of America way up north in Washington, D.C. So he had the flag-draped box, weary now of its travels, brought to Washington and buried in the cemetery reserved for great heroes, at Arlington. Marita wished that it could have been nearer Benedict, so that she might visit her husband's grave. But she was content, really. And she had named the infant Angel, after all, in spite of the other Angel's objections that day of the wedding.

None of this the guests could know now as they laughed and danced and ate and sang, and the small children screeched and ran and darted under the tables and gobbled bits of cake.

The music of the guitarras grew louder, more resonant. "Come along home now, honey," Bick said. "We can go now. I've had enough of this and so have you."

He rose from the crowded table, and Leslie with him. Angel, the bridegroom, and Marita, the bride, seeing their guests of honor about to leave, started toward them in smiling farewell.

It was then that Jordy Benedict stood up, too, and to the amazement of the wedding guests he put his arm about the girl Juana's shoulder. He was very pale and his dark eyes seemed enormous.

He spoke formally in Spanish. "Ladies and gentlemen! My mother and my father! Friends! I have not spoken until now because I did not want to intrude on the festivities of this wedding of my friends Angel Obregon and Marita Rivas. But now I can tell you that yesterday morning Juana and I were married in the rectory of the Church of the Immaculate Conception in Nopal. We are husband and wife."

He spoke without his usual stammer. No one noticed this. Though perhaps somewhere in his mother's stunned mind it registered.

28

SPRAWLED COMFORTABLY on a veranda chair, Bick was deep in talk with Judge Whiteside and Gabe Target and Pinky Snyth and Uncle Bawley. Cattle, oil, politics were the primary subjects of discussion as always in a group of Texas males. Wars and the end of wars; nations and the fall of nations; human lives and the shattering of human lives; all these were secondary.

"My family and I live just the way we've always lived here at Reata. All that black grease in the far lot," Bick said contemptuously, "hasn't made a mite of difference. Plainer, in fact. Look

417

at the Big House where I was brought up, compared to this little shack."

"That's right," Pinky Snyth agreed. A gleam of malice danced in the seemingly guileless blue eyes. "Just like in the old-timey days, that's you, Bick. Nature is all. God sure was good to you Benedicts to hand you a seventy-five-foot reinforced concrete swimming pool set down in the brush right in your own front yard."

Bick good-humoredly joined in the laughter. "Well, now, it's a health measure. Leslie's in and out like a seal. And the young folks. We'd have had that pool in time, oil or no oil."

Gabe Target was a realist. "Like hell you would! That twenty-seven and a half percent exemption on oil fetched all the little knicknacks around your country here like swimming pools and airplanes and Caddys and whole herds of fifty-thousand-dollar critters. And that goes for the rest of the state, too."

"Depreciation," Pinky Snyth mused. "It's wonderful."

Judge Whiteside spoke pontifically. "One of the finest laws ever passed in Washington, that oil-well depreciation."

There was the sound of light laughter from the shadow of the vines at the rear of the veranda. The heads of the five men turned sharply. "That you, Leslie?" Bick called.

Her voice, a lovely sound, came to them though they could not see her. "I get starved for male conversation. I'm in the harem section pretending not to be here."

"Whyn't you move down here where we can look at your pretty face, not only hear you," suggested that ancient charmer, Uncle Bawley.

She came out of the vine shadows then and stood a moment, waving them back to their chairs. "No, I'm not staying. Relax. I was just wondering about depreciation in first-class brains. My father, for example. He's way over seventy now, he's given his life to saving other men's lives. He's a weary old gentleman now, and not well. What about depreciation exemption there?"

Gabe Target, bland and benevolent, undertook to clear this

feminine unreason. "Oil is a commodity, and valuable. How you going to measure the value of a man's brains!"

"By his record." Her voice was crisp now. "When a country considers oil more important than the spirit of man, it's a lost country."

"Now Leslie." Bick's tone was fond, but a trifle irritated too. "Get down off that stump. Someday a short-tempered Texian is going to take a shot at you."

"All right. I'm off." Her voice was gay but her eyes were serious.

"Where you going, hot of the day like this?" Pinky asked.

"Stay here," Uncle Bawley pleaded. "It rests my eyes just to look at you."

"Gentlemen, I'll tell you this privately," Bick announced, "old Bawley's always been in love with my wife."

"Who hasn't!" The heavily gallant Judge Whiteside.

Straight and slim as she had been more than twenty years ago. A misting of white in the abundant black of her hair. "I wish I didn't have to go, but I've promised. Luz and I are driving Juana and little Jordan over to Bob Dietz's new place. Bob's got a new lamb to show Jordan, he's never seen a lamb."

"All these Jordans around here," Gabe Target said, "I should think you'd get mixed up."

"His name isn't really Jordan, you know. Jordy and Juana named him Polo, after his grandfather. But Jordan began to call him Jordan——" Laughing, she gave it up.

"Dietz's place," Bick said, and shuffled his feet a little. "That's a far piece for the kid to go, day like this."

"He's tough."

Bick's frown cleared and he wagged his head. "He sure is. I sat him up front of me on my horse yesterday, just to see what he'd do, and when I took him down he began to bellow to be put back up again. Kicked me."

"Well, real Mexican——" Pinky began. Then he stopped abruptly.

Brightly, but looking them over with a clear cool gaze, Leslie said her polite farewells. "I'll be back by six. You know the way Luz drives. Won't you all stay for supper? And tell me what you've talked about while I'm away. If you dare. Just what are you five evil men up to now, I wonder. And don't you know you'll have to pay for it in the end?"

She vanished into the house. The five men looked at each other.

"Leslie's always been real sharp talking," Judge Whiteside said, and his tone was not altogether admiring.

Uneasily Bick dismissed the criticism. "Leslie doesn't mean it. When she gets going I just come back at her with some mild questions about the South and Tammany in New York and a few things like that."

The men sat quietly a moment. Reata Ranch sounds came to them on the hot Gulf wind—humming metallic sounds now, different from the sounds of a quarter century ago. The men pondered this, too, as they sat seemingly relaxed but actually tense with a kind of terrible Texas tenseness born of the fierce sun and the diet of beef and the runaway pace of prosperity.

"Don't hardly ever hear a horse nowdays," Gabe Target observed.

"Do when I'm moving around," Bick said.

Pinky eyed him keenly. "Thought you didn't gallop around as much as you used to."

"Leslie's always after me to take it easy, but I pay it no mind."

"Everything and everybody taking it easy now," Gabe Target mused. "Reach in the deep freeze for food. Lunch counter right in your own kitchen like a café—pie, coffee, sandwiches. Bump gates, touch 'em with the nose of your car, out they open and bingo they close. Bulldozers. Stingers. Jeeps. Planes in the back lot like Fords."

"My twins," Pinky said, "they went zooming down to Houston yesterday, and back—slacks and their hair in curlers—said they had to get them some lobsters, they had the girls coming for a card party they'd set their hearts on these lobsters Luggen's store just flew in special from up in Maine. They thought nothing of the trip, three four hundred miles each way, like running to the corner grocery."

Uncle Bawley often sat with his eyes shut, listening. His fingers tapped a tuneless rhythm on the chair arm. Now he opened his crepey lids and surveyed the younger men. "Oil! What do folks use it for! In the war they were flying around shooting up towns of women and children. Now it's lobsters from Maine. Got to have lobsters. And streaking hell-bent in automobiles a hundred miles an hour, going nowheres, killing people like chickens by the roadside. Pushing ships across the ocean in four five days. There hasn't been a really good boatload of folks since the *Mayflower* crowd."

"You don't get around enough, Bawley," Gabe Target argued. "Look what it's done for the state! Look what it's done for Houston and Dallas and Hermoso and Corpus and a hundred more. Look at the people there!"

"Yep. Look at 'em. The girls all got three mink coats and no place to wear 'em. And emeralds the size of avocados. The men-folks, they got Cadillacs like locomotives and planes the size of ocean liners, and their offices done up in teakwood and cork and plexiglas. And what happens! The women get bored and go to raising pretty flowers for prize shows like their grammaws did and the men go back to raising cattle just like their grampappies did a long time ago. Next thing you know mustard greens and corn bread'll be fashionable amongst 'em, instead of bragging about how they eat at the Pavilion Café and the Twenty-One Club when they go to New York. My opinion, they're tired of everything, and everybody's kind of tired of them. They made the full circle."

"Well, anyway, Uncle Bawley," Pinky Snyth protested, grinning, "you can't object to the breed of beef cattle that oil money has raised up here on Reata."

"Can," declared Uncle Bawley. "And do. I was thinking yesterday in that big tent Bick set up there, selling off bulls and steers. All out of that big black bull Othello, scares you to see him, a black Kashmir bull with all those greeny-white cows it's miscegenation. Priced fifty thousand dollars, he is."

"Sixty," Bick said. And he thought, Oh, shut up for God's sake will you, Uncle Bawley, I'm tired and edgy.

"Fifty—sixty—when you get up into those figgers for a he-cow what's the difference! Like Jett Rink's holdings. Has he got a thousand million or only a hundred million? What's the diff? It ain't money any more, it's zeros. There they stood, those critters in the auction tent, solid square, low-slung like a Mack truck, legs just stumps, all beef and more of it in all the right places than any beef animal that ever was bred up on this earth."

"Yes, well now look, Uncle Bawley——" Bick interrupted.

"—And it put me in mind of the fat women in the circus," the old man continued, unheeding. "Fattest Woman on Earth, the fella says, hollering about how big she is. And sure enough, there she sets, enormous, she's all female, she's got more of everything in the right places than any woman on earth. But who the hell wants her!"

A yelp went up. Even Bick, annoyed though he was, joined in the laughter. "You'll eat those words along with that steak we're going to have tonight for dinner."

"Don't know's I will, at that. Looking at two three those animals yesterday that you keep aspecial for family feeding. Looked like a string of freight cars standing there. One of them had laid down with his legs kind of splayed out instead of doubled under and by golly it couldn't get up. They finally had to buckle on ropes and chains and straps and haul the thing up standing. I've et steaks off those behemoths. They've had the flavor bred right out of them."

"Tell you what, Uncle Bawley," Pinky suggested. "Maybe one the boys'll go out rustle up an old Longhorn that's been hiding somewhere in the brush these past fifty years. Leslie'll have you a good old-time leather steak cut off of that."

The calm low tones of Gabe Target's voice undercut the talk and laughter. The cold grey eyes grew opaque, expressionless. "Now boys, this is very pleasant, sitting here gabbing and joshing in the hot of the day. But I'm due back home tonight, and this isn't what I came down for. You want to state your situation, Bick? Not that we don't know it. But just between us, off the record, cut down to bare bones."

Bick Benedict hunched forward, his hands clasped in front of him between his knees, his arms resting on his thighs. "Here it is, straight. We didn't realize, when we let out the oil leases, how many oil workers were going to swarm in on Reata. There's a mob of them. I've got nothing against them, big husky fellows, work hard and spend their money. They know they have to keep away from me and I keep away from them. Well. At first it was work and sleep and eat and live in those shacks just anyhow, for them. But now the whole outfit has sort of shaken down, they've brought in their wives and kids and so on. At first they stuffed their houses with refrigerators and radios and gadgets. But now they've got together in a bunch called The Better Living Association."

"Better living!" snorted Judge Whiteside.

"How many of them?" Gabe Target did not waste energy on emotions.

"Oh, good many hundreds by now. Swarming all over the town and county."

"Dissident votes," Pinky Snyth announced, like a checker of lists. "Right in this precinct."

"They're yelling all over the district they want what they call decent schools for their kids and a hospital for the sick and injured and so on, and homes for their families. And the oil property— about a hundred and fifty thousand acres of it—is in my precinct here. In the town of Benedict. If they vote—and they will—and carry it—and they will the way it stands now—they don't want my—the old Commissioner. They want him voted out and a new Commissioner in. There'll be a new tax rate on every acre of land hereabouts. That tax on a couple of million acres can just about cripple Reata. They win, and it'll spread to your Double B, Pinky. And you know it."

He unclasped his hands, threw them open, palms up. The

lines in his forehead were deep, the eyes strained and bloodshot. Pinky Snyth, looking at him, thought irrelevantly, Vashti's right, like she said Bick's letting Reata eat him up alive.

Judge Whiteside cleared his throat. "You talked to the Azabache crowd about this, Bick?"

"What do they care! It doesn't affect them. They said Jett Rink heard of it, he laughed his crazy fat head off."

Silence. The hot wind rustling the vine leaves. The drum of a powerful motor somewhere far off on the prairie. One of the nearby workboys calling in Mexican-Spanish to another busy at the pool. The five men sat eying each other. Waiting.

Smoothly, benevolently, Gabe Target broke the silence. "Well now, Bick, we don't want anything that isn't perfectly legal and aboveboard, of course."

"Course," the four echoed, and their eyes never left his face.

Silence again, brief, breathless. "I suggest—and of course I'd want the sound legal opinion of our good friend the Judge here— I suggest a very simple feasible plan, Bick. Now first I'd like to ask you a couple questions. You don't need to answer if you don't see fit. But my little plan kind of depends on the answers."

Goddamned old pompous fool, Bick's inner voice yelled. Aloud, "All right, Chief. Shoot."

"Plainly speaking, the County Commissioner's your man. That right?"

"Right."

"The Mexicans on your place—vaqueros and so on—they vote right?"

"They vote—right."

"All of them?"

"Yes."

"I heard some of the younger Mexican fellas since the war's over they've come home and haven't settled down right, they've been rabble-rousing, shooting their mouths off, getting together saying they're American citizens without rights and that kind of stuff. They want to be called Latin Americans, not Mexicans any more. I hear they're getting up organizations, the boys who fought in the war, and so on. Spreading all over, they say. Got some fancy names for their outfits with America in it to show how American they are."

"Well?"

"Can you handle them?"

"I can handle them. Always have. They'll quiet down."

"The full vote is needed to carry your candidate. Am I correct? Without it, he's out?"

"Out."

Gabe Target's eyes were flat disks of steel sunk in the caverns below his fatherly brow. "Well, my boy, you don't want a crowded big noisy city sprung up around this beautiful Reata——"

"As fair a piece of Nature's bounty," Judge Whiteside intoned, by now somewhat piqued at finding himself shorn of his accustomed curls of peroration, "as there is anywhere in this Great Commonwealth, and I may say, anywhere—North America, South America, the uncharted wastes of Asia——"

"If you think Asia's uncharted, Judge, after this last war," Pinky Snyth interrupted somewhat pertly, "you better get set for a shock to your nervous system."

"Boys, boys!" Gabe Target's kindly chiding tones like those of a gentle schoolmaster.

Bick held his temper by an effort. "Let's just hear Gabe out, will you? This is pretty important. I know a few millions don't matter much any more in Texas. But Reata matters to me more than anything in the world."

Pinky thought, By gosh he means it. More than anything in the world.

But Gabe was talking in that quiet reasonable voice so that everything he said sounded plausible and right and somehow beneficent.

"That's a mighty fine sentiment, son, and it does you credit as a real Benedict and Texian. Now then. These boys in the big oil outfits—and I don't doubt they're good fine boys, though maybe mistaken some ways—they ought to have their own town. They've

425

earned it. Hard-working boys. And keep Benedict the way it is, population and layout and nice little town government and all. And taxes. The same. Just have the precinct lines rearranged and the town line set to where it was before oil. B.O. There's a big enough population sprung up there outside to make a fine little town of their own, the oil crowd and their wives and all. Get 'em incorporated, all fair and aboveboard—before they know where they're at. Town line. Board. Commissioner. Everything in good order. They could call the town—for example, if they were so minded—Azabache. Or town of Jett Rink. And leave him build the schools they're bawling for, and the hospitals and the city hall and the gymnasiums and pave the streets and put in the water. And let Jett Rink pay the taxes."

Silence. Gabe Target's eyelids came down over the flinty eyes, giving him that aspect of benevolence again.

Finally Bick spoke. "You really think it can be done?"

"Judge Whiteside here will bear me out I think. Won't you, Judge? Bick wants to know if it can be done."

Judge Whiteside cleared his throat. His voice had the finality of one who is the Law. "It's as good as done this minute. You can forget it."

"Little drink would go good," Pinky suggested.

Everything had been conducted in the approved fashion. Like the concocting of a well-made Texas barbecue sandwich. The preliminary conversational chitchat was the blandly buttered under slice of bread. Then the quick hot spiced filling of meat and burning sauce. And now the layer of pleasant aimless talk again. The top slice of bread.

Bick reached for the little bell on the table at his side. Almost before its tinkle had died away on the hot restless air the two Mexican girls appeared, one with the tray of bourbon and ice and water, the other with the coffee.

Solemnly the men drank, the talk was more desultory now, their voices as always low, pleasant, almost musical. Gabe looked at Bick Benedict, he thought the man's russet coloring was now like a lacquer over a foundation of grey. "Bick, how's Jordy working out as a doctor?"

Bick hesitated a moment before answering. When he spoke it was with a wry lightness. "Oh, you know young folks today. Jordy takes after Leslie's side of the family, more. Her father."

Blunderingly, Judge Whiteside must satisfy his own curiosity, now that Gabe Target had inserted the entering wedge in a topic that the Benedicts' social circle considered closed to discussion. "I suppose this Guerra's office he's in—I suppose Jordy's starting off using the Mexicans like a clinic, more. For experience—observation—so forth."

Bick did not reply.

"I can't get the right of it," the Judge persisted. A thick unctuous layer of virtue was spread to conceal his sadism. "Only son and all. Where's his feeling about Reata! To say nothing of his pa and ma!"

The little crooked smile on Bick's lips did not deceive the four keen-eyed men. "Oh well, Judge, you can't tie a kid to a horse. His talents lie another way, that's all. I'll make out. I'm not quite through—yet."

Judge Whiteside blustered reassuringly. "You! Why, Bick boy, you're good for another fifty years hard riding. Look at old Bawley here! A thousand, ain't you, Bawley! And spry as a gopher."

Gabe Target's cool measured tones cut through this persiflage.

"Bick, you ought to get you a good smart solid young fella, now the war's over, knows stock and range and feed and all. Modern —" hastily—"like yourself. Train him into manager to do the routine hard over-all work. College type but with his feet on the ground. And I mean Texas ground."

Pinky Snyth spoke up. "That's Bob Dietz. Say, I tried my best to steal him off you, Bick, years ago to work the Double B. He wasn't hardly more than a kid then. Wouldn't come."

Bick's gaze went out and out, past the veranda and screening, on and on to the distant line where the dome of the sky met the golden-tan curve of the earth. "I offered him the job. He wasn't

427

interested. He as much as said I was old-fashioned. Said this was
the time for pioneering in advanced range management tech-
niques. That's what he said. Said he was interested in ranching
as a way of life for the many, and not to make big money. He
said people who wanted big money ought to try the stock market
or the oil industry or most anything but agriculture and stock."

A stunned silence followed this recital of heresy.

Judge Whiteside cleared his throat. "I don't aim to appear
nosy, but I heard around that this Dietz and your Luz were running together a good deal. Dietz isn't invited to parties and places,
but a lot in her plane and his car and hamburger joints talking,
and so on."

Bick shrugged in an effort at carelessness, but his brow was
thunderous. "Oh, kid stuff. Dietz is smart enough, but he's one of
those know-it-all kids. Luz is a real rancher, she'll talk to anybody who'll teach her something new. The Dietz kid—or anybody."

"He's no kid," Uncle Bawley announced, suddenly awake,
wide-eyed. "He's getting along."

The guffaw that this brought forth lightened the heavy resentment of Bick's tone. "Well, anyway, this ancient Bob Dietz, he
says the big ranch is doomed. The feudal system he calls it. That's
you and me, Pinky. Says that with artificial insemination and
modern long-term reseeding, pretty soon you won't need to feed
your stock a pound of hay or cake. You'd think to hear him talk
he was the one first discovered Lehman's love grass and yellow
bluestem and sideoats grama and blue grama and all. He's got
a piece about twenty sections now, down near the Valley, he calls
it a trial range unit, he says he——"

"How about water?" scoffed Judge Whiteside. "He got water
fixed to eat out of his hand too?"

"Oh sure. He says no reason why water can't be harnessed and
led across the continent. In the future. Says the Tennessee Valley
showed us a little something. Says they'll find a way to take the
salt out of salt water and hitch the whole Gulf of Mexico to
Texas. That's in the future too. He says."

"If they ever get water into Texas," Gabe Target said, "God knows what'll happen."

"I'll tell you what," Uncle Bawley announced in his gentle musing voice. "The youngsters will cut Reata into pie slices and raise up a steer to the acre."

29

EVEN AFTER all these years Leslie Benedict always felt a distinct shock as she came out of the dim cool rooms of the Main House to meet the full blast of the Texas sun. The Big House hummed with air conditioners but here at the Main House the family relied on the massive old walls for protection. Leslie often had suggested a cooling unit for Bick's bedroom but he said he'd as soon sleep with a woman who snored as that thing. He even refused to have one in his office.

"Let the barbecue shacks have them," he said, "and the Houston and Hermoso zillionaires, and Neiman-Marcus and the

431

Hake Hotel. I was brought up on Texas heat. Sun and sweat have
made Texas."

Luz said, pertly, that he was beginning to sound like Uncle
Bawley.

Now Luz and Leslie in the front seat, Juana and little Jordan
in the back, the four were off for Bob Dietz's ranch in the Valley.

Leslie cast an anxious eye toward the child. "It'll be cooler as
soon as we begin to move."

"And we're really going to move," Luz threatened as she released the brake and they were off.

"Now Luz, no stunts. It's two hours out and two back, even at
your speed. . . . Juana, you don't think it's going to be too much
for Polo, do you?"

Juana glanced down at the child beside her. "He loves it. He
was so excited this morning he wouldn't eat his breakfast."
Juana's English was spoken with precision. Her voice was soft
and low and leisurely, unlike the strident tone of many Mexican-
American women. Old Polo stemmed from Spanish blood and his
granddaughter's skin had a creamy pallor, the dark eyes were soft
and the black hair was fine and abundant. About her throat she
always wore a strand of pearls that Leslie had given her—Benedict family pearls—and the luminous quality of these seemed reflected in her skin. But the child Polo had the café-au-lait coloring
of his Mexican grandmother and great-grandmother; and their
Mexican hair and eyes.

Now the car rounded the curve in the long driveway and passed
the Big House. Three or four people were descending the broad
stone steps and there were cars waiting in the drive. Almost automatically Leslie bowed and waved and smiled, though she knew
only vaguely who the guests were this week or this particular day.

"It seems to me," Luz remarked, "that our visiting strangers
get stranger and stranger. Who's that lot?"

"I don't know, really. Not very important. Two of the boys
have been delegated to take them around. But next week!"

"I hear it's a king and queen. Doesn't it sound silly!"

"Yes, poor darlings. And a swarm of other people. It's a weird list. Somebody must have slipped up on it—Jordan's secretary or somebody. They can't all be interested in cattle."

"Who?"

"You won't believe it, even for Reata. Uh, let's see—there's a prize fighter and a Russian dancer and a South American Ambassador. And a movie queen who's bought a ranch in California and wants to stock it. And her husband. I don't remember who else. And I'm afraid your Aunt Maudie and your Aunt Leigh are descending."

"I may suddenly be called away."

"Now Luz! Anyway, they're all invited to that big thing at Jett Rink's new airport."

"Oh, that! I may hop over for a look at it but I wouldn't be found dead at the idiotic howling dinner."

"Your father would like you just to show up, and Jordy, too, and all of us."

"That's ridiculous! What for?"

"Because everybody is going to be there, and if we stay away it will look queer. Anyway, there's a political reason of some kind. He doesn't like it any better than you do. But Roady asked specially that we all go—you and Jordy and Maudie——"

"Me!" asked the child's eager voice from the back seat.

Leslie turned, she held out her hand to the child and smiled at him. "No, you don't have to be political, my darling. Not yet."

The child looked at her solemnly, the great dark eyes almost mournful. "I'm hungry."

"There!" Juana said. "Because you didn't eat your breakfast."

"I want my breakfast now."

"Listen, Snooks," Luz called to the child, "wait till we get out of Benedict and past Nopal."

"But I'm hungry."

"In a little minute, mi vida," Juana said to the child. "Near the Valley where it is quiet. You will have milk and we will drink coffee. And we will have lunch at Bob Dietz's house."

"And I will see a baby lamb!"

They had whirled through the streets of Benedict. The old

433

main street had become a business section that branched in all directions. Plate-glass windows reflected, glitter for glitter, the dazzling aluminum and white enamel objects within. Vast refrigerators, protean washing machines, the most acquisitive of vacuum cleaners. There were three five-and-dime stores and the dime had burgeoned into a dollar. All day long in these stores mechanical music droned a whining tune sung by a bereft crooner. Why do you make me feel so blue? he complained. Don't you want me as I want you? Mexican women with four small children, the woman always pregnant, wandered up and down the crowded aisles, fingering the gaudy wares piled in tempting profusion. The children touched everything with slim caressing dark fingers. Plastic things, paper things, rayon things. Gadgets. Pink panties marked 59 cents. Machine embroidery on these depicted a lewdly winking yellow sun with He Loves Me stitched in pink and blue around its rays.

The leather shop of Ildefonso Mezo was little more than tourist bait now, for Ildefonso was long gone. Tourists from Iowa and New York and Missouri stopped to buy stitched high-heeled cowboy boots in which their offspring hobbled back into the waiting family car.

The moth-eaten Longhorn steer still stood in his glass case morosely staring out at the procession of motorcars streaming along the road which in his lifetime had known only the quick clatter of horses' hoofs and the bellow and shuffle and thud of moving cattle.

As the Benedict car flashed through the town and out Leslie's quick glance darted this way and that. "How it changes! Almost from day to day. You should have seen it when I came here a bride, before any of you were born."

"Well, I hope so, madam!" Luz exclaimed virtuously.

"That first week! I'll never forget it. I rejected just about everything—except your father. The—the vaqueros' horrible little shacks were worse than the Negro cabins in my Virginia. Texas food was steak and the steak was sole leather."

"Still is," Luz observed.

434

"But not at our house. And there are all those modern houses in the barrios now. And they're talking about a new hospital here in Benedict and a new school."

Juana's voice was very low, for the child had fallen asleep against his mother's side. "The school for the Latin American children is a disgrace."

Leslie turned in her seat to face her daughter-in-law there at the rear of the car with her lovely sleeping child. "I know, Juana darling. We must keep on working."

Their speed on this flat endless road would have been terrifying to anyone not a Texan. Past the fine new house of Fidel Gomez in Nopal. Fidel Gomez, wallowing in oil, scarcely bothered now to manage the business of bringing the Mexican migratory workers, men women and children, into the Valley for the seasonal crop picking at twenty-five cents an hour.

Nopal was changing, too. TORTILLA FACTORY a sign read in the town where once the pat-pat of women's hands had sounded from every little dwelling. The dry-goods store was a department store now, it boasted a plate-glass expanse of its own and in the window a large printed sign announced LADY CASTLEMERE SHEETS! ADVERTISED IN LIFE! And staring into the window a black-garbed Mexican woman with four children tugging at her skirts, and it was plain to see that she never had lain between such sheets, nor would; and that Life as she knew it had always been lower case. There were motion picture theatres offering Westerns. *Border Bad Man. Wagon Wheels West.* Coals to Newcastle, Leslie thought as the great car swept through the small towns and out again into the open road.

"There isn't any open road any more," she announced. "Just the other day I read that a hundred years ago—less than a hundred—Congress voted money for camels to be sent to Texas. They came from Syria and Alexandria and Constantinople with the camel drivers, to be used in the United States Army. Imagine some Texas pioneer woman looking out of the door of her little shack and suddenly seeing a camel chewing its cud in the open prairie under the Texas stars."

435

"I want to see a camel!" little Polo demanded.

"The camel has gone away, my pet. Look at that enormous thing with all those aluminum chimneys or whatever they are. Acres of it."

"Lexanese plant," Luz said.

"They couldn't have run it up overnight. But I don't remember having seen it before. I must get about more. I'll turn into a homebody if I'm not careful."

"If you weren't so stubborn about letting me take you up in the little plane," Luz reminded her, "you'd see the world."

"You and Jordy don't really see the world. You've learned your geography from planes. You think the world is little blocks and squares with bugs wriggling over them. To you Tennessee is a red and pink checkerboard, and Louisiana is a smear of purple and black. And the Mississippi is a yellow line slithering through it all. I don't think you ever really see anything from the angle of the ground. What with horses and planes and cars you never set foot to earth."

"Bob says you forgot to teach me to walk. But anyway, what I see from the air is mighty pretty, missy. Which is more than you can say down here."

"Tell me, what's Bob's new house like? Is it attractive?"

"Attractive as a box car. You could put the whole thing in our pantry."

"Modern pioneer, h'm?"

"You and Pa are a little worried about Bob Dietz, aren't you?"

"Well, no, not worried. I think he's a wonderful young man. I don't suppose you plan to marry every man who interests you."

"No. Only one. Bob and I have talked about it. He says he wouldn't marry any girl who has Reata hung around her neck." The girl's voice was even and her eyes were on the road ahead but something intangible asked mutely for guidance.

"Your Aunt Luz, that you were named after, thought that Reata was more important than marriage." Luz said nothing. They drove on in silence. Luz just turned her head, then, to glance at her mother, and again her eyes came back to the road.

In a tone of somewhat dry reminiscence Leslie went on. "She was in love with Cliff Hake—that was Vashti Snyth's father—and he was in love with her. But he wouldn't come to live at Reata and she wouldn't go to live at the Double B, and they wouldn't throw the two ranches into one. So she lived at Reata an old maid. And died there."

"I'm still young," Luz said, her voice airy, "even if I am over twenty. Young in spirit, that's me. . . . I danced with Jett Rink the other night."

"No, Luz!"

"It was only for a minute or two. He was drunk but not violent. It was last week when I went to Houston for the party. We were having dinner at the Shamrock, Glenn McCarthy came into the Emerald Room with a bunch of Big Boys and Jett Rink was one of them. He looked quite handsome in a Mississippi Gaylord Ravenal kind of way. He had the nerve to come up to our table and ask me to dance. I decided it would be better to try it than to risk his going into one of his slugging matches with one of our men."

"What did he say?"

"Sort of babbled. Still mad at the Benedicts but not you and not me, as nearly as I could gather. A lot about you. And then he suggested it would be nice if I'd marry him. What an ape!"

"I'm hungry!" Polo was wide awake now.

Leslie turned to reassure him. "All right, my precious. We'll stop somewhere."

"I want my breakfast," the boy demanded.

Luz called back to him, "Sweetie, there's a kind of monotony about your conversation. Juana, there's a nice clean new place about a mile further on. Bob and I stopped there for a sandwich the other night. They toast them. Quite good. I could do with a Coke, myself."

There were a dozen cars outside the little roadside lunch room. A radio whined. Trucks and passenger cars and jeeps mingled affably in the parking place. "You go along in," Luz said. "I'll park away from these bloodthirsty trucks." Leslie took the boy's hand in hers as he walked with his uncertain staggering steps. He looked proudly up into her face. She loved the feel of the velvety morsel in her palm. "Now, my pet. We'll all have something good, but not much because Bob Dietz will want us to eat lunch at his house, he won't like it if we're not hungry."

"Won't he let me see the little lamb?"

"Oh yes, he'll let you see the lamb. Now then. Up the little step."

A coffee counter. Metal tables with chairs upholstered in scarlet imitation leather. A harassed middle-aged woman behind the counter, a red-faced shirt-sleeved man behind the cash register; a waitress wiping a table top with a damp cloth. Truck drivers at the coffee counter, women and children eating at the tables.

They stood a moment, Leslie, Juana, the child, in the bright steamy room with its odors of coffee and fried food. "That table in the corner," Juana suggested. "Perhaps there is a high chair for you, mi vida."

"I don't want a high chair, I am a big boy."

They sat down. "What's keeping Luz?" Leslie said, and tucked in a paper napkin at Polo's neck which he at once removed.

"We don't serve Mexicans here."

They did not at first hear. Or, if they heard, the words did not penetrate their consciousness. So now the man came from behind the cash register and moved toward them. His voice was louder now. "We don't serve Mexicans here."

Leslie Benedict stared around the room, but the man was looking at her and at Juana and at Polo. Leslie was frowning a little, as though puzzled. "What?"

"You heard me." He jerked a thumb toward the doorway. "Out." The men drinking coffee at the counter and the people at the nearby tables looked at the two women and the child. They kept on eating and drinking, though they looked at them and glanced with sliding sidewise glances at each other.

Leslie rose. Juana stood, too, and the child wriggled off the chair and ran to his mother's side. "You can't be talking to me!" Leslie said.

"I sure can. I'm talking to all of you. Our rule here is no Mexicans served and I don't want no ruckus. So—out!"

The worried-looking woman behind the lunch counter said, "Now Floyd, don't you go getting techy again. They ain't doing nothing."

Leslie felt her lips strangely stiff. She said, "You must—be out of your mind."

"Who you talking to!" the man yelled.

Luz came blithely in, she stared a moment at the little group on whose faces was written burning anger; at the openmouthed men and women at the counter and tables.

"Heh, what's going on here!" she said.

The man glanced at the golden-haired blue-eyed girl, he pointed a finger at the two women and the child, but Leslie spoke before he could repeat the words.

"This man won't serve us. He says he won't serve Mexicans."

Even the jaws at the counter had ceased champing now.

The scarlet surged up into Luz's face, her eyes were a blazing blue. Leslie thought, with some little portion of her brain that was not numb, Why she looks exactly—but exactly—like Jordan when he is furious.

"You son of a bitch!" said Miss Luz Benedict.

The man advanced toward her.

"Floyd!" barked the woman behind the counter.

"Git!" shouted the man then. "You and your greasers." And he gave Polo a little shove so that he lurched forward and stumbled and Luz caught him.

Luz reverted then to childhood. "I'll tell my father! He'll kill you! Do you know who my father is! He's———"

"No! No, Luz! No name. Come."

As they went they heard, through the open doorway, the voices of the man and woman raised again in dispute.

"You crazy, Floyd! Only the kid and his ma was cholos, not the others."

"Aw, the old one was, black hair and sallow, you can't fool me."

Leslie put a hand through Juana's arm, she took the child's hand in hers.

"Come, children. Sh! Don't cry!"

"That is a bad man," Polo said through his sobs.

"Yes, darling."

"I am hungry I want my breakfast."

They were climbing into the car now. "Grandma will sit back here with you. That man didn't have nice milk to drink. Luz will get out at the next place and she'll get you a bottle of milk and some crackers and you can drink the milk through a straw as we ride along and you can see the little lamb all the sooner. Won't that be fun!"

30

SHE HAD their promise. All the way to Bob Dietz's ranch and all the way back they had argued. But in the end Luz and Juana had promised.

"Please," Leslie had implored them, "please not until after that horrible Jett Rink party is over. Please Luz, please Juana, don't tell your father don't tell Jordy don't tell Bob until after that. You know they'd do something—something hasty, it would get into the papers, it would be all over the state. All those guests at the Big House, and a thousand people going to the party.

There'll be publicity enough. Please just wait until next week, then we'll all talk about it quietly, together."

"Quietly!" shouted Luz. "I'm going to tell Bob the minute we hit the house. He'll kill that baboon."

"Luz, I promise you it won't be left like this. I promise. But it can't be now. This is the wrong time. It's got to be handled through proper channels, carefully. Your father and Gabe and Judge Whiteside."

"Judge Whiteside!" Luz scoffed. "That belly-crawler!"

Quietly Leslie said, "We're furious because of what that ignorant bigot did. But we all know this has been going on for years and years. It's always happened to other people. Now it's happened to us. The Benedicts of Reata. So we're screaming."

"All right," Luz snapped, "then let's hit it."

"Yes. But not now. Please. Not just now. It's the worst possible time to make a public fuss."

And deep inside her a taunting voice said, Oh, so now you're doing it too, h'm? After twenty-five years of nagging and preaching and being so superior you're evading too. Infected. Afraid to speak up and act and defy. Hit the rattlesnake before it strikes again. Tell them now, tell them now, what does it matter about the silly guests and the ranch and the oil and the banquet and the talk and the state? It's the world that matters.

At six that evening Bick Benedict, sprawled on the couch in their bedroom, regarded his wife with the fond disillusioned gaze of the husband who is conditioned to seeing cold cream applied to the wind-burned feminine face.

"What the hell went on down there at Bob Dietz's?" he inquired. "You girls came home as sore-acting as if you'd been scalped by Karankawas. Juana looked as if she'd been crying and Luz stamped past me without speaking. Just glared. Did the two girls quarrel or something? What the hell went on down there, anyway?"

"Nothing," Leslie replied. "Just tired, I guess."

"Uh-huh. All right, keep your girlish secrets. You don't look so good yourself, by the way."

Leslie continued to pat the cold cream on her cheeks. "Thanks, chum. There's nothing like a little flattery to set a girl up before dinner."

"The boys decided not to stay. Except Uncle Bawley. He's not going back to Holgado until tomorrow."

"Did you finish your business? That private business you were all so cagey about?"

"Uh, yes. Yes."

"I thought you all looked as guilty as kids who were going to rob an orchard. Did it turn out all right?"

"Fine. Fine."

"What was it all about?"

"Oh, nothing you'd be interested in, honey. Town business. Elections coming up. Stuff like that."

Tell him now, the Voice said. Tell him his wife and his daughter and his daughter-in-law and his grandson were kicked out of a roadside diner and it's his fault and your fault and the fault of every man and woman like you. But she only said, aloud, "We brought the little lamb back with us in the car. Bob gave it to Polo."

"You trying to make a sheep man out of a Benedict! Don't let that get around the cow country."

"He insists on keeping it in a box in his bedroom. Juana's having quite a time."

He laughed like a boy at his mental picture of this. Then he fell silent. When he spoke he was serious, he was urgent. "Leslie, I wish they could live here at Reata. Not only little visits like this, but stay. Do you think they might? The kid loves it here."

"Of course he does. He thinks it's heaven. Wouldn't any child who'd lived in a three-room New York apartment while his father went to school?"

"Speak to Juana about it, will you? Maybe if Jordy sees how happy she and the boy are here he'll leave Vientecito and give up that stinking clinic, settle down here at Reata where he belongs."

Agreeably, quite as though she did not know that what he suggested was hopeless, she seemed to fall in with his plan. "Wouldn't that be lovely! I'll speak to Juana tomorrow."

He sighed with a sort of deep satisfaction as if the impossible were already accomplished. "Let's have a little drink up here before I have to go down and start arguing again with Uncle Bawley." After she had given the order, "What's Dietz's place like?"

"Compact as a hairbrush. You wouldn't know it was Texas. Everything planned to the last inch like a problem in physics. It's planted right up to the front door, I expected to see grass growing in the house."

"Did, huh? See his stock?"

"Yes. Some. It looked—what's that word?—thrifty. Bob said it was solid beef cattle, he wasn't going in for collectors' items."

"Snotty kid."

"Let's be fair. Bob's more than that. Jordan, maybe this boy has got hold of something so fundamental that it's enormous."

"You sound as if you'd been talking to your daughter Luz. I want to know what you think of him."

"Bob's a fine man. And more than just smart. For the rest, perhaps he's just a le-e-etle bit too earnest for my taste, and not enough humor. But maybe that's the mark of future greatness. Great men are usually pretty stuffy. Except you."

The Mexican girl came in with the tray and placed it on the table beside him. Bick opened the bourbon, cocked an eyebrow at Leslie, she nodded.

"That's mighty pretty talk, missy." But he was not smiling. "Look. Is she going to marry him?"

"I don't know. Neither does she. He won't marry Reata. I'm sure of that. Not even if he has to lose Luz. And he's crazy about her. But not that crazy."

He put down his glass. "Heh, wait a minute! This is where we came in, isn't it?"

"Sort of. We talked a little about her Aunt Luz today. I told her about Luz and Cliff Hake—before he was old Cliff Hake."

He got up and began to stride about the room. "Oh, you did, eh?"

"Yes. I thought she might be interested to know what happens to a woman, sometimes, if she doesn't marry because of some unimportant thing like a ranch, for example."

"She doesn't want to marry that dirt farmer. Anyway, she isn't going to. Not if I can help it."

"Twentieth century. Remember?"

Moodily he stared at her. "Oh, let's forget it. I'm tired. This has been a stinker of a day."

Instantly she was alert. "What happened?"

"Nothing. Everything. After the boys left I sat there talking to Bawley a while. He looked like an old hundred-year turtle, mopping his eyes and mumbling. I love the old goof but he sure can drive you crazy. Talking. He thinks he's one of the Prophets or something now, the way he talks."

"But what did he say that upset you?"

"Nothing. Nothing that made sense, that is. It was just the whole stinking day. I got to thinking about this damned Rink shindig next week. Bawley said he wouldn't be seen dead there, oil or no oil. And to tell you the truth I'd rather be shot than go."

"That's wonderful! We won't go."

His shoulders slumped. "We've got to. Because everybody's going. If we stay away we'll be the only outfit for a thousand miles around that isn't there. Everybody's going and nobody wants to—nobody that is anybody. Stay away and we'd be more marked than if we went to the party naked. . . . To think that that cochino could make decent people do anything they don't want to do!"

"He can't. We don't have to go." She faced him squarely, hairbrush in hand, she gesticulated with it as she spoke. "You keep on doing—we keep on doing things we're really opposed to. You just can't keep on doing things against your feelings and principles."

Belligerently, "You don't say! What things?"

"You've just said it. This hideous kowtowing to a thing like

445

Jett Rink. But that isn't so important. It's a thousand other things. Oil. And the ranch. And the Mexicans. The bigotry. The things that can happen to decent people. It's going to catch up with you. It's taken a hundred years and maybe it'll take another hundred. But it will catch up with you. With everybody. It always does."

"Go join a club," he said wearily, and turned away from her and threw himself again on the couch, his boots scuffling the silken coverlet.

She came over to him and sat beside him. "Bick, do you feel ill?"

He stared at her. "You called me Bick."

"Did I?"

"Why?"

"I don't know, Jordan. I didn't know I had."

"You've never called me that before. Never. Everybody else did, but you've never called me anything but my name, since the day we met. Say, that's kind of funny. Maybe it means you've kind of finished with your husband Jordan."

She sank down against him, her cheek against his, her arm across his breast. "Jordan's my husband, darling. Bick's my friend."

"Tell your friend to get the hell out of my wife's bedroom." But he was not smiling. He lay inert, unresponsive to her. After a moment he began to talk, disjointedly, as though unwillingly admitting the doubts and fears that for months had been piling up against the door of his consciousness. "I guess it's kind of got me . . . the Boys this afternoon screwing around . . . and the whole damned oil crowd . . . it's like any dirty boom town now, Benedict is. . . . And on top of everything Jordy turning out a no-good maverick. . . . Oh well, no real Benedict, anyway. . . . Doctor Jordan Benedict! Can you imagine! Down in Spigtown with the greasers in Vientecito, a shingle on the door right along with a fellow named Guerra. . . . Juana and the kid . . . Juana's all right she's a decent girl she's Jordy's wife Jordy Benedict's wife and the kid looks like a real cholo . . ."

446

"Darling, don't say things like that! They're terrible. They're wrong. You don't know how wrong. You'll be sorry."

"Yeh, well I know this much. Things are getting away from me. Kind of slipping from under me, like a loose saddle. I swear to God I sometimes feel like a failure. Bick Benedict a failure. The whole Benedict family a failure."

She sat up very straight, she took his inert hand in hers, his brown iron hand, and held it close to her. "Jordan, how strange that you should say that just today!"

"Today?"

"Because today was kind of difficult for me too, in some ways. And I thought, as we were driving along toward home—Luz and Juana and little Jordan and I—I thought to myself, well, maybe Jordan and I and all the others behind us have been failures, in a way. In a way, darling. In a way that has nothing to do with ranches and oil and millions and Rinks and Whitesides and Kashmirs. And then I thought about our Jordan and our Luz and I said to myself, well, after a hundred years it looks as if the Benedict family is going to be a real success at last."

As he turned, half startled half resentful, to stare at her, the man saw for just that moment a curious transformation in the face of this middle-aged woman. The lines that the years had wrought were wiped away by a magic hand, and there shone there the look of purity, of hope and of eager expectancy that the face of the young girl had worn when she had come, twenty-five years ago, a bride to Texas.

447

Aline Cooper	Nov. 12
Helen Eaton	Nov. 26
Betty Harden	Dec. 10
Margaret Holt	Jan. 14
Katherine Jordan	Jane.28
Louise Foley	Feb. 11
Grace Maynard	Feb. 25
Iris McEwen	Mar. 11
Hallie Ragsdale	Mar. 25
Hazel Sellers	Apr. 8
Lynda Sharpe	Apr. 22
Cammie Spikes	May 13
Rouse Steele	May 27
Annie S. Stratford	June 10
Helon Tucker	June 24
Georgia Wilson	July 8
Betty Carr	July 22
Emma Carroll	Aug. 12